Praise for *NO ONE HEARD HER SCREAM*

"A dynamite debut! Plain thriller country!"
Publishers Weekly

"A compelling page-turner!
Pulling no punches with this exciting debut,
Jordan Dane quickly establishes
her credentials as a promising new star."
Romantic Times magazine

"Terrific debut. Jordan Dane has got the goods
and she delivers them with a knock-out ending.
A great new author to watch."
Crimespree magazine

"Jordan Dane has crafted a debut novel
with thrills, chills, and emotions.
She's not to be missed!"
Heather Graham, *New York Times* bestselling author

"Jordan Dane's debut romantic suspense sizzles.
Intense and satisfying."
Allison Brennan, *New York Times* bestselling author

"High stakes romance, riveting,
gritty suspense, and engaging characters.
A fabulous new voice!"
Cindy Gerard, *New York Times* bestselling author

"Jordan Dane is a brand-new star on the horizon
of women's fiction. Her style is gritty—
her writing sharp and concise.
A roller-coaster ride of nail-biting suspense
and heart-stopping emotion."
Sharon Sala, *New York Times* bestselling author

Praise for *NO ONE LEFT TO TELL*

"Rising star Dane really showcases her talents.
The characters in this gritty tale
are vivid and real, with emotions
that range from love to twisted evil.
Riveting reading!"

TOP PICK *Romantic Times* magazine

Praise for *NO ONE LIVES FOREVER*

"Rarely does an author make such an impact
in such a short span of time."

TOP PICK *Romantic Times* magazine

By Jordan Dane

Evil Without a Face
No One Lives Forever
No One Left to Tell
No One Heard Her Scream

Coming Soon
The Wrong Side of Dead

JORDAN DANE

EVIL WITHOUT A FACE

AVON

An Imprint of HarperCollins*Publishers*

This is a work of fiction. Names, characters, places, and incidents are products of the author's imagination or are used fictitiously and are not to be construed as real. Any resemblance to actual events, locales, organizations, or persons, living or dead, is entirely coincidental.

AVON BOOKS
An Imprint of HarperCollins*Publishers*
10 East 53rd Street
New York, New York 10022-5299

ISBN 978-0-06-147412-5
www.avonbooks.com

First Avon Books paperback printing: February 2009

Printed in the U.S.A.

10 9 8 7 6 5 4 3 2 1

To my Mom & Dad,
who supplied plenty of fodder for fiction.
Look Mom, no duct tape required.

ACKNOWLEDGMENTS

I used to live in Anchorage, Alaska (ten years), and I love that *Evil Without a Face* weaves in and out of that setting. Alaska will always hold a special place in my heart. And as is usually the case, the plot was influenced by a real crime that happened 2004 in Florida. This is my take on it. I'm particularly fond of the main character in this book, my Fugitive Recovery Agent Jessica Beckett. She's scarred both physically and mentally by her past, yet her inner strength is resilient. Her scars are the imperfections in us all. But one of her most endearing traits is that she's a real smart-ass. Normally, I fall in love with my male characters, but this woman has stolen my heart on many levels. I hope you take her under your wing and show her some love.

And if my whiz kid Seth Harper had to rely on me for his computer savvy, he would have been assigned to a remedial class. But thanks to the Mystery Writers of America loop and Patrick Murray, Harper could fake it. And special thanks go to a real computer genius, Tom Radcliffe, who had the good sense to marry well.

For me, living in Alaska was the adventure of a lifetime. I've been to the charming town of Talkeetna many times for softball games, Moose Dropping Festivals (to honor the many uses of moose poop) and winter cross-country skiing. And Talkeetna's Roadhouse is a special place to hang out and grab a great bite to eat. But two wonderful friends from Anchorage helped remind me that when you get out of your car in Alaska, you are fair game—just another part of the food chain. Special thanks to Alaskan residents David Boelens and Janet Rodgers for sharing their logistical expertise and sick humor. And for the fictional purposes of this book, I ignored the fact that the St. Lawrence Island has no trees and blessed it with evergreens near the NE Cape.

And for those who know me, you know that blowing up stuff on paper is a blast for me, especially with the help of my murder and mayhem buddy, weapons expert Joseph Francis Collins, a talented aspiring author. Joe, thanks for being my "tail-end Charlie." And for the best friend a new author (or anyone) could ever have, I'd like to publicly declare my heartfelt thanks to Charlotte Worsham, owner of the Around the Corner Restaurant in Edmond, Oklahoma, for her unflinching support. When she says she cooks with love, she means it.

Finally, I'd like to thank some special folks in my life. To my husband and best friend, John—you never cease to amaze me. To my family circle—thanks for weathering my influence all these years and keeping me thoroughly entertained. To my agent, Meredith Bernstein—you are a savvy businesswoman with a classic sense of style. But it's your never-ending appetite for life that I admire most. And to my editor, Lucia Macro, and everyone who contributed to this book from the talented staff at Avon Books/Harper Collins—thanks for your commitment to excellence in all things. You have touched my life and I'm so very grateful and blessed to know you.

CHAPTER 1

Talkeetna, Alaska
Mid-June

Seventeen-year old Nikki Archer knelt on the floor inside her dark closet, rolling another T-shirt to stuff into a canvas duffel bag, her hands shaking. She'd drawn the thick drapes of her bedroom to block the enduring daylight common this time of year and chose to work by a meager light. The darkened space gave her the illusion of privacy and the solitude she desperately needed. Still, she strained to listen for the familiar creak outside her bedroom door, an early warning signal she had unwanted company.

The closet door stood open a narrow crack. She needed the light, but in case her mom came looking for her, the partially closed door would give her time to react and hide what she was doing. She worked until she couldn't take the shakes anymore. The dim light from a distant lamp on her nightstand seeped in to find her. Its pale glow cast a steady luminous ribbon across her arms.

The reality of her intentions had closed in, seizing Nikki with a rush of guilt, and she stopped and clutched the handle of the duffel to steady her trembling fingers. But it wasn't enough. Perspiration beaded on her forehead and upper lip. Feeling light-headed, she found a corner at the back of her closet and cowered deep into its shadows. In the cramped space, her heartbeat echoed and her breathing filled her ears, muffling everything except the nagging doubts that had surfaced again. Part of her wanted to stay put, burrowed into her clothes and mementos with the faint scent of her favorite perfume in the air. But she had made up her mind more than a week ago, and the final details would be worked out tonight.

This time she had a plan. She had somewhere to be. And she knew her mother would never understand.

Her computer sounded a ping. With the noise, her heart leapt. She knew who it would be. She shoved out of the corner and rose to her feet. After doing her best to hide the duffel, she slowly headed for her computer, closing the closet door behind her. Her eyes fixed on the monitor across the room. When she got close enough, she recognized the Instant Messenger name on the screen.

SnowMaiden

Her friend, Ivana Noskova from Chicago, was of Russian decent and loved the bittersweet tale of the Snow Maiden. In the story Ivana told her, the fifteen-year-old maiden in the popular Russian fable was the daughter of Spring Beauty and Grandfather Frost. As the maiden grew, she yearned for the companionship of humans in a nearby village, particularly a young shepherd boy, but her heart was incapable of affection. Her mother eventually took pity on her and gave her the ability to love. But as soon as she did, the maiden's heart warmed and she melted. Love and her yearning for something more had destroyed her.

A sad story, but in her own house, Nikki knew this never would've happened. Her mom and pity were complete strangers. Yet she *could* identify with the maiden's wish for more than she had.

SnowMaiden: U there?

Until she moved the cursor, the chat box blinked its bluish light into the murky room and onto her sweater as she sat at her desk. Nikki knew the conversation they'd have next would set wheels in motion. She took a deep breath, but before she answered, her eyes found a framed photo next to her monitor, shoved to the back of her desktop. She reached for it and wiped a thin layer of dust from the glass with her fingers.

A remembrance of her thirteenth birthday, the day she officially became a teenager.

On a bright perfect day, she grinned and squinted in front of The Moose Nugget. The sun had made a rare appearance, making her feel even more special. Her mother had an arm around her shoulders, and Uncle Payton held up two fingers behind her head with his signature goofy smirk on his face. He always made her smile. Even now. Even with everything as it was.

Her family. All she had left, anyway.

But her grin faded when she touched the glass, running a finger down the face of her mother. They started fighting for real that year, and it hadn't let up since. Her mom instigated most of their yelling matches with her ridiculous and smothering rules. Nikki clenched her jaw, the rage still fresh from their last argument. A friend had given her a belly ring that she proudly displayed once too often. With small-town gossip, word had gotten back home and the great debate over body piercing began.

Nikki slammed the photo facedown. Her mom would believe this all had something to do with the ongoing friction between them. True, it started there, but now she had her own reasons for leaving. She grabbed the mouse and positioned the cursor to answer her friend, then pulled the keyboard closer.

Her Instant Messenger name didn't have much of a story behind it, nothing as interesting as her Chicago friend, SnowMaiden. Nikki had picked a name during the winter months when the sun was a rare commodity in Alaska. Now the IM handle stuck year-round, more in keeping with her mood.

DarkdazeGirl: bak—411?

She typed the code they used—"Back at keyboard. You have the information?" If everything went as planned, she'd probably feel like changing her IM handle real soon. But only if her cyber friend SnowMaiden played her part without a hitch.

Providenija, Russia

The old man sat in his small apartment, hunched at a kitchen table, half listening to the loud argument of a couple down the hall and the grating rumble of a truck outside his window. He'd almost learned to block out such annoyance when he worked. Absentmindedly, he scratched through the gray stubble of his chin, trying to peel the last crusty layer of a scab near his lip. The pungent smell of sardines and onions, remnants of his dinner, mixed with the overshadowing odor of cigarettes. He took another drag of his smoke and jammed the butt into an overloaded ashtray, his fingernails yellowed with nicotine stains. Ashes spilled onto the table, but he didn't bother to brush them aside.

A slow smile emerged on his face as he typed the last message on his laptop keyboard. At first the cryptic language of the American girl took him a while to learn, but over time he had mastered it. Now his fingers swept across the keys with confidence. No hesitation.

SnowMaiden: dw 143 cus

He punched the keys and hit Send to a message that translated to, "Don't worry. I love you. See you soon." In cyberspace he could reinvent himself, become anyone. He'd taken on so many aliases that he now maintained cryptic records to keep his lies straight.

DarkdazeGirl: 143 2, cya f2f ☺, bff

The spoiled American girl had replied, "I love you too, see you face-to-face, best friends forever."

This week would prove to be quite profitable, with another delivery on its way. He preferred to think of the girl as nothing more than cargo. Where there was demand, he filled the need with his bountiful supply at no risk to him. The system worked and allowed him to operate in secrecy, but the anonymity worked both ways.

By design, he knew very little about his contact down the line, except that the man lived in Chicago. The American had let that slip once, but he was much too smart to let that happen to him. His contact only knew him as Ivan Andreyevich Krylov, an alias of his own choosing. The name meant nothing to his capitalist counterpart. The man was probably no more than an uneducated pig.

Known as the Russian Aesop, his namesake Krylov was an accomplished author of satirical Russian fables who died in the mid-1800s. Many of his stories and characters still resonated with the pop culture of his country today.

But the American would not know this.

Still, it made a fitting name for him to use. And he was fond of fables, hence his use of SnowMaiden when he first contacted the girl in a chat room. In truth, she had made the first move. He'd learned it worked better that way, to dangle the bait and linger with patience. He made a respectable living from his skill, amidst such rustic surroundings.

The remote seaport of Providenija was nothing more than a crude airstrip and a modest harbor located at the base of a mountain range on the southeast coast of Chukotka Peninsula. The larger landmass projected into the waters of the Chukchi and the Bering Seas. Just under forty miles separated Russian land from St. Lawrence Island near Alaska, part of the United States. In Providenija, housing consisted of tenements and prefabricated metal structures barged into port in the off season when the ice flows permitted. And the main source of income came from the sea and hunting.

Although he prided himself on his enterprising means to rise above such a livelihood, he remained cautious not to call attention to it. Once he had enough money saved, he would move to Moscow under an assumed name as a man of means once more, or perhaps leave the country, bound for someplace warm. That thought pleased him.

He knew from experience that he was only a cog in a much larger wheel. Any message from Ivan Krylov would be funneled down the line. Safer that way. He didn't care how things worked or why anyone wanted these overindulged children. He only cared about getting paid. He spent enough money to keep him in food and cigarettes, with a roof over his head and the occasional acquisition from the black market when it suited him. Mostly, he saved for the better life he deserved. After all, he had need of comforts, especially at his age.

The old man pulled up the Web page to Globe Harvest, a site with a note that it was under construction. The notice had been there for as long as he remembered. He hit the keystrokes to open the site, a predesignated arrangement. An ID and password box flashed onto the screen. He typed his unique code and hit Enter. After a few seconds a mailbox appeared. No emails waited for him, but he sent one of his own to *info@globeharvest.com.* He typed a simple message and embedded it into a digital photo of Alaska he'd taken off the Internet. Another agreed-upon security measure.

Delivery from AK on its way to Chicago as agreed. ETA two days.

His American comrade might not know who Krylov was, but he would know what to do when he got this message. The old man got to his feet and stretched his back. After lighting another smoke, he trudged across his kitchen, heading for the toilet down the hall. The onions had soured his stomach, and his bladder required attention. He reached for the newspaper thrown onto a bookshelf near his apartment door and tucked it under his arm.

But a ping sounded, calling him back. His computer. When he returned, the old man glared at the screen.

GR8OZ: Hey man how r u?

The chat box blinked. A young flamer from Calgary, Alberta, in Canada, full of tattoos and both ears pierced. The blond-haired, blue-eyed gay boy had sent photos of himself last week. And his ears weren't the only places he had punctured. Perhaps the boy thought to entice him with his provocative and depraved ways. He reached for the prints he had made and glared at the young man's nakedness. It had taken time to earn this one's trust, but now that he had it, he knew what to do. It wouldn't take long.

Perhaps in some small measure he made a living from fishing after all. The old man stared down at his flashing laptop, blowing smoke from his nostrils. A smile strained the contours of his face.

Yes, there was little doubt. Money would be good this week.

South Chicago
9:50 P.M.

The cheap motel room reeked of cigarettes, stale beer, and pizza. The best thing Charlie Swain could say about the four walls that closed in on him now was that a heat wave kept his AC cranked. And he had the TV blaring to cover up the sound of sex from the next room. The woman was a real screamer.

He loved sticking it to a woman who knew how to scream, but having to listen to someone else do it left him frustrated, with no options except a five-finger spankfest. He raked fingers through his thinning hair and lit another cigarette, pacing the floor.

This dump had been his home for five days, but for the last two weeks he'd lived out of a suitcase, moving from place to place. While he waited for new ID and a gig with a connected dealer up North, he'd severed all links to his old life, including giving up his wheels. Buses had become his new mode of transportation, to stretch his limited funds. Fake ID would cost him serious coin.

But Charlie knew boredom would be the real test. When his cell phone rang, he wanted nothing more than to answer it, breaking up the monotony. Instead, he let it roll to voice mail, cautiously screening his calls. He finished the last of his warm beer and sat on the edge of his mattress until curiosity needled him into retrieving the message. He didn't recognize the phone number, but the caller had left a message.

A woman's voice. Crying. Cursing. The melodrama made him chuckle until he heard a familiar name. The message was intended for his ex-girlfriend, the bitch. He replayed the call, trying to make out the words between the curses and sobs.

"Leave my Danny be . . . he got me pregnant . . . and when I find out where you live, Annie Rae Miller, I'm gonna . . . What the hell kind of name is that?"

He might have found the whole thing entertaining, except that Annie had dumped him before his life went into the crapper. And now everything made sense. That whore had been cheating on him with Dan the Man.

"Shit." He threw the beer bottle across the room, shattering it against the wall.

When his cell phone rang again, he looked at the display and recognized the number. The same woman was calling back. This time he answered it.

"Yeah."

The woman didn't say anything at first, but he heard her crying. In a soft voice, she finally spoke.

"I'm sorry. I m-must have the . . . wrong number. Do you know wh-where I can find . . . Annie Rae Miller?"

"I got your last message," he offered. "You think your man's with her now?"

"Hell, yeah. I know it for a fact. That's why . . ."

Rage flooded through him like water hitting a fast boil. He didn't even listen to what the woman said. "What's your name again?"

"Sophie."

"Well, Sophie girl, I know this is gonna sound crazy, but please . . . come and get me. I don't have a car at the moment, but I know where you can find that bitch," he pleaded. "But you gotta come pick me up first."

It took him time to convince the woman that he was on the level, but she eventually agreed to pick him up. *Women! Sometimes, they were real gullible.* He gave her directions, and twenty minutes later he heard a knock. He crept to the door and peeked out the peephole, checking out the woman dabbing her eyes with tissue.

Not bad. He smiled. If things worked out, he might have a screamer of his own before the night was done. But when Charlie flung open the door, he came face-to-face with the business end of a .357 Magnum Colt Python.

"Hello, Charlie." The woman grinned, aiming the weapon

between his eyes. "Looks like my man Danny isn't the only one getting screwed."

Taller than he was, she was lean and athletic, glaring at him with unflinching dark eyes. The woman wore a windbreaker with the top of her Kevlar vest showing, prepared for business. And she had a scar above an eyebrow, the jagged mark too nasty to ignore. No shrinking violet, the bitch would have been intimidating even if she weren't carrying a gun.

"You're under arrest for jumpin' bail. You skipped a court date." She flashed her badge. "Now turn around."

Over her shoulder, she yelled, "I've got him."

She wasn't alone. Resisting arrest would land him in more trouble with the law, not to mention getting the crap beat out of him. He'd heard stories about bounty hunters and even seen them in action on cable.

He took a deep breath and did as he was told. She shoved him against the wall and cuffed him, frisking him for weapons after she'd subdued him. He heard her speaking to someone he couldn't see, but when she shoved him toward a blue van outside the motel room door, he realized he'd been tricked again.

"Shit! You were working alone." He launched into a tirade of curses.

"Not exactly, Charlie. I've got my summer intern with me . . . and if you don't cooperate, he might give you a paper cut."

Charlie shut his eyes and kept walking toward the van, conceding his fate.

After securing her prisoner in the back, Fugitive Recovery Agent Jessica Beckett jumped into the front passenger seat next to Seth Harper, a new hire she jokingly called her "summer intern." She hadn't lied about everything.

Harper greeted her with a big grin, handing her ten bucks. "I'm not betting with you anymore. All you had was his cell phone and an old girlfriend's name and you still tracked him. Un-fuckin'-believable."

"Just remember the horn dog factor, Harper." She took his money. "You can always track a guy through his woman. The love muscle is nothing but an Achilles' heel. Beckett rule number one."

Charlie Swain was a no account scrub—a fringe dweller on the edge of humanity—hustling drugs and stolen merchandise. He was wanted on two warrants, including skipping a court date on robbery charges. A real charmer, but relatively harmless in her world. She made a note to the file she'd compiled on the guy, a record of the case and her authorization for the arrest—a certified copy of the warrant.

Top-notch Fugitive Recovery Agents got paid better working directly for specific bondsmen. Most were ex-military or former police officers. She didn't have the qualifications, discipline, or temperament to land her anything more than being a freelancer, catching the odd jobs that usually didn't pay as much. She had to work twice as hard to make ends meet, earning her negotiated percentage of the bond money.

As a woman, building a reputation in this business had been tough. She realized she could have done better, but kissing ass wasn't her thing, not even if the ass was Grade A prime. To date, cops had been her biggest critics, mostly because she had to live down the cable TV bounty hunter image. Yet she had to admit that some of her rep had been well-deserved.

It had been a gamble to hire Harper, but she hoped that with the proper training she might gain an eventual partner to help with the tracking aspects of each case. The quicker she gathered intel, the better the cash flow would be. Although she'd never put him at risk by placing him in the line of fire, Harper had been the one asking to come along on her arrests.

"Call it in, will ya? And let's get this guy to the cops. A

girl has gotta pay the bills." Jess took a long swig of water, listening to Harper as he made the call to the bondsman for the Swain job. "God, this heat is killer. I'm sweatin' like a pig with an invite to a luau."

To cool off, she took off the Kevlar vest that she wore under a windbreaker as Harper finished up. After he started the van and pulled from the motel parking lot, she got another call on her cell. She recognized the phone number, even though NO NAME appeared on the display. Fingering the scar above her eyebrow, she prayed the call meant what she thought it would. She took a deep breath and answered.

"Yeah."

"I got a lead on Lucas Baker, but it's gonna cost ya. And you have to move tonight. No guarantees he'll be there tomorrow."

After a quick glance at her watch, Jess clenched her jaw and pictured the face of Baker. The image triggered a flood of dark memories that she thought she had under control . . . until now.

"Gimme what ya got." Jess grabbed paper and pen. "I'm ready . . . more than ready."

CHAPTER 2

Chicago, Illinois
Mid-June

On the other side of midnight, the nasty oppressive heat lingered and made the air dense and sluggish. It clung to the body of Jessica Beckett like a film of wet gauze, stifling her breath. The customary cooling effect off Lake Michigan cowered from it, avoiding the thick and stagnant mass of unseasonable heat. Dressed in dark jeans, a black tee under her Kevlar vest, and a ball cap, she jogged down the street, keeping to the shadows, then made her way across the road. Her gaze shifted to the second floor as she did, counting the windows so she'd know which room. A dimly lit one had its shades partially drawn.

A man inside.

She'd paid good money for the tip that the bastard had a room here, living off the grid, trying to escape his pathetic excuse for a life. And she had done her best to contribute to his problems, targeting Lucas Baker with her obsession. He had been one slippery weasel to corner, but she recognized his ugly mug, even from the street below.

Once Jess got across the street, she headed for the side entrance, down and to the right. Nearing an alley, she reached for her .357 Magnum Colt Python with its four-inch barrel and a trigger as smooth as butter. With gun in hand, she thought of a thousand other places she could've been tonight, but being a woman on a mission left her little choice. And she wasn't one to squander an opportunity.

"You see our target?" She spoke into a two-way com set with a radio on her belt, a mic clipped to a sleeve of her tee, and an ear bud. With a shoulder to a brick wall, she peered down an alley to make sure everything was clear, and maintained her position.

"Affirmative." Her backup, Seth Harper, cleared his throat and nearly blew her eardrum with the sharp abrasive noise. She winced.

"Uh, 10-4," he added.

Jess fought a smile when she heard Seth dishing out the cryptic lingo, resisting the urge to add "good buddy" after everything he said. She could picture him now. The kid was situated in his old beat-up Econoline van across the street and down an alley, probably using binoculars.

"Talk to me. What's he doing?" she prompted, keeping her voice low. "He got any company?"

Out of habit, she traced a scar along her right eyebrow with a finger, an old injury from a lifetime ago.

"Negatory. Target at a table, working on a computer. Laptop, I think."

Baker would have his life on that computer. She could score big if things went as planned.

She wanted to avoid the clerk at the front desk. The tip she got on Baker's whereabouts had warned her the sleaze was tight with the so-called management of the joint. She had to find another way in. With plan B in mind, she ducked into the dark alley and crept along a brick wall, dodging Dumpsters and broken bottles, keeping a firm grip on the Python. The faint stench of puke invaded her nostrils, the rank odor made more caustic with the heat.

She held her breath and moved on, hoping she hadn't stepped in it. With her luck, she'd be wearing it home.

As Jess neared the back of the dilapidated hotel that rented rooms by the hour, she flipped her black White Sox ball cap backward, rally style. Sweat-drenched strands of her dark hair stuck to her neck, aggravating her mounting discomfort. She wiped her palms down a pant leg. Carrying a weapon, now was no time for a slick grip.

Once she got to her destination, she tested the alley door into the old hotel. Locked. After slipping the Python into the custom holster she carried at the small of her back, she pulled out a lock pick kit from her pocket. She didn't need a light to work by. She'd done this a thousand times. When the door creaked open, she stashed the kit and reached for her weapon again.

"I'm going inside. Let me know if he moves," she muttered into her mouthpiece. "No matter what happens, you stay put until you hear from me. You understand? No heroics, Seth." She repeated the instructions she'd given the kid an hour ago. "Call 911 if things get dicey. Going to radio silence now."

"Dicey. Got it."

Seth did his best to maintain radio silence, in his unique way, but his heavy breathing into the mouthpiece reminded her of a late night call from a pervert. The kid held the mic too close to his lips and didn't always release his transmit switch when he was done, another practice she had to correct.

Eventually, Seth broke the silence.

"Define dicey."

With no time to set him straight, she slipped through the back door and shut it behind her, grimacing at the creak of its rusty hinges. Time to get to work.

Jess squinted as she got inside, looking toward the front for a way to the second floor. The hallway looked as dismal as the alley she'd left behind. Gang signs were spray-painted on the walls in an array of colors. And trash was strewn along the baseboards and over a stained ratty carpet that had definitely seen better days. Shoddy wall sconces were positioned down the hall, but with every other bulb burned out, the old hotel looked more like a cheap horror flick. Maybe the dim lights were a blessing in disguise.

Jess walked past each door with caution, not ruling out an ambush, but the place had one purpose for most of its patrons. The sleazy hotel rented by the hour. At the next door that thought was reinforced with the unbroken rhythm of a bed squeak and the steady bang of a headboard against a wall inside the room. A woman's breath caught as she panted her encouragement.

"Yeah, baby, do it." She tossed in a theatrical moan and a gasp. "Harder, that's it. Oh, you're so good."

It didn't take long for the woman's companion to cry out, a loud pitiable groan. Prone to a cynical nature, Jess wondered what Mr. Stopwatch would do with his remaining fifty-five minutes. She rolled her eyes and kept moving toward the stairs in front. Her weapon held in a two-fisted grip, she drifted down the hall with eyes alert.

Until—

"Jess? Target's on the move. You read me?" Seth cried out through her earpiece. "He's spooked."

Her eyes grew wide. Baker must have heard the noisy door hinges or been warned by the front desk. She broke into a sprint toward the stairs and collided with an old wooden banister as she rounded it, bruising a hip. *Damn it!*

From the front desk of the hotel a sleazy guy in a wrinkled T-shirt and a scraggly beard yelled after her. "Hey, where're you goin'? I'm callin' the cops, lady."

Jess looked over her shoulder, her sarcasm on full throttle. "Then you better flush the hookers. I'd hate to see you lose your Triple A rating."

She barely had time to respond to the clerk's warning when she heard Seth screaming in her ear, "He's out the door. I can't see him, Jess. What do you want me to do?"

She heard the panic in his voice, but a door slammed on

the second floor and drew her attention. She had to move. Fast.

She bounded up the stairs, taking two steps at a time, gripping the banister with her left hand to propel her body up. When she got to the top, she raised her weapon, ready for anything. The stainless steel of the Python glinted under the pale light as she moved the barrel right, then hard left.

That's when she heard the footsteps down the hall, running away from her. She rounded a corner in time to see Baker slip through a door marked EXIT, but not before he turned to grin. A shaved meaty head set atop no neck on a square muscular body, the physique of a wrestler. *Scumbag!* Baker had a lead and the laptop under his arm.

"Not gonna happen, asshole!"

Jess chased after him. She knew he might stage an ambush at the exit door, but it didn't matter. She'd risk anything to get this jerk. *Anything!*

"He's going out the back. The fire escape." She took time to let Seth know what was going on. Otherwise, the kid might do something she'd regret later. "Hold your position. Don't do anything."

She ended the communication, but muttered under her breath, "This bastard's mine."

Jess grabbed the door and shoved through it with a shoulder. Once she got on the other side, she slammed it quick, not wanting to make herself a target silhouetted against the light. She aimed the gun down the grated metal steps. As her eyes adjusted to the sudden darkness, she searched the shadows below for any sign of movement.

Nothing.

Baker could have her in his sights even now and she wouldn't know until it was too late. With her heart throttling her ribs, Jess steadied her breathing. She crept down the steps, her back to the wall, with the business end of the Python trained down the alley. Adrenaline had her wired, but she didn't want to make a mistake. Having a bad day in her line of work could put her in the hospital or the morgue.

When she got to the bottom of the fire escape, she looked up and down the alley, unsure where he'd gone. He had a lead, but not enough for him to lose her. The hair at the nape of her neck stood on end. More than likely he lurked beyond the light, waiting for her to turn her back. The safest course for a sane person would be to walk toward the street in front, sticking with the light. Instead, she followed her gut instincts and headed deeper into the alley—into the dark.

Sanity was highly overrated.

She listened for anything out of the ordinary, but the sounds of the city made that nearly impossible. Her feet crunched over glass and gravel. She couldn't afford to look where she stepped, not taking her eyes off what little she could see. He'd hear her coming but it couldn't be helped.

Still, she pressed on, the Python in her grip.

Suddenly, she heard a faint rustle coming from inside a Dumpster up ahead. She held her breath and crept closer, straining to hear a repeat, but nothing. Had she only imagined it? She swallowed hard, knowing Baker might leap out at any second, ready to shoot. She adjusted her grip and kept moving. The metal bin loomed dead ahead, with so many places for him to hide. Doubts surged through her brain, mixed with a strong dose of self-preservation, but she struggled to stay focused.

Jess heard the frailty in her breath and felt the sharp thrash of her heart. In a second she'd know if Baker hid inside the trash where he belonged. To get a drop on him, she had to raise the lid, fast. Any hesitation could get her killed. She eased a palm to the heavy lid, took a deep breath, then shoved with all her strength.

"Unghh," she grunted and threw back the lid, pointing her gun into the shadows.

"Yowwgrrrr."

A loud shriek crawled under her skin and up her spine.

Movement deep in the shadows. A dark cat leapt from the bin and bounded over her shoulder. Its claws found her face and neck. The sting of the attack sent shivers across her skin like tiny needle pricks.

"Shit!" she cried out and leapt back, almost losing her footing on a broken beer bottle. The glass shot across the alley and shattered against the wall.

"Jess? What's going on? Can you hear me?" She heard Seth's voice in her ear as if he stood right behind her. A startling sensation. Almost creepy. She was used to working alone.

She looked down into the Dumpster and frantically searched the outside. Baker wasn't there. She'd lost him. She nearly collapsed against the brick wall behind the trash bin, sweat streaming from every pore. Bending over, she braced a hand to her knee to keep from falling over, loosening her grip on the Python. Shaking her head, she couldn't believe her lousy luck.

"I'm okay, Seth. But . . . I think I lost him." She gulped the hot moist air, her throat raspy. "Gonna keep looking. Stay put."

Jess replayed the chase with Baker in her head. It had all happened so fast, but she couldn't believe she missed him again. Shaking it off, she raised her weapon and headed for the rear of the alley. That's when she heard it.

An engine.

Headlights flashed on, drilling her in their spotlight. She squinted and raised a hand to shield her eyes. The screech of tires jolted her heart. And the smell of burning rubber hit her nose. When a cloud of dust kicked up, it drifted in front of the headlights like an eerie fog. She knew it was Baker behind the wheel of the dark SUV even though she couldn't see his ugly face.

He'd hit the gas and headed straight for her.

Jess had a choice, but not much of one. She could leap for the Dumpster, hoping he wouldn't ram into it and crush her against the wall. But another option had more appeal. And she was pissed enough to do it.

She gritted her teeth and planted her feet, took in a deep breath and let it out. She held up the Python in both hands—rock steady—aiming for the faceless driver behind the wheel. If she were going down, she'd take Lucas Baker with her.

Time to play chicken with six thousand pounds of steel.

CHAPTER 3

Seconds.

Precious seconds.

The SUV barreled down on her, the engine revved. No more time.

Jess held her ground, the Colt Python clutched in her hands. The muscles in her arms taut, her grip solid. Adrenaline surged through her system like coiled lightning.

"Jess? Are you okay?" Seth's fear-stricken voice shot over her earpiece.

Without hitting her com switch, she held her concentration and muttered under her breath, "Not now, Seth."

Glare from the headlights nearly blinded her, but once the SUV got close, she could finally see. The bastard's face came into focus through the murky haze of the windshield. That's where she aimed—between his eyes. When she saw his sudden panic, she squeezed the trigger.

The Python bucked in her grip. Once. Twice. A fierce plume of fire streaked from the muzzle. Deafening blasts echoed down the alley, magnifying the intense explosions.

Her ears rang then muffled everything that followed as holes punched through the windshield with a weighty pop.

The glass splintered, sending fissures across the once smooth surface. With one last measure of desperation, she aimed at his crankcase and let the Python do its worst. Baker collapsed behind the wheel and the vehicle swerved. It hit the wall to her right, spraying shards of brick. The shriek of metal stabbed her eardrums, rippling goose bumps across her skin. In a fiery display, sparks showered the air, a giant sparkler on the Fourth of July.

Jess leapt to her left, narrowly escaping the metal behemoth. The SUV came to a grinding halt down the alley from where she lay sprawled on her stomach, facedown in the filth near the Dumpster. The engine revved, sounding like Baker still had his foot on the gas. But in the shadow of the SUV through the back window, she couldn't see him. No silhouette. The headlights pierced the night. Smoke drifted from the engine and across the beams with bugs lured to the light. Still no Baker.

She got to her feet, holding her weapon in both hands. On unsteady legs she crept toward the vehicle from the rear, prepared for the worst. Even though her skin felt raw from scrapes, and sweat trailed down her back like unwanted fingers, she kept her eyes fixed on the driver's front seat. No movement inside.

But as she got closer, all that changed.

Baker loomed in the shadows. He rose from where he'd slumped and hit the gas again, trying to break free of the wall. Metal whined as it grated against brick and mortar.

"Oh no you don't, you sick twisted jerk!"

Jess secured the Python into its holster and took off running. A full-out sprint. Baker had a lead. If he got out of the alley and into traffic, she'd lose him. In the suffocating heat, her lungs strained for air. Her legs burned with lactic acid at the sudden burst of speed. *Shit!* Baker punched the gas and made it to the mouth of the alley. But as he turned hard left, he nearly collided with a van.

Seth's blue monster.

Baker slammed on his horn and yelled obscenities as if he had the right of way. Surprisingly cool under fire, Seth lurched the van forward when Baker tried to drive around him. It gave Jess time to catch up. She lunged for the handle and flung the passenger door open just as Baker hit the gas. She grabbed for anything to keep her upright but lost her battle. Her hand found an armrest, and with the other, she wrapped a wrist tight into a seat belt. She ran as fast as she could until her feet gave out.

When Baker picked up speed, she struggled against being pulled under the SUV. Her ankles and legs battered against the ground. The friction made them feel on fire. As her fingers strained with the weight of her body, Baker swerved. The door flew wide, pulling from her grip.

"Let go, bitch!" he screamed, his eyes maniacal and cruel.

In the background, Jess heard police sirens growing louder. Baker heard it too. A mean vicious evil swept across his face. He had to ditch her, fast.

He swung the SUV left at the next turn. Her body swept wide, whipping her back against the door. Her spine nearly snapped in two. Although she knew she couldn't hang on much longer, letting go wasn't an option until she got what she wanted. If she couldn't get Baker, she'd take the next best thing. Her eyes fixed on the laptop lying on the floorboard.

"Ummphh."

With a grunt, Jess shoved from the door handle and swung toward Baker. He reached for her and pressed a hand to her face, blocking her air. Blind, she grappled for the laptop, her body suspended only by the seat belt.

When she grasped the computer bag, she pulled at the strap and let gravity do the rest.

Baker screamed, *"Nooo!"*

He lunged for her, and the SUV veered right. She tried to break free of the seat belt, but Baker held her wrist, almost wrenching her shoulder out of its socket. Jess yanked the laptop to her chest, clinging to the hardware like a lifeline.

He tugged at her arm, pulling her inside. Without her footing, she had nothing to leverage against, and he gained an advantage in their battle of tug-a-war. Police sirens blared from everywhere now. Speeding onto a street with more traffic, Baker drove with one hand and yanked at her with the other. He craned his neck behind him looking for flashing lights. They were an accident waiting to happen.

In a minute he'd get her inside—and have his computer back. Damned if she'd let that happen!

Baker didn't care what happened to her, she reasoned. He only wanted his property. And with the cops closing in, he wouldn't risk slowing down. She'd have one chance. She had to make it count.

When he had her balanced on the edge of the passenger seat, he let go of her arm and wrestled for the computer she now clutched to her chest. It was the break she'd been waiting for.

She bit into Baker's hand until he let go.

"Aarrgghh!" he shrieked. "Shit!"

He pulled back his hand in reflex, and she rolled toward the open door and fell out the moving vehicle, still gripping the laptop. Her hip hit the street, jarring her teeth and neck. Out of control, her body careened across the road, tumbling and scraping the pavement. Still, she held onto the computer, sheltering it from damage with her arms and chest. For that, she paid the price. It jabbed her ribs and elbows, sending shock waves of pain through her, but her Kevlar vest insulated her from more damage.

When Jess slammed into a parked car, stars burst behind her eyes and through her skull. She struggled to stay conscious, her eyes seeing only a blur. A police car sped past her—siren blaring and lights flashing—hot after Baker. The first cop led the pursuit, but she knew he'd radio the others to find her. Other cops weren't far behind. Not much time before they caught up to her and she'd have to answer a lot of questions.

Jess shoved the computer into the shadows under the parked car that had stopped her perilous fall from the SUV. With great effort, she lifted herself off the pavement, every bone and inch of her skin aching. With a pronounced limp and chest heaving, she hobbled to the curb and stumbled down the block, away from the prize she'd stashed from the cops.

When she looked down to assess the damage, she only shook her head and kept walking. Her lungs burned. Everything hurt. Insult to injury, Baker had torn her T-shirt and she smelled like puke, but topping her WTF list, she'd lost her White Sox ball cap. *Damn it!* She wanted to collapse at the curb but had to put distance between her and Baker's computer. She wanted a crack at it before the cops.

As a distraction from the pain and insult, Jess reached for her com set. The earpiece and microphone dangled from her shirt, out of place, but the unit itself had stayed put. A regular miracle that ranked right up there with how she'd survived another clash with Baker.

"Seth? You . . . there?"

"Where are you?" he cried, worry heavy in his voice. She heard the sound of his engine in the background. He was on the move.

"No time . . . to explain," she gasped, out of breath. "I stashed . . . Baker's laptop."

She quickly told him where to look. "Cops are gonna . . . take me into custody soon. I'm not gonna make it hard for them . . . to find me, but don't worry. Just get that computer. Start working on it. You got that?"

"Yeah, but Jess—"

"No buts, Seth. Just work your magic, genius. I'll catch you later."

With every muscle in agony and protesting, Jess took off her com set and ditched it under a withering shrub in front of a house up for sale. The ramshackle dump didn't look like hot property, so her equipment was probably safe until she could pick it up later. She was in enough hot water. No need calling attention to Seth, her Boy Wonder and resident Einstein with a computer.

Besides, she had bigger problems.

A siren closed in. They'd be on her soon. Jess heard the crunch of gravel under a tire as the patrol car pulled to the curb. She kept walking, keeping her back to the cops. No sudden moves. Spiraling red and blue lights filled the dark sky with color. Party time. She slowed down, nice and easy, heard the cop's voice pierce the fog building in her brain.

"Stop right there." A stern voice. "Put your hands up. Now!"

"Okay, okay. I'm all about cooperation here."

She did as she'd been told, stopped and raised her hands, still not turning around. She knew the cop had a gun on her. Protocol. She wouldn't do anything to provoke a fight with the boys in blue.

"Get on your knees, hands behind your head. Do it!" Another voice. A cop and his partner.

Feeling beat up and raw, Jess didn't have any more fight in her. Sinking to her knees, she yelled over her shoulder, "Officers? I'm a freelance Fugitive Recovery Agent. And I've got a permit to carry and a Colt Python under my shirt. I can explain everything."

"Yeah, I bet you can . . ." one of them said. "Bounty hunter."

The cop said the words like he'd just been forced to eat raw monkey brains on a cracker at gunpoint and couldn't spit it out. She hated the term "bounty hunter." Cable TV hadn't done her profession any favors. And today her obsession with Baker hadn't helped.

Ignoring the cop's cynicism, she closed her eyes as they manhandled her to the sidewalk, yanking her hands behind her back to fit her into cuffs. And, of course, they took her gun. Back at the local cop shop, word would get around she'd been at it again. Her crusade against Lucas Baker would be under harsher scrutiny.

Jess appreciated the challenge of talking her way out of this, but knew she'd never fool one set of dark eyes. Detective Samantha Cooper had her number. And they went far enough back to make lying impossible. If Sam got called in at this hour, Jess knew her night had only just begun.

For a cop, the ringing of a phone in the middle of the night meant only one thing—bad news.

Samantha Cooper awoke as if waiting for it. Her eyes popped open on the first ring. No need to wait for cobwebs to clear. In the dark of her bedroom, she reached for the phone on her nightstand, her voice steady and calm.

"Cooper." Already on the job, she answered like an on-duty cop.

"Hey, Sam. Sorry to wake you. Miller here."

She recognized the voice of the night desk sergeant, Jackson Miller, a top-notch cop cruising to retirement.

"Yeah, Sarge. What's up?" Raised on one elbow, she flicked on the light and squinted as she grabbed the pen and paper she kept handy by the phone. "I'm not on tonight."

"I know, but I got something you might want to hear. Something personal." He paused only a moment before he continued. "It's your friend Jessica Beckett."

Sam's heart lurched. She tossed the pen on her nightstand and slumped back onto the pillows, pulling the covers to her chest. Her stomach suddenly felt queasy, like the aftereffects of a roller coaster free falling from its pinnacle on full tilt. A part of her had known this day would come, when she'd get the call in the middle of the night telling her Jess had crossed one too many lines in the sand. Maybe her friend had been living on borrowed time from the day they'd met.

Fearing the worst, Sam couldn't stop the flood of memories from invading her mind, dark childhood images that had changed her life forever. In truth, they were never far from the surface. They had marked her and stripped away what remained of her innocence. Scars buried deep. But in her mind it had been far worse for Jess, who dealt with the scars she carried on the outside, visible for all to see.

"Is she . . . ?" Sam shut her eyes, catching the emotion in her voice. She cleared her throat. "What about her, Sarge?"

She waited for him to spit it out.

"She had another run-in with that scumbag Baker. And it ain't going well, if you know what I mean."

Sam breathed a sigh of relief, but shook her head. Baker served as the catalyst for a longtime crusade Jess had against sex peddlers in all shapes, sizes, and perversions. And her childhood friend had elevated pissing people off into an art form. Jess never knew when to quit. Most days, she admired her for it. No, the word "envied" described it best. That kind of attitude not only emblazoned the way she lived her life, but how she had survived what happened to her.

But in the solitude of her heart, Sam knew the truth. Jess had become her Achilles' heel, the focus of a pervasive guilt that made it impossible to turn an apathetic shoulder to her friend. She knew it. And at times she suspected Jess used it against her—all for the greater good, of course.

"I'm coming in. Who's got the lead on this?"

"You're not gonna like it, Sam."

She felt the start of a tension headache tighten at the base of her skull. No way to start the day, but sidestepping it was out of the question. She knew what Sergeant Miller was going to say before the words were out of his mouth.

"The chief has taken a personal interest."

"This time of night?" With brow furrowed, she glanced toward her alarm clock. "It's almost three."

"He got called in on a high-profile murder that happened two hours ago. Some rapper I ain't even heard of. A gang thing." The sergeant lowered his voice. "Anyway, once the press left, he caught your friend's case. Bad luck for her."

Sam shut her eyes again and took a deep breath. She worked at Harrison Station, the Eleventh District. Last year, Harrison took top prize on the most murders in the Chicago metropolitan area. A dubious distinction her fellow detectives would have preferred to pass on. The chief's personal concern over this statistic did not surprise her. The media would be all over this one, dredging up the station's marginal record once again.

As a member of the metro police department, Sam worked in Vice Control under the Detective Division of the Bureau of Investigative Services. She'd been working her way toward Homicide for the past two years, hoping to catch a break into the more prestigious unit. She didn't need this. Butting heads with the chief, her boss's boss several times removed, was not her idea of a smart career move.

Within BIS, the chief headed up her entire division and had five deputy chiefs reporting to him. Plus, the man had shot up through the ranks like a regular golden boy, garnering the favor of the superintendent and many others during his meteoric rise.

How far would she go to get Jess off the hook this time?

Her personal connection to Jess was already known within the CPD, but no one knew the reasons behind her loyalty. Her pact with Jess had gone unspoken, a commitment born as much from her own burden of guilt as the love she felt for her headstrong friend.

But Sam's career in law enforcement meant everything to her. It had become the focal point to her life, giving her a sense of worth. Would she be forced to choose between her life's blood and the friend she loved like a sister?

Sam prayed it wouldn't go that far.

"I'm coming in, Sarge." She tossed back the covers and sat on the edge of her bed. "Be there in thirty."

Talkeetna Alaska
River Park Campground
1:00 A.M. AKDT

On the northwest side of town, Nikki hid in the scarce shadows by the public restrooms of the campground, waiting for her ride. This time of year, the sun merely dipped below the horizon, leaving behind a wedge of time where the night sky was as dark as it ever got—a deep dusk that would eventually turn to morning.

The best time to make her escape.

Her duffel bag lay near her feet as she paced with hands in her jacket pockets. In the distance she smelled a campfire, and saw its glow through the trees. Soft voices and the lingering aroma of a late night dinner drifted toward her, making her stomach growl. She hadn't counted on this. Who would be up and cooking this time of night? She rolled her eyes at the ridiculous question. Why should she care?

In no time she'd be gone. All she had to do was keep a low profile until then.

In the background the confluence of the Talkeetna and Susitna rivers surged against a steel gray sky. Normally, the white noise of the water would be soothing, but not tonight. The unsettling rush made her more anxious. Dressed in a royal blue windbreaker and jeans, she wished she wore another layer. It felt chillier by the river, and a brisk evening breeze had kicked up. Maybe nerves had more to do with her shivers. A silver Subaru Outback would pick her up, and the signal of flashing headlights had been prearranged.

She knew after tonight her life would change forever.

"Come on," she whispered under her breath.

She'd done all her thinking. No regrets. She didn't see the point in having second thoughts. Drained, she finally slouched onto the canvas bag, straddling it. She kept her eyes on the drive into the park. And to ward off the cold, she rubbed her thighs with her hands.

Nikki hated making her ride drive through town to pick her up, but the campground wouldn't draw many locals this time of night. And since it was close to her home, she wouldn't have to lug her duffel far. It made sense at the time she arranged it through her friend Ivana, but now she felt out of place . . . and alone.

In the fanny pack around her waist she carried the essentials she'd need for the trip. She'd been told to leave any credit cards and her cell phone behind, making it impossible for her mother or the law to trace her once she got where she was going.

She had followed her instructions to the letter, severing all links to the life she'd left behind.

This should have felt liberating, but it only reminded her of the deceitful way she skulked out of the house in the middle of the night. She left her mom a cryptic note, saying only that she had gone and would contact her when she could. Anything more would have been trouble.

But a strange mix of dread and relief came when headlights pierced the gray murkiness, flickering between the tall stand of evergreens. A car eased toward the park. At that distance and angle, Nikki couldn't make out the color or make. She stood and craned her neck for a better look. About the time she poked her head up, a young man emerged from the trees to her right. He barged down the trail without a care in the world.

"Oh shit," she gasped, nearly leaping out of her skin. "You scared me."

"Sorry. Didn't know you had this section of the park staked as private property." He grinned. "Just here to drain the lizard. You okay?"

Between the river noise and the distraction of the car, she hadn't heard him coming down the path. The guy was tall and lean, with dark hair. He had a nice smile and kind, soulful eyes. She gauged him for late teens or early twenties. With her heart still racing, her judgment meter was way out of whack. Normally, he would have been her type, but she had more on her mind.

"Yeah. Why wouldn't I be?" Nikki sneaked a peek past him toward the headlights. She had to ditch him fast or all bets were off. "I had to use the restroom, that's all."

The kid chuckled. "Yeah, right. So why'd you lug the duffel with you? Planning on staying awhile?"

Nikki swallowed and blinked—caught in her lie. After a quick second, she collected her thoughts enough to glare at him with hands on hips, going on the offensive.

"Why don't you go and take care of your . . . lizard." She raised her chin in defiance. "I got better things to do than talk to you."

Pretty lame, but it was all that sprang into her head. The guy smirked and walked by her with a shrug, more amused than pissed. But before he got near the men's room entrance, he glanced over his shoulder and checked out the car driving up. Maybe in the shadows and the glare of the headlights, he wouldn't see much. Or God willing, the whole incident wouldn't register with him. He vanished into the darkness of the men's room, but not before the damage had been done.

She had overreacted. Chalk it up to a bad case of nerves, but now someone had seen her and the car. Her only prayer was that the kid would be gone in the morning, before the search for her had begun.

As planned, the vehicle parked and flashed its lights twice. From this range and through the headlights, Nikki couldn't see inside. Almost sick to her stomach, she reached down to pick up her duffel bag and hoisted the strap over a shoulder. She looked up the footpath and down, to make sure no one else saw, then ventured from the trees. She walked toward the car, gravel crunching underfoot. Even up close she still was unable to see the driver's face. And no one got out. When she reached for the door, doubt kicked her heart into high gear and throbbed in her ears.

She knew once she got inside there'd be no turning back. After taking one last breath of the crisp night air, she opened the rear door and tossed in her bag, then slipped into the front passenger seat and shut the door behind her.

She didn't want to believe in regrets.

Harrison Police Station
3:25 A.M. CST

After Sam got to Harrison Station, Sergeant Miller filled her in on what had happened and directed her to the holding room where they'd detained Jess for questioning. Detective Ray Garza was interrogating her now. Baker had been taken into custody but was kicked loose. No arrest.

So why were they still questioning Jess?

Sam was digesting all the details of her friend's encounter with Baker and the aftermath when she opened the door to the adjoining observation room. She found Chief Nathan Keller dressed in a pricy suit and standing in the darkened room with only the light from the adjacent interrogation room shining through the two-way mirror. He glanced at her with little acknowledgment and turned his attention back to the interrogation without saying a word.

Sam contemplated the possibility of slinking from the room, but for the sake of her friend she took a deep breath and joined the chief, standing shoulder-to-shoulder in the dimly lit room.

When she caught her first look at Jess, her eyes widened with shock. She fought to stifle her reaction.

Jessie was battered and bruised. Cuts and scrapes on her face were stark under the fluorescent lights, making her skin appear ghostly pale. Jess stared at Detective Garza, sitting across from her, her face unreadable, her eyes blank. Sam knew that look. Jess had survived worse than Garza could dish out in his wildest imaginings. No way the detective would break her.

A voice came over the speaker overhead, sounds of the interrogation.

"Tell me one more time, what were you doing at the hotel?"

"I already told you."

Jess sounded tired, but there was an underlying intensity to her demeanor, a shrewd feline ready to pounce on its prey. At times Sam could read her friend, but only if Jess let her.

"I came to talk to Baker. I got a tip he'd be there."

"Talk? About what?"

"A private matter, between me and him."

"Since when do you talk with a Colt Python in your hand? The hotel clerk said you chased after Baker, carrying a weapon."

"In that neighborhood, I'd be foolish not to protect myself. And you gotta admit, a Colt Python is a pretty nifty ice breaker." Jess shifted in her seat. "Are you gonna arrest me? If not, I think I've had enough fun for one evening. I need my beauty sleep."

Sam understood her friend's sarcasm about her looks. When Jess looked in the mirror, she only saw the scars. And any man interested in her only wanted one thing, according to Jessie. She gave it when she had the same urges, but the room had to be completely dark and on her terms. No romance. No talking. No future. Jessie had no time for complications.

"She's a cagey one." The chief finally said. "Your friend should consider exercising her right to remain silent."

"She may have the right, sir, but she sure doesn't have the ability."

She caught Chief Keller glancing down at her with a faint look of amusement.

"What's your interest in this, Detective?"

The man turned his attention to Jess in the next room. Sam did the same.

"Personal, sir."

Jess wasn't the only one who knew about cagey. Sam's answer was the equivalent of saying, "With all due respect, none of your business, sir." She tightened her jaw, waiting for his response.

Silence filled the tight quarters. Sam felt the tension as Chief Keller stiffened beside her. The occasional voices carried over the speaker above, but the noise was muffled in her head. She was too distracted to register what was said.

After a long moment the chief spoke.

"Understand this, Detective Cooper. If you expect to advance your career, you must avoid the negative perceptions of others by steering clear of controversy. Your personal friend in there is mired in it. Par for the course, from what I can see."

The man knew more about her relationship with Jess than she had given him credit for. She shut her eyes tight. None of this bode well for her career. The chief continued, dropping another bombshell.

"You may have to make a choice, Detective. That is, if you truly want to make the leap into the homicide division."

He knew about her political maneuverings inside the department, lobbying for Homicide. She swallowed, hard. This was either a very good thing or she had completely blown it.

As if reading her mind, he added, "I've got my eye on you, Samantha. I expect your help in persuading your stubborn friend to let things cool between her and Baker. For both your sakes, I hope she listens to you."

He turned to go, but Sam couldn't resist another question. "What happened with Baker, sir?"

She already knew the answer to her question. Sergeant Miller had briefed her, but she wanted to see if the chief would lie. Unfortunately, the man had a third option in mind. He completely ignored her insubordination.

"Process her out and get her home, Detective Cooper. Mr. Baker is none of your concern."

Chief Keller left the room. And Sam never turned around.

Next door, Garza had given up and left Jess alone. Her friend sat rigid in the chair, not giving an inch. Eventually, she shifted her gaze to the mirror, knowing someone stood behind it. With stubborn defiance, Jess glared at the glass. Sam wanted to smile but knew the pain behind those eyes. The defense mechanism it took to hide her true emotions had been borne from years of abuse and the unflinching will of a survivor.

Sam debated how much to tell Jess about what she'd learned about Baker. In the end she decided she could never talk Jess out of her personal vendetta, nor did she want to.

Anchorage International Airport
3:20 A.M. AKDT

Claire Hanson had already been on edge, but when the young girl didn't say much during the drive from Talkeetna to Anchorage, it made the trip seem like an eternity. Her attempt at conversation died on the Parks Highway when the girl avoided eye contact and kept to simple answers, if she replied at all. Her young passenger merely stared out the side window onto a murky blur of scenery.

And the chill in the morning air closed in on them both.

Claire didn't know what to expect, given the girl's special situation. But the poor kid needed help, leaving her little choice but to do what she could. Besides, the resemblance was uncanny. Even if she'd wanted to call the whole thing off, she couldn't—not after seeing the girl's face.

The airport terminal was busier than she expected, with the first bank of red-eye flights departing Anchorage. After pulling to the curb marked for departures, Claire parked the Subaru and turned off the engine. She leaned toward the girl and forced her to make eye contact this time.

"Everything's going to be okay now. You'll see."

She reached out and stroked a loose strand of hair off the kid's face, a familiar gesture that clouded Claire's eyes with painful memories. The girl nodded, her eyes brimming with the start of tears, but she said nothing.

"Here's your ticket and ID. You know what to do, right?" Handing over an envelope, Claire tried to keep the tension from her voice. "I mean, he told you what to do, didn't he?"

"Yeah, I know what to do." The troubled kid managed a fleeting smile. "And thanks."

After a long moment burdened by the silence between two strangers, the girl looked at her plane ticket, then opened the car door and got her belongings from the backseat. While she did, Claire searched her mind for something to say. Anything to make one last connection. She wanted nothing more than to ask the girl to call her when she got where she was going—a mother's instinct. But she had no right to ask that. She knew this would be the last time she'd see her.

Knowing she'd done the right thing had to be enough.

After the car doors slammed, the girl walked into the airport terminal looking small and unprepared, lugging her big duffel bag. A breath caught in Claire's throat when the girl turned to look over her shoulder and waved. At that moment—for the first time—she felt a twinge of doubt.

If she had done the right thing, why did it feel so wrong?

Nikki had wanted to tell the woman not to worry, but Ivana had warned her not to talk to her. Her father had made the arrangements and could get into a lot of trouble if she did. Best friends don't rat each other out, she'd told her. Besides, Ivana and her father were only trying to help.

Despite what she'd been told, Nikki couldn't help but make one final gesture to the woman who had driven her to Anchorage. She turned to catch a glimpse of Claire through the huge airport window and waved one last time. Red taillights disappeared down a departure ramp against the backdrop of a pale gray morning. A part of her felt rooted to the spot, yet another part yearned to make her first step toward a new beginning.

Finally, she slung the duffel bag over her shoulder and headed for the airline check-in counter. Soon she'd be in Chicago to meet her friend Ivana Noskova and her father. When she walked by a bank of public pay phones, she stopped and glanced down at her watch. She checked her plane ticket once again and knew she'd have time before her flight took off.

Nikki tossed down her bag and pulled out some coins, but not before she retrieved a special remembrance from her fanny pack. The photo off her desk. It was from her thirteenth birthday, one of the last days she'd been truly happy. She couldn't leave it behind.

She gazed at the photo and placed the call.

She knew that receiving a call at this time of morning would trigger a sense of panic in most people that something bad had happened—but not Uncle Payton. With him, there was a fifty-fifty chance he'd be home at all. He lived on the lunatic fringe of humanity. A restless soul. Nikki couldn't resist reaching out to him. She knew why she split from her mother, but Uncle Payton was another story. She hoped he would understand that she had to do this.

As the phone rang, she held her breath. If he answered, she wasn't sure what she'd say. Mostly, she just wanted to hear his voice, and she wasn't disappointed.

"I'm screening my calls to avoid someone. Leave a message, but if I don't call you back, then it's you."

A long beep followed Uncle Payton's gravelly voice. Despite her situation, Nikki smiled at his latest message. And his voice sounded so good. But with a lump in her throat, she clutched the receiver, barely able to speak. A tear slid down her cheek.

She left Payton a message, the only words she could manage. And after a long moment, she hung up the phone and stared at the family photo in her hand.

Even amidst a crowd, she had never felt so alone.

Chicago
6:35 A.M. CST

With the veil of night lifted, the overcast sky shed its dull pewter glow along a landscape of urban sprawl. The dismal smell of rain made the air muggy. Normally, mornings like this would have challenged Sam to leave the comfort of her bed—an everyday occurrence if she lived in Jess's hood. She turned off the Stevenson Expressway onto Cicero Avenue going south. Jess had barely said a word the whole trip, no doubt her mind entrenched in her next moves, if Sam knew her friend.

And she did.

"Did you hear what I said about Baker? He's a snitch for one of the detectives in Vice. Unless he blatantly breaks the law and gets caught doing it, we won't be able to touch him, Jessie."

Sam heard the word "we" come out of her own mouth and hoped Jess would ignore it. Too much to hope for.

"Don't worry, Sam. *We* won't, but I might feel the urge to reach out and touch the bastard in my own special way."

After a long moment of silence, Jessie added, "He's probably only getting rid of his competition by ratting them out. I'd say the guy is vermin on two legs, but I wouldn't want to insult the rat population."

Sam had to agree with her assessment. No way she'd have someone like Baker as a snitch. She would have picked another way to obtain information off the streets. The guy didn't deserve the Get Out of Jail card the CPD had reluctantly granted him. She gripped the steering wheel and stared out the windshield, unsure what to say next.

Under the rumble of Midway Airport, just southwest of downtown, the normally bustling thoroughfare was quiet by comparison to what it would be in an hour. Commercial fast food, gas stations, and minimarts lined the avenue, crammed in and competing for space. In her mind, the exhaust fumes of the heavily traveled street and the annoying roar of the flight path of a busy airport created a mix of sights and sounds that had all the aesthetic appeal of a greasy oil slick. The marginal businesses choked out the small homes and apartment complexes, casting a dingy pallor across the older residential neighborhood.

Totally depressing.

"Things never change here in paradise."

Sam couldn't resist the jab as she pulled into an apartment parking lot off the main drag and headed for an empty slot marked for visitors near the rental office. A small two-story complex had been converted from an old motel into apartments. Oatmeal gray paint peeled off the exterior walls, suffering from an overdose of neglect. The only color in a sea of apathy, gang signs were painted across the rusted metal mailboxes located near the door of the rental office, right under the nose of an indifferent management.

"Yeah, I pinch myself every day."

"What? Hoping you wake up from your self-inflicted nightmare?"

Her sarcasm didn't get a rise out of Jess, but they'd had this argument before. And she was in no mood to rehash it.

"You okay for money? 'Cause I can—"

"Don't . . ." Jess interrupted. "Please don't say it. I don't need money."

Sam caught the flinch of her jaw, and Jess crossed her arms, looking as if she hurt, on the outside and in.

"It's just that Baker is not a bail jumper. Unless you know something I don't, you won't earn a dime from chasing his miserable ass. You're fixated on him, and I'm . . . I'm worried about you, that's all."

"I've got my reasons, Sam. And sometimes it's not about money. I thought you got that."

She definitely got it. She wasn't going to retire early on what she made as a cop, but she couldn't imagine doing anything else.

"I do, Jessie," she muttered under her breath. "I do get it."

She parked the car but kept the engine running, figuring Jess had seen enough of her company. She often wondered why Jess had chosen an apartment in this neighborhood when she could afford to live elsewhere. If pressed for an answer, she believed her friend had convinced herself she didn't deserve better. A reflection of a low self-esteem that had been thrust upon her, a feeling that Jess couldn't outrun or overcome.

Maybe her choice had been a form of penance, a self-inflicted punishment because she thought she didn't deserve any better. Or her matchbox existence provided the bare minimum roof over her head at a cheap price. Either way, Sam knew that living here would be a self-fulfilling prophecy for Jess. Her surroundings would wear her down, whether she realized it or not, like a hostile subliminal message.

To live with the dark memories of the abuse she had survived, Jess focused on eradicating those who preyed on the weak, one two-legged vermin at a time. Sam understood this, but some days her friend's antics were harder to accept, like living in a low rent dump and shunning anyone who got too close. And even though Jess invested all her energy into the pursuit of her worthy mission in life, she lived in complete denial that she was part of the walking wounded.

"Why are you still living here?" Sam asked. "This place is a dump."

"You know me. The price was right. I'm saving up for that summer home on the lake." Jess opened the car door, a sad, distant smile on her face, but she didn't move. Instead, she turned toward Sam as if she read her thoughts. "Besides, you know how much I love the cozy atmosphere."

To punctuate her cynicism, a jet bellowed overhead, nearly drowning out her words.

"Yeah, this place is a real gem." Sam smirked and raised an eyebrow.

Even as tired as Jess looked, she broke down into a smile that turned to a soft chuckle, her unfailing humor another quality Sam admired.

"Come up for coffee, sista," her friend offered. "Being grilled by the cops always makes me hungry. If you sweet-talk me, I might rustle up some breakfast for both of us."

"No sweet-talking required. Somebody's got to patch you up." Sam grimaced. "Of course, all this comes after you take a shower. Did I say you smell like a college frat house?"

"Now I *know* you're being kind."

With a grin, Sam turned off the ignition and followed Jess to a place she knew all too well. Her friend trudged up metal stairs to the second floor landing and headed toward the back of the complex. Her apartment was down and to the right, a unit overlooking a narrow alley and a commercial storage enterprise. She wondered if Jess got a discount for the crappy view.

But as they rounded the corner, Jess stopped Sam cold, thrusting a hand across her body, holding her back.

Her front door gaped wide, busted open, splintered at the lock. Jess nodded and kept her silence as she reached for the gun she kept holstered at the small of her back.

Sam pulled her Glock 17 and shoved Jess behind her, a cop performing her duty. The move irritated her friend, but there would be no argument. Sam inched closer to the doorway and peered into the dark with weapon raised. She listened for any noise that told her the intruder was still inside, but the damned airport and traffic along Cicero Avenue made that impossible.

Staying low, Sam made a quick move across the threshold to get to the other side of the doorway. Facing Jess, she caught her friend's eye and gave her silent instructions, letting her know she'd take the lead and Jess would follow.

Peering into the shadows inside, Sam rushed through the door with weapon drawn and Jess at her shoulder. But the sight of the room snatched her next breath.

CHAPTER 4

A shambles.

Nothing remained unscathed.

An overturned bookshelf had its contents scattered around the room, picture frames lay shattered on the carpet with photos torn apart. Her bills and personal mail had been strewn over the floor. And a knife had shredded her small sofa, tufts of foam yanked out and thrown across the room. Her possessions were piled high, touched by the stranger who had invaded her home. And the carpet smelled of urine. Nothing would be salvageable. Jess knew the malicious break-in was more than a mere robbery the moment she saw it. This was an act of sheer rage.

Lucas Baker had left her a message.

She was aware of Sam staring at her, expecting a reaction. But she couldn't move. And nothing came from her mouth, although inside she felt like screaming. Eventually, Sam left her side and continued her search through the tiny apartment, checking for intruders. It wouldn't take long. She remained behind in the living room, completely stunned.

Her body ached from the fresh bruises, but nothing hurt worse than this cold violation of her privacy. Her eyes began to water, but she choked back the emotion. She didn't have much to her name, but what she owned now lay in tatters, a lifetime ripped to shreds in a matter of minutes. The degradation only brought back the fear—the mind-numbing fear she despised.

When Sam rejoined her, Jess barely heard what she said. She crossed her arms to stop from shaking.

"I'll call it in if you want, but there's something you gotta see first. In your bedroom."

Sam touched her arm, forcing her to finally move. By the time she got back to her bedroom, she was numb with loss. It looked the same as her living room. None of her possessions were recognizable, heaped in piles like so much garbage. And insult to injury, the bastard had taken her backup gun. A sweet .45-caliber Glock 21 with thirteen ACP rounds in the mag and one more in the chamber. Angry words were smeared across the walls in her lipstick, mixed with death threats. If there was any doubt of the intruder's intentions, Baker's coercion became perfectly clear with the harsh words scrawled across her dresser mirror.

YOU KNOW WHAT I WANT!!!

Written all in caps, she could hear him screaming in her head, a replay of what happened hours before. The sound mixed with other voices from her past, a paralyzing recollection. And with haunted eyes and her face bruised and cut, Jess stared at her own reflection in the mirror through the scrawl, feeling lost and alone. The rage of a lifetime swelled inside her, on the brink of breaking loose. She'd worked so hard to keep the past behind her. To control it. But now it glared at her through accusing eyes. Her eyes.

While the police held her for questioning, the scum bucket had plenty of time to rip apart her life. The anger threatened to burst inside her, a seething pool of heat. The urge to cower in a corner like a lost child waged its quiet war against grabbing her Python to hunt Baker down like a crazed vigilante.

Jess gritted her teeth, fighting off the itch to nail Baker—now.

"He stole my backup gun. A Glock 21," she muttered.

"Do you know what he wants?" Sam asked. When Jess didn't answer right away, Sam grabbed the cell phone clipped to her belt. "I'm gonna call this in. Get a team over here to dust for prints."

Jess held out her hand to stop her overzealous friend.

"No, don't. Let me handle this, my way." She locked her gaze on Sam, but turned away the minute her friend opened her mouth.

"You know more than you're letting on. I know you. What's this all about, Jessie?"

Sam didn't stop there. She ranted on about reporting her stolen weapon and about not taking the law into her own hands, but Jess stayed focused on the problem at hand, struggling to regain her composure. Baker wanted his property back, but she couldn't tell Sam everything about her recent skirmish with the bastard. At least not yet. She had to respect Sam's position as law enforcement. And her friend had done too much already, risking her job to tell her about Baker. This was her problem, and she'd deal with it her way.

With Seth's help, she'd get her shot at Baker's computer. By the looks of her place, she'd paid a hefty price for the right to invade his privacy, returning the favor he'd just bestowed on her. But she had no intention of getting Seth more involved than he already was. With Baker acting as an informant to the cops—a fact she hadn't known until today—one of them might have leaked the information on her address. And that thought scared the hell out of her. She didn't have the heart to tell Sam what she suspected. And no way would she drag Seth into this cesspool. After the kid dissected Baker's laptop, he'd be out.

"Aw, Jessie." With her voice laden with disappointment, Sam shook her head. Her eyes filled with the sympathy of a friend—absent the judgmental glare of a jaded cop who knew better. "What have you gotten into now?"

Getting in hadn't been the problem. Walking away in one piece would be the real challenge. She always figured that if you're gonna walk on thin ice, you may as well dance. And she and Baker weren't done with their time on the dance floor.

Outside Talkeetna, Alaska
Mid-morning

Warm sheets felt good against his bare skin, especially with the soft patter of rain tapping its sweet music along his rooftop and windowpanes. He'd always been a sucker for rain, Nature's version of a lullaby. Behind closed eyelids, Payton Archer pictured a steel gray morning, heavy with the smell of rain, commonplace in Alaska this time of year. The summer sun rarely made an appearance through the constant and dense cloud cover, even with the longer daylight hours.

With eyes shut, Payton could imagine his world a different place. Rapt in the last vestiges of sleep, he lay perfectly still, clinging to the twilight before he opened his eyes to the reality of his life. He listened to the sound of his breaths as if they came from someone else. A slow steady rhythm. The simple ebb and flow of a man who didn't know failure.

Today, things might be different. Maybe *he'd* changed.

Like hell.

The serene moment of complete denial didn't last long. When he rolled to one side, the top of his head nearly exploded. Shooting pain charged up his shoulders and neck, burrowing behind his eyes like it had a perfect right to be there. And who was he to argue? Hell, his brain took up prime real estate in his skull and certainly wasn't working hard enough to pay its own way.

"Shit." His rumbling baritone vibrated through his aching head with all the finesse of a shrill air horn at close range.

Bleary-eyed, he squinted across his small cabin, propped on an elbow. Every detail rolled in and out of focus—clothes strewn along the floor, an old liquor bottle with its spilled contents, and his bed pillows, which had migrated across the room. Strands of his dark blond hair hung over his eyes, masking much of the upheaval from last night. A good thing. He'd never get high marks from *Good Housekeeping*, even on his best day.

To clear the haze, Payton ran a hand over his face and scratched the stubble on his chin. Every bone in his head throbbed with a dull pain. Even his teeth hurt. And his throat felt like someone had jammed an old sock down it, foot and all.

"You're up. Good. I thought you might be dead."

Payton jerked his head when he heard the man's voice. The sudden move punished him. A shadow stirred, a dark shape sitting at a wooden table next to his stove. A blur of red flannel and a slick navy windbreaker beaded with rain.

Gradually, the deadpan expression of Joseph Tanu emerged from Payton's self-induced fog. Oval face with dark skin and long black hair streaked with gray. Joe's deep-set eyes looked like dense volcanic glass, shiny obsidian reflecting the man's ancient Haida lineage. Age lines furrowed his face, but Payton had no idea how old Joe was. He never asked; it never seemed important. He'd known the Native Alaskan since his early teens. Being a local trooper at the time, Joe had been the one who told him and his sister Susannah about their parents—right after his father's Cessna slammed into the mountain range outside Juneau. The worst day of his life. And that was saying something.

"Thanks for the concern," Payton grumbled. He sat up in

bed and raked fingers through his hair. Every muscle and joint bellyached from old gridiron war wounds, a persistent pang made worse by his self-inflicted booze bullet to the brain.

When Joe shoveled a fork full of eggs into his mouth—*his eggs*—Payton put two and two together.

"Hey, you eating my food?"

"I was out of bacon." Joe shrugged without contrition. "And if you woke up dead, I wanted dibs on your stuff. Bacon and eggs seemed like a good place to start."

Payton scrunched his face. "Can't argue with *that* flawless logic, but I've seen bag ladies with better shit than me."

Joe leaned back in his chair and looked around the room, as if seeing it for the first time.

"You've got a point." He nodded, pursing his lips. "Guess I better raise my standards."

"You don't have any. That's why we're friends."

A rare smirk flashed across Joe's face. "I made you breakfast. Get your sorry ass over here."

"Not hungry. It's too early."

Payton stood on wobbly legs in his boxers and trudged to the bathroom. Not bothering to close the door, he took care of business.

"In some countries, you might be right. But here, the morning's already come and gone."

Thinking over the vague memories of last night, Payton flushed and washed his hands and face, then looked over his shoulder as he toweled off.

"Hey, how did I get home last night? You took my truck keys, right?"

Joe chuckled under his breath and shook his head. "You were in no condition to drive. Your truck's out front. You gotta gimme a ride home. But last night, that Jessica Alba look-alike offered to tuck you in bed personally."

"Sandy Kirkwood? I must have been drunk . . . *and* out of my mind."

For a woman, Alaska was a target rich environment, with the male to female ratio nearly four-to-one. With her looks, Sandy could have her pick. Yet for some bizarre reason, she had culled him out of the herd, targeting her red hot brand on his hindquarter. The feeling wasn't mutual.

"She's got all the subtlety of a sledgehammer. I didn't get married last night, did I?" He quickly brushed his teeth.

"No, you turned her down flat and walked home. That really pissed her off, but I got a feeling she considered it foreplay." Joe narrowed his eyes and crooked a lip. "Playing hard to get, that's not a maneuver most guys can pull off. And Sandy's not the kind of gal who hears no too often. You've got balls of brass, boy. Speaking of an overdose of testosterone, what got into you last night? You nearly tore my place apart."

The brawl at The Moose Nugget nudged his conscience. Joe's bar and grill, his pride and joy. After rinsing his mouth, Payton stood in front of the sink and stared at the stranger in the mirror. The harsh light made the dark circles under his blue eyes worse. And the bruises on his jaw were raw and swollen. *Nice, real nice.*

"Sorry about that." Payton winced. "I'll pay for everything."

"Yes, you will, but that doesn't answer my question." Joe walked over and leaned against the doorjamb to the bathroom, his face reflected in the mirror over Payton's shoulder. "You let that loudmouth jackass get to you. What happened to the Iceman?"

Joe referred to the nickname he'd been given when he played pro football for the Dallas Cowboys. Folks in Texas thought everyone from Alaska lived in friggin' igloos and mushed dogs, so the name stuck through the end of his career. His last stop had been with the Chicago Bears, a period of his life that had gone from bad to worse in a hurry. After Chicago, he wanted to crawl into a hole and forget he ever played the game.

But he'd been dubbed the Iceman mainly for his nerves of steel in the pocket, in the face of a fierce blitz. A quarterback who could take the punishment of a linebacker freight train. Those days were long gone. He'd pissed them all away, with no one to blame except the man in the mirror.

"The Iceman is nothing but urban myth. The agony of defeat replayed over and over on some TV sports channels." Payton grimaced in the mirror, his blue eyes turning stormy gray.

His gut gnarled. And it had nothing to do with "the morning after" or the nauseating smell of bacon and eggs lingering in the air like a hostile cloud. He was a has been at the ripe old age of thirty-two. Natural athletic ability, scholarships, and prime opportunity, he'd been handed keys to the gates of heaven—to make something of his life after the tragedy of his parents' death. But he'd fucked it up, for him and for his sister Susannah. And every day he looked in the mirror, it reminded him of the betrayal to his parents' memory. Utterly pathetic.

"You were always hardest on yourself, Payton. Even growing up, you always set the bar so high. That attitude kept you reaching for the impossible. But when you fell, you fell hard, boy. I never wanted that for you. I wish—"

"I know, Joe." He brushed by the old man and reached into a trunk to pick out a T-shirt, jeans, and an oversized blue flannel shirt. Mostly, he couldn't look Joe in the eye.

As Payton dressed, Joe talked.

"You're alone even in a crowd. I can see it in your eyes, you've tossed in the towel. Your whole life is in front of you and you act like it doesn't count." Joe stuffed his hands into his pockets but kept his eyes on Payton. "You need to come out of the locker room with a second half, son. Don't make it about your parents or anybody else. Make it about you, what you want."

"Hell, what if this is all I've got, Joe? Livin' day-to-day off the bankroll of my glory days. Maybe I'm fresh out of comebacks and you're the one who needs to adjust his thinking." Payton poured himself a cup of coffee, took a sip and muttered, "Get used to it. I have."

Bitterness tainted his mouth, and it had nothing to do with lousy coffee. For a long moment Joe stared in silence. But when the man opened his mouth to speak, Payton's phone rang, saving him from round two.

He gladly picked it up and ignored the red blinking light of his answering machine, the signal that he had messages waiting.

"Yo. Speak to me."

"Thank God . . . Payton."

A sob swallowed her voice. At first, in his alcohol-addled brain, he didn't recognize the caller, even in the stillness of his cabin. Eventually it came to him—his sister Susannah. Most people didn't give thanks when they crossed his path these days. Susannah was at the top of a short list of folks who tolerated him. But something in her voice made him grimace, triggering a throbbing headache.

"Hey, sis. What's—"

She interrupted. "Nikki's gone, Payton. She took her clothes . . . a duffel bag. And the state troopers are treating this like a missing person case, not an AMBER Alert." She choked on her last words. "I can't go through this again."

More tears. A crying woman always ripped him apart, but his sister's pain provoked a rush of dark memories. He shut his eyes, wanting all of it to go away. Grief had torn a hole in his heart, one he never filled. Together they endured the loss of their parents at far too young an age. Emotionally, it cut the legs out from both of them. He wasn't sure he could do it again.

Especially if something happened to Nikki, his only niece.

All those years ago, Payton had been the one to buckle down and take charge after their parents died, to make the difficult decisions and get their lives back on track despite Susannah being a few years older. He had no choice, really. It had been that way ever since. His sister relied on him for everything. She and Nikki were the only family he had left.

"Have you called her friends?" he asked. "Maybe Nikki's staying overnight somewhere, like the last time."

Joe Tanu stepped closer, urgent concern on his face. Payton shrugged and shook his head. Susannah's only child was seventeen, a strong-willed girl with a mind of her own. Nikki had run away before, but something in his sister's voice triggered a bad feeling.

This time would be different.

"Nikki packed a lot of clothes," she cried. "She left a note, but it didn't say much. I'm scared, Payton. This time she's meeting someone, a stranger off the Internet. And I have no idea how to find her."

Payton ended the call and rushed to his truck, with Joe riding shotgun. With his mind elsewhere, he forgot about the red blinking light on his answering machine.

CHAPTER 5

Talkeetna, Alaska

Payton turned onto the gravel road that led to his sister's front door, his mind working overtime on what he'd say to a mother whose only child was missing. He drove through a stand of evergreen trees, with the sound of stone crunching under his tires filling the cab of his truck. He was resisting the urge to gun the accelerator. Kicking up rocks and riding in like the cavalry would do nothing for Susannah's frayed nerves. Over the years, he had learned that his sister needed his calm reassurance, no matter how he felt inside.

Joe rode next to him in the front seat, not saying a word over the last few miles. Having him along gave Payton a sense of strength, one he could pretend for his sister's sake. And the man understood he needed time to think. But even now, every little noise plucked at his resolve and played on his mind like an annoying guitar string off key and out of sync, grating on his nerves. Even the quiet patter of drizzle on his windshield made him on edge as it outpaced the steady thump of his wiper blades. He had a bad feeling. And no amount of macho bullshit or testosterone overload would make it go away.

But for Susannah's sake, he had to put on his game face.

Up ahead, his sister's house looked stone cold. The curtains were drawn and the place looked empty, but he knew better. Susannah would be inside, waiting for him to find the elixir that would cure her misery and bring Nikki back.

"You're not in this alone." Joe's voice came when he needed it most.

Payton nodded. Never one to mince words, his friend always knew how to slice through the clutter and make each word count. He parked the truck and took a deep breath, unable to take his eyes off his sister's door.

"Déjà vu sucks, Joe." He caught the movement of a curtain from inside. "And I'm not sure I can be the rock she needs this time. If something happens to Nikki—"

"Don't borrow trouble, Payton."

"Hell, who needs to borrow it?" He pinched the bridge of his nose to fend off a welling headache, then raked a hand through the blond hair that had fallen into his eyes. "Trouble gets off on kicking me in the ass. I got no say."

Joe fortified him with a hand on his shoulder. Susannah opened the front door wearing a bathrobe and a nightgown. She waited for him to come inside, her face red and puffy, glistening with tears. But as Payton got out of the truck, any resolve he'd had drained from him like sand through his fingers.

When he crossed the threshold, Susannah collapsed into his arms. He held her tight, soothing her with whatever came to mind, whispering lame reassurances in her ear.

"This can't be happening, Payton. I think I've lost her this time." His sister sobbed harder now, her body trembling. "Maybe I lost her a long time ago. I just don't know anymore."

Joe caught his eye. And he understood the man, without so much as a word spoken between them. Getting his sister to focus might make all the difference.

"Catch us up to speed, sis. What happened?"

She pulled away, wiping her nose with a tissue. That's when he smelled the liquor on her breath. Alcohol had become the weapon of choice in his family, when self-flagellation beat the alternative of facing the truth. His friend must have smelled the liquor too.

"I'll make us some coffee." Joe nudged his head toward the sofa, directing Payton to get Susannah off her feet.

With his arm around her shoulder, Payton walked her to the living room as she talked, rehashing it all in her head.

"You don't know how it's been with that girl. Communicating with her these days is like talking to a stone. If I get any conversation at all, it comes in one-word mumbles with that annoying roll of her eyes. But you wanna know the worst thing? Whenever I saw her resentment, I'd blow a gasket." She gulped air, taking a breath hindered by a sob. "I'd see myself lose control and I couldn't stop it from happening, Payton."

The bitterness in her voice had melted away, transformed by a wave of prevailing doubt as he helped her to the couch and eased her down.

"It's been playing over and over in my head like some continuous loop that I can't stop. Damn it, how did it come to this? You don't know how much it hurts to know your daughter hates you, to be rejected by your own kid. God, I suck as a mother."

"She doesn't hate you, Susannah." Kneeling at her feet, he wiped the tears from her cheeks. With his voice steady and calm, he added, "The double shot of raging hormones and the strong Archer stubborn streak are hard to overcome. But Nikki loves you. I know she does."

In the way he always preferred to remember it—in hindsight filtered through love and loss—he and his sister never went through the teen war zone with their parents. A part of him wished they had. That would've meant his mom and dad hadn't died in that blasted plane crash just as they'd hit those difficult times. Teen angst and the drama of rebellion seemed like such a small price to pay to have them longer. The stark reality of their death forced him to grow up way too fast. And after the shambles he made of his life, he was pretty damned sure he never got it right.

"When did you notice her missing?" he asked.

"This morning." Fresh tears mixed with a powerful guilt. "But her bed wasn't slept in and she took clothes with her, more than she did the last time. And a duffel bag is missing too. I think she left last night." She looked into his eyes. "I'm scared, Payton. Really scared."

"Stay with me, honey. For Nikki's sake." He gripped her by the shoulders. "You said she left a note. What did it say? Do the state troopers have it?"

She nodded. "Yeah, they've got it, but it didn't say much. Only that she left on purpose. Said she'd call when she got where she was going." She wrung her hands, her knuckles drained of color. "I can't get my head wrapped around this, Payton. Nikki did it for real this time. She really did it."

Disoriented, she wiped her face with a sleeve from her bathrobe. Smudges of mascara left dark circles under her eyes, and her skin was covered with red blotches.

"I need a drink." She grabbed for the armrest, trying to stand, but Payton stopped her.

"Joe's got coffee coming, honey. Remember?"

"It's almost done," Joe called out from the kitchen. Payton knew he'd been listening.

"You said she met someone off the Internet. Why do you think that, Susannah?"

"I know what goes on, Payton." His sister slouched back but kept a grip on his arm. "All those secret codes. She didn't want me to know."

"What are you talking about? What codes?"

"I'll show you."

She struggled to get off the sofa. Payton helped pull her up, then followed her to the stairs. He kept a hand to her back so she wouldn't fall. Susannah had more than a few drinks, but who was he to judge? Suffering a hangover, he had no right to say anything. When they got to Nikki's room, she moved to the desk and grabbed a stack of papers by the computer.

"See? She's been talking in codes." She choked back the emotion of her daughter's betrayal. "She didn't want me to know. She did all this to blindside me."

Nikki had run away before, staying at a friend's house in town. She wanted to hurt her mother and had succeeded in a big way until Susannah took to spying on her. She found chats on Instant Messenger where her daughter had made arrangements to escape maternal oppression. She tracked Nikki down and forced her to come home that time, erecting a wall between them. Trust on both sides had decayed, a complete breach of faith.

When Payton looked at the printed pages Susannah gave him, he saw where his niece had thwarted any potential for her mother's espionage attempts. This time she meant to disappear for real.

"This looks as cryptic as one of my old playbooks," he muttered, staring at one of the pages. "Where did you get these?"

Joe had followed them upstairs. Payton handed him the pages, sharing an apprehensive look. When he turned back to Susannah, she looked sick.

"Off the computer." She swallowed and avoided looking him in the eye. "I'm not proud of what I did, but . . ." His sister struggled to find the words. "I put software on her computer, to spy on her activity. I used it the last time, but I swear to God I had no intention of—"

"No one's judging you here, sis. You and Nikki have history. I'm not gonna pretend to know what it's been like."

"I thought I could trust her again. I wanted to. God, I didn't think I had to keep doing this."

His sister was pale, the skin of her face a ghastly gray.

"Nikki did this on purpose, to shut me out." Susannah collapsed onto her daughter's bed. "I should've taken the computer away for good, but I was afraid." A strange amusement drove harsh laughter from deep in her chest, a nervous outburst that sounded out of place. "Afraid I'd make things worse. Can you believe that?"

Her eyes filled.

"I was just trying to establish boundaries for her. I thought I was doing the right thing. If this ends up being my fault, I won't . . . I just can't . . ."

His sister grabbed for her daughter's pillow and clutched it to her face, breathing in the scent of her only child. It broke Payton's heart. He reached out a hand and stroked her head. Nothing he could say would help, but he had to do something.

"We need a recent picture of Nikki." When she looked up at him through dazed eyes, he said, "So we can make flyers to post around town. We're not gonna leave Nikki in the hands of the local law without helping all we can."

Not waiting for her permission, Payton looked around the room and found a picture of his niece. Smiling, the young girl looked so much like her mother, but something in the eyes hinted of Nikki's father, a guy Payton knew nothing about. Susannah had her only child without the dubious benefit of marriage, and she'd never confided the sperm donor's name.

It reminded Payton of the troubled times following the gaping wound caused by the tragedy of their parents, when his already fragile link to his sister nearly swirled down the drain too. The memories came at him in a rush, like a blitz he never saw coming. At the time, he had put his life on hold and took control, helping Susannah deal with the unexpected pregnancy. All this came on the heels of pro football scouts courting him. The added pressure, coupled with the instantaneous celebrity, had not been a good mix. He knew that now, but back then he thought he was bullet-proof. Mr. Teflon.

He stuffed Nikki's photo into his shirt pocket, but an empty frame on the desk by the computer caught his eye.

"What was in this frame?" He held it up, showing it to his sister. "Didn't she used to have—"

"The photo of her thirteenth birthday, yes." Susannah reached for the frame with trembling fingers, using both hands to hold something precious to her. "I remember."

"Maybe she took it with her, sis. That's got to mean something, right?" Payton sat beside her on the bed, putting his arm around her shoulders again. The unexpected glimmer of hope bolstered his spirits too. Nikki hadn't completely severed the link with her mother.

"Tell me what happened with the state troopers."

"One of them came here, took a report and a photo of Nikki. He also took something of hers for fingerprinting and asked about dental records. Said they'd post her picture on the Internet and get the word out through some kind of database clearinghouse for bulletins."

He knew the trooper's request meant something more. Dental records and fingerprints were used to identify a body, if it came to that. The gravity of their situation hit him hard. And by the look on his sister's face, she knew it too.

"Before, you said they were handling this like a missing person case. Why aren't they treating it like an AMBER Alert?" Payton asked.

Joe stepped in, to save Susannah from having to explain something she probably didn't fully comprehend in her condition.

"Nikki has a history of running away," he said. "And she left a note and took clothes. Not good. If they don't have evidence of an outright abduction, they make a judgment call to treat this like a missing person case." Joe set his jaw and fixed his gaze on Payton. "Plus, she's seventeen. Different jurisdictions have lower age restrictions. It varies state-to-state."

"What difference does that make?" Payton asked.

"An alert may not get transmitted across every state line." Joe crossed his arms, a pained expression on his face. "They make rules about AMBER Alerts for a reason. Overuse of the system would undermine its effectiveness. I know it's hard to understand, but—"

"No, I tell you what's hard to understand, Joe." Susannah's face had turned bright red. She pointed a finger at the former lawman, aiming all her anger and frustration. In the quiet room, her raised voice shocked him. "The law is supposed to help. My little girl is out there somewhere with a stranger. For all we know, it could be a sexual predator. And no one is lifting a finger."

His sister had made the leap toward blaming someone else, a convenient lifeline in a raging sea of desperation.

"Susannah, Joe is only trying to help," Payton whispered, and stroked her hair. When she settled down, he kissed the top of her head and pulled her to him. "We're gonna find her, but we need your help too."

He glanced up at Joe.

"Joe and me, we're gonna get answers from the state troopers' office. Then we're gonna plaster this town with posters, even into Anchorage. But I need you sober, sis. Joe made coffee. Use it. If Nikki calls and wants to come home, I want you to contact me on my cell."

"You think . . . ?" She looked up at him. The fragile hope glistening in her eyes wrenched his heart. "Please find her, Payton. All I want is one more chance to make it right. Please."

"We're gonna find her. I promise you'll get that chance, Susannah."

He had no business making that promise, not with his track record, but his heart pulled rank over his good sense. When he stood and caught the eye of Joe Tanu, the harsh reality of their undertaking took hold, and his belly churned hot with the prospect of another failure. But he didn't see the sense in shoving his sister off the same cliff. For now, he had no qualms with letting her believe he could do it.

"You comin', Joe?"

His friend lifted a corner of his mouth—his version of a smile—and handed him the pages of Nikki's code.

"Just try and stop me."

Payton stuffed the computer printouts in a pocket of his flannel shirt and headed for the front door, but by the time he got there, the phone rang. He stopped dead in his tracks, and for a split second stared at Joe and his sister. It didn't take long for him to jump to some pretty dark conclusions. He knew this call could change everything.

For the mother of a missing child, every phone call could bring life or death. His sister raced to the phone after the initial shock wore off.

"Hello." Susannah held the phone tight, her knuckles white with the strain. She shut her eyes tight—to block out the rest of the world—and fresh tears squeezed onto her cheeks. After listening for a long moment, she fixed her eyes on Payton and shook her head.

He stepped closer, feeling the weight of Joe by his side. Payton reached for his sister's hand and locked his fingers in hers.

"Can I put you on speaker, Trooper Fitzgerald?" she asked, her voice trembling. "I've got my brother and Joe Tanu here. I need them to hear this too."

By the look on his sister's face, Payton wasn't sure what to expect.

CHAPTER 6

Susannah punched a button on her phone and spoke again.

"Go ahead. You're on speaker." She wiped the tears from her face with both hands and took a ragged breath.

Payton recognized Dan Fitzgerald's voice when he came on the line.

"I know you folks are waiting for good news, but I just wanted you to know we've had a break. And in cases like this, we gotta run down every lead." The trooper cleared his throat. The sound came across far too loud in the quiet room. "Hey, Joe. Long time."

"Yeah, Fitz. What's happening? You got something to chase?" Joe kept the man on track, but by using his nickname, he reminded the trooper of their personal connection.

"Yeah, it seems some kid from Anchorage spotted Nikki getting into a car up at River Park around one. He was camping there with friends and he told us Nikki tried to pretend she was using the restroom, but she had a duffel bag with her, hidden in the bushes."

"And where'd you find this kid? Could he be blowing smoke? Maybe he's trying to divert the search." Joe's take on the case deflated Payton's fragile spirit.

He knew Joe had made valid points, but only wished that Susannah didn't have to hear them. She looked desperate and in need of encouragement. Reality would come soon enough. The trooper's voice broke in and pulled him from his morbid thoughts.

"Nah, some folks in town have seen this kid and vouched for him. And he recognized her from the photo we used to canvass the town. A lucky break, I'd say, 'cause he was fixin' to leave today. We caught him packed up and eatin' breakfast at The Moose Nugget, Joe."

"Did he remember the car? See anyone inside?"

"Too dark to see anyone inside, he said, but he remembered it was a Subaru and gave us a partial on the plate." Fitzgerald described the Subaru in more detail, then asked, "Any of you recognize the description? Would Nikki know someone who owned a Subaru like that?"

Payton shrugged and looked at his sister, who was shaking her head.

"Susannah says no, Fitz," Joe replied. "Did you run the tag?"

"Yeah, we did. I got Anchorage looking into it now."

Joe narrowed his eyes, an uncharacteristic look of concern on his normally stoic face. With the Alaska State Troopers main headquarters located in Anchorage, Payton suspected Anchorage troopers would get involved sooner or later, but this soon? By Joe's expression, it looked as if he had the same question.

In most states, troopers focused on traffic and highway patrol duties, but due to the limited accessibility and government presence within the state, the Alaska State Troopers enforced all criminal laws too. They served as primary law enforcement for most Alaska residents. For the Anchorage headquarters to get involved so soon after Nikki's disappearance, Payton drew one conclusion. The troopers had begun to realize that Nikki wasn't just another runaway.

"Not that I'm complaining, but why is Anchorage involved so soon?" Joe asked.

"It appears we got enough of a partial to ID the vehicle, so we're running a background check on the owner of record. It's registered to a local schoolteacher in Anchorage. They're bringing her in for questioning. I'm heading there now, but before I leave town, do you know any reason why Nikki would get into the car of a woman teacher from Anchorage?"

Payton turned to his sister. By the look on her face, he knew she was thinking the same thing. The implication of Nikki being taken to Anchorage by a stranger chilled them both.

"I want in on this, Fitz. Stay put. I'm heading your way." Joe didn't hesitate. Nor did he ask Payton and Susannah for consent to get involved. After all, family didn't need permission.

Joe ended the call, not waiting to hear the man's objections. "We need you by the phone, Susannah, in case Nikki calls. Can you handle it alone?"

His sister nodded, her eyes filled with cautious hope. "Do you think she's there, Joe . . . in Anchorage? With this teacher?"

"We won't know until we question the woman, but anything is possible. We'll call you when we know something." After Joe gave Susannah's arm a reassuring squeeze, he fixed his dark eyes on Payton. "You're driving, hotshot."

Payton leaned over to give his sister a kiss on the cheek, but before he pulled away, Susannah grabbed his arm.

"Please . . . find her, Payton. She's all I've got." Fresh tears filled her tired eyes.

Payton wrapped her in his arms and held her. "You've got Joe and me on your side too, sis. We'll find her."

He only hoped he sounded more confident than he felt.

Downtown Chicago

The late afternoon sun poked through the clouds, resurrecting her mood from the depths of where it had been, but not by much. Still, it felt good to get out from under the dismal clean-up of her apartment. Sam had helped until her shift at Cop Town. Together, they had made progress, but after Sam left, the task became torturous. Once Jess got her front door replaced and secured, she had to get out. And only one thing dominated her mind.

Baker's damned laptop. And Seth Harper had it.

With feet planted on the sidewalk of Lake Shore Drive, she reread the street address scribbled in her own handwriting, completely stumped. When she looked up to confirm the number, the exclusive condominium project and the spectacular view overlooking the glistening waters of the Chicago harbor baffled her. Scrawled on a piece of torn paper, the address had been taken from her employment record of one Seth Harper, her first and only new hire. And from the outside of the building looking up, she counted the floors to make sure her suspicions were correct.

"Well, I'll be damned." She didn't believe her eyes.

At the light, she walked across the street, making an effort not to limp. Her body still felt battered, one of the reasons she covered up with a long sleeve tee and jeans. In her condition, she'd be a sure standout where she was going, no matter what she had on. The imposing bright red awning and elegant black and gold double doors loomed ahead. She tried not to be intimidated by the fancy real estate. Seth had Baker's laptop, and maybe by now some of his secrets.

Once Jess got inside the small foyer of imported marble and inlaid gold, a set of security doors barred her access unless she buzzed the correct residence. Seth had given her number 602 as his place. Just as she thought, the little weasel laid claim to—

"The penthouse, my ass." She crumpled the scrap of paper with his address, jamming it into her pocket.

Most of the other residents had surnames listed beside a button. Hit the buzzer, say your name, and the security doors opened. Simple. Except suite 602 didn't have a name listed. She buzzed it anyway. Once. Twice. On the third try, she kept her thumb on the buzzer, replicating SOS in Morse code. Still no Seth to chat her up on the intercom or buzz her in.

"Well, I don't have all day, Harper. Time to improvise," she muttered under her breath.

One by one she went down the row, punching buttons, like playing Russian Roulette with the rich and famous.

"Publishers Clearinghouse. Prize patrol."

No reply. She went on to the next one.

"Candy Gram."

Still no answer.

"Domino's Pizza. In thirty minutes, I'm hot and ready."

Buzzzzz. The security door clicked open.

Jess rolled her eyes as she caught the door and went inside, still pondering her new hire. Seth probably lied on his job application, but she had no room to cast stones. She wasn't above stretching the truth herself. Not too long ago she'd gotten the idea to post a job for a "summer intern" with the weekly *Chicago Gazette* advertiser. She had stretched reality paper-thin on the job post. And crappy wages was all she could afford, so why pay for an ad? Free was firmly within her budget. If she got a nibble, she'd reel the sucker in. It was worth a shot.

Her subtle subterfuge had been completely free of guilt. After all, who would look for a career worth having in a free paper?

Only one applicant applied. Seth Harper.

To legitimize her freelance Fugitive Recovery enterprise, she actually had the gall to interview the kid, giving her an option to toss his vague pencil-written application if he turned out to be a real flake. In the end, she liked his easygoing nature, and his eagerness charmed her, so she hired him on the spot.

But standing in one of the trendiest locales on the Chicago loop, she found her ego rearing its ugly head—a clear case of double standards she fully condoned. Duping him was fair game, but the other way around was nothing less than insulting.

Damned straight!

"If you lied about living here, Seth, I'm gonna kick your punk ass all the way to Gary, Indiana."

Once inside the elevator, she punched the button for the penthouse suite. Overhead, a chandelier tinkled as the elevator rose and a high-pitched violin played classical music ad nauseam over the speakers. The overdose of pretentiousness made her edgy. She felt out of place like a decked-out hooker at High Mass, especially when she caught her own reflection in the shiny elevator doors. Even pricy light fixtures did nothing for her appearance.

One side of her face—the already scarred side—had a raised welt at her cheekbone, the size of a fifty-cent piece. The dim lighting didn't help. If the little ferret misrepresented his home address, she'd make a fool of herself knocking on the door of the Grand Poobah of the posh suites. Mr. Moneybags in 602 might use the boys in blue to give her the bum's rush from his doorstep. And she didn't need another beef with the cops.

But when the elevator door opened at the top floor, a sound caught her attention. On massive imported rugs costing some serious coin, she walked toward the noise while gaping at the high ceiling with its elaborate crown molding. Deep rich cherry-wood doors were gilded by gold hardware, and exquisite artwork was displayed under subtle lighting.

Only four suites occupied the floor. And music came from the one down the hall, suite 602. It was a song she recognized—and one she had a hard time picturing the Grand Poobah gyrating to the driving beat. "The Only Song" by Sherwood blasted through the door. The base rhythm rocked the walls. Someone played it loud and proud, and it penetrated through the sound-dampening acoustics of the top-notch construction.

Jess fought a grin. "Harper? If I'm about to make an ass of myself, at least I'm doing it to damn fine tunes."

When the music died down, ready to shift songs, Jess took a deep breath and punched the doorbell. For good measure she whacked the fine cherry wood with the heel of her fist. From inside she heard the song end and nothing new replace it. She cocked her head and pursed her lips, waiting for someone to open up.

For an added element of mystery, she pressed a thumb to the peephole. Her version of an icebreaker. In no time the door cracked open and Seth peeked over a gold chain.

"Jess, what are you doing here?" He undid the chain and threw the door open, his face in shock when he got a good look at her. "Are you okay? Did the police do that?"

He grimaced and pointed. His eyes took in the fresh damage to her face.

"Don't be melodramatic, Harper." She stepped inside and resisted the urge to gawk at his digs. "Cops use rubber hoses. The bruises don't show as much. Remember that."

After taking a good look around, she whistled in complete admiration of more than just the panoramic view of Lake Michigan. The kid lived in a regular Taj Mahal, Chitown style. A damned museum. The best of the best. Exquisite oil paintings and top-of-the-line furnishings were no doubt picked by the hand of the finest interior decorator money could buy. And someone was a big game hunter. Exotic animals in all shapes and sizes adorned the luxury suite, forever frozen with their fierce eyes and barred teeth. Stephen King would have appreciated the eerie cross between *House Beautiful* and *Creep Show.*

"Way to go, Harper." She nodded her approval. "How did you score this place?"

The kid jammed his hands into his jean pockets and barely looked at her, giving her an open invitation to yank his chain again.

"And better yet, it doesn't look like anyone objects to your ear bleedin' noise decibels. In my hood, the cops would come knockin' for sure."

Seth shrugged. "No one else lives on this floor. The other suites are empty."

Jess narrowed her eyes and studied him. The kid looked like a visitor here, wholly out of place and alone. And he definitely tipped the scales on the forgotten side.

"That's 'cause not many people have the jack to live here," she said.

Her voice echoed into the penthouse suite, a hollow, empty sound. And she got a sense that he lived alone. She wasn't sure how she knew this, but the feeling hit her strong. CDs and DVDs were strewn across a fancy rug near a mile-long velvet divan in the formal parlor dead ahead. Baker's laptop lay on a sheet of plastic on the rug. But other than that incidental clutter marring the picture perfect decor straight out of *Architectual Digest*, she couldn't be sure Seth really lived in suite 602 either.

"It's not what you think. I just know . . ." He avoided her eyes again. ". . . certain people."

"Okay, now you're sounding like someone off *The Sopranos*. Are you 'connected,' Seth?"

Jess hooked her fingers in air quotes and grinned, but when his only reply was another lame shrug, she let him off the hook.

"If you don't wanna discuss it, that's cool. But just remember, you're talkin' to a very stubborn woman. If I wanna know somethin', all I gotta do is exercise my keen investigative skills."

She winked and turned her back on him to snoop for real

this time. But in a huge beveled mirror in the ostentatious foyer, she caught his reaction. Tall and lanky, Seth's cheeks blushed with embarrassment. Tousled wavy dark hair curled at his neck, making him look like he'd just crawled out of bed. And she would have killed for his large brown eyes framed by thick lashes, a picture of innocence she could never pull off. The kid was dressed in faded jeans torn at the knee and a black Jerry Springer T-shirt.

Yep, Seth Harper was a real charmer—and one snappy dresser.

But a part of her suspected she shouldn't envy him. Appearances weren't always what they seemed. He had an inherent sadness behind those incredible eyes. And that was something she knew about. The kid was a kindred spirit with an ancient soul. Cutting him slack, she changed the subject to relax the poor guy.

"I see you're working on Baker's laptop. Does that mean you got through his ID and password?"

He brushed by her, pumped with a sudden rush of adrenaline. He flopped to the carpet sitting cross-legged with the computer propped on his lap. He was wearing thin gloves, no doubt to keep fingerprints off the computer keyboard while trying to unlock Baker's secrets.

"Yeah, sort of," he said.

"Let's hear the 'yeah' part first. I'm not in the mood to deal with 'sort of.' "

"Well, to get past all the security on the laptop, I took out his hard drive and hooked it up to another computer as a second drive, using my own operating system, not his. That bypassed the need to hack into his passwords."

"Wow. That seems simple." She grinned. "Does that mean you got the key to his magic kingdom?"

Seth scrunched his face. "Not exactly. Once I got into his hard drive, there were plenty of files to access, but every last one of them was encrypted, of the 256-bit encryption variety. He's a pretty cagey bastard. Definitely paranoid."

"256 sounds like a lot of bits." She pretended to understand his geek speak. "You have any luck hacking into his business?"

"I'm working on it." He frowned and shrugged. "But can you please refrain from using the word hack in my presence? When cats cough up a hair ball, they hack. What I'm doing takes a little more finesse."

"Well, excuse me, Mr. Sensitive." Jess narrowed her eyes at him. "I'll try and remember your skill level is a stroke above a cat with a fur ball."

"Apology accepted, I guess." He gave her a sideways grimace. "Normally, getting into a computer is no big deal, not with some of the software I've got. But the guy sure knows how to lay down barriers."

Standing over him, Jess absentmindedly checked out the CDs strewn along the carpet. She had originally thought they were music CDs, but after a closer look, she noticed the shiny disks were marked with black scrawl. Nothing legible, only a cryptic numbering system to identify the bootlegged software, all except for one. But she knew enough about what a crimeware program did to wonder how the hell Seth got his hands on the stuff.

"I thought only identity thieves used crimeware." She reached down to pick up one of the CDs. "How did you get your hands on this sort of program?"

Seth barely looked up, pretending to focus on his keystrokes.

"I told you. I know . . . people."

"People," she chimed in as she laid the CD down, glad the boy was on her side.

"I thought it might come in handy," he added, continuing to work.

But after thinking about it, Jess took a second look at his pricy digs and wondered.

"That's not how you make a living, is it? 'Cause you

wouldn't be livin' here on the coin I pay you. You do know identity theft and fraud are against the law, right, Seth?"

He stopped what he was doing and glared at her. Jess stood her ground with arms crossed, returning his stare. Deadly serious.

"I can't believe you had to ask." He softened his stern expression. Hurt swept over his face. "I get that we really don't know each other, but what do your instincts tell you?"

He held her gaze without flinching. Seconds on the clock dragged through the quagmire of time, not cutting her a break. She felt the weight of her accusation. Heat rose up her neck and spilled onto her cheeks.

"We're good." She nodded. "I mean, yeah, I trust you."

After a long awkward moment, Seth turned back to his work and Jess breathed a quiet sigh of relief. She didn't want to live in a world where innocents like Seth Harper could be seduced to the dark side, but that was the reality of it. Good judgment filtered through her powerful cynicism, a reliable measure of human nature until now. She only hoped she wasn't wrong about him.

"So did you find out anything else?" she asked.

"Yeah, I think so." He sat with his back against the fancy sofa and his eyes glued to the glowing monitor, ignoring her as she sat across from him in a wing-back chair.

"I sniffed out this strange IP Baker visits. The guy's not stupid enough to bookmark it, but I noticed he comes to this site—a lot."

"Strange IP, huh?" She couldn't resist moving closer, unsure whether he'd let her. "What the hell is an IP? Translate, genius. 'Cause I'm gonna need subtitles in Harperworld."

The intrigue of Baker's files drew her in. She invaded Seth's personal space by sitting shoulder-to-shoulder with him on the carpet. The kid was so enthralled with the computer that he didn't seem to mind. And apparently he didn't hold a grudge.

"Harperworld." He grinned with eyes on the monitor. "Good one. Well, an IP is an Internet Protocol address. It's unique. The computer version of X marks the spot in cyberspace. Only it's not that simple."

With a bad case of the yammers, he went on, working the keyboard and waving his hands in the air as if he could blow the confusion off her face. When he looked at her, he stopped and took a different tack.

"Every Internet provider tags their users with an address or block of codes. Every time the user gets on, the ID can roll and change through a shared block. If you query the IP number, the physical location might bounce to different locales. In other words, there are limitations on what you could learn about an IP. And this information will only take you so far . . ."

When he went into a spiel on proxy servers, routers, ISPs, reverse DNS lookups, and anonymizer services, she felt her eyes glaze over. For all she knew, the kid made it all up, except no one could fake the kind of enthusiasm he held for all the technogeek speak.

"Yeah, but did the pervert leave any incriminating proof we can turn over to the cops?"

Jess knew the chain of evidence had been broken and any proof on Baker's laptop would be inadmissible in court, unless she found a clever way to turn over his property and still keep her and Seth out it. When the time came, she knew what had to be done and would see to it.

"I've got nothing so far, but like I said, Baker had plenty of trips to this one strange site on the Internet, an IP address through something called 'Globe Harvest.' The site's under construction. But I took a look at the source code behind the site and found an embedded login if you hit the control shift key and type in the letter O. Here, let me show you."

Seth pulled up a Web site with the name Globe Harvest emblazoned across the screen. A note indicated the site was under construction. But after he hit a few keystrokes, a box popped up, requesting the user to log on.

"I don't have the login yet, but I'm working on it."

"For a site under construction, that seems weird." She narrowed her eyes.

"That's what I thought. Usually a site like this is a blind to allow the Web designer to work behind it until the site is officially published and operational."

"If you get into this thing, can you get a physical location for these people?"

Seth shrugged, disappointment in his eyes. "Like I said, simple it ain't. An IP address might be a stand-alone proxy or it could be shared by multiple client devices, part of a common hosting Web server."

The kid was speaking in tongues again, and she knew her face reflected her confusion. He tried another explanation.

"Okay, okay. Think of this like one big telephone system. The use of a main number can act as the proxy, with extensions behind it that are shared. You get it?"

"That kind of makes sense . . . in a geek alternative universe." She raised an eyebrow, clearly content in her ignorant bliss.

He continued, "These unique addresses are created and managed by the Internet Assigned Numbers Authority or the IANA."

"Can we cut with the alphabet references? I think I'm developing a tumor."

Seth ignored her and went on.

"Superblocks in cyberspace are kind of like real estate. They can be subdivided into smaller lots and distributed to various Internet providers. What I'm trying to say is, it's gonna take time to dig through the spiderweb of info he left behind."

Seth looked her in the eye and kept going.

"Even if I narrow it down to a real network and registration, we might be dealing with a server out of the country that allows anonymous e-mails. If I was working it, that's what I'd do. If the U.S. government can't coerce another country to cooperate, what are the odds we're gonna do any better in getting a physical address on Baker's organization? It'd be like fishing for Moby Dick with a cane pole."

When he started to talk about real people and fishing analogies, she interrupted him.

"Harper? Let me worry about concocting a fish story. If you give me the phone numbers to contact these cyberspace realtors and I can talk to a live human being, I've got skills you haven't seen yet. Trust me, I'll get what we need if I have to speak Swahili."

"Now why doesn't that surprise me?" It was his turn to smirk. "Any woman who'd bulldog a moving SUV earns *my* respect."

"That's about the nicest thing any man has ever said to me. Thanks, Harper."

"But here's the bad part. Baker knows we've got his shit." Seth turned toward her. "While I'm dicking around with this, I'm afraid he's shut it all down. From anywhere, this guy can make contact and change passwords, he can get the word out. Hell, for all we know, he may have already closed shop."

Jess gritted her teeth, knowing he was right. But she did have one advantage.

"There's one thing we can count on, Seth. Maybe this organization is international and pretty computer savvy, but I know Baker. He's a friggin' idiot. Most criminals are. People like him are not exactly MIT material. You feel up for the challenge?"

"To beat an idiot?"

"Worded like that, I have complete faith in you."

"Thanks." He furrowed his brow. "I think."

Jess tried not to smile. "The point is, we've got Baker's portal to a bigger organization. Find me the hole in his dike, Seth."

"Ditch the dike hole analogy, will ya? It scares me."

He hit a few keystrokes and pulled up a file.

"Before I forget, I got something else for you." He grinned, a crooked lazy smile. "Baker had a digital photo open when he tore out of that room, something sent via e-mail. So far, I've got nothing on the origin of the e-mail itself, but embedded at the end of this picture file was a message. I figured these jerks wouldn't be sharing their Alaskan vacation slides for nothing, so I looked for a reason he'd have this one open and found the embedded message. I saved it to the drive."

Seth flipped the monitor toward her. Jess read the message on the screen. One line from a man named Ivan Andreyevich Krylov.

Delivery from AK on its way to Chicago as agreed. ETA two days.

"A Russian?" She cocked her head and stared at the screen. "And maybe a connection to Alaska."

"Actually, I Googled the name and got some Russian fables and folklore dude. I don't think that's a coincidence. We're not gonna find these guys using their real names."

Seth shrugged and kept talking.

"On the surface, this message isn't incriminating. Granted, the wording is a little cryptic, but for all we know, he's addicted to the Home Shopping Network or he's got an eBay delivery coming from Alaska. However, when you couple the way this message was transmitted in a digital photo file with the use of aliases and international IP addresses, I'd say the whole setup reaches outside the U.S. in an impressive array. At the risk of using a redundant fish analogy, I'm thinkin' Baker may be a guppy in a very big pond."

Jess reread the embedded message from the Russian.

"ETA two days." She backtracked the date and looked at her watch to confirm her suspicions. "That means whatever is being delivered to Chicago is coming in today."

If Seth was right and Baker closed up shop, this last bit of intel might be the only link she would have to his organization. This so-called shipment had been set in motion. Did the bastard have time to call it off or would this be her best shot at nailing him?

"I've got to play a hunch, Seth. It might be a stretch, but I'd bet money he's bartering in human lives. The delivery may be some poor unlucky kid caught up in Baker's web of lies."

A worried look spread across Seth's face. "So what are you gonna do?"

"I don't know yet. I gotta think."

A scheme started to form in her mind. Baker would still want his property back, so his laptop could be a bargaining chip. She touched Seth's arm to get his undivided attention.

"Hypothetically speaking, I may be forced to return Baker's property to get another crack at this guy. And that thought makes my blood boil unless I have the upper hand." She took a deep breath. "If I knew someone really connected to certain people, could this computer-savvy guy install software on this laptop? I want to track Baker's movement in the cyberworld from inside his own computer."

Seth stared at her a long moment.

"I see you've got pliable ethics when it comes to turning the tables on Baker using my crimeware bootleg stuff. The all-important end justifies the means, is that it?"

He didn't let her squirm long. Fighting a smirk, he cocked his head and raised an eyebrow in a good-humored challenge. What the hell could she say?

"Hey, you got me. When it comes to Baker and his perverted world, I guess my ethics take a backseat. Sue me."

"That's okay. I understand. I'm just sayin' . . ." Seth grinned, a totally wicked smile, and let it go. "Hypothetically speaking, of course, such an absolutely freaking genius could load a Trojan horse the guy would never see coming. Keystroke loggers can collect sensitive data, steal his new passwords and store them on his own system, leaving cyber bread crumbs to follow. Once Baker accesses those encrypted files I was telling you about, we're in too."

Seth's eyes radiated light. This stuff really turned the boy on.

"Plus, we could add bells and whistles to allow us remote access or even redirect his browser to a counterfeit link of our choosing. He'll think he's logged into his site, but he'll be talking to us. Very cool stuff. And I may have one or two other tricks I can add. Is that covert enough for you?"

"Perfect, just like you." She pinched his cheek, and flaming red streaks shot across Seth's face. But then she got serious. There was too much at stake to trivialize what they were about to do.

"I really need this to work, Seth. Rig his laptop with your Trojan horse. I got a feeling it'll be our last shot at Baker."

"I'm on it. I'll have it done and tested before you step out that door. Maybe if I have time, I can kick in something extra."

Seth turned his attention to the computer in his lap, leaving Jess rapt in her thoughts.

If Baker was in the process of severing his links to the old setup, the delivery to Chicago—some poor kid—might turn out to be a sacrificial lamb. She had no way of knowing where or how the "delivery" might be coming. No leads at all, except for the e-mail reference to Alaska. Hell, she didn't even know if she could trust the intel. There'd be no way to intervene, so she had to do the next best thing.

Her instincts told her to focus on stopping Baker—for the greater good—but could she ignore the feeling that a faceless kid's life hung in the balance? She hated how that made her feel. No doubt about it. Life sucked on a grand scale, a fact she understood better than most.

Even if Sam could work her cop magic this late in the day and check the flight manifests for all inbound planes from Alaska, the odds weren't good that her friend would have the resources to go much further. They wouldn't even know what to look for. And if the CPD knew she was connected to Sam's search, everything would come to a grinding halt. Besides, given the time of day and the duration of a flight from Alaska, the plane was already gone, narrowing her odds for success considerably.

She knew she was on her own—as usual.

In no time, Seth had Baker's laptop rigged and ready to go. He packed it back into the computer bag it came in and handed it to her, the thin gloves removed.

"Call me on my cell if you think of anything else," she asked.

"Yeah, okay." He nodded.

Jess got to her feet and headed for the door. "You got my number, right?"

"Yeah, programmed into my cell." He stood and followed her. His hands fumbled through his pockets, pulling out coins, cash, and a set of keys.

"Let me walk you out. I gotta meet a friend for drinks." He shrugged and added, "It's gotta be five o'clock somewhere on the planet, right? You're welcome to join us."

"Thanks, but no. I gotta motor, but can I get a rain check?"

"Yeah, no problem." Seth locked the door behind them and walked with her to the elevators. They chatted as they rode down to the ground floor, the idle chat of two people getting to know one another. For Jess, it felt good to act normal for a change.

He walked her out the building and stood on the sidewalk by the front door, but before he took off, she wanted to make a point. Seth's part in the computer Trojan horse wasn't over.

"One last thing. I gotta ask you a big favor." She winced, realizing the magnitude of what she was about to ask from a new hourly employee. "I'd like you to track Baker's activity once he gets his property back. I know I've got no right to ask, but—"

Without hesitation, Seth replied, “Sure, I’ll do it.”

“Wait, before you commit, you gotta know. With a low-life like Lucas Baker, I have no idea when or for how long that will be. I’ve gotta scare him up first. You still in? Even with all the flaky hours?”

“Count on it. I’m in.” Again no hesitation.

Jess grinned and shook her head at her employee. “If you’re buckin’ for a raise, Harper, you should probably consider playing harder to get. You’re too easy.”

“And for a guy, there’s no such thing as being too easy.” Seth smirked. Jess had a sneaky suspicion the boy wasn’t talking about the almighty dollar anymore.

“Before I forget . . .” She grabbed her cell phone off her belt loop and thumbed the menu to her contacts page. “Give me a phone number where I can reach you. Now that you’ve volunteered for duty, I’ve got to reach you twenty-four/seven.”

He gave her his cell number and she keyed it into her phone.

“I’ll stay in touch. And thanks, Seth. You’re a good man.”

She tugged at a loose strand of his hair, and her show of affection sent a blush across his cheeks. In return, he rewarded her with a quirky grin and a shrug. Cute. Damned cute.

With Baker’s laptop slung over her shoulder, she left Seth to carry on and headed for her car, mulling over her situation. Her mind raced with things beyond her control. Under the circumstances, Baker would be laying low, not hanging out at his usual haunts. It would now be a major waiting game—waiting for him to contact her or hunting him down again. Only this time he’d be warier and harder to find.

Hell, what choice did she have?

And from the looks of her apartment, the guy had anger management issues. Baker was beyond pissed. She had a feeling trashing her place was only the first installment to his payback. It wouldn't be so bad if this was only a head-on collision between her and Baker, but she knew it wasn't that simple. Other lives would be at stake, and that thought weighed heavy in the pit of her stomach. Whatever was going to happen, she had to pull her part off clean.

As Jess crossed the street with Baker's laptop slung on her shoulder, she squinted into the late afternoon sun, unable to shake the image of Baker's angry face. Even in broad daylight the man triggered a deeply rooted jumble of rage and degrading fear in her—an all too vivid taste of her past. She knew she'd have to find a way to control such feelings or he would have the upper hand.

With other lives at risk, she had to come out on top. And instinct told her time was running thin. *Real thin.*

CHAPTER 7

Payton drove to a building at the junction of the Talkeetna Spur Road and Parks Highway where the state maintained a small troopers' office only fifteen miles from Susannah's place. He couldn't get his mind off the mysterious Anchorage schoolteacher who'd driven Nikki out of town. Taking a kid in the middle of the night, without the knowledge of her mother, was completely irresponsible. No way the woman could claim the incident was one big misunderstanding. What would compel a complete stranger to do such a thing?

But his more immediate problem would be Trooper Dan Fitzgerald.

How could he convince the man to trust him—to allow him to accompany the troopers when they talked to this teacher? He quickly came up with a simple plan. When they entered the troopers' office, he would let Joe Tanu take charge. It made perfect sense. It was Joe's turf, and he appreciated Joe's influence with an organization he'd worked with for years.

When they walked in, they were greeted by a familiar voice.

"Hey, Joe. Figured we'd see you sooner or later." At her desk behind a counter, Bernice Fleming looked up from her dispatch duties. "Sorry to hear about Nikki, Payton. Susannah and her daughter sure got their share of trouble."

Bernice shook her head. The older woman's face was a mix of concocted sympathy and the righteous superiority of a regular churchgoer.

Payton didn't want to talk about Nikki with Bernice. He had no patience for it. For whatever reason, the woman thrived on other people's misery. Some folks were like that. Given the woman's reputation, the implication he heard in her voice was that his niece had probably brought this on herself and Susannah played a hand in it, though he also knew that his hangover had tainted his perspective.

"Thanks, Bernice." It was all he could get out.

With the incessant pounding in his head, anything from his mouth echoed like a bass drum inside his skull, triggering other painful twinges. He caught a sideways glance from Joe, who picked up on his mounting irritability. In his understated manner, Joe zapped him with a heavy dose of "stick eye." His friend had practically invented the disapproving look.

Payton shrugged and heaved a sigh.

Let Joe handle this part, jackass! You're in no condition to play nice.

A handful of folks in town still treated him like a celebrity, leaving him with the empty ache of knowing he never measured up. Bernice Fleming was one of those people who probably thought she meant well, but the way she expressed her sympathy, it seemed she straddled the fence between good intentions and the idle curiosity of a rumor monger gathering intel and a good head of steam. He had no time to sift through the merits of her intentions. Truth told, he preferred outright hostility, something he could deal with, like a beefy lineman hungry to humiliate a cocky young quarterback on a one-way ego trip.

"I suppose a second time doesn't make it any easier," Bernice went on. "How's Susannah holding up?"

"Well, how would you—" He stopped and reigned in his attitude, then took a deep breath before he continued. "She's doing the best she knows how."

What the hell? Like a mother would ever get used to her daughter running away?

He knew she was fishing for the real dirt behind Nikki's disappearance and pushing his buttons to get it, but he wouldn't give her the satisfaction. No one else needed to know the nightmare of his sister's pain.

Even living in Alaska, where a guy's idiosyncrasies were considered normal and his past was respected as private, most folks in Talkeetna went out of their way to speak their minds about him. And he'd brought the same attitude down on his sister by default. For some reason, both their lives were fair sport. And contrary to the norm, many folks had an opinion.

He'd gotten used to it, but Susannah had been an innocent bystander. She deserved better.

His own downward spiral had sucked his sister in—guilt by association—but he received the worst of it by far. To his face or behind his back, it didn't matter. Most people openly looked upon him as a major disappointment—quite a fall from the celebrity they'd heaped on him not too long ago. Now, he was nothing more than a drunk, a brawler, and a failure. He could see it in their eyes—and his own when he looked in a mirror.

People saw what they wanted to see. He guessed he was no different.

But if Joe hadn't come along today, he wasn't sure how much help he'd be to Susannah. He'd worn out his welcome with the local law.

"You need to speak to Trooper Fitzgerald?" Bernice stuck to protocol with the formal title. Her question had been directed to Joe, but she kept her eyes on Payton.

"Yes, we do." Joe nodded.

The woman glanced over her shoulder, then stood, her chair squeaking with the effort. From behind the plexiglass window, she stepped toward them and rested her elbows on the worn Formica countertop that separated the secured offices from the waiting area.

"He's on the phone. No telling how long he'll be." She forced a smile. "I got some coffee brewing, fresh. Can I get you boys a cup while you wait?"

"Not for me." Joe shook his head. "Thanks, Bernice."

Payton did the same, mumbling a distracted reply under his breath.

"You almost missed him. He's heading to Anchorage, but I'll slip him a note to let him know you're waiting. Just have a seat."

After Bernice ducked behind a closed door, Payton glanced back toward the visitor chairs. With the adrenaline pumping through his veins, he couldn't imagine sitting while the trooper got off the phone. His impatience had taken a firm grip.

Pacing the small room, he found his eyes unable to settle on any one thing. Flashes of Nikki's face plagued him, along with erratic sound bites from their last conversations. He'd been so rapt in his own misery, he hadn't spent much time with Susannah or Nikki; something else to fuel the fires of guilt.

"God, I hate this."

Payton wasn't sure he'd spoken aloud, but when he spotted Joe from the corner of his eye, he noticed his friend standing and watching him. Cool and rock steady as still water, Joe's dark eyes never gave away his thoughts. Most days, Payton envied the man's self-control. Yet there were other times he thought holding a mirror to Joe's nose might tell him if the man actually breathed like normal people.

"Trooper Fitzgerald will see you now." Bernice opened the door to let them come in.

By the time he and Joe walked down the hall to Fitzgerald's office, the trooper was standing by his desk, ready to leave. He had plans to make their visit short and anything but sweet.

"Look, I gave you the courtesy of staying put until you got here, but I can't let you come to Anchorage. This is police business, Joe. And last I looked, you weren't on the payroll."

Fitzgerald looked intimidating enough in the authoritative duty gear troopers wore, and he had a way of staring that cut lesser men to the bone. His practiced glare came with the job, but being tall and athletic with broad shoulders, Dan Fitzgerald had slid into his late forties with plenty of good miles left. The only signs of his age were thinning dark hair and creases around his pale blue eyes. His seasoned face gave the trooper character and allowed him to readily flip a switch between harsh and merciful at his choosing.

But Joe came from the same cut of cloth. He squared off with Fitzgerald in his own simple way.

"Don't tell me you'd sit back and twiddle your thumbs if this happened to one of your girls, 'cause I know better."

Payton hung back and didn't attempt to break the tension. Eventually, the trooper caved. He showed it in his eyes first, then lowered his chin and relaxed his shoulders.

"Look, don't make me out to be the bad guy here, Joe. I'll call you the minute I know something. Besides, Anchorage could be a wild goose chase."

"It's the only lead we got, and you know it." Joe kept his voice steady and his eyes fixed on Fitzgerald. "I ain't asking for much. If I got a marker left with you, I need it now, Fitz. Payton and I can observe from the next room. The teacher won't even know we're there. And who knows? We might even shed light on what she's tellin' you, knowing Nikki the way we do."

The trooper stared at Joe, letting silence do his talking until Payton broke the stalemate.

"Look, Dan, you know how it is. We gotta do something. Nikki is out there . . . with strangers. Susannah is afraid some outsider off the Internet has taken her only kid. She's sick with worry."

He stepped forward, but kept his voice low and in control.

"Please . . . I promise. You won't even know I'm there. And Joe is a trained investigator. Doesn't it make sense to have another good man on this case? It would give Susannah peace of mind, something she hasn't had much of lately."

The trooper tightened his jaw and glared through ice blue eyes until his stern expression softened. He let out a sigh and tapped a finger to Payton's chest.

"I'm gonna hold you to that promise, Archer. You're gonna follow orders. No questions asked. You hear me?" After Payton nodded, the trooper shook his head and brushed by him, muttering, "Let's get this traveling circus on the road."

Anchorage

The late afternoon sun struggled to make an appearance, but lost its battle to a stubborn band of clouds and a steady mist. A dull gray cast its pallor on Payton's already sullen mood. On the drive in from Talkeetna, dark thoughts about Nikki's whereabouts crept through his mind on a continuous loop. And the gloomy day exacerbated the feeling that he might have already lost her for good. These days, he didn't feel like a lucky man. His old cocky self was long gone, replaced by someone he wasn't sure he wanted to know. And worse, he craved a drink so bad he actually smelled his favorite single malt scotch. The power of suggestion triggered a need he thought he had under control—until today.

When they got to Anchorage, Fitzgerald drove to the Alaska State Troopers' headquarters on Tudor Road. Once in the building, Fitzgerald vouched for him and Joe Tanu, saying they'd merely observe the interview with the teacher.

The assigned Anchorage trooper, Clive Stalworth, narrowed his eyes and exchanged a questioning look with his Talkeetna counterpart, but didn't object since the missing person report had been initiated by Fitzgerald.

Stalworth informed them that the schoolteacher, Claire Hanson, had already been picked up and waited for them in Interview Room 5. The Anchorage trooper led them through a corridor to an adjoining room where he and Joe could observe through a two-way mirror. The only light came from next door, the room where the teacher sat alone.

Once he stepped into the room, Payton fixed his eyes on her, unable to look away.

Claire Hanson appeared to be a woman in her forties and was dressed in a floral skirt, white blouse, and navy blue cardigan. She wore glasses and looked unassuming with her straight dark hair pulled back in barrettes. Payton stared at her face, unsure what he had expected. Secretly, he hoped to find a subtle menace behind her eyes. It would have been easier to picture someone the troopers could badger for the truth and incarcerate if they found her guilty.

Yet even though the woman in the interview room didn't appear to be malicious, something about her gave him a bad feeling that festered in the back of his mind.

"I'll be conducting the initial interview, but Fitzgerald will remain here with you in case you have questions during the proceedings." Trooper Stalworth stood by the doorway. "Can I get you any coffee before we get started?"

"No, thank you," Joe replied, and waved a hand.

Payton shook his head, only half listening. After the trooper closed the door, he kept his eyes on the woman next door until he felt someone by his side. Fitzgerald must have been reading his mind.

"I know this schoolteacher doesn't exactly fit the mold of a hardened criminal, but don't worry. If she knows anything or is hidin' somethin', Stalworth'll find it. And if she broke the law, it won't matter if she's Mother fuckin' Teresa."

"You always were a politically correct kind of guy, Fitz." Joe Tanu smirked, but his expression grew more solemn as he turned toward his old friend. "We wanna thank you for doing this . . . regardless how it turns out."

The last part of what Joe said struck Payton—a hard dose of reality, one he wasn't sure he wanted to hear.

In the adjoining room, Stalworth had entered and greeted the woman sitting at the table. Their words were mute until Joe turned up the volume on the speaker system. Payton listened as the trooper started the interview by identifying Claire Hanson for the session recording and confirming details of her background. With each question, the schoolteacher grew more anxious.

"I still don't understand why you've brought me here. What's this about?" she asked.

Stalworth obliged her with an answer.

"We have witnesses who've placed you in Talkeetna early this morning, around one, picking up a young girl named Nikki Archer. We'd like to know where she is."

The sudden change in direction took the woman by surprise, and it showed. Claire Hanson tried to recover, but it was too late. Her body language had given her away. Stalworth had stretched the truth about the number of witnesses. And he had lied about Claire being spotted. Payton knew that in the interview process, cops sometimes embellished the facts to get results. By law, they could do this. And judging by the look on Claire Hanson's face, the trooper's subterfuge had gotten her attention.

"Nikki Archer?" Even though the schoolteacher stalled with a question, Payton suspected the woman knew more than she wanted to admit.

"Don't bother to deny it. We have witnesses who will put you at River Park with the missing girl. If you cooperate and help us to find her, a judge might go easier on you."

Panic spread across Claire Hanson's face. "Missing girl? I didn't do anything wrong."

"That's not how the District Attorney will see it." The trooper glared, not giving an inch. "He tends to frown at kidnapping."

The word kidnapping shocked her.

"Oh, my God, this can't be happening." She wrapped her arms across her waist and rocked in short erratic movements. "Do I need a lawyer?"

"Not if you haven't done anything wrong, but you gotta help me out here." Stalworth softened his tone. Switching from bad cop to good, the trooper leaned forward, resting his elbows on the table. A look of sympathy replaced his stern authoritative expression.

"Look, Nikki's mother is worried sick. We just want to get to the bottom of this and bring the girl home safely. Maybe you can help us."

"I swear, that's all I was doing, trying to help." Claire Hanson began to cry. Red blotches spread across her cheeks and she swiped her nose with the back of her hand. "Oh God, I didn't mean to . . . I thought I was helping."

"Who were you trying to help, ma'am? You don't look like the kind of woman who'd take the word of a kid without first checking with a parent."

Payton stepped closer to the observation window, hands in his pockets. Claire Hanson hadn't denied taking Nikki, but he still couldn't imagine why.

"He told me about this girl, an abused kid. He never told me her name, to protect her identity, he said. But she needed help to get out of a bad situation."

"Who is this guy you talked to?" Stalworth handed the woman a tissue from a box on a nearby shelf. "You better tell me what happened, from the beginning."

Claire Hanson told the trooper about meeting Mark Russo in a chatroom, a support group for grieving parents. Claire had searched for solace of any kind after the death of her only daughter, Tami, in a car accident at the hands of a drunk driver. At first she only knew Mark as a member of the group. But after she'd gotten the courage to confide the depths of her grief, Mark singled her out for one-on-one chats. He'd also lost a daughter to violence, and his wife eventually divorced him when he grew so depressed that he wasn't able to deal with his emotions. He finally found his road to recovery through a program that allowed him to reach out to others. A "no questions asked" hotline for troubled teens. Mark shared his story of healing, making her feel special that he had chosen her to confide his very personal journey.

Hearing Claire's story gave Payton a thread of hope. As the teacher continued to tell her side, he turned to Trooper Fitzgerald and spoke in a hushed tone.

"Maybe Nikki misrepresented her situation, exaggerated her side in order to get someone to help her leave the state. She might've connected with Mark Russo through that teen hotline."

Payton knew he was grasping at straws. Nikki wasn't the type of kid who would do such a thing—to use a stranger to get what she wanted. But believing his niece was in control gave him hope that Mark Russo was legit.

"Look, I know what you're thinking, but don't delude yourself. I think you have to be prepared that Russo might not be his real name." Fitzgerald prepped him for the worst. "Online predators have gotten sophisticated in how they hunt on the Internet. They're master manipulators and find other people to do their dirty work. Makes it harder to prove their guilt in a court of law."

Fitzgerald stared at the woman in the next room. "It'll be up to the D.A. to decide if he's gonna press charges against this schoolteacher, but my gut tells me Claire Hanson is a victim too."

"What are you talking about?" Payton asked.

"We'll check into Mark Russo, but I got a feeling we're gonna be looking for a ghost. An online predator creates a persona and a back story that no one questions until it's too late. And this guy can change his name and move on. Even if we track the real person down, he or she may live in a foreign country, making it nearly impossible to trace. The Internet breaks down international barriers, which can be a good thing. But in the wrong hands, it can erect walls for criminals to hide behind. If a predator is smart, the Internet is a perfect hunting ground."

In the next room, Payton heard Claire Hanson say, "Mark had me buy a one-way ticket to Chicago for some poor girl he'd been trying to help. She lived in Alaska, he said. I didn't say yes right away, but he eventually convinced me I was her only hope. I made the reservations under my daughter's name and used her ID, paying for it with my own money. Her flight left a little after five this morning."

The woman glanced at her watch and shut her eyes tight, taking a deep breath before she went on.

"The girl said the man had told her what to do once the plane landed. I assumed she meant Mark, but thinking back, I guess she never mentioned a name." The teacher wiped her eyes and sobbed, dabbing at her cheeks with the tissue Stalworth had given her. "I tried to get her to talk to me during the ride from Talkeenta, but she refused. She looked so lost, it broke my heart. And she looked so much like my . . . my little girl."

"Oh my God, Chicago?" Payton looked over his shoulder at Joe. "We gotta stop that plane. When does it touch down? It's gonna take time to get the Chicago PD involved. We gotta call now."

Fitzgerald checked his watch, but the look in his eyes confirmed what Payton already feared. It was probably too late.

"I'll call the airline . . . just in case. But don't get your hopes up." The trooper left the room, leaving Payton alone with his desperation.

Joe Tanu stepped closer and gripped the back of Payton's neck. In the darkened room, his friend spoke quietly, trying to reassure him.

"We're gonna find her."

Payton kept his eyes on Claire Hanson, staring through the two-way mirror as he spoke.

"Nikki flew to Chicago, Joe, one of the largest cities in the U.S. and a major hub for the airlines. Hell, if the plane's already landed, she could catch another flight anywhere." He shook his head. "This all happened too damned fast. I don't even know what to tell Susannah."

"Tell her Chicago is beautiful this time of year. And that we're not leaving Nikki in the hands of some overworked cop in downtown Chicago. No, sir."

Payton caught the glimmer in Joe's eyes, a hint of the cop he used to be. For his friend's sake, he forced himself to smile.

"You're right. We're not playing against a clock that's gonna run down. Nikki's still out there and she needs our help." Payton kept up his show of optimism. "We're not waiting for a commercial flight either. If Fitzgerald tells us Nikki's plane has already landed in Chicago, then we better have a backup plan. I've got money and the connections to get us there fast."

"Now you're talking." Joe smiled. A real smile. "You still have those pages from Nikki's computer? I'd like to see if Fitz can analyze them for us. Maybe Nikki and her friend left a cyber trail we can follow. We can attack this from another angle."

Payton reached for the pages in his shirt pocket and handed them to Joe, thankful his friend had kept a clear enough head to remember the printouts. After Joe left the room, Payton stood alone in the shadows and watched Claire Hanson, suddenly seeing her in a different light.

Gone was the demon he had imagined before. Now, all that remained was a timid, frightened woman caught up in something she didn't understand. He wanted to hate her for what she did, but pity was all he felt. Because of her grief, she might have been duped into becoming a pawn in a bigger game. But if a guy using a phony name in a chat room had manipulated her in such a heinous way, Nikki might be in the hands of a very dangerous predator.

An old sensation returned, hitting him hard.

From the moment he first saw Claire Hanson, something about the woman had given him a bad feeling. He hadn't understood why until now. If this woman had no idea what happened to Nikki—and if her story turned out to be a complete lie conjured by a practiced online predator who knew how to cover his tracks—then Claire Hanson would be a dead end.

A damned dead end!

Wishful thinking would do no good. No matter how fast they got to Chicago, the trail would be cold.

CHAPTER 8

Chicago O'Hare Airport

The plane had arrived ten minutes early with the help of a good tail wind. Nikki navigated a smaller concourse, following the signs for the main terminal and baggage claim. Outside, Ivana Noskova would be waiting with her father in a car her friend had described. If they weren't there, Ivana had given her a backup plan that Nikki hoped she wouldn't have to use.

She desperately wanted this to work right the first time, without a hitch.

Walking at her own pace, she nibbled absentmindedly at her lower lip and played with the zipper of her fanny pack. She had a feeling that once she was truly on her own, she'd discover many things about herself, not the least of which would be her preference for freedom in smaller doses. Meeting Ivana would go a long way toward making her feel more comfortable in a town as big as Chicago.

She had been through O'Hare a handful of times, but never without her mother. And call it stubborn pride, but she didn't want to admit that her newfound independence might turn out to be a double-edged sword. Both fear and exhilaration played a part in making her edgy.

Shake it off, Nik. You're not a kid anymore.

PA announcements overhead mixed with snips of conversations from passengers carrying rolling luggage. The place was huge and crowded. She felt invisible, and cocooned in a time warp that made her feel like she was standing still. Everyone else had someplace real to be. People darted by her with tight connections to make. Others stopped in her path to check computer monitors. She was an amateur at all this, and it showed.

But one thing might get her out of her weird funk. Eating.

She thought about grabbing a quick bite. The smell of french fries, cinnamon buns, and pizza by the slice tempted her, for sure. Whenever she got nervous, she had a tendency to eat junk, but she didn't want to keep Ivana and her father waiting. She'd promised not to draw attention to herself, but there was one stop she had to make before getting her bag.

A pit stop.

Nikki hit the public restroom and took care of business. But when she was done, a dark-skinned woman in a navy janitor's uniform, hardly more than a girl, caught her eye. She was cleaning one of the stalls. Nikki saw her in the mirror as she washed her hands, and she tried to smile, but the woman only stared through her, her eyes dull and vacant. Hard to tell her age, but she didn't look that much older than her. Nikki tried not to stare but couldn't help it. The woman was too young to give up on the rest of her life. And what about dreams? Did she ever have any?

How did people let these things happen? she wondered.

She watched the woman work for a while longer, until an odd sensation settled in the pit of her stomach. The girl suddenly made her feel uncomfortable and anxious. She didn't understand why she felt this way. It wasn't like she was alone with her. Other people had been there, and the cleaning woman posed no threat. Yet something came over her that was palpable and strong. All she knew was that she couldn't stay any longer. She rushed from the restroom, heading for baggage claim and Ivana.

As she walked, Nikki picked up her pace with one thought repeating over and over in her head. She'd done the right thing by coming here, damn it. She had dreams and a new life to start. And she wouldn't let anything stand in her way.

Nothing.

Outside baggage claim, the passenger pickup lanes were swarming with activity. He'd counted on the buzz to blend in. People were coming and going. Skycaps were hauling bags on wheel carts, dodging traffic. And a taxi wrangler whistled and waved a cab up from the waiting line to drive a suit downtown to an overpriced hotel. That's what he figured anyway.

He knew fresh meat when he saw it. They all looked clueless, and he could spot easy pickings a mile off. The instinct was hard to kick, but he had a new gig now. And it sure beat hustling for chump change.

Alert, the man kept his eyes on the rearview mirror and out his windshield, looking for a face he'd committed to memory. When he found what he was looking for, he smirked, then keyed a speed dial number on his cell phone. His call was answered on the third ring.

"Yeah, you got somethin' for me?" A low guttural voice with a Russian accent came on the line.

"She's definitely a looker." He narrowed his eyes. A girl craned her neck, looking down the row of waiting vehicles. When she spotted his car, the kid headed toward him.

Bingo.

Speaking into his phone, he added, "With any luck, we'll have options with this one."

He looked right, expecting the sullen girl sitting next to him in the front seat to move, but she didn't.

"Hey, hold on a sec." He put a hand over the phone, glaring at the girl beside him.

Still the bitch didn't move. She picked at strands of her thin brown hair, tugging at split ends. Sometimes she could get under his skin, like now. He poked her scrawny arm with a knuckle and barked an order.

"Hey, go make nice. You know what to do. Get her into the car, both of you in the backseat. Once we get her home, I wanna see that fanny pack. And she better not have a cell phone."

Ivana shifted her attention to him, her dark green eyes the color of dull moss with the luster gone. And her skin looked blotchy from too much makeup, her attempt to cover acne scars.

"No problem. Jus' remember, I do this thing for you. I help you, yes?" Sometimes Ivana slathered on the Russian accent like it was butter. It used to turn him on.

"Yeah, yeah. Now get goin'."

She got out of the vehicle without saying another word, returning his stare over her shoulder. Once outside, she perked up for the performance and waved to the new one, calling her over. The girls hugged. It gave him time to finish his call.

"I got appointments for her tomorrow. Who knows? Maybe if we get lucky, I'll be sending her to you real soon. Kind of a shame she may've come all this way, but you know the drill. I'll give you a heads-up when I can."

He ended the call and got out of the car, forcing himself to grin at the kid, real friendly.

"Hey, Nikki. Welcome to Chicago. I'm Ivana's father. Lemme take your bag."

She smiled and handed over all her possessions. Real trusting. They all had fresh young faces that he never got tired of seeing.

"Thanks, Mr. Noskova. I really appreciate—"

He didn't let her finish.

"My name's not—" He stopped and stared at the girl. He could have corrected her, but it didn't matter what she called him. "Just call me Mike."

The new girl narrowed her eyes and gave him a questioning look. Before she could ask anything, he took her duffel and placed it in the trunk.

"You girls go ahead and get in the backseat. I'm sure you've got a lot to talk about." He smiled again and waved them off. "Go ahead. We've got a bit of a drive, so get comfortable."

He shoved her bag into the trunk of his car and closed it. When he got into the driver's seat, he heard the kid talking to Ivana. Looking in the rearview mirror, he watched for traffic to clear, but the new girl did a better job at holding his interest.

"I've never lived anyplace as big as this." Nikki struck up a conversation with her friend, but the whole thing felt awkward with her father listening. And she caught the man snatching glimpses in the mirror.

"You like livin' here, right, Ivana?" she persisted.

Her friend looked at her and forced a smile. "Yes. You will see."

As Ivana's dad pulled from the curb and into traffic, Ivana crossed her arms and turned away, gazing out the window.

"So are you excited about tomorrow?" Nikki tried again to make conversation.

"Yes, it will be good day," the girl replied.

Nikki was so anxious to talk about tomorrow that her friend's indifference didn't register at first. Mr. Noskova had pulled strings to get them both an appointment with a prestigious Chicago modeling agency, one with connections to New York. Apparently, they had liked a photo posted on her blog. And they wanted to see Ivana too.

Ivana's dad merged into freeway traffic, taking Interstate

190E, then south on 294. The road signs flew by, not catching her attention. Her focus was entirely on what tomorrow would bring.

"I hear if they like you, they take head shots . . . with a real fashion photographer. I've never done anything like that. Do you think someone will be there to help us with makeup? 'Cause that would be so cool, you know?"

She was talking a mile a minute now—excited to finally share her dream—but Ivana only stared back, barely nodding or shaking her head in reply. An unreadable face with vacant eyes. Her reaction caught Nikki by surprise.

A cold slap of déjà vu.

In her friend's apathetic eyes she found remnants of another face—the cleaning woman—the one she thought looked defeated and used up. But before she could ask Ivana what was wrong, Mr. Noskova interrupted.

"Tomorrow is a big day for you girls. I got a feeling it's gonna change your lives."

He stared at Nikki through the mirror again. Although she heard a smile in his voice, the man wasn't what she expected.

But then, neither was Ivana.

Talkeetna, Alaska
Hours later

While in Anchorage, Payton had arranged for a private charter to make the trip to Chicago later that evening, but he couldn't leave without first seeing Susannah and explaining what had happened with the schoolteacher, Claire Hanson. Once he got home, he'd have just enough time to pack, see his sister, and pick up Joe on his way to the Talkeetna airport. He'd arranged for the charter to meet them at the small local airstrip, saving him a trip back to Anchorage by car.

When he walked through his front door, he gazed at the mess he'd left behind, remnants of his self-indulgence. A life without consequence.

"You're a piece of work, Archer," he mumbled to himself.

He tossed his truck keys on a kitchen counter next to a half-empty bottle of Macallan scotch and noticed the red blinking light from his answering machine. His first thought was that the message might be from Susannah. Without hesitation, he punched the button to hear it.

With garbled noise in the background, it took a while for a voice to come on the line.

"Uncle Payton . . . I love you."

The faint voice of his niece caught him by surprise.

Knowing how she'd left town, he recognized the background noise as the Anchorage airport, with part of a flight announcement recorded. He checked the time stamp for Nikki's call and a cold fist of sadness gripped his heart.

She'd called when he was out drinking. If he'd been home, would things have turned out differently? Had this been her attempt to reach out one last time? Anger and frustration surged under his skin.

"And you picked me, Nikki. God help you."

He grabbed for the bottle of scotch, not bothering with a glass, and took a long pull. It burned his throat all the way down, the heat swelling through his chest and belly. Gasping, he came up for air and wiped his lips with the back of his hand. Guilt closed in without mercy.

Until now, he thought he'd only done harm to himself with the choices he'd made, but that wasn't true. He'd cut himself off from the people he loved, and there had been consequences.

How would he face Susannah?

Chicago
Early evening

From Seth's place, Jess drove to a library on the way to her apartment to access the Internet. Her home computer had been a casualty of Baker's deranged payback.

She checked into flights leaving Anchorage bound for Chicago that day. Several carriers fit the bill, with destinations to Chicago's O'Hare, Midway, and Rockford airports. If Baker had a kid booked on an inbound flight from Alaska, most arrivals had already touched down. And the odds weren't in her favor for the few remaining flights. Even if she picked the right airport, she couldn't be in two places at once. She and Madame Luck had parted company in a big way.

"Shit."

She wasn't sure why she tortured herself with the flight information. It wasn't like she could do anything. Even if she narrowed the search, she was only playing a hunch about Baker and his so-called Alaskan delivery to Chicago being an unfortunate kid.

More than likely her diversion to the library had been nothing more than procrastination, pure and simple. The wasteland of her apartment awaited her attention.

"Let's get it over with." She left the library and drove home to suffer the indignities of a full-blown pity party. Once and for all, she had to face clean-up duty, deal with it and get on with her life.

Back at her place, Jess worked for another couple of hours, filling the apartment complex Dumpster with the remnants of her life. It pained her to do it, and little remained after Baker's rampage. Her apartment almost echoed with emptiness. She never had much, but until now hadn't appreciated her mixed bag of furnishings and a lifetime of remembrances. And having a lunatic in her home had brought back a familiar sense of violation that would be hard to shake.

Sam called mid-shift to see how things were going, and Jess lied.

"I'm okay. I needed new stuff anyway." She had sloughed off her friend's concern so she wouldn't worry, but mostly Jess knew she needed to convince herself that she could get her life back to normal, whatever the hell that was.

"When I get off duty, I'm bringing Chinese takeout and the two of us will finish cleaning up, okay? Nothing says love like Kung Pao." Sam did her best to keep the pity from her voice, but Jess knew better.

"Sounds good. And I've got you a new key to my seriously humble abode." She took a deep breath, exhausted after her stressful day. "See you soon, sista. And . . . thanks."

Jess ended the call and took out another couple of trash bags. Tomorrow she'd get a fresh start hunting Baker. She'd look under every rock for the lowlife weasel, contact his known associates, and visit his old haunts to search for leads. She'd found him once before, she could do it again.

But now all she needed was a hot bath, something to eat, and time to heal—in that order.

Her body had taken a beating from her confrontation with Baker. And the trips up and down the stairs hauling garbage and maimed furniture hadn't helped. To catch her breath, she leaned against the railing outside her apartment door and stared down at her life in a Dumpster.

She ached down to her soul. It had been one helluva day.

Overhead, a jet engine rumbled. A Southwest Airlines Boeing 737 reflected the molten orange of sunset against its fuselage until it faded into the horizon. That's when she finally took stock. Her arms glistened with a thin layer of sweat and she felt perspiration on her forehead and down her back. And with the sun going down, a cool breeze had inspired a wave of goose bumps. She needed a long soak in a tub to scrub away the remains of her butt ugly day.

But it wasn't meant to be. Clipped to a belt loop, her cell phone rang. Caller ID displayed the name.

Seth Harper.

She grinned as she answered the call, an interruption she didn't mind.

"Don't tell me. You've done a scientific study and found clarity of mind comes after three Rock Bottom lagers," she teased with a grin. "What did you forget, hotshot?"

"He forgot to mind his own business. So did you." A man's voice. "Have you missed me, darlin'?"

What the hell? The slithering voice jolted her heart and carved a notch from her nerves. She didn't have to locate Lucas Baker. Like a train wreck waiting to happen, he stood in her path, braced for their inevitable collision.

One thought was crystal clear, and it made her sick to her stomach. If the twisted bastard had Harper's phone, then she was responsible for placing Seth in Baker's crosshairs. And for that, the kid might pay a terrible price—*meant for her.*

CHAPTER 9

Jess struggled to keep panic from her voice. Career criminals like Baker smelled fear and knew how to draw first blood.

"Yeah, guess you could say I've missed you . . . about as much as I'd miss a frontal lobotomy with a Phillips head screwdriver." Taking the first shot, Jess went on the offensive. Anything short of that would've been a sign of weakness.

"You sound pissed. Don't tell me you didn't like the way I redecorated your shit hole. With that dump, I was doing you a favor."

The sleaze bag had the nerve to gloat. Baker had a smile to his voice mixed with a heavy dose of contempt, enough for her to picture his ugly sneer.

"You had it comin', but we ain't done yet, darlin'. You got somethin' of mine and I want it back. I figure we'll trade for it."

She heard a heavy scrape and a loud thud in the background. But the muffled gasp and moan of a guy's voice put her over the edge. She forced herself to breathe.

Baker came back on the line. "I got your boy. Seth Harper, the one who's a fan of *Jerry Springer*."

If she'd had doubts before, Baker knowing about Seth's T-shirt made her a believer. Baker had Harper. And she had to keep the man talking to divert his attention from the kid.

"Out of curiosity, how did you make the connection between me and him?"

"You delivered him on a silver platter, sweet thing. It all started when I watched you and your cop friend walk through your busted door." He laughed. "I gotta tell ya, it was worth the wait to see the look on your face. But contrary to what you might think, I ain't stupid. You both had weapons drawn, and your friend's a cop. I seen her at the station. And believe me, I know how to fly below radar with the cops. Shootin' one of 'em is no way to earn brownie points."

Baker embellished his story, enjoying himself.

"Hell, I knew you didn't have my property with you. And you sure as hell didn't have it stashed at your dump or I would've found it. So I figured all I had to do was wait. You'd lead me to it eventually."

In the background she heard Seth cry out again. What the hell was Baker doing to him?

"Leave him alone, Lucas. You've got my attention, so talk already." She pressed. "Tell me. How did you cross paths with Seth?"

"Well, pretty boy here, he was a gift. I must be living right, but you, not so much. I followed you downtown, having no clue where you was going. But when you came out of that fancy pile of bricks with this guy in tow, I recognized him right off. He'd collided into my SUV with his shit blue van that night you was chasin' me. I ain't good at math, darlin', but even I could put two and two together. You wanna talk to the kid?"

An interminable moment of silence. Dead still. Jess swallowed hard, then heard Baker bellowing in the background, angry words muffled and distant.

"You better speak up, asshole, 'cause I can make you

pay in ways you can't even imagine. You'll be beggin' me to kill ya."

She clung too tight to her phone, straining to hear every word. In her mind she pictured what Baker might've done to Seth, the image pure torture.

"J-Jessie? I'm s-sorry." Seth. It was definitely Seth on the line.

She let out the breath she'd been holding.

"What has he done to you? Are you okay?" Both were stupid questions, but she was running on impulse and not thinking straight. That would have to stop. She needed to focus.

"Just give him what he wants. It'll be o-okay."

Seth could talk, but he sounded seriously messed up. Yet despite his condition, he had the wits to send her a clear message: Give the bastard what he wanted because he'd rigged the laptop. They'd be able to track Baker's moves online. Sooner or later the jerk would make a mistake.

All she had to do was make the exchange and get Harper back. Then her boy genius could exact his own brand of retaliation—revenge best served cold.

Baker got back on the line. "Your toady is still breathin'. That's gotta be worth somethin'. I expect you to show a little appreciation for my . . . generosity."

"If you lay another hand on him, I swear—" she began, but the scumbag didn't let her finish.

"You act like you're in charge. Well, don't you have balls." The man laughed again, an abrasive sound. Baker using Seth as leverage took their feud to a whole new level and the bastard reveled in it.

"No, but I'll have yours if you lay another finger on that kid. I could use the target practice. And you already know I can make your life a livin' hell."

The line went dead silent. By the time Baker regrouped, his amusement had vanished.

"Our swap ain't open for discussion. I want what's mine and I'm gonna get it. And you'll get the kid back, but in how many pieces will be up to you." His voice lowered to an icy whisper. "The way I see it, you got no say how this'll go down, bitch. Now . . . listen up."

Jess shut her eyes tight and listened to the man's demands. With the timing, Baker wasn't cutting her much slack. One more night without much sleep and she was heading for another rendezvous with a not so distant cousin to *Homo erectus.*

Given the situation with Seth, she wanted Sam as backup, to be on the safe side, but had no idea how to cover up her involvement with Baker and his laptop. She'd crossed the line and breached protocol with the evidence she knew would be on the man's computer. Back into her apartment, she stared at Baker's property, sitting by her front door, where she'd put it after coming in.

She'd painted herself into a pretty tight corner, and now also had to think about Sam. If she told her friend what was going on, Sam would be in the middle of her mess, forced to decide whether to turn her in. And if Sam brought the CPD into it, they might decide their informant's contributions far outweighed her flimsy speculations. Jess knew she had no proof. At best she'd be back to square one. At worst she might do jail time if the Chicago police wanted to teach her a lesson. Neither had much appeal, and she'd come too far to let it happen.

She figured it was a chicken or an egg scenario. Either way, poultry always got screwed. And with most things in life, she'd learned it was far better to ask forgiveness than permission. An idea started to take shape.

Jess looked at her watch. She'd have to come up with a plan on the fly. Part of that plan included Sam getting off shift a little early, if Jess could find a way to avoid telling her everything. She had to think. Lucas Baker held all the cards, especially with the location he'd picked, and Madame Luck had dealt her and Seth a lousy hand.

But it was time for her to summon her *own* brand of good fortune.

An alarm should have gone off in Nikki's head long before Mr. Noskova pulled up to the closed fence of an old warehouse. The place looked run-down. Weeds lined the perimeter of the fence and had cropped up through cracks in the asphalt. A deserted guard shack with shattered windows and chipped paint stood by the front gate and an old faded sign at the main entrance indicated the warehouse used to be a textile manufacturer: GOODVILLE TEXTILES.

She had been talking to Ivana, lost track of time, and didn't pay attention to where they were going, especially after nighttime closed in and they turned off the interstate. Lights glittered on the distant horizon, a small town. But here, everything was black. Even the moon had conspired against her. Only the headlights of their vehicle lighted the way, drawing insects from the gloom.

"What is this place?" she asked.

Nikki leaned forward in her seat, her eyes peering through the darkness. Ivana turned away and stared out her window at nothing, ignoring her question. She raised her voice to get Mr. Noskova's attention in the front seat.

"Excuse me, Mr. Noskova, but where are we? I thought we were going . . . home. Your home."

"We've got a stop to make." He offered nothing more.

He lowered his driver's side window and swiped a card key through a reader. The cyclone fence jumped to life and slowly rattled aside. An uneasy feeling swelled inside her, threatening to cut off her air. Realization hit as a cruel blow, flooding her mind with every detail that had led her to this place.

Ivana had lied . . . about everything.

"Is Ivana even your real name?" Nikki whispered to the

girl by her side, suddenly afraid of the man in the front seat. But the girl didn't turn her head, much less give her an answer.

She was alone with two strangers and had no idea where she was. She stared through the front windshield. The man behind the wheel drove through the gate and across a massive parking lot. The shadows of the old warehouse were more imposing under the faint glow cast from a sliver of moon, giving the illusion that the inky black heaved and swelled with a life of its own. Her mind played tricks on her, conjuring images from all the horror slasher movies she'd ever seen.

Only now it was happening to her.

Oh, God. Please help me. Her heart pounded faster, punishing her eardrums from inside. And a slow bead of sweat trailed from her temple.

Slowly, Nikki groped in the dark for the door handle. She stared straight ahead, not wanting to give away her attempt at escape. When she found the handle, she pulled it hard, prepared to shove the car door aside and roll out. But the handle wouldn't budge. She tried the lock next, but it wouldn't open.

They had locked her inside. She had nowhere to go.

"Please . . . don't do this." She whispered her plea to no one.

The car drove by a large group of loading bays and pulled up to another card reader that led to a secured subterranean parking garage. The garage door opened with a swipe of the driver's card and they drove inside, swallowed into the bowels of the old building.

As the garage door closed behind them, Nikki stared at the girl beside her, perhaps seeing her for the first time. In the dim glow from the headlights, she caught the glimmer of a tear in Ivana's eye. And without a sound, the girl finally looked at her and mouthed the words, *I'm sorry.*

All Nikki wanted to do was scream, but now, who would hear her?

Chicago's South Side
11:00 PM CST

Little known fact, but Lucas Baker owned part of a bar and pool hall on the south side of Chicago with a cousin he despised. The place was located in a rough part of town. Jess had discovered the tidbit in her latest search for him. As far as she could tell, he almost never came to the joint. Why he chose tonight to make an appearance would remain one of life's mysteries, mainly because she didn't care enough to ask the son of a bitch.

The name of the place was The Cutthroat. In pool, cutthroat was a game designed to take advantage of the odd man out. The game's objective is for a player to eliminate his opponents. In Baker's case, life had a strange way of imitating art. The man never played by the rules, except for his own, so cutthroat described the way he operated to a tee.

The pool hall's air was thick with cigarette smoke, a heavy country twang coming from a jukebox, and testosterone—a combination that left Jess thinking a root canal might've been a better choice. But Baker hadn't given her an option, and Seth needed her.

When she walked into the crowded dung heap, every eye shifted to her. An image popped into her head. She pictured herself doing a fast dog paddle in a river teeming with piranha, flailing before the inevitable. Men of every shape and size cocked their heads her way, and not a Brad Pitt look-alike in the bunch. There were a few women, but she had nothing in common with them. She still had her own teeth and had never taken advantage of the two-for-one special at the local tattoo parlor.

"Nothing like being the center of attention," she mumbled under her breath and turned her head to scope out the place.

"I'm reading you loud and clear." Sam's voice came over

the ear bud Jess had hidden under her hair. Her friend would be listening whenever she keyed the mic, her only form of censorship. "Maybe you should tell me your safety word . . . in case you get lucky. I'd hate to intrude."

"Very funny. Just for that, your name's going on the men's room wall . . . unless it's already there." Jess headed for the back of the main room, navigating an obstacle course of biceps, pectorals, and beer bellies. Baker had told her where he'd be.

"And for the record," Sam said, "I hate this plan. I should be in there with you. Meeting Baker on his turf is like playing Russian Roulette solo. When the gun goes off, you're on your own. No one to pick up the pieces."

"Nice visual. And thanks for the vote of confidence."

"What are friends for?"

Jess had already shared her thoughts with Sam, her justification for leaving a cop parked on the curb outside a seedy bar. On the drive over she'd told Sam that her gig with Baker was private. Her friend respected that, but not enough to lay off the third degree. Jess had to come up with something more.

She'd told Sam that Baker had a beef with an old girlfriend, a former hooker trying to turn her life around. Baker had been abusive, not much of a stretch to believe. And Jess helped hide the woman a month ago, despite the fact that she wouldn't press charges. Baker had been trying to strong-arm Jess into telling him where the woman had moved.

She knew that the best lies came from elements of the truth. A year ago she'd helped a woman get rid of her ex, two hundred pounds worth of mean. She could relate to the woman's plight, since she'd come by her own scars honestly, both inside and out.

Even so, it scared Jess how easily she conjured a lie, especially to an old friend. But in her mind, Sam needed protecting too. She had her career to think about. If Sam didn't witness her exchange with Baker—or know anything about that damned laptop—she wouldn't be called to testify if things turned ugly.

So far, Sam had bought her gloss over, but Jess knew that wouldn't last long.

All she needed was time. Time to get Seth away from here and to a hospital if he needed it. And to do that, she needed Sam's help as backup. If she didn't have the added complication of Seth, she would've come alone and dealt with the consequences.

"The office is straight back by the cigarette machine." She spoke to Sam on the communication link. "Hang tight till you hear from me."

Word on the street was that Baker was neck deep into a string of missing kids. That's what set Jess on his trail, but she had no proof—yet. There'd be no bounty on this case, but as she told Sam, some things were more important than any stash of cash.

"You ain't goin' anywhere, honey." Some jerk outside the office stopped her. A beefy hand reached out with splayed fingers pressed to her chest, copping a feel. "Not without a strip search. Rules of the house."

The guy smirked and looked real impressed with himself.

Jess locked eyes with Baker's muscle, feeling the weight of her .357 Magnum Colt Python at the small of her back. A square-jawed cowboy dude in a tight white tee, wranglers, and a no frills burr cut blocked her path. He had a knife clipped to his jeans pocket, made to look like a money clip or key chain to the untrained eye. Lucas had to be behind the cheap theatrics, and she had no patience for it.

Enough was enough.

Sam couldn't sit in Jess's car any longer. She got out and paced the sidewalk under a glow of red and blue neon, catching movement to her right. Night shift lowlifes remained faceless in the shadows, but she felt their eyes on her. And a hooker glared with suspicion then walked around the corner, taking her business down the block. She probably smelled cop.

So much for keeping a low profile.

Sam's eyes darted across the street to the front door of The Cutthroat. It had only been ten minutes since she last heard from Jess, but ten minutes in her friend's world could mean plenty of trouble. Besides, instincts born of a lifelong friendship had started to niggle at her belly.

"Jess? Are you okay?" She keyed her mic. "Talk to me."

Radio silence. Nothing.

Sam wanted to respect Jess and her reasons for confronting Baker alone. Even if she didn't buy the whole story, she trusted Jess to do the right thing. But now that trust was being tested, and her cop instincts told her something didn't feel right.

Jess was supposed to speak up if she got into trouble, but was her silence the equivalent of sending up a flare? Sam clipped her badge to her belt, preparing to go in. And with steady fingers, she touched the service weapon under her jeans jacket, an old habit.

"Damn it, Jess. What's going on in there?"

Jess narrowed her eyes at the brute standing in front of her, his hand pressed to her breast. He squeezed to see if she'd react and the bastard wasn't disappointed. She grabbed his hand and twisted his thumb backward. In reflex, he bent over and turned his back to her, writhing in pain. When he did, she shoved a hand hard against his elbow and thrust his arm up between his shoulder blades.

"Aarrgh," he cried out. "You're gonna break it."

"Good. I was afraid you wouldn't get the point."

She shoved the jerk into a wall with a sharp crack, pinning him in place with the weight of her body and the awkward position she held his arm. He twisted against her grip so she wouldn't wrench his shoulder, but he couldn't break free without doing serious damage. He grunted and let out another yelp. By now all eyes were on her again. Jess held firm and glared at each face.

"What are you looking at?" she demanded, yelling above the blaring music from the jukebox.

For an instant she thought someone from the crowd might interfere, until a sound came from near the bar. One guy started to clap, then another. As the room erupted into a standing ovation with whistles and shouts of encouragement, Jess turned her head to the door marked OFFICE, still grappling with the bouncer.

"You're comin' with me."

She kicked at the door and waited for someone to answer. When it opened a crack, she shoved the cowboy through it, using him as a shield as she walked in with gun drawn. Beef Boy sprawled to the floor in a huff—all under the wary eye of his boss.

"What the hell?" Baker jumped to his feet and pulled his weapon.

Jess yelled, "Hey now, hold your water, Lucas. Let's not get crazy."

She aimed her weapon between Baker's eyes but kept her voice calm, trying to defuse the situation.

"I came here to trade, but you're the one who left that bulldog outside," she persisted.

Two men stood near the desk with guns drawn. Their eyes shifted between her and Baker, waiting for orders. Although she was clearly outnumbered, she gripped her weapon and held firm. In an instant things could have gone very wrong. Someone had to make the first move.

Jess decided it should be her.

She raised her weapon toward the ceiling and relaxed her grip, both hands in the air. After a very long minute, Baker followed suit. He ordered his men to stand down with a nod and a disgusted look meant for the cowboy at her feet.

"Shut that door. And get off the damned floor, Gary," he demanded. "You're making me look bad."

"And that you can do on your own," she said, holstering her weapon as one of Baker's men shut the door behind her. "Where's Seth?"

Still standing, Baker tightened his jaw and glared at her. After a long beat, intended to intimidate her, he finally nodded to one of his goons, who went to a side door and opened it.

In a dark closet, Seth had been bound to a chair with duct tape.

He squinted into the sudden light, his face swollen and bloody. His shirt was drenched in sweat and his skin looked mottled and bruised under the fluorescent light. And Baker had cut his lip. But when the kid's vision cleared, he found her in the crowded room and his eyes filled with relief, tinged by fear from his time with Baker.

Innocence destroyed, the look on his face broke her heart.

He'd been beaten because of her vendetta. And she'd been careless, leading Baker to him. She wanted to rip away his restraints and help him out of this rat hole, but she knew these men would never allow it, not until they concluded their business.

Before she could speak to Seth, Baker intruded. "I noticed you came here a little light. I don't see my property."

"There's nothing wrong with your eyesight, Lucas," she replied with her gaze still glued on Seth.

"Well, your boy ain't leavin' here without that laptop, so what's it gonna be?" He cocked his head.

"That's fair." She shrugged and turned. "I came to trade, but I've got a new deal."

Slowly, she stepped toward Baker. "This time we're playin' it my way."

CHAPTER 10

"You're a real pain in the ass, Beckett." Lucas Baker shook his head, royally pissed. "But I'm sure you've heard that before."

"Coming from you, I consider that a compliment." Jess forced a faint smile. "I thought you had the market cornered."

One of Baker's boys smirked, a flinch behind the man's back. She reached into her pants pocket and pulled out something to hold in front of Baker's nose. He narrowed his eyes.

"A key? What the hell am I supposed to do with that?"

"Generally, keys open locks. And if you hurry, you can use this key to retrieve your property tonight." She handed him a note that she'd prepared beforehand after making a stop on her way to Sam's place. "Here's an address and locker number. It's a nearby skating rink off Greenwood." She gave him the cross streets. "The place closes at midnight. Your laptop's there."

"How do I know you're not just blowin' smoke?"

"'Cause you know where I live and I'm not going anywhere." She fought to keep her expression unreadable. "I don't want any more trouble. You've made your point. I'm done."

She had to convince him that she'd rolled over and he had won. The bastard glared at her, trying to decide if she was telling the truth.

"The locker could be empty," he pressed. "Hell, there might not even be a skate rink at this address."

"Look it up," she challenged with arms folded.

Baker snapped his fingers and held out her note. Cowboy Gary made himself useful and took the paper. He started pulling open the drawers to the desk. In short order he had a phone book spread on the desktop and was flipping through the yellow pages to confirm the address.

"It's here, boss. Just like she wrote."

"Clock's ticking, Lucas. They close at midnight." Jess stood in front of his desk with hands on her hips.

"Then you better have a seat and pray Gary don't get lost, 'cause you ain't leavin' here until he gets back." Baker handed her note and key to the wannabe cowboy, then continued, "Go on. Sit. That ain't exactly a request."

Jess clenched her jaw and plopped into a seat, her arms folded. Now she had a dilemma. First off, Gary looked to be one bronco shy of a rodeo. It wouldn't be a stretch to imagine him getting lost on the painted pony of a merry-go-round. Second, Sam would be getting impatient about now.

Jess hadn't counted on Baker holding her and Seth until he got his laptop back. *Damn it!* She wanted to leave and take care of Seth, but that idea looked shot to hell. She had to face reality. Even if she made contact by radio, what could she say in front of Baker that wouldn't stir up questions from Sam? And as paranoid as Baker was, he'd probably think SWAT was right outside. No, she'd have to let the chips fall, and knowing Sam, she wouldn't have to wait long.

Even expecting it, the knock on the door jolted her heart. Jess shut her eyes tight.

Oh, hell! Right on time.

Baker grimaced and shot her a nasty look.

"If this brings trouble down on me, you and your friend here won't like how fast shit trickles downhill." He snapped his fingers at Gary. "Open the damned door."

As she figured, Sam wasn't a patient soul. Her friend stood in the doorway, not saying a word, at first. She shifted her eyes around the room, trying to puzzle out what was going on. Jess had seen the look before, and she held her breath, waiting for Sam to open her mouth.

"Well, I'm not selling Girl Scout cookies. And this doesn't look like a Kiwanis Club meeting. Are you all right, Jess?"

"Yeah, everything's fine." She nodded. "We were about to head out."

"We?"

"Yeah, he's coming." Jess pointed to Seth. "Introductions will have to wait."

Seth waved a finger, trying to look casual in duct tape. "Hey."

Sam grimaced at the kid, but before she got a good look at him, Jess stood and blocked her view, turning to Baker.

"Lucas has an appointment to get to, but we're all done here, right?"

The man took a slow breath and narrowed his eyes—more intimidation—but after a long moment, he flinched. That's when she knew she had him.

"Yeah, I gotta go. Cut the kid loose. But our business better be done and over, Jess. Neither of us wants a repeat." Then he pointed a finger. "Do I make myself clear?"

"Crystal." Jess headed for Seth and helped him to stand once he got free. She wedged a shoulder under his arm. "Oh . . . and Lucas? I'd like my gun returned. You know, the one you borrowed from my place?"

He smirked, his eyes shifting from Jess to Sam. "I don't know what you're talking about. Sorry."

Jess clenched her jaw. Her Glock 21 would be a casualty, but at least she had Seth back.

"What happened to him?" Sam asked. "Was it nickel beer night if you came dressed in duct tape?"

Before Jess could reply, Seth intervened.

"I picked a fight and got out of control. The duct tape was for my own good."

"Yeah, right. You look like a real animal." Sam crossed her arms and cocked her head. "So what happened that got you all riled up, sport?"

"A guy took offense to my *Jerry Springer* tee." Seth winced as he walked toward the door. "And nobody slams Jerry."

Real tough guy! Jess almost smiled. Seth looked like a total flounder out of water in this dump. He would never have come here on his own. And by the look on Sam's face, she wasn't buying any of it, but to her credit, she let things play out. She seemed to appreciate their urgency to leave.

"Next time, be more careful, young man." Baker laid it on thick, but he didn't show a speck of amusement. "We can get a pretty rough crowd in here. You're lucky no one pressed charges."

"Yeah, I feel real lucky." Seth didn't bother to hide his cynicism and never looked back.

When Jess got him to the door, she handed Seth over to Sam. She wanted to make sure business with Baker was concluded out of Sam's earshot. Jess looked back at him and tapped a finger to her watch.

"Time's a-wasting. We done here?"

"We better be." The man scowled, rooting her where she stood. "'Cause if I get that déjà vu feeling from you, you're gonna find yourself on the wrong side of the turf."

Jess wanted to say something clever as she turned to walk out the door, but nothing came to mind. She knew Baker meant every word.

* * *

On the drive home, after Seth insisted he'd be okay without a trip to the emergency room, Jess introduced Sam to the kid and told her about how she'd hired him. Given what had just transpired, the thought of Seth punching the clock like an hourly employee sounded ludicrous to her. Sam heard it in her friend's voice as Jess tried to explain why she'd crossed paths with him in the first place. Any other time she might have found humor in Jess's version of a "summer intern" job, but not tonight.

The situation only made her sad.

Road noise and the sounds of Chicago traffic had filled the void in conversation over the last ten minutes. Sam had picked the backseat to put distance between her and Jess. She stared out the window, the ebb and flow of street lamps washing over her. Seth Harper rode shotgun in stone cold silence. Apparently, he sensed the rift and kept his mouth shut. Smart boy. And although she had no concrete reason to believe Jess had lied about her confrontation with Lucas Baker, she knew it in her bones.

And that hurt worst of all.

Jess had always been a loner. Sam knew this, but being hit with the harsh reality that her best friend would never completely trust her had hurt all the same. Jess maintained her privacy like a miser hoarded coins, and Sam wanted to respect that. Her friend had come by that philosophy honestly and with good reason. But when Jess kept her at arm's length under a misguided attempt to protect her, Sam hated not being included in the decision.

Jess did things her way. End of story. Sam had no idea how to break into her world, and after tonight, she realized she might never get a passkey.

"Pull over, Jess. I need to walk."

Jess slowed the car and looked in the rearview mirror, making eye contact in a flash of light, but she didn't question her need to be alone. Of all people, Jess should understand that. Sam was close enough to walk the last couple miles. When Jess pulled to the curb of the older residential neighborhood, a street lined with small well-kept bungalows, Sam opened the car door with some parting words to Seth Harper.

"If you need it, I can put you in touch with a twelve-step program for *Springer* addicts. The first step is recognizing you have a problem."

"Yeah, very funny." He nodded with his head down, not looking back. "Good to meet you, Sam. And thanks."

From the backseat, she tousled his hair and got out of the car. Jess followed after putting the car in park and leaving Seth to wait.

"Are we all right?" Jess faced her in the dark, hands in her pockets.

Sam wasn't sure how to answer. After an awkward silence, she began to put her feelings in perspective.

"You know, I get the fact that you'll never let me in, but it still hurts."

"I didn't intend—"

"No, you never intend to hurt me, Jess, but that doesn't mean I'm bulletproof." Sam took a deep breath and stared into the night sky. "Look, I'm tired and you need to get him patched up. Let's talk . . . tomorrow. I gotta get some sleep, but I've got things to sort out first."

Jess stared at her for a long moment, looking as if she wanted to say something real, but then changed her mind. Moonlight painted pale blue streaks through her hair, giving her an ethereal quality. The image disturbed Sam, as if she was staring into the face of a ghost. Jess nodded and turned to walk away without saying another word, then hesitated and looked back over her shoulder.

"You know, I trust you with my life."

"Yeah, but not with what's in your heart, Jess. I mean, I know you love me like a sister, but you sure don't trust me with who you are as a person. That, you keep all to yourself." She tried to smile but it wouldn't come. "And this obsession of yours is consuming you, but you just don't see it. I don't know what you have going on with Baker, but . . . you've changed. And not for the better."

After a long moment of silence between them, Sam let it go.

"Good night, Jess."

She turned to walk away, but as Jess drove by, she watched her go. Something had changed between them tonight. Jess had stepped over a line with their friendship, and she only hoped she could get past it the next time—if there *was* a next time.

At ten minutes before midnight, when Lucas Baker pulled in, the skating rink parking lot was quiet. It was on the way to where he'd be spending the night. Jess Beckett had been a regular pit bull, latching onto him and making his life a living hell over the last several weeks. Living out of a suitcase was no fun, but he had a feeling he was finally on the downhill side of the ordeal now. Pretty soon it would be business as usual.

Before he got out of his vehicle, he looked around to case the place. With his engine and radio off, he heard the steady thump of muffled music coming from the rink. A few vehicles were still parked in the lot, and a group of kids hung by the entrance, talking it up and smoking cigarettes. Nothing looked out of the ordinary, so he got out of his car and locked it.

As he headed for the entrance, he fumbled in his pocket for the key Jess Beckett had given him, along with the note for the locker number. He clutched them in his hand, ready to make his stop quick. As a precaution, he reached down to touch the butt of his .45-caliber Glock 21 tucked in a belt holster under his suit jacket.

You're a real piece of work, Beckett. This damned trip, along with everything else, had been a royal pain in the ass. While he was out of commission, he'd found a temporary way to get online, but only on a limited basis. Beyond the strict instructions he'd been given when he first got his laptop, he had never strayed from protocol—until now. He'd restricted his usual routine, being on an unsecured setup, but hell if he'd call attention to his fuck-up. He would handle things his way but needed to get back online pronto.

Still, he had to admit, Jess Beckett picking this place had been a smart move on her part. With the rink closing at midnight, she knew he'd have to hustle to make it. And the locker had been a stroke of genius. If she'd walked into The Cutthroat toting his laptop, he had a whole different scenario planned for her. That would now have to wait for a time when she least expected it.

Baker smirked when he thought about spending quality time with that bitch.

The skate rink looked run-down, a reflection of its surroundings. The older neighborhood had a reputation for being rough, but Baker remembered a day when that hadn't been the case. As he came closer to the group of black kids near the entrance, they grew quiet and watched him with wary eyes, as if he had a tattoo on his forehead marked with the word "outsider."

When he got inside, the lights had been flipped on and the last customers were getting ready to leave. Rap music blared on the overhead speakers. There was no one behind the ticket counter, but he spotted the location of the lockers and began his search for the number written on the paper.

"We're closed, mister." A guy pushing a broom and picking up garbage yelled at him from across the rink.

"I'll only be a second. My kid forgot something." Baker turned his head, not giving the guy a clear look. He didn't like the attention and had hoped to get in and out without notice.

After he found the right number, he stuffed Beckett's note in his pocket and tried the key. When the locker opened, he saw his black computer bag inside. He pulled it out, unzipped it, and turned the laptop on. It had enough juice to power up. He wanted to check the desktop to make sure it was actually his, but the damned manager or janitor kept watching him. Baker knew he wouldn't have much time.

The monitor kicked its blue light across his chest and face as the screen popped on. After a minute, he had his answer. The laptop was his. But to drill down further, to see if the bitch had tampered with his stuff, he'd have to do a closer inspection elsewhere. He packed up his gear and headed out, shifting the shoulder bag tight under his arm and away from prying eyes.

He made a quick exit and walked by the kids who were still standing out front, fighting a growing smile on his face. But that changed when someone stepped out of the shadows in his path.

"You taking up a new hobby, Lucas?"

In the dim light he almost didn't recognize the man, but the Russian accent was unmistakable. Then he remembered seeing him before.

"I don't have time for hobbies. What are you doing here? I told you I'd fix the problem."

"Yes, you did. And yet, here we are. I had to see for myself."

Baker showed the man what he had slung on his shoulder. "I got my property and I'm back in business. End of story."

"I wish it were that simple, but you broke protocol. You called attention to our . . . organization." The man kept his voice low and steady. And he moved against the light behind him to keep his face in the shadows, making eye contact impossible.

"What's the big deal? In the grand scheme of things, I only lost a day, nothing more than a hiccup."

"The point is you showed poor judgment, Lucas. You accessed our site by an unsecured means and you allowed strangers to jeopardize this operation. Secrecy is how we survive, but I don't think you fully appreciate that. And what if this happens again. What then?"

The man's voice was nearly a whisper. Baker felt his cheeks blush, and his skin tingled with adrenaline.

"I tell ya, it won't happen again. I'm gonna take care of that bitch."

"This bounty hunter . . . Jessica Beckett, yes?"

"Yeah, that's the one."

"And who do you think she's talked to, Lucas? How much does she know?"

Baker didn't answer right away. The face of Beckett's detective friend popped into his head, but if he mentioned the cop, the Russian wouldn't understand.

"Beckett knows nothing. And even if she did, no one would believe her. The bitch has no credibility. She's a hothead who goes off half-cocked, flying by the seat of her pants."

"Yes, unfortunately, I'm familiar with the personality type. Go on."

Baker understood what he was implying and resented it, but the arrogant bastard was too dangerous to dismiss. The man was more than just a reflection of his boss. Like a psycho, the Russian enjoyed his work, and it showed. He'd seen him in action, once. And once was enough.

"She's got some kid that works for her. Seth Harper. I don't think she talked to anyone else. I can take care of him too."

"Then I suppose her police detective friend isn't a concern for you?" The man inched closer, sticking to the shadows. "She is to us."

Baker clenched his jaw, his breath caught in his throat. He inched his hand closer to his weapon.

"Even after I told you I'd handle the situation, you checked up on me?"

"Think of me as quality control." The man laughed, sounding genuinely amused. "My superiors ask questions, I must have answers. That is all."

Baker relaxed a little and forced a smile. The Russian still made him edgy, but it looked as if he'd get through this.

"Tell them things are under control."

"Yes, that is my hope." The Russian grinned, his silhouette defined by a distant street lamp behind him. "Good night, Lucas. No hard feelings, yes?"

Baker took a deep breath and shrugged, happy to be done with him. It had been a long night. But when he walked by the man, he felt a hand at the back of his neck. The Russian spun him around to face him in the dark and pressed something hard to his rib cage.

He felt a punch to his chest. Then another. It staggered him.

What the hell? He looked down, catching the first blooms of red. His eyes grew wide and a chill raced through his body. With it came fear, raw and undeniable.

He'd been shot.

Numb and in shock, he tossed the computer bag down and reached for his Glock. The Russian got to his gun first and grappled it from his hand. For the first time, he noticed the man wore gloves.

"Fucking coward," he muttered.

In the murky haze, everything blurred and faded out of focus. The kids at the entrance to the rink ran for cover. And in the background he heard shouts, the rumble of engines and the squealing of tires. Yet his world spun cock-eyed and sluggish, in slow motion. He dropped to the ground, catching a glimpse of the Russian standing over him.

"You're nothing . . . a damned coward." Baker's voice cracked. "You couldn't even . . . face me like a man, asshole."

His chest heaved for air but he couldn't fill his lungs. And the coppery sweet smell of blood made him nauseous and light-headed. He fought to stay conscious, but his arms and legs had grown numb and the pain hit him in powerful waves.

"Is this man enough for you?" The killer raised his weapon and aimed at Baker's face.

In the split second he knew he would die, Lucas Baker felt the pounding of his heart, but he defied death with a sneer, saying, "Fuck you."

Muzzle flash was the last thing he saw.

Alexa Marlowe had been on the trail of Lucas Baker for a week, but she'd gotten sidetracked after receiving a tip. Some woman bounty hunter had put out word on the street, looking for Baker too. Curiosity got the better of her and she'd looked into Jessica Beckett, hitting pay dirt when the bounty hunter scored a solid lead on Baker before she did. Alexa had been relegated to playing catch-up, a game she normally refused to play, but now she was determined to make up lost ground.

Following Lucas Baker had been easy. She knew where he was going.

With surveillance gear, Alexa had eavesdropped on his intimidation tactic with the gutsy bounty hunter, all under the nose of the cop who waited outside The Cutthroat. Afterward, she hung back in traffic and forced herself to be patient. Baker had been so focused on getting his laptop back, he hadn't paid attention to the dark sedan tailing him. He had the ego of a predator, not the prey.

And she had counted on that.

But after a man stepped out of the shadows to speak to Baker in the skate rink parking lot, she realized she'd been just as careless and egotistical. She hadn't seen the incident coming, but then again, the intruder hadn't seen her either. After spotting him with her night vision binoculars, she had covered her blond hair with a knit cap and left the anonymity of her vehicle to creep closer. She edged along the shadows in the parking lot with her .45-caliber H&K MK23 drawn.

The two men talked in the dark, but she never got a good look at the second man and had no time to do a proper surveillance of their conversation. When it looked as if their business was concluded, Baker headed for his car. That's when the stranger pumped two in his chest. The muzzle flash took out her night vision capability, blinding her for a second. By the time she recovered, it was over.

The sudden savagery shocked her. *Who the hell are you, my deadly friend?* The man had taken a life without hesitation. A seasoned killer.

And just like that, Lucas Baker had become a dead end, literally. Those who lived by the sword, died by it, she thought. One day she might not be so cavalier about that kind of fate, but she had no sympathy for a guy like Baker. Preventing his murder required incentive and opportunity, and she had neither. And saving Baker's life hadn't been in the cards. Now, given the new scenario, she had to adapt and improvise.

She kept her eyes on the man who had killed Baker using her night vision gear. He picked up the computer bag and his shell casings, then dissolved into the shadows, as he had come. Carefully, she weighed her options. The man would have to report to someone.

In the next parking lot over, she saw him get into a dark BMW sedan. He headed out of the lot without his headlights until he got to the main road, doing the speed limit. After yanking the knit cap off her head, she pulled from the curb, minding all the traffic laws.

Trailing a killer was a gamble, but one she was willing to take. The stakes were too high to play it safe.

She lagged behind him, not wanting to spook the guy. When he merged onto the Dan Ryan Expressway heading south, she blended with traffic, not wanting to stand out. She calmed her heart and settled in for a long, steady pursuit.

But when the bastard swerved off the Calumet Expressway, heading for the Indiana state line, all that changed. He picked up speed. And off the freeway it would be harder to lurk behind him this time of night.

"What the hell?" she said aloud. "Did you spot me?"

She had to be careful now. He might have picked up speed to watch his rearview mirror to see if anyone followed. But even if she kept her composure and didn't panic, she still had a dilemma. She could lose him if she lagged too far behind, but if she sped up, he might spot her. This section of road had less traffic.

"Cagey bastard."

Baker's killer might have eyes in the back of his head, but if she didn't hit the accelerator, she'd lose him anyway. She took a calculated risk and sped up. Barreling through the dark, the BMW sedan flashed in and out of overhead streetlights ahead. And she used his red taillights to keep her eyes on him.

But in a dark section of road the taillights disappeared. It took her a moment to figure out what he'd done.

"Shit."

Playing hardball, the guy was running without lights, making him hard to see. A dangerous game. The killer had upped the stakes, leaving her little choice. She gripped the steering wheel and floored the gas pedal, dousing her headlights. Until she could confirm the man knew he had a tail, she had to play by his rules.

"The gloves are off, baby. Let's play."

CHAPTER 11

Her eyes adjusted to the darkness, but not nearly enough. Speeding, Alexa gripped the steering wheel and glared through her windshield, navigating by moonlight. Just her luck. Mother Nature hadn't cooperated. What she wouldn't give for a full moon and a clear night. She barely saw the center lane stripes and had to guess at the curves in the road.

Spotting the BMW, she gunned her vehicle to keep up. Her target's dark shadow loomed dead ahead, still running without lights. Few cars remained now. And only two drove at breakneck speed.

At the last minute he veered onto a dark frontage road, forcing her to pull the wheel hard right. Momentum shoved her against the car door. Her seat belt locked across her chest. She prayed the car wouldn't flip, putting her in a ditch. The bastard knew where he was going, but she could only react—a formula for disaster.

No pretense anymore. The guy knew he had a tail. She turned on her headlights and pushed the car faster. Tall grass and fence posts blew past, caught in the tunnel of her headlights. She got close enough to see the back of his head through his rear window, but he never turned around. A man with long dark hair, from what she could make out.

He broke from the frontage road and hit an entrance ramp. She followed hard left.

"Damn it." With her chest heaving, adrenaline pumped through her veins like a drug.

Up ahead, an overpass glimmered in the dark. More traffic.

"Oh, shit."

The guy hit the exit ramp doing eighty. At the busier intersection ahead, a traffic light turned red, but he didn't hit the brakes. He blasted through it, forcing cars off the road. One hit a guardrail with the grinding tear of metal. She slammed on the brakes, barely missing a car in the intersection.

The bastard put too many innocent people at risk, and she refused to compound the problem. He sped away without lights, leaving her at the traffic light. Her heart pounded her ribs, pumping her full of juice. *Damn it!* She throttled her steering wheel with the palm of her hand until it ached. Losing wasn't part of her vocabulary.

"This isn't over, you son of a bitch."

She'd gotten close enough to get his license number, but didn't have high hopes for DMV to give her answers. A guy who killed the way he did wouldn't be caught so easily. Round one went to him, but their fight had only just begun. She'd run DMV to see if she got a hit, but had money on her long shot—the bounty hunter.

For whatever reason, Jess Beckett had kept one step ahead, making her the odds-on favorite to come up with another hot lead. Hedging her bet, Alexa had placed a GPS tracker on Beckett's car outside The Cutthroat, after her cop friend went inside. If nothing else, she'd track the impetuous woman to make sure she didn't get in the way. At least that was how she preferred to think of it. In reality, if she came up empty, she didn't want to explain why a damned bounty hunter had gotten a jump on her again. It was only a matter of time before Garrett Wheeler, covert liaison to the Sentinels, would know she had ignored his advice and pursued her personal agenda to Chicago. When that happened, she'd have questions to answer, but until then, making progress was key.

One way or another, she would find another way into Globe Harvest. The stakes were too high to fail.

Stanislav Petrovin kept his eyes alert, parked off the shoulder of a rural frontage road near a stand of trees. Preferring the anonymity of the dark, he sat in his BMW with engine running and lights off. Several times, he had detoured and hid his vehicle in the shadows to watch traffic and make sure he'd lost his tail. Now, convinced the chase was over, he pulled back onto the road with headlights on, thinking about what he would report to his superior, Anton Bukolov.

Eliminating the threat of the vehicle tailing him had not been an issue. Few had the stomach for driving as if they had a death wish. Disregarding the risk to himself, he was more concerned with what his pursuer had seen and known about this segment of Bukolov's organization. Lucas Baker had become a liability. He'd been right to kill the man, but had the damage been done?

Bukolov would expect his assessment. What would he tell the old man?

He'd learned a valuable lesson long ago. The success of a mission always outweighed his personal safety. He preferred to stare death in the face on his terms than to place his life in the hands of Bukolov if he failed. His superior was not known for his mercy.

And he hadn't become second in command by playing it safe. So far, the rewards tipped the scale in his favor, at least in his judgment. In this country, he had power, saved from a life of mediocrity.

But tonight's unexpected encounter set Petrovin on edge.

Despite the setback, perhaps evacuation of their local facility would be in order. They had a plan for such an eventuality. It would not hurt to be ready. Severing a gangrenous limb to save the body made sense.

Yet one course of action was quite clear to him. At a minimum, the bounty hunter and her connections would be eliminated. He'd take this task on himself, along with a team of handpicked men. Failure would not be acceptable.

For the second time in two days Sam jolted awake from a call in the middle of the night. She flipped the light on and squinted, groping for the phone on her nightstand. She recognized the number displayed by caller ID.

"Yeah . . . Cooper here."

"Hey, Sam. Sorry to wake you." The voice of night desk sergeant Jackson Miller stirred a repeat of her worst fears for Jessie. Miller had been on duty when her friend was pulled in for questioning the other night.

"No problem, Sarge. What's happening?" She forced herself to remain calm.

"Thought you'd want to hear. Lucas Baker is dead."

The words resonated in her head like a harsh slap to the face.

"What?" She sat up in bed, her face in a grimace. "How? When did this happen?"

"I don't have details yet, but with Baker connected to Harrison Station as an informant, Garza is on his way to the scene now. At this point all we know is that the guy got gunned down outside a skate rink."

Miller gave her the nearest intersection and Sam's mind flashed on the location. The place wasn't far from The Cutthroat. The coincidence was too much to ignore. *Damn it!* Could Jess be connected to a murder? If the thought occurred to her, then other cops would make the same leap. And Detective Ray Garza had been the one who'd interviewed Jess the other night. He'd have the incident fresh on his mind.

Without a doubt he would bring Jess in for round two. Only this time she might need a solid alibi.

Sam looked at the clock on her nightstand; just after two in the morning. South Chicago Station would still be working the scene. She threw off her covers and sat on the edge of the bed. Waiting until her shift started wasn't an option. She had to know more now, especially the timing of Baker's murder. Had she been with Jessie and Seth—or had it gone down after they dropped her off?

Even if she could serve as Jessie's alibi, she'd have a hard time explaining what happened at The Cutthroat. She didn't have all the facts herself. And during the course of an investigation, detectives retraced the victim's whereabouts prior to the murder. She didn't see how she'd avoid getting pulled into the case. And if that was going to happen, she needed real answers from Jessie this time.

But before she got off the phone, Sergeant Miller conveyed his true reason for calling.

"You might wanna steer clear of this one. The timing of your friend's run-in with Baker could backfire on anyone standing in the way. And Chief Keller will be interested in how this turns out. You get my drift?"

"Yeah, I do." She took a deep breath and dragged fingers through her dark hair. "Thanks for the heads-up, Sarge. I owe you one."

"I'll add it to the list." He had a smile to his voice that quickly faded. "Watch yourself, Sam."

"Will do. And thanks, Jackson."

After she hung up, Sam stared through the shadows of her bedroom, thinking about Jess and her possible involvement with Lucas Baker. In her heart of hearts she wanted to blindly trust her childhood friend, but as a cop, blind trust wasn't an option. And because she did know Jessie, she had to admit a fraction of doubt lurked in the back of her mind.

* * *

Sam spotted the crime scene up ahead. Red and blue bursts of color strafed the walls of nearby buildings, coming from police cruisers strategically parked to block off side streets. And yellow crime scene tape set up the police barricade, with floodlights coming from the back parking lot of the skate rink. Beyond the perimeter, techs bagged and tagged evidence, dressed in uniform vests. The Mobile Crime Lab was present, which meant ET-South would be working the scene, forensics investigators of an evidence technician unit assigned to the area.

A group of curious onlookers cast a shadowy obstruction, blocking her view. And TV reporters, operating from the perimeter, capitalized on the dramatic backdrop of the investigation as cameras rolled. She parked down the street and made her way back to the scene with her badge clipped to her belt and visible.

Nearing the police barrier, she was stopped by a beat cop in uniform, one of the few assigned to crowd control. When he saw her badge, he waved her through with a nod. She'd seen him before. Detective Ray Garza was talking to an evidence tech across the way, and Sam headed toward him, negotiating her way around the main activity. In her hand, she had a large cup of coffee. This time of morning, java never hurt as a goodwill gesture.

When Garza saw her, he had plenty of questions.

"I know why I'm here, but what about you? You got a good reason for the extracurricular?"

"Come on, Ray. I came to see you in action. I'm interested in moving out of Vice."

"If that's true, you should avoid this case." He grimaced. "For you, this one has got career suicide written all over it."

"Thanks for your heartfelt concern, but why don't you let me worry about that."

"It's your neck, Coop. And a damned fine one at that."

Garza took the coffee she offered without a thank-you, keeping his eyes on her. His words had been flirty, but the expression on his face said otherwise. The man was all business. When he looked like he wanted to ask her another question, she beat him to the punch with her own agenda.

"When did this go down?" She reached into her pocket for a pair of latex gloves and pulled them on. "What did the M.E. say about T.O.D.?"

She wanted to establish Baker's time of death, to confirm that she'd been with Jess when the man was killed. Across the parking lot, the body had been bagged and lay on a gurney, ready for a trip to the morgue. The medical examiner stood nearby, giving his preliminary assessment to an investigator. If Garza wouldn't cooperate, she had other options. One way or another, her morning trip would pay out.

"I don't think I want you at my crime scene, Cooper. The way I figure it, you've got a conflict of interest. And until I figure out how your friend Jessica Beckett is involved with Lucas Baker, that's too much coincidence for me to swallow."

"This isn't your case, Ray. South Chicago's got lead."

"You don't want to push this, Sam. Trust me."

She forced a smile. "All I want are the facts, Ray. If you can't handle that, then I'll find someone who can."

After taking a gulp of coffee, Garza glared at her. She returned the favor and didn't blink. Eventually, he caved and answered her question, bare minimum.

"Witness accounts put T.O.D. around midnight. Anything more, you get from the lead investigator. I don't want any part in whatever agenda you've got. And I won't play a hand in flushing your career down the toilet, even if you don't give a damn. Thanks for the coffee."

Detective Garza walked away, distancing himself from her. She'd be on her own.

With Baker gunned down close to midnight, Sam knew she couldn't rightfully claim to be with Jessie. She was walking home at that hour. Seth might work as Jess's alibi, but a skeptical detective could be convinced that both Jessie and the kid had gone looking for Baker after they'd dropped her off, trying to even the score or settle unfinished business. At The Cutthroat pool hall, she'd had the distinct impression that she interrupted something bigger than a misunderstanding and a barroom brawl.

Until she knew more, she wouldn't mention any of this to Ray Garza. Putting Jess in the vicinity of Baker's murder at the nearby Cutthroat would have piqued the detective's interest, enough for him to bring Jessie in for questioning. And Sam wanted first shot at the truth. Her stubborn friend would play hardball with Garza and dole out her version of what happened, filtered through her considerable self-preservation skills. Who knew how that would turn out? No, she needed to get to Jessie first, but not without more intel to strong-arm her friend into cooperating.

To confirm what Garza told her about Baker's time of death, she spotted a forensics tech she knew, a guy named Greg Walters, working the blood evidence. Walters confirmed the eyewitness accounts of the incident that had established a reasonable time of death.

"So who reported the shooting?" she asked.

"The manager of the rink. He only saw the shooter for a few seconds. He called 911, then took cover. The guy was scared shitless." Walters nudged his head toward the body bag. "You need to see the body? If you've got a weak stomach, I'd pass."

Although she would have preferred to avoid a look at the corpse, she needed to keep the tech talking. And acting squeamish on the job wouldn't cut it. She planned to take notes, supporting her claim to Garza that she came in the interest of advancing her career—instead of imploding it, which was the more likely outcome.

After the tech unzipped the body bag on the gurney, he directed the beam of his Kel-Lite onto the face of Lucas Baker. The stench took her breath away, and Sam recognized the smell. At the time of traumatic death, the muscles relaxed and the bowels emptied. She clenched her teeth, trying not to react, but even worse, she knew the gore would haunt her.

Baker had been shot in the eye—a pitch-black hole drilled through a misshapen skull. No doubt the bullet and its exit wound had done extensive damage to the man's brain, causing his head to appear lopsided. The other eye—wide and accusing—had turned milky white. Seeing him alive only a few hours ago took its toll. She didn't have to respect Lucas Baker to have an appreciation for the fragile nature of life.

Thankfully, Walter's voice pulled her from the brink. He had launched into a forensics spiel as if he were at a cocktail party talking about the weather and munching on pigs in a blanket.

"He took two to the chest, but the shot to the eye killed him." He pointed to the fatal bullet hole as if she could miss it. "There's stippling marks around the entry wound. Judging by that tight array of tiny hemorrhages, I'd say the shooter had to be up close and personal, no more than two feet away."

"But far enough away to leave those marks, right?" Sam's natural curiosity took over.

"Yeah. If our killer had put the gun barrel up against the vic's head, hot gases and particulates would have gone directly into the skin and charred it. Plus, the impact would have torn a starlike pattern around the wound. But see? There's no tearing or charred skin, only this distinctive tattoo effect."

Walters continued, "And from the trajectory, I'd say the shooter stood over the vic as he lay on the ground. We're recreating what might have happened, but judging by the blood splatter and cast-off, that's my theory."

"So whoever did this stared down at him, then pulled the trigger. That feels personal to me."

"Yeah, I'd say so. Hell, if I was Lucas Baker, I'd take it real personal." The man chuckled, but Sam found it hard to fake any amusement. *Back at the lab, I bet you slay them over the water cooler, Greg.*

"What caliber?"

The man zipped the body bag as he replied, "From the entry and exit wound, I'd say .45-caliber."

"You find any casings? A bullet for comparison?"

"No shell casings so far, but we retrieved a round embedded in the asphalt. The fatal shot cleared the skull. Not sure we'll get much, given the condition of the bullet, but a Firearms ID tech may tell us more. In autopsy, the M.E. will recover what's in his body. And we're still working the crime scene. We could get lucky."

"So, you got any theories on what happened?"

"Between what witnesses have told us, we can piece together what happened and compare it to blood evidence, but no one saw the shooter's face and we've got varying reports of height, weight, you name it. A couple of 'em swear they saw two people. One might've been a woman who drove from the scene, but that's up to the investigator to figure out."

Walters went over the crime scene and pointed out the blood evidence to support his speculative theories. Evidence techs had recorded every drop and splatter of blood with a yellow numbered marker with digital photos taken of each one.

Sam nodded, but as she thought more about the setup at the rink, she wondered something more basic.

"The vic was ID'd as Lucas Baker. How did they determine that?"

"They ID'd him from his driver's license. He still had his wallet loaded with cash, so the shooting wasn't a mugging."

"Anything else on the body?" she asked.

"Actually, now that you mention it, I think they found a note in his pocket."

Sam flinched at the news. "Can I see it?"

"Yeah, I guess so."

Walters stepped over to the Mobile Crime Lab and disappeared inside. When he came out, he carried a plastic evidence bag with a piece of paper clearly visible. As soon as Sam saw it, she recognized the handwriting. Jess had written the note, but her name didn't appear anywhere on the paper. Her heart throttled into high gear but she kept her voice steady.

"I recognize the address of this place, but what's the number written beneath it?" she asked.

"A locker number . . . inside. The manager of the rink said Baker had a key to one of the lockers."

"Wait a minute. You mean he had the key going in?"

"Yeah, he had it with him heading in, but coming out, he'd left it behind. According to the manager, Baker pulled out a black bag, but the guy never got a good look at it. And so far, no one's found the bag. The shooter might've taken it. It's the only lead we have for motivation."

"Interesting." She nodded, trying to act nonchalant.

But the case had taken a turn for the worse. Would they find Jess's fingerprints on the locker key? On the note? And what did Jess have to do with Baker and this black bag? Sam knew how the investigation would go, and she had a strong suspicion that the clock was ticking on her friend's freedom, especially if a couple of witnesses swore they saw a woman. She had no time to lose if she intended to get at the truth enough to help Jess—if that were even possible.

"Thanks for your time, Greg. Here's my card." She handed him her business card. "If you learn anything new, I'd appreciate a call."

"How are you involved in this case again?" he finally asked. "You're over at Harrison Station, right?"

Her smile had gone a long way to distract Walters until now.

"Yeah, and Lucas Baker was an informant. I've got a personal interest in the case." She didn't exactly lie. "I'll be making a few notes before I call it a night, but you've been a big help. Thanks again, Greg." She touched the man's sleeve and smiled again.

Walters grinned and got back to work, leaving her alone to make her final notes. She made a quick diagram of the crime scene, estimating distances and detailing the locations of the building and parked cars in relation to the body.

From across the parking lot, Detective Ray Garza eyeballed her. She did a double take when she noticed those dark eyes staring back. Any other time she might have appreciated his interest, but she felt more like the mouse to his tail-swishing cat. Garza was savvy. Once he got his teeth into something, the man had an unparalleled taste for blood when it came to criminals. And right now Jess might satisfy his need.

Sam yanked off her latex gloves and stuffed them into a pocket before heading to her car, unable to look Detective Garza in the eye as she left the crime scene. Her friend had no idea that her world was about to shatter, but Sam knew.

With Garza on the case, it was only a matter of time.

The question was: How far would she go to help a friend she loved like a sister? At the moment, she couldn't answer that question. She only hoped that whatever Jessie had going on, it would be worth it.

The man Ivana had called her father took Nikki by the arm and pulled her into a waiting room, keeping hold of her while he hit a buzzer on the far wall near a door. It didn't take long for two men to arrive. They took charge of Nikki and her duffel bag. When she turned around, Ivana and her so-called father were gone. The men, who would be her keepers, hauled her down a long corridor without saying a word.

From the outside, the underground facility looked like an old abandoned warehouse, but inside, the lower vault surprised her. It was like a maze, dimly lit corridors fanning out, with intermittent doors leading to many rooms.

"Where are you taking me?" She tried to resist, but they tightened their grip on her arms and yanked her along. "Please . . . you're hurting me."

As they walked, Nikki tried to memorize the layout, hoping she'd find a way out. But when she caught glimpses of other kids escorted under guard, she lost the last of her defiance. They looked as frightened as she was, and it scared her. What was this place? The men took her to the end of a hallway and pushed her into a dark room. Up ahead, a solitary lightbulb hung low. Her handlers navigated through the murky room, but she knew the spotlight was meant for her. When they shoved her under the light, she squinted and raised a hand to block the glare, but one of the men smacked her arm down.

Nikki shook all over, partly from the cold, but mostly from fear. And she felt sick to her stomach. While she was held in place under the spotlight, faceless strangers pawed through her things, dumping her clothes to the floor at her feet. In the room, she felt the presence of others and heard their low voices murmuring in the background, but they stayed hidden in the shadows. She had no idea how many. Their voices echoed in the large chamber, sounding as if they came from everywhere at once.

But eventually one voice stood out from the rest.

"Take off your clothes," the man demanded.

Nikki gasped and struggled against their hold on her. "Please," she begged.

She heard footsteps approach, but the man remained hidden in the dark. She still couldn't see his face.

"You will do this thing, or my men will rip them off you. And trust me, you will not want that to happen." The man had an accent like Ivana's. Russian, she guessed.

She waited for what seemed an eternity, but eventually gave in. Tears streamed down her face. Piece by piece, she stripped down to her panties and bra. But when that wasn't enough, her mind blurred with the details of what followed as the men manhandled them off her. In the end, she stood before these men, naked and crying. They inspected her and took pictures, making her turn around for every humiliating angle. And they took pleasure in her misery. The more she cried, the more they took photos, the flashes of light blinding her.

In her mind, she screamed, *Make it stop. Please make it stop!*

But it didn't. Not for a very long time. And a part of her was deathly afraid that when it did stop, something far worse would replace it.

After her ordeal, her keepers hauled her naked and screaming down the main corridor and threw her into another room. She'd only seen a quick glimpse of the inside when they shoved her in. Once they shut the door and locked it, she fumbled in the dark, crawling on all fours, reaching for the mattress and blanket she had seen.

The room would have been pitch-black but for the sliver of light that seeped in from under the door. She was left alone there for what felt like hours, but even as exhausted as she was, she couldn't sleep. She lay naked on a thin mattress shoved to a corner, using a shabby blanket to ward off the chill radiating from the concrete floor and brick walls.

And the tears had not stopped. The memory of her degradation played over and over in her head. A lifetime would not be enough for her to forget.

Shaking and unable to get warm, she clutched the blanket to her chest, her feet ice cold. But she kept her eyes on the light under the door, jumping at every noise, no matter how loud. Eventually she heard distant footsteps approaching echoing down the corridor outside her room. Nikki sat up and cowered in the corner, gripping the blanket tighter. She found herself praying they would walk past her door to prey on someone else.

But that wasn't meant to be. When a shadow eclipsed the light under the door, she heard a key in the lock and knew.

They had come for her again.

CHAPTER 12

Like a painful out-of-body experience, Jessie watched the frail little girl she used to be feel her way through the musty dank basement. The dark chasm never ended in her nightmares. Even without light, she saw it happening again and could do nothing to stop it. The girl's heartbeat and faint gasps for air matched her own as if they shared one body.

And as before, a deeply rooted futility made her feel listless and spent, nearly robbing her of hope.

Nearly.

In her dream, she headed for a dim stream of light coming from a small chink in the wall, a gap she had dug out with a piece of broken glass until it shattered and cut her fingers. Bright red blood was the only color of her recurring nightmare. Everything else washed to black and white with deepening shadows that threatened to swallow her. The crack to the outside had become her lifeline to a world that had forgotten her, her only source of fresh air—and something more.

Little Jessie peered through the hole from a safe distance. If she got too close to it, the light hurt her eyes, burned them like acid and made them water until she couldn't see. She had been in the dark far too long.

She remembered another child had seen her. At least, she thought the kid had seen her finger poke through the hole. Had her brief encounter been real or only imagined? She remembered that she tried to call out but her voice came out raspy, from lack of water and not being used in a very long time.

But mostly she was afraid he would hear her. The man had ears that heard secret thoughts. And he had told her before that other little girls would be punished if he caught her being bad. She remembered the screams—heard them still in her dreams. They would start deep in her head and the ear-splitting noise would grip her heart with terror, but the silence that followed made her even more afraid.

Despite her fear, little Jessie risked poking a small finger through the hole she had made. And for a second she dared to smile. The cool air on her skin felt good. And maybe the little girl outside would see her for real this time.

Thump. Thump.

"Oh, no." She knew that sound . . . and the crack of the floor above her. She knew the weighty steps were his.

"Oh God, please," she ventured a prayer no one would hear. Jessie pulled her finger from the hole and cowered into the darkest corner of the dank cellar, making herself small.

"Oh please . . . please . . . please."

Thump. Thump. Thump.

Her body trembled, violently. And she rocked at an erratic pace, chewing on her nails until they bled. The man was coming. He had found out her secret.

The little girl outside would never find her now.

Not now. Not ever.

The cold basement swept away, replaced by an inky black memory she never wanted to remember. She heard a little girl's scream and realized it came from deep in her own throat. Her arms were sluggish and unable to move, as if she were drowning in quicksand. The more she fought, the harder it became for her to breathe at all. Going under for the last time—when her lungs were burning—she finally saw a glimmer of light and focused on it.

She opened her eyes, tearing at her bed sheets, which were drenched in sweat. Gasping for air, she sat up and stared into the dark, her mind still anchored in the past.

"No. Can't be happening . . . make it stop." She sucked air into her lungs and coughed, her throat parched.

When she finally knew where she was, the old terrifying basement morphed into her apartment bedroom. One just as dark as the other, but with her apartment, the old man wasn't coming for her. He didn't have his hands on her again. And the little girl who had seen her poke a finger through the hole—that little girl didn't exactly save her back then, but had played a part in her recovery. Sam had been her friend from that horrible beginning, and she knew the ugliness Jess hid from others. And Sam carried her own memories of how their paths had crossed.

As a kid, Sam had seen her poke her finger out of the dark basement that day, but she didn't mention it to her parents or anyone else. Later, Sam admitted it struck her as strange, but as a kid she had no idea the old man in that house could have done such a thing. The cops eventually rescued Jess, but not before weeks of abuse continued and another little girl had been taken. It took her a long while to understand why Sam hadn't acted and done something. Eventually, she reasoned that innocent kids had a hard time fathoming adult sins. But Sam had held onto the guilt of not telling, and as easy as that, the old pervert claimed another victim.

Now, the resurgence of old childhood memories had stirred that damned recurring nightmare—a nasty dream Jess hadn't had in quite a while. But as images of Sam as a child flashed through her mind, an ugly aspect of the dream remained.

Thud. Thump.

The sound shocked her, holding her firm—mired in the horrific terrors of long ago.

"What the hell?"

Jess listened in the dark, for a repeat of the noise that made her heart lurch. After a second she heard the pounding again, followed by her doorbell.

Damn it! Someone was at her front door. She glanced at the clock near her bed. Almost five in the morning and her bedroom was black, without a hint of sunrise. Who the hell would be rapping on her door this time of morning?

She flung back the covers and got out of bed, then reached for the Colt Python stuck in her nightstand drawer. She didn't bother to throw on a robe. Her plaid PJ bottoms and T-shirt would have to do. This didn't sound like a social call. Gripping her weapon, she headed down the hallway to her door. With her back to a wall, she peeked out a side window to avoid looking through the peephole. If her caller was armed, she didn't want to get shot through the door. When she got a good look at her early morning caller, she lowered her weapon.

The irony wasn't missed on her when she saw Sam at her front door, bridging the gap in time from that horrific day so long ago to now. Jess slowed her heart and opened the door with as much composure as she could muster.

"You forget that you've got a new key?"

Before Sam walked in, she stooped down to pick something off the landing. Sam might have interrupted her sleep, but at least she came bearing gifts. Jess smelled coffee and pastries coming from an IHOP bag.

"I respect my friendships, unlike some folks I know." Sam went straight to her kitchen and pulled out two large coffees, handing one to her as she set down her Colt Python on the breakfast bar.

"What's that supposed to mean?"

"It means we're at a crossroad, my friend. I don't like being lied to by someone I love like a sister." Sam rummaged through what was left of Jess's dishes, plated a couple of cheese Danish, and grabbed napkins. "In case you haven't noticed, I carry a badge and a gun. I can handle myself and I don't need you to protect me."

She brought the pastries and her coffee to the kitchen table and sat, waiting for Jess to join her. When she did, Sam got a second wind.

"Most days, it's hard to figure out where you end and I begin, we are that much alike. But on other days, I firmly believe you should come with a warning label." Sam took a sip of coffee and glared over the rim of the cup.

Jess knew the look. "Yeah, but people like me keep churchgoers in business."

"Funny, Jess. But I'd settle for a little Laverne and Shirley, instead of the constant life or death drama of Thelma and Louise. I've got my shift in a couple of hours, so don't screw with me. I don't have time for games."

"What are you talking about?"

Jess knew she was a toxic influence on those around her, but she didn't know how to change. The circumstances of her childhood set her on a collision course with life, and there had been consequences, but she wasn't the type to take the easy way out for herself. Some things were worth fighting for, even if it meant she had to go it alone.

"You used me to back you up yesterday, but you didn't tell me the whole truth about Baker. You know it and I know it."

When she didn't answer quickly enough, Sam jumped in.

"Why Baker? What's going on between you and this particular loser? What's the trigger that sets you off? I think you know what I'm talking about." She set down her coffee cup. "Does it have something to do with—"

"Please . . . don't go there." Jess got to her feet, too antsy to sit. She dragged fingers through her mussed hair. "I don't want to talk about that."

Sam had been the only person she had shared the darkest moments of her life, something no one else should know about another human being. Yet they'd remained friends through it all. She knew it took courage for her to keep Sam in her life, a living reminder. But there were times when she wondered if her childhood friend had become part of her penance, an odd form of self-abuse.

"I think we need to, Jess. That situation with Baker could have turned ugly. And Seth Harper would've been caught in the middle."

Jess knew she was right, but it didn't make it any easier to hear. She took a deep breath and ventured onto treacherous ground.

"I don't want to be defined by my past anymore. It's not who I am. I've left that part of me behind."

"Have you, Jess? Have you really?" Sam pressed. Her voice raised, it echoed in the stark silence of early morning. "Ignoring the past isn't dealing with it. You've shoved the tough stuff so deep that you've convinced yourself it's gone. But every time another Baker comes along, something goes off in your head that turns you into a crazy person. Your judgment gets . . . clouded."

Sam voice's softened. "Maybe it's not about leaving the pain behind. Maybe you have to face it head on."

Jess leaned against a wall, staring across the room without seeing anything in particular. Morning had edged its way onto the horizon, and a dull gray leached through the blinds.

"Have you talked to anyone else?" Sam asked. "I mean, about what happened back then?"

Sam's subtle way of asking if she'd undergone any recent therapy. When she was a kid, after she was rescued, she'd become a ward of the state of Illinois and had her fill of third-rate therapists and counselors to last her a lifetime. No thanks.

"No, you're the only one who . . . really knows how it was." Jess closed her eyes, taking comfort in the quiet. And Sam let her find words, in her own time. "Most days, I distance myself from it until someone like Baker stirs it up again. Then you're right, I'm out of control. Sometimes I can't even breathe, I get so . . . sick that it's never gonna be over."

The abuse she had endured as a kid had left its marks, literally. No human being should endure that kind of shame, especially a child. She had dug deep for the courage to survive, but she still had nightmares because of it, instigated by any number of triggers.

"I hate this . . . the fact that I can't shake it?" she finally admitted.

"You're a survivor, Jess. And I'm proud of who you've become, but being a survivor is not a sin that you have to atone for the rest of your life."

Sam reached for her hand, forcing her to sit.

"Look, I know we're not going to solve any of this tonight, but I did have a reason for coming here, Jess. I know about the skate rink and what you put into the locker. You should have told me the full story about Lucas Baker."

She flinched enough for Sam to notice.

"Wait, how did you—" She stopped herself. She could have kept up the charade, but why? Sam was right. It was time to come clean with her friend. Frankly, she was relieved.

"I needed proof, Sam. No cop was gonna believe me without concrete evidence. And that laptop is the key. Baker is up to his eyeballs with an international organization that is bartering in kids. I just . . . know it."

"And what exactly did you figure would happen?"

"I had every intention of giving his damned computer back. Hell, it practically fell into my lap when I tried to wrangle his SUV. What was I supposed to do? I had to take a peek at what he had on his computer. But then the bastard got his hands on Seth and forced an exchange. He beat the kid up, for cryin' out loud." Jess took a swig of black coffee, then reached for a cheese Danish and pinched off a small bite with her fingers. "But by that time, Seth had already rigged Baker's laptop with his Trojan horse program."

Nibbling on breakfast, Jess shrugged and went on.

"I just figured we'd give the computer back and track the bastard's movements firsthand. You know, not breaking the chain of evidence. Baker would have his laptop back and we'd track him using Seth's really sweet software. Eventually, I figured we'd get the proof we'd need to put him away and save some troubled kids. A pretty slick idea."

"What makes you think Baker is running kids? If the man is working as an informant with CPD, don't you think we'd know what he was up to?"

Jess knew Sam wouldn't want to hear about Baker running a scam on the CPD. The man didn't flaunt his business in front of the law. He had played it smarter than that, flying below police radar, from what she could tell. She had a theory he was operating outside Chicago, keeping his nose clean in town. The guy didn't piss close to home. And for the CPD's efforts, he gave them a token lead every now and then, probably throwing them his competition. *Sweet deal when you can get it.* But it was time for the CPD to take a hard look at the bastard, and she hoped to convince Sam to be her messenger.

"Well, where Baker is concerned, someone better open their eyes." She set down her coffee cup and wiped her mouth with a napkin. "'Cause the guy is dirty. Seth found an e-mail on his computer, saying a delivery from Alaska was coming to Chicago yesterday. And the sender had a Russian name. The delivery was probably some poor kid. But with all the flights scheduled, no way I could cover 'em all. He's running kids, Sam. I know it."

"From Alaska, you say."

"Yeah. Probably Anchorage. And the sender used a Russian name that was probably fake. It was linked to a classic Russian fable. Seth looked it up." She might have laid it on a little thick about her theories on Alaska and a Russian connection, but she had Sam's ear and took advantage of it. "Baker's involved with a big operation, an international organization with a Web site called 'Globe Harvest.' He hits the site all the time. A site under construction, I might add. You'll see. When Seth gets a login for Baker, you'll see the whole setup for yourself. Baker's not exactly a brainiac. He won't outsmart my resident genius."

"Baker won't be logging on anywhere, Jessie."

"Yeah, he will. He's got his laptop back. In fact, I'm expecting a call from Harper anytime."

"Baker's dead, Jess. He got gunned down outside the skating rink."

"What?" Jess slumped back into her chair. "When did this happen?"

"Sometime around midnight."

"Who did it?"

"Eyewitnesses weren't clear. Some even reported seeing two shooters, maybe even a woman." Sam crossed her arms. "Besides being dead, Baker's got another little setback. His laptop is missing. Until now we didn't know what was in the black bag. Thanks for filling in the gaps."

"Damn it! I thought I had him this time. Shit!" It didn't take long for her to do the math, but when she did, she narrowed her eyes and glared at Sam.

"Wait a minute. You set me up. You knew about Baker, but you wanted to see what I'd say. You played me like . . . a suspect." She thought about it for a minute, then added, "You've been hanging around me too long. I don't know if I should be mad or damned proud."

"Well, two can play the bluff game, but that's not how friends should treat each other. Right now, you and me need to stick together. Detective Ray Garza is running his own investigation on the murder of Lucas Baker. And as of now, you top his list of suspects."

"But I didn't do it. You know I didn't do it." She knew she was preaching to the choir, but she couldn't help jumping to her own defense.

"When he looks for fingerprints on that note you slipped

Baker and that locker key, I've got money that he'll find yours."

Jess thought about it for a second, then winced. "No bet. Shit! I'm totally screwed."

Sam leaned forward and grabbed her shoulder.

"I know you didn't kill Baker, but the way I see it, we've gotta stay one step ahead of Garza. Will Seth work as your alibi? If Baker was killed at midnight, you were with Harper, right?"

Jess shrugged, but after thinking about Harper, more than a few things didn't add up about her boy.

"I'm not exactly sure what Seth actually does for a living. Believe it or not, he's not getting rich on what I pay him, but he may not stand up to close scrutiny from the local cops . . . if you know what I mean."

"Oh, that's just great, Jess. You do realize how much trouble you're in, right? You need an alibi. And preferably not somebody on the FBI's Most Wanted list."

Jess got up to pace again.

"Hell, for all I know, Seth has pulled up stakes. I nearly got him killed, Sam. I practically handed him over to Baker on a silver platter. If it were me . . . I would've quit me." She dragged a hand over her face. "And the address I have for him may not be . . . exactly his."

"I swear to God, Jessie. You know the strangest people."

"Don't forget, you're at the top of my Christmas card list. Don't be casting stones at my peeps."

Sam grimaced, then looked at her watch. "Look, I've got time before my shift. Get dressed. Let's see if we can track down Harper. First and foremost, you need a legitimate alibi."

"I do have his cell phone number. Let me try calling first. If he ignores the call, I might consider that a very bad sign."

Jess went to her bathroom and took her phone off the charger to place a call to Seth. She walked back into the kitchen as his phone rang. On the fifth ring it beeped and rolled into voice mail without an outgoing message. She tried again and got the same result. Not having a good feeling about all this, she didn't leave a message.

When Sam narrowed her eyes in question, Jess shrugged and said, "Strike one. He didn't answer my call."

"Well, it's bottom of the ninth with bases loaded. And it doesn't look good for the home team, Jessie. We gotta find Harper."

Before she got dressed, Jess wanted Sam's take on her chances, being a glutton for abuse.

"Sam? What if we can't find him? Without an alibi, when would Detective Garza come looking for me?"

"Hard to say." She shrugged. "He won't know the note is from you. I recognized the handwriting and didn't say anything. And it'll take time for the lab to lift prints, but he'll find a fingerprint match when he conducts his usual database searches. He'll score a hit on your permit to carry the Python."

Sam took a swig of coffee and continued speculating.

"But you're already on his list of suspects after your recent beef with Baker. He could act on that alone and bring you in for questioning as a person of interest. And I'd say you're gonna look awfully bad when he backtracks Baker's time prior to his murder. Folks will remember that fight you had at The Cutthroat. Another run-in with Baker on the night of his murder won't sit well with Garza."

Jess crossed her arms, feeling a sudden chill in the air. "Damn it! I almost forgot about that."

"I could lie for you, Jess, and say I was with you until after one," Sam offered without hesitation, looking her straight in the eye. "Harper's the only one who'd know otherwise."

"Ah, Sam." She hugged her friend and whispered in her ear, "That's a tempting and generous offer, but I can't let you do that."

After she pulled back, she added, "Nice to know you'd

drive my Ford Bronco if I ever needed a lame getaway. But if I get dragged into this, I want a cop in good standing to help me. Taking down Baker's organization is a bigger picture worth pursuing. I hope I can convince you of that."

After thinking about her predicament, Jess offered her hand.

"I promise. No more lies, Sam. I mean it." She gripped her hand and shook on their pact. "Now let's find Harper. Maybe I'm only being paranoid about the kid. He's probably right where I left him, licking his wounds. My luck has got to turn sometime."

Jess headed to her bedroom to change, sounding more confident than she felt. Her future rested on Seth Harper—whoever he was.

Downtown Chicago

"Shit, I can't believe this!" From the secured foyer, Jess tried the buzzer to the penthouse suite again. Nothing. Seth was either gone or not answering. Neither prospect bode well for her. And out of respect for Sam, she didn't try her usual antics to get buzzed into the building unannounced.

"Are you sure this guy lives here?" Sam asked. "Hard to imagine a kid like that . . . here. This is a real upscale neighborhood. I doubt any of these people have even heard of *Jerry Springer*."

"Yeah, I thought the same thing when I first came here. Damn it! I should have listened to my gut instincts."

"Yeah, I bet the next time you hire an intern as slave labor, you'll go through a legitimate temp agency to find the next sucker . . . I mean, employee." Sam slathered abuse on thick. "Well, what now? You have any clue where to look for him?"

Jess plopped down on a marbled step inside the secured foyer with her elbows propped on her knees.

"No. I tried his phone on the way down, but no answer. I've got nothing."

Sam joined her on the step. "I hate to say this, but maybe he saw the TV news coverage on the shooting. Being hauled into a murder investigation tends to test the loyalties of a new employee, especially during probation period."

"God, I'm never gonna hear the end of this, am I?" She shot a sideways glance at Sam and grimaced. "Harper's a damned wimp. How could I have been so wrong about that guy?"

"Look, knowing you, you're thinking of the many ways to break into the penthouse, and an officer of the law wouldn't make a good accomplice, so I'm gonna vacate the scene of the crime. I want to get to work early today, see what I can find out." Sam patted her knee with affection and smiled, not a very convincing display of reassurance. "Call me if Harper shows, and I'll give you a heads-up if I learn anything new."

Jess nodded, and her cop friend headed out the glass door. After she left, Jess stood and walked up to the row of buzzers again, cracking her knuckles like a concert pianist. She wasn't done with Seth Harper. Not by a long shot.

Jess eventually got inside Harper's building again and went straight to his penthouse suite, but Seth didn't answer the door. She didn't take the snub personally. To show no hard feelings, she let herself in by way of a lock pick and made herself at home. But once she got inside, her worst fear became a reality. Seth Harper was nowhere to be found, and there was no trace of him, not a speck of proof that he'd even been there.

No trash. No scraps of paper. Nothing. She even hit the redial button on the suite phone and got 411 information. The place was as pristine as if no one lived there at all. Harper was a damned ghost. She thought about staking out the place to see if he came back, but she knew he'd cleared out for good.

"Damn it, Seth. Who the hell are you?"

Jess tried his phone again, but only got voice mail. This time she left a message, though she didn't give her SOS much chance of getting to him. Being in the dumper had become a full-time job for her, and she'd never felt so low.

After getting into her car, she drove to her favorite breakfast joint to grab some coffee and read the newspaper for more on Baker's murder.

Nothing like a little murder over easy with a side order of bacon and home fries at Red's Grill, a little hole in the wall joint off I-55 on South Kedzie Avenue. She'd discovered the place during a stakeout three years ago. Decent food priced cheap, and patronized by corrections officers, local cops, and the folks they should have been monitoring. A real microcosm of the universe.

Sitting in a booth, she was nearly done with the paper, saving the funnies for last, when her cell rang. She recognized the number.

"Please tell me you're gonna make my day."

"First things first. Did you find Harper?" Sam asked.

"No. Not even a precious hair off his thick skull. And I've left messages for him on his cell. Nothing. I think he pulled a rabbit on me."

"Well, then maybe what I've got will lift your spirits. I don't know what this means, but it doesn't exactly suck." Sam had an edge of excitement to her voice.

"Go on. Try me, babe. I could use some good news."

"Chief Keller announced this himself at our shift briefing. You better sit down."

"Enough with the buildup already." Jess rolled her eyes and shook her head.

"We got a missing person bulletin today. Get this. There's a missing girl from Anchorage and they think she's in Chicago. She flew in yesterday. That's too much coincidence for us to ignore, Jessie."

She grinned. She couldn't help it. "I knew it."

"Yeah well, don't get all worked up. I mean, on the surface

it gives me a pretty good idea you were right about Baker's e-mail on that delivery from Alaska, but we need more than a hunch to point a finger at a dead guy. Allegedly speaking, you didn't happen to keep a copy of that pilfered e-mail, did you?"

"No. Harper's got it, allegedly." She heard the sigh on the other end of the line. "So what do we do now?"

"It would be nice to get our hands on that laptop and find a direct link to Baker, but that's not likely to happen. For all we know, someone in the crowd stole the computer before the cops got to the murder scene. If that happened, we may never find it."

She knew Sam was right. The laptop was a long shot, especially with Harper going missing. But when Jess hit the lowest point of her morning, feeling like she'd been dumped back at square one, Sam came up with something new.

"Look, I got an idea, but I think I should pursue it on my own. If you get involved and Garza hears about it, you're toast."

"Spill it, Coop. What's your idea?"

"Chief Keller mentioned the missing girl, Nikki Archer, has relatives who flew into town this morning from Alaska. They're staying at a hotel in Oak Brook. Get this—she's the niece of a former pro football quarterback, Payton Archer. They said he used to play here in Chicago, but I've never heard of him, have you?"

It took Jess a while to place it, but the name eventually rang a bell—and not in a good way.

"Yeah, I remember him. Media blitzed the guy, but as I recall, he deserved the abuse. He had an ego the size of Alaska coupled with a drinking problem. That's a nasty combo when you fuel the fire with the kind of money those jocks get paid."

She added one more thing to her recollection. "And from what I remembered, he couldn't keep his mouth shut."

"Boy, that sounds familiar."

"Hey, watch it."

"Well, I'm playing a hunch of my own, Jess. I volunteered to be Archer's contact here at CPD. I'm working the case with him while he's here, see if it goes anywhere. It might be worth a shot."

"You what? Why would you want to saddle yourself with an egotistical media junkie like Payton Archer? He's nothing but a prima donna in a jock strap with a penchant for grandstanding. The guy practically turned trash talk into an art form."

"It's my time to waste, and the damage has been done. I've already been assigned to the Archer missing person case. End of discussion. I'm heading to meet him now. He's staying at the Marriott in Oak Brook."

"Well, you just keep Jockboy away from me. Someone like Archer could be a real distraction that I don't need right now. Don't get me wrong. Chasing down one poor kid is a good thing, Sam, but Baker had a much bigger gig going on. And that, I'd like to sink my teeth into."

"Guess you'll have your hands full with chasing Harper." Sam's voice turned somber. "But Jess, if anyone at CPD gets wind of you nosing around Baker's business again, it'll get back to Garza. And he doesn't need much of an excuse to haul you in. Don't make it easy for him."

"I swear." Jess put cash on the table for her tab with the phone crooked against her shoulder. "I'll behave myself."

"Oh God, this is gonna get worse before it gets better. I just know it."

"O ye of little faith." Jess chuckled as she slid out of the booth and headed for her car. "Like things have been going good till now? How much worse could it get?" She scrunched her face. "Wait, don't answer that, but I could use a favor."

She asked if she could use Sam's home computer and phone to search for Seth Harper. She had a spare key and needed a place to work since Baker had trashed her own computer. But mostly, she didn't want to make it easy for Detective Garza to find her.

After Sam agreed, Jess ended the call with her mind tumbling around ideas on how to track down Harper. Hell, she was a Fugitive Recovery Agent. If she couldn't find one scrawny but cute intern, she might as well land a real job. Nine-to-five.

"Yeah, right," she said to herself. "That'll happen."

CHAPTER 13

Seth Harper was an enigma. Jess realized she hadn't been far off the mark when she imagined him to be nothing more than a ghost. After conducting searches on his background from Sam's home computer—queries she hadn't felt the need to do when she hired him—she came up with a series of dead ends. The kid lived off the grid, a move that appeared deliberate.

He had no history of utilities registered in his name. His cell phone had been prepaid. He had no current or prior address. No credit cards. And amazingly, she struck out with DMV and insurance queries too. Even the schools he listed on his employment application had no information under the name Seth Harper. To dig deeper, she needed time and out-of-the-box thinking.

"Who the hell are you, Harper?"

She wasn't any closer to finding her man, the guy who could serve as her alibi and help put her back on the track of Baker's missing laptop. But as a plan B began to form in her mind, her cell phone rang. When she looked at the display, no name came up and she didn't recognize the phone number. Taking a chance, she answered it anyway.

"I sure hope you're not a waste of my time."

"Depends on what you consider wasteful." A soft chuckle. "I'm more of an acquired taste . . . if you lower your standards."

It took her a moment to place the voice, but when she did, she had to grin.

"Well, I'll be damned. Where have you been, Harper? I've been . . . looking for you."

"Yeah, sorry about that. I figured with Baker on my ass and knowing where I lived, it was a good time to lay low. I ditched my old phone number too."

"Yeah, I noticed."

A part of her wanted to hit him with all the questions floating in her brain about his nonexistent background. And one day she would have that conversation, but more urgent needs took priority. The point was, he'd reached out to her, and if he had planned to disappear, he wouldn't have called.

"Have you seen the news?" she asked.

"Yeah, barely. It took me most of the night to hustle out of my digs and find a new location, so I slept in. I didn't see what happened until a little while ago. You probably thought I bailed on you."

"Not me. I had complete faith."

"Liar."

She heard the amusement in his voice.

"Hey. I thought you should know," she added. "The news coverage wouldn't have mentioned this, but the laptop is missing. According to Sam, the cops never found it at the scene. It might have been stolen."

"What?" he said. "That's not possible."

Jess grinned. "I never took you for gullible, Harper. Why would you find it so difficult to believe someone stole it? Granted, taking it off a dead guy is a little cold, but—"

"Jess, that's one of the reasons I called you. I didn't expect the laptop to be running this morning after Baker kicked it, but someone has been poking around. And they sure don't need a road map."

"What are you saying?"

"By the keystrokes, I could swear Baker is still alive. Whoever has his computer really knows what they're doing. You and I need to talk."

In the darkened room, Ethan O'Connell kept his eyes on the bank of computer monitors in front of him as he sipped coffee, freshly brewed from the kitchen. Dim lighting made the screens easier to see. He sat alone at the control center, an elevated workstation that overlooked his handpicked staff, charged with local system maintenance and data entry for Globe Harvest. The business end of the U.S. domestic operation was situated belowground in an abandoned textile manufacturing plant.

On-screen, data updated in real time, a living, breathing online entity with international connections. Behind the facade of a Web site under construction lay a vast encrypted network accessible only through proper security authorizations. Part of the system was dedicated to tracking the influx of "assets" into the existing inventory, while other aspects focused on the more complex side of the business—the disposition of inventory by myriad disposal options. The extensive on-screen display of numbers was nothing more than supply and demand in action on a grand scale.

They bartered in human lives, and everything had a price.

"Bidding starts in twenty minutes, sir." A man's voice came from below.

"Thank you," he replied, catching a glimpse of his watch.

Bidders on an encrypted system were ready to transact after reviewing a comprehensive profile on each asset that included a current medical record. A fully automated system.

The sex trade, and other more inventive endeavors, had turned high tech, protected by the obstacle of multijurisdictional borders and the anonymity of cyberspace. And with the organization compartmentalized, he had no idea how the computer system actually ran or who might be responsible for facets of the business. Anonymity had its advantages, both ways.

"Are the recent acquisitions included?" he asked. "Those medically certified, that is."

"Yes, sir." Another voice came from across the room. "We're set."

Acquisitions underwent a screening process, with recruited Internet operatives looking for the young, inexperienced, and disassociated kids who met a specific profile and wouldn't be missed until they were in "the system."

Enticed by exciting opportunities and money, kids with low self-esteem or a faltering relationship with their parents made for easy picking. To them, money could represent a powerful solution to their problems. And there was adventure and big money to be made during the summer at Alaskan fish canneries. Or perhaps the promise of marriage to a rich American or an international modeling job with free room and board, and pay in tax-free dollars, would be enough of a lure. The promises didn't matter.

Once a kid became a part of the Globe Harvest system, they'd be moved again and again until all evidence of their true location was covered up without a trace. Cops had a hard time tracking kids across a multijurisdictional landscape, especially when each case appeared random and without similarity—just another runaway kid for the auction block.

"And I understand we have two new bidders. Are they operational and online?" he prompted his staff.

Markets were given unique numbers and set up elsewhere to maintain their anonymity. Once orders came through and property was awarded, he would only know certain aspects of the shipping destinations, nothing more. And if an intermediary for shipment was utilized—which many markets took advantage of—he knew even less about the final disposition of the asset.

"We have confirmation they are certified for online access. And the two new bidders are in queue, but only one is currently online."

"Give me an update when that second bidder joins the party," he said.

"Will do, sir."

Once the online auction started, things would go quickly and the outcome for each asset would be determined within minutes. Handlers would be assigned and transactions executed with money wired instantaneously. All transactions took place in an automated clearinghouse, with orders filled by the end of the day. On today's online global forums, anything could be bought. And Globe Harvest had taken this theory to a whole new level.

Business, pure and simple—*but not always for him.*

Ethan went to the screen posting the latest profiles. Whenever he did this, the rest of the control room melted away to nothing. Explicit photos were always a major turn-on—one of the perks of the job. He found himself getting aroused. His cock strained against his pants. On occasion he got to sample the goods as a bonus—the incentive that had lured him to the organization in the first place.

Globe Harvest fed his addiction.

"You are nothing but fox in charge of chickens, yes?"

Ethan jumped at the sound of Stanislav Petrovin's voice coming out of the darkness. When he looked over his shoulder, the long-haired Russian stood over him, gazing down at the photos on the computer monitor.

"A fox in charge of the hen house, Stas," he corrected. "But this fox knows better than to sample the goods, unless he has permission."

He didn't like the way the Russian always appeared from thin air and without making a sound.

"If this is true, you are stronger man than I," Petrovin said.

The Russian grabbed control of a screen and looked through photos of the new additions. He muttered in his native tongue anytime he found a profile that he liked, but after a look at the man's face, Ethan didn't need a translation.

He knew Petrovin didn't always abide by the rules when it came to the handling of assets. What the Russian wanted, he took without permission, leaving him to clean up the damage. He suspected Stas had been granted sanction from a higher authority, but he was too afraid to challenge the man. One look in the dead eyes of the Russian gave Stas all the authority he'd need, as far as Ethan was concerned.

Leaning over the console, Petrovin scrolled through the photos and kept his eyes on the screen as he talked.

"Lucas Baker is no longer problem. His laptop . . . it is in our hands."

"Yes, I heard you brought the computer back. It wasn't hard to imagine what happened to Baker. The bag had blood on it." Ethan slouched in his chair and swiveled. "My people are going over it now, to see if it's been tampered with."

"Yes, good. But we have another situation," Petrovin added, turning his intense focus on Ethan. "I must eliminate another threat from the Baker incident. A bounty hunter and two others, but one is a cop."

"A cop?" He leaned forward in his chair. "Do you think that's wise?"

"Baker left me with no choice in the matter. Anton agrees." When the Russian noticed the worried look on his face, he added, "Don't worry. I know how to make it look like hazard of job, but I may need your . . . cooperation."

Petrovin's understated style made him a difficult man to read. He maintained a somber expression, part of his nature. Yet now, Ethan noticed a subtle change in his demeanor. Cool under fire, the man never panicked. So when Petrovin asked for help, his request came with a certain sense of urgency.

"Whatever you need," Ethan said, "consider it done."

The Russian crooked his lips into a smile, the humor never reaching his eyes. At times Ethan found himself mesmerized by the awkwardness of that expression, but most days, he wished to block the man's face from his mind altogether. He slept better that way.

Downtown Chicago
Midday

Located on the "Magnificent Mile," the Peninsula Chicago on Superior Street was one of the city's most luxurious and sophisticated five-star hotels, set in the heart of the city's exclusive shopping scene. In contrast, the posh hotel stood beside the historic Water Tower, a uniquely eye-catching and ornate limestone structure that looked more like a small chapel at first glance—the old and new set in perfect harmony.

Jess had driven around the block three times before she decided to avoid the grand porte cochere entrance with its intimidating display of flags, uniformed valets, and couture-dressed patrons. Instead, she parked down the block and hiked back, contending with a brisk wind. When she got to the hotel, the stiff breeze swept across the front entrance like a wind tunnel, buffeting her clothes and hair. Sensitive to her disheveled appearance, she regrouped once she made it to the valet station outside the main entrance.

Yet again Seth Harper had surprised her with his new digs. And he'd promised to meet her in the lobby since his accommodations required card-key access to the secured floors.

"Card-key access, my ass," she muttered under her breath as she pushed through the revolving glass door, running a hand through her tousled hair. Once inside, she searched the lobby for her enigmatic boy genius. When she spotted him, Jess did a double take, unable to contain her grin.

"Well, I'll be damned." She raised an eyebrow and cocked a hip.

Nice dark slacks and a blue open-collar, button-down shirt had replaced his *Jerry Springer* tee and worn jeans. He'd even combed his hair for the occasion. Harper was a damned chameleon. If not for the bruises on his face and for his cut lip, she might have mistaken him for someone else. With her arms crossed, she waited for him to come to her.

As she got a closer look at his face, she grimaced and asked, "Are you okay?"

"Yeah. My macho pride took a beating, but you know what they say. Anything that doesn't kill you makes you stronger."

"That's just another way of saying, 'Man up and get over it.'" She took a good long look at Seth from head to toe. "Well, I have to say it. You clean up nice, Harper. But I'm still reporting you to Springer. Where's your loyalty, man?"

Harper didn't bat an eye. He opened a button to reveal a Jerry tee under his shirt.

"Never question my sense of loyalty, Jess. I may surprise you from time to time, but some things about me never change."

"I'm beginning to appreciate that fact, Harper." She smiled. "Lead the way, uptown boy."

Seth escorted her to the top floor and into the most fabulous suite she had ever seen. Jaw dropping gorgeous. Massive windows in every room offered stunning panoramic views of Lake Michigan, the Water Tower, and Chicago's historic Gold Coast district. Without waiting for her reaction, he headed for an impressive study, leaving her to explore—something she couldn't resist.

Painted in gold tones and creamy ivory, the suite had two living areas, one casual and the other more formal. If a patron ever got confused about which was which, the grand piano served as a focal point to the formal one. She had no idea if Harper played, but nothing would surprise her about the guy anymore.

The rest of the upscale quarters had fireplaces everywhere and a private exercise room. But the most amazing sight was the outdoor terrace with its ornamental garden and hot tub, a relaxing oasis in the middle of Chi-town. She walked onto the terrace and gazed across the cityscape with the warm sun on her face and the hum of traffic below. The breeze rustled through the small trees and shrubs of the terrace garden and messed with her hair again. Yet despite having to contend with Mother Nature, she enjoyed the view at the top of the world. To the west a dark bank of clouds loomed on the horizon. A storm building its case. The sun wouldn't last, but from Seth Harper's spectacular vantagepoint, he'd soon have a prime seat for the unfolding drama.

Breathtaking.

"Man, I love this town." The constant and underlying vitality of downtown Chicago never ceased to amaze her.

When she came back inside, she noticed once again that Harper didn't look like he actually fit here. Granted, it had only been one night since he'd moved, but he made use of only a fraction of the suite, leaving little trace of himself behind. An efficient and practiced lifestyle, if it could be called living at all. She got the sense he could vacate the premises in a heartbeat, needing only scant time to undertake his skillful disappearing act.

For now, she accepted him as is, noticing he didn't respond well to an overabundance of questions. Neither did she, but since he obviously didn't need her lame job, why had he reached out to her at all? She had the feeling he didn't have a huge circle of friends and had grown accustomed to his solitary life, yet the question persisted in her mind: Why had he picked her?

Fixing her windswept hair, Jess joined him in the study and leaned against the open French doors.

"Your view is absolutely stunning."

Harper barely looked up from his laptop. "Yeah. It's nice." Spoken like a man who had grown accustomed to an address on easy street. "Here . . . come check this out. And I've got a confession to make."

"No . . . really?" She exaggerated her reaction as she looked over his shoulder behind the desk. "Don't tell me you've been keeping secrets from me, Harper."

She hadn't noticed it before, but he had an array of equipment on the desk, alongside his usual assortment of pirated computer software. Batteries, wiring, and what looked like two metal briefcases with control panels inside.

"What's all this?" she asked.

"I wanted to surprise you."

She raised an eyebrow. "You've done nothing *but* surprise me since we've met. What are you talking about?"

"When I installed the tracking software onto Baker's laptop, I thought of something else to give us an edge. Remember I mentioned I might have time to kick in something extra?"

By the apologetic look on his face, she wasn't sure she'd like what he had to say, but she kept her mouth shut—nothing short of a miracle.

"Well, I hid a long range transmitter in the computer bag and sewed it into the lining, so we could trace the physical location of it. I figured you for the impatient type, not wanting to wait for Baker to login." He raised both eyebrows. "I hope that was okay."

After a moment of stunned silence, Jess laughed aloud, the sound echoing through the suite.

"Okay? Harper, I'd kiss you, but I couldn't afford a sexual harassment suit. Way to go, genius!" She grinned and waved a hand to prompt him. "Come on. Show me how it works."

"I will, but I want to explain the keystrokes first." He breezed through his laptop to bring up the data he'd recorded, taken from Baker's computer when someone had logged into it. He explained what had happened and the conclusions he drew from it all. "You see what I mean? Whoever has Baker's laptop knows what they're doing. These aren't the maneuverings of a novice."

While she pondered the significance of what he'd said, he clarified his point.

"We installed the tracking software figuring Baker wasn't savvy enough to know it was there. But I can tell by the keystrokes that whoever has the laptop really knows their stuff. They may find what I've done."

"Meaning, if they find the embedded software, they'll wonder who tampered with it. Eventually, someone in Baker's old organization will point a finger at us."

"Yeah. Yet another reason to support my Houdini vanishing routine." He nodded. "But you . . . it may not be safe for you to go home. At least, not until we figure this out."

"And you know, there's another piece to this puzzle I gotta think through. Sam told me the police don't have the laptop. They thought it was stolen at the murder scene." She thought about it for a minute, wanting to make sure she had it right in her head. "You know, if you're correct, I think Baker's organization took him out. That's the only thing that makes sense."

"Globe Harvest?"

"Who else would know so much about navigating that computer? The theft was no coincidence, Harper." She furrowed her brow. "I think if we find that stolen property, we're gonna find Baker's killer . . . and get our foot in the door to something much bigger."

It wasn't just a case of hunting down a laptop. That computer served as a back door into an online conspiracy linked to missing kids. There had to be big money involved too. A lot at stake. But had Lucas Baker been killed because she'd taken his computer in the first place?

"I hate to say this aloud," he said, "but if the people behind Globe Harvest are willing to kill one of their own to keep their secret, they won't have any trouble taking care of outsiders threatening their business."

A cold chill shot across her skin, and not just because the AC was too high.

"You better show me how this gear works."

Suddenly, their preparation took on a more ominous urgency.

"Yeah . . . guess I better," Seth said. "Here's the basic setup for the tracking system."

He explained how the long range tracking system worked, transmitters with a receiver range of up to twenty-five miles on the ground. And he'd gotten his hands on a law enforcement package that would allow two people to track and cover more territory in the process—receivers, transmitters, directional antennas with RF frequencies, headphones, the works.

"The plan is to drive until we pick up an initial signal that we can track. That signal should lead us to the exact location of the laptop." He pointed at a map of the Chicago area. "We'll stick to the freeways to cover the most ground. Don't veer off until you've got a signal to chase. You'll start here and work your way in, and I'll do the same coming from this direction. When we get a hit, we'll contact each other. I know this has been a crash course, but do you think you can handle the equipment on your own?"

"I think so." She forced a smile.

"But when we find the computer, you're gonna contact the police, right?" he asked. "I mean, it's evidence in a murder now. All we're gonna do is track it, right?"

"Yeah, sure. I've already talked to Sam." She nodded and grimaced a little. "Speaking of the police, I may need you to do me a favor. Detective Garza doesn't think very highly of . . . my behavior with Baker."

"You mean, when you stalked and hunted the asshole down with a gun?" Harper raised an eyebrow.

"Yeah . . . that." She shrugged. "He might want to question

me about where I was the night Baker was killed. Would you be willing to come forward and be my alibi if all this goes down? I don't expect you to lie. Just tell the truth about what happened that night."

"All of it?"

"Yes, all of it." She tried not to act insulted that he'd suggested lying would be a better option. "I'll take the heat for what happened, but personally, I think being wrapped in duct tape makes a pretty good argument for extenuating circumstances in your case. And Sam can attest to what happened."

Seth narrowed his eyes and slouched back in the desk chair. "If you need me . . . yeah, I'll do it. But Jess, it wouldn't be my first choice for . . . entertainment. Believe me, it's not that I object to helping out, but . . . I've got my reasons."

"Yeah, kind of figured as much." She nibbled her lower lip. "Well, let's hope it doesn't come to that. Besides, if we get lucky locating Baker's computer, the heat will be off me, and Sam can finish the rest. Finding stolen evidence in a murder investigation should make her look pretty good in front of CPD brass too."

She thought of something else. A precaution.

"Listen . . . in case we get split up . . . when we find the location of the laptop, we'll contact Sam and let her know. I promised her no more secrets. And we don't want to take possession of stolen property. It'll screw with CPD's chain of evidence." She found a pen and used a pad of hotel stationery to write down Sam's number. "So it might be a good idea if you had her cell number too. Just in case."

"Yeah . . . sure." When Seth tried to smile, he winced and reached for his cut lip. "Don't mistake me for a lightweight, but— *Ow!*"

With humor, he'd taken everything in stride, but his grimace gave her an opening.

"Listen, Seth. I'm sorry for getting you into all this. I

don't know why you're still . . . helping me, but I really appreciate having you as a friend, you know?"

"Yeah . . . I know."

"But I gotta ask. Why are you doing this? I know it's not for the big bucks I'm paying you."

He stared at her a long time and finally answered, "Not everything is about . . . money."

She wanted to laugh aloud when she heard nearly the same words that she'd said to Sam the other day. Seth Harper was more than a kindred spirit. He was a damned mind reader.

"I couldn't have said it better myself." She grinned and patted his shoulder. "Let's do this."

She helped him pack the equipment, and it took time to carry it down to their vehicles and make sure the gear was operational. This time of day, they would hit the early outbound commuter traffic. And by the drops of rain on her windshield, the drive would be ugly and slow moving. But as she drove out of downtown Chicago, following Harper, she had more on her mind than the weather.

She wondered what they'd find when the search narrowed to a single location. If Lucas Baker wasn't the tip of a very nasty iceberg, then why did she feel like the captain of the *Titanic*?

CHAPTER 14

Nothing. She hadn't found a damned thing. And from their last call, neither had Seth.

Although the tracking system kept interference to a minimum, it didn't block out frequency noise completely. Every time the gear would register a blip of sound, it made her heart race until it cleared, getting her hopes up for nothing. And the system didn't operate real-time. It had a slight delay. That meant she had to learn how the equipment worked the hard way—trial and error coupled with emotional highs and lows.

And to compound her stress, when she turned on her car headlights at dusk due to overcast skies and steady rain, she fell victim to a dismal funk that left her exhausted. The darkness exacerbated her sullen mood, and thumping wipers competed with noise coming off the receiver, making matters worse. Long hours and sleepless nights had caught up with her and she was nearly on empty, in more ways than one. She hadn't eaten since morning and would soon have to find a gas station. None were in sight.

A road sign ahead gave her the miles to the Indiana border, reminding her she'd slipped farther southeast than she had planned. They hadn't discussed crossing state lines into northwest Indiana or heading north into Wisconsin, but that made more sense than driving through rural Illinois or driving into states to the west. Instinct had played a part in her thinking, considering Baker had been murdered in South Chicago and that Globe Harvest might want close proximity to Chicago airports.

Jess glanced at her gas gauge when she saw a road sign for a station ahead. Time for caffeine and a call to Harper. After taking a pit stop and buying a large cup of black coffee, she leaned against the outside of her vehicle to stretch her legs, sipping java and talking to him.

"I've got nothing. With a twenty-five-mile radius, I'm not sure how far to take this."

She gave him her location on I-57 south and they talked about her state line theory. Seth had used his instincts too. He'd driven west until his gut told him to try north, with the same result. Nothing.

"We may have to call it a night, try again tomorrow . . . early," he suggested.

"No. What if they move, take it farther away or destroy the transmitter? I don't think we can risk it. Thanks to you, this is our best shot, Harper." She knew how she sounded. Desperation had leached into her voice and she couldn't control it. Seth must have picked up on it.

"You've got to be tired, Jess," he said. "You've had a rough couple of days."

"I'm okay . . . really." She sighed and took a sip of coffee, ignoring her dull throbbing headache. "I'll call you in a half hour. If I get a signal, I'll call sooner." She recognized wishful thinking when she heard it. "I've got a fresh tank of gas and my java juice. I'm good to go."

After Jess left the gas station heading north, the receiver got a faint hit. She almost missed it, and once the sound registered in her mind, she downplayed it. No sense getting her hopes up until the signal showed real signs of life. When it got stronger, she was certain she'd hit pay dirt. She pounded her steering wheel with a fist, fighting the grin on her face. As soon as it was safe to make a call, she contacted Harper.

"I got a hit, Seth." She gave him her approximate location, but had no idea where the transmission would take her.

"Pull over at a good spot and wait for me."

She knew he was on the other end of Chicago. What if the computer bag was on the move? Should she stop and risk losing it? And once that Globe Harvest computer geek found Harper's tracking software, could the transmitter be far behind? She had a feeling the clock was ticking down on her opportunity to tap into Baker's illegal enterprise.

"I don't think that's a good idea, Seth."

She kicked up the speed of the wiper blades as the rain got worse. The sound made it harder to hear the receiver, but it couldn't be helped. Peering through the windshield, she leaned forward and looked over a dark horizon dappled with a blur of glittering lights. Their colors bled across the glass in streaks. Her heart was racing, pumped full of adrenaline and a fresh jolt of coffee.

"If I have to get off the interstate, I'll call you again and we can talk, but I gotta stick with this. That bag may be on the move. I don't want to lose it."

"Oh, I think you've already lost it. And I'm not talking about the laptop," he said. "Is it raining where you are? I hear rain in the background."

She ignored his question. A discussion about the weather would only make Seth worry more.

"Funny, Harper. You ever thought about taking your act on the road?" She smirked. "Hell, I guess you're doing that right now."

She heard him sigh.

"Come on. I've got a full tank of gas and I'm driving the interstate. What could possibly happen?" She cringed, hearing the jinx come out of her mouth.

"Okay, we'll do it your way. But Jessie, you better stick to this. You call me once you leave the interstate and you stay put until I get there. You got it?"

Even through the rain pummeling her vehicle, she heard the concern in his voice. The worsening weather would only aggravate their situation.

"Yeah, Seth. I've got it. I'll see you soon." She took a deep breath. "And thanks."

Payton Archer wasn't the kind of man Sam had expected. After speaking to Jess and getting her take on him, she pictured of a loudmouthed jock whose favorite topic would be sports and himself—and not in that order. But Payton Archer had nothing on his mind except for his missing niece, a girl he loved without question.

No, Archer was quite different. And that distinction also reflected in his choice of friends. Even if she hadn't learned about Joe Tanu's law enforcement background with the Alaska State Troopers from their introduction, she would have sensed it. Tanu had the eyes of a cop.

Tanu carried a .45-caliber Glock 21 in a holster under his windbreaker and a .380 Walther PPK/S strapped to his ankle, along with a lawful affidavit giving him authorization to carry a concealed weapon in Illinois. The man had been up front about it, showing his authorization before she had to ask for his license. She had no objection. Having a retired state trooper along might prove useful.

After a quick meeting at Archer's Oak Brook hotel suite, the men shared information on Nikki's disappearance and, together, they had come up with a game plan. Their first stop had been O'Hare Airport. Although Archer's niece had already arrived in Chicago, showing her photo to airport personnel might have turned up a clue, and they hit a solid lead when airport security played surveillance video taken outside, at the customer pickup area.

Sam was able to isolate an image of a man and a young woman who had picked up Archer's niece. And although the young woman had not been identified, after Sam e-mailed the digital photo downtown for review, she learned that the man in the video had an extensive arrest record.

None of this bode well for Archer's niece, and by the look on his face, the man knew it.

"So what now?" he asked.

He sat next to Sam in her front passenger seat, looking out his window, watching other airline passengers coming and going from her parked vehicle. She felt the weight of disappointment in his voice. A town as big as Chicago had plenty of places for a felon to hide a young girl.

"I've put out an APB on the guy. And I've got one of our detectives looking for his known hangouts. We'll find him," she replied as she pulled away from her parking space. "For now, we need more to go on."

Although she was confident they'd eventually find the bastard, she had no idea when. And her gut told her something else—the longer the clock ticked on Nikki's time with the man in the video, the worse her situation would become.

From the backseat, Joe Tanu made a suggestion.

"The Alaska State Troopers are analyzing Nikki's online chats. They faxed prelim comments to our hotel earlier today and there were local Chicago references made. Maybe you can help us decipher the significance."

"Good idea." Sam merged with traffic heading out of the airport, hitting her wipers to clear the rain from her windshield. "You have them with you?"

"Yes, I do."

"Great. Then let's head downtown. Maybe we can—" The sound of an incoming call on her cell phone interrupted her.

Keeping an eye on the road, she pulled the phone from her belt and looked at the number displayed, not recognizing it. With all the strange things happening with Jessie, she decided to take the call.

"Excuse me. I should take this." She held the phone to her ear. "Yeah, Cooper here."

"Sam, it's me. Seth Harper." It took her a moment to register the name, but before she could respond, the guy got down to business. "Jess is tracking Baker's missing laptop and I don't have a good feeling about this. I think we're gonna need your help."

"What? Slow down, Harper. I think you'd better explain."

Seth told her what had happened. At first Sam got angry at Jess for bending her "no secrets" agreement, but after she filtered her irritation through her friend's warped version of logic, she realized Jess probably didn't feel that she'd strayed from the concept. Thank God Seth had taken the initiative to call her, but even that was part of Jess's plan, so again she couldn't fault her friend.

"Give me her last location, Seth." After he did, she said, "I'm heading there now, but don't you make matters worse. Both of you sit tight until I get there. Tell her I may have to bring Detective Garza into this. She's given me no choice. Jess will know what I'm talking about."

After hanging up, she tried Jess's cell. It displayed an out-of-service message. The weather probably didn't help. She wasn't sure it was any cause for alarm, but something in her gut told her Jess was onto something big. A cop's instinct.

Payton Archer turned toward her, waiting to hear what had happened, though he had no idea that the laptop Jess was tracking might break a murder investigation—a case that could be linked to Nikki.

If Jessie had been right about that e-mail on Baker's computer, Nikki Archer might have been the delivery from Anchorage. The coincidence was significant enough to make Sam a believer—enough to volunteer for the chief's assignment with Archer and Tanu in the first place.

She knew she had to find Jess, and she had no time to

take Archer and Tanu back to their hotel. A part of her wanted to give these men hope. They had a right to know what was going on.

"Change of plans, gentlemen." Merging into heavier traffic, she hit the gas pedal, heading south. "And I've got a lot of explaining to do on the way."

"Stas. We need you in the control room. Now."

The urgent voice of Ethan O'Connell came over the intercom in Petrovin's private quarters. The Russian reached to press the button to respond, heat rising to his cheeks.

"I will come . . . five minutes," he panted.

Naked, he lay spread-eagle on his bed, gazing at the frightened young girl ministering to his need. She crouched between his legs, her soft pale body completely exposed to his ways. Her head bobbed up and down, her lips warm and moist. For an instant after he'd gotten O'Connell's message, the girl had looked up with tears glistening in her eyes, still holding him in her mouth. Perhaps she had hoped he'd ask her to stop, saying he had to leave.

That never happened.

"Five minutes . . . plenty of time." He reached for the whimpering girl, gripping tufts of her hair in both hands. She would need his help to finish.

By the time Petrovin got to the control room, O'Connell did not look pleased with his delay.

"You said you'd come in five minutes."

"Yes, I am a man of my word." The Russian smiled. "What is so urgent, Ethan?"

"Baker's laptop. One of my men inspected it and found it had been tampered with. Keystroke-tracking software had been installed, the kind identity thieves use. That bounty hunter must have done it."

Before he had a chance to explain more, Petrovin asked, "Did your man access sensitive areas that could be detected with such software? Are we exposed?"

"No, thank God."

The Russian almost laughed aloud at O'Connell's reference to a higher power. With the storm outside, perhaps lightning would strike the man.

"You better hope there is no God, Ethan. For your sake . . . and mine." He smirked. "I do not understand your urgency. Simply destroy the computer and be done with it. Very soon, this bounty hunter will no longer be a problem."

"Not soon enough, I'm afraid." O'Connell waved him over to the computer in question, lying on top of a desk. "Doing a thorough job, my analyst also found this."

When O'Connell tore back an inside corner of the computer bag, Petrovin knew why the man had been concerned. The Russian recognized a transmitter when he saw it. Anger flushed through his system like a deadly toxin. If Lucas Baker were not already dead, he would do the honors again in a much more painful way. But since this would not be possible, he focused his anger where he could.

The bounty hunter had planted the transmitter, placing his entire organization at risk. And worse, the life he had cultivated in this country would come to an abrupt end at the order of his superior if this debacle compromised Bukulov's grand design. Failure was not acceptable.

He clenched his jaw, seething with anger.

"I haven't destroyed the transmitter yet, but I'm using a frequency counter to block it." O'Connell said. "At a minimum, we need to get the word out to our key people. We're in lock-down mode until further notice."

"Yes, I agree. Do it now. But on my order, be prepared to evacuate. We can't take chances. You know what to do."

When Petrovin reached for the computer bag, O'Connell asked, "What are you doing with that?"

"Perhaps with the right bait, I learn to fish, no?"

With the computer bag in hand, Petrovin headed for the control room door. If the bounty hunter came looking for the computer, he would make sure she found it—and more.

"I need five of your best men. Now. Have them meet me . . . the weapons room."

At the exit, the Russian looked over his shoulder at O'Connell.

"Tell your men . . . we are hunting."

CHAPTER 15

Lightning split the night sky in frenzy. And with every crack of thunder, Jess tensed with her heart in her throat. Rain pelted her windshield, hard. She'd been tempted to pull under an overpass to wait the storm out, but that felt like a waste of time. With visibility poor, she had to lower her speed to a crawl.

She drove until the signal became faint. She turned around at an overpass and headed south again, but before too many miles realized it was time to divert off the interstate and head east. Rather than arbitrarily picking a route, she decided to drive the frontage road that paralleled I-57 to see where the signal was strongest. Soon it became clear that a farm road heading east, a route meant for local traffic, was the most promising. And she couldn't see any lights in that direction, not even a farmhouse. Had they lost power in the area?

"Damn it."

Any other time, she might have followed the road without hesitating, but she'd made a promise to Seth . . . and to Sam. She pulled into an abandoned gas station situated next to the turn off, with the interstate clearly in sight. Harper would see her headlights from the highway if he knew where to look. And the station's overhang gave her a break from the steady rain. A good spot to wait. She took a deep breath, thankful for the relief.

"Okay, Seth. Let's find out where you are."

She tried his cell phone. With the bad weather, service was marginal. After a couple of tries she got his voice mail and left a message. In a few minutes she tried again and got through. When he answered, she didn't bother with formalities.

"Hey, it's me."

"Where are you?"

She gave him her location, using exit numbers and estimated mileage. Although the old gas station wasn't much, it made for a decent landmark.

"I'll keep my car running and the headlights on. As you're heading south, I'll be on the frontage road to your left, the east side of the road. This place looks like one of those old funky gas stations from the fifties."

"Looking at the mile markers, I'm only a few minutes away. That's great."

"Can you read the signal, Seth? You should pick it up, right?"

"Yeah, I've got it. You did good, Jessie." He sounded relieved. "Stay put. I'm almost there."

She ended the call, but had to admit it felt wonderful to hear his voice, and knowing he was minutes away felt good too. She kept her eyes on the interstate, looking for that damned blue van. The rain blurred everything, but she kept watch anyway. When he got there, she'd get them both suited up in Kevlar. No sense taking any risk. She had a couple of vests in the trunk.

But when the transmitter signal suddenly got stronger—out of the blue—it caught her by surprise. She shifted in her seat, focusing all her attention on the tracking gear.

"What the hell?"

Now the signal was steady and clear. If she didn't know

any better, she could swear she was right on top of the thing. Seth said that once they found the location, they'd know it, without a doubt.

But this? She was in the middle of nowhere. It made no sense.

"What's happening?" Her hands groped the control panel in the dim light off her dashboard.

But a sharp tap on glass jolted her heart.

"Shit!"

She turned and the glare of a flashlight blinded her. She shielded her eyes. What was Harper doing? How did he . . . ? It dawned on her too late. No way Seth could have gotten there so fast. A motion across the headlights caught her eye. And to her right, another flashlight invaded the darkness. A group of men surrounded her car. She couldn't see how many.

They were dressed in black like a paramilitary unit, and their faces were covered. But one man approached from the shadows near her front door. In his hand he held something she recognized.

The black computer bag.

"Oh . . . my . . . God." It was all she had time to say.

Jess reached for her Colt Python, but the man with the bag beat her to the punch. She stared down the barrel of his weapon, knowing she couldn't beat the odds. For a heartbeat, she left her hand on the butt of her gun, but soon raised her hands. She swallowed, unsure she could even breathe. The man gestured for her to open the door.

Slowly, she looked down. Yes, her door was locked, but it went against all her survival instincts to give in. How could she help them? When the man decided she wasn't moving fast enough, he took matters in his hands. He shouted an order.

Crack! The passenger window exploded.

Glass shattered across her face and hands. She felt the sting of cuts. In defense, Jess wrapped her arms over her head. From both sides her car doors flew open. They'd unlocked the doors. Hands groped her body, tugging at her. The men yanked her from the car, kicking and screaming. Like a pack of animals, they came at her, punishing her for resisting. They dragged her into the cold rain. And a fierce chill took over, making her teeth chatter out of control.

One of the men shoved her against a hard surface, an edge cutting across her back.

"Arrgghh."

A sliver of hope. That's all she had. If she held out long enough, Harper would see what was happening and call for help.

"Who are you?" She tried stalling. "What do you want? There's been a mistake."

The men circled her now. No one answered her questions. Their shadows eclipsed the light from her headlights. One man looked to be the leader. The tall one with long hair. When he stepped closer, she thought he might speak, but instead he reached out and gripped her by the throat with one hand, the move quick. With brutal force, he pressed hard and shoved her against a wall, smacking the back of her head. She nearly lost consciousness. Blood slithered down her neck.

She felt her body lift. Her feet no longer touched the ground. She couldn't breathe. Struggling for air, she clawed at his arms—punching and kicking him—but the others held her down. Stars burst like fireworks behind her eyes. And the blackness came. He was going to kill her . . . right here . . . right now.

And there was nothing she could do about it.

CHAPTER 16

The rain had finally tapered off, and Seth took the change to be a good sign. He dialed back his wiper blades to stop the annoying sound they made on high speed. Finding Jess had become his top priority, so when he noticed a change in the transmitter signal, the notion barely registered; he dismissed it.

Maybe the rain and the dark made him worry more than he should, but Jess had a way of attracting danger. Even in the short time he'd known her, he could tell that she lived on the edge. And something drove her from deep inside—something she held close.

Lucas Baker had been different from the other scumbags she hunted for bounty money, but there had been no time to talk about it, assuming she'd open up to him at all. He'd never met anyone like her.

A road sign caught his attention. This was it. According to Jess, at the next exit he would follow the frontage road to the overpass and hit the turnaround to catch her on the other side. She'd also told him her headlights would be on and he could spot her from the interstate.

Seth peered through the rain, finding the old gas station,

as she'd described it. And he grinned when he saw her car with headlights blazing. But his smile quickly faded. In the dim light, off to the right, a group of men huddled—some kind of fight.

"Damn it!" He hit the accelerator, gripping the wheel with both hands.

His eyes searched the dark for the exit, then went back at the old gas station. He'd never make it in time. Jess needed him now. There was only one thing for him to do. He veered to the left lane, looking for a spot to cross. When he hit the median, his van almost bottomed out. He didn't have time to search for level ground. And with the excessive rain, his tires hit mud and spun. A high whine mixed with the sound of heavy splatter.

"Shit! Not now!" he yelled. "Not now!"

Finally, the van lurched forward, nearly jostling him out of his seat. When he got to solid road, he reached for the cell phone clipped to his belt and hit redial.

"Come on . . . come on." He prayed Sam would pick up. She couldn't be far behind, not after he'd called to tell her where Jess would be. When she answered, he blurted out, "Jessie's in trouble. Those men—they have her."

"What's happening, Seth? Talk to me." Sam heard his panic and it gripped her heart in a tight fist. In reflex, she gunned the gas pedal and barreled down the interstate, looking for the exit. "Seth? Can you hear me?"

She heard road noise over the phone and Seth cursing in the background, but he sounded far away. After what seemed an eternity, he got back on the phone.

"They took her car. She's gone, Sam."

Now she heard fear in his voice.

"Who took her, Seth? What's going on?" she asked. Archer leaned toward her, concern on his face.

She punched the accelerator as she spotted her exit ahead.

"I'm almost there, Seth. Hang on."

But he didn't hear her. "Sam, I'm keeping my cell phone open, but I gotta drive. And I can't do it in the dark."

"What are you talking about?" she asked.

"I know where they went. I followed their taillights, but now I gotta drive without my lights so they won't see me. And I'm already too far behind, I may lose them. They've taken a farm road east, the one near the gas station. You'll know it when you see it. And I'm driving a blue van, but Sam? In case something happens to me, track my phone. I'll leave the line open."

Seth's meaning was clear . . . and ominous. Now all she could do was listen to him drive, but she had to keep the connection open. The gas station was ahead to the right.

Turning to Archer, she said, "Please . . . make a call to Detective Garza. He should be on his way."

She gave him the number, hitting the turn onto the farm road and gunning the engine. But unlike Seth, she kept her headlights on, trying to make up time. Archer made the call using his personal phone and handed it to her. When Garza got on the line, Sam filled him in.

"Jess is in trouble."

"Wow, something new. I'll alert the media."

"I don't need your sarcasm, Ray. Seth Harper is following the men who've taken her. Have someone trace the GPS on Harper's phone, we may need it." She gave him the phone number for Seth's open line. "I'm on the farm road by the gas station. Heading east. Find me."

Sam ended the call and handed the phone back to Archer.

"Sorry I got you both into this." She wasn't sure what else to say to Archer and Tanu. If anything happened, she'd get them to safety first, but she'd cross that bridge when the time came.

Archer fixed his gaze on her, his profile silhouetted by the dim lights off her dash.

"If these men have Nikki, then this is my fight too," he

said. "Don't apologize. I just hope your friend is okay. She sounds like a gutsy woman."

Sam kept watch for Seth's blue van, but she couldn't get her mind off Jessie.

"You have no idea."

Jess opened her eyes, her head spinning and in pain. Everything blurred around her, fading to blackness then in bright focus again. Bile rose from her stomach. She heaved but nothing came. And behind her eyes, pinpricks of light spiraled out of control, making it difficult to see anything at all. From experience, she suspected she had suffered a concussion, judging by her symptoms.

And the cold, her body ached from it. She gasped for air, her throat bruised inside and out.

"What . . . ?" She tried to speak but only a raspy whisper escaped her lips.

When her eyes cleared enough for her to trust what they saw, she found a harsh light hanging overhead with nothing but darkness around her. She sat propped against a wall, her wrists cuffed above her head. And they had stripped her and taken her clothes. She surged into a sudden and uncontrollable panic, tugging at the handcuffs until her wrists nearly broke, screaming as loud as she could. Primal fear for survival had taken over.

"*Aaarrgghhh* . . . noooo!" She felt the warm trickle of blood down her arms. Her hands and wrists were already numb.

Her body reacted in frenzy and she couldn't stop it. A flood of desperate memories clouded her mind, yanking her back to a time she only wanted to forget. No longer a grown woman, she was forced to suffer the unimaginable torment of her childhood once again. And the jagged scars across her body—faded with time yet fresh in her mind—were plain for anyone to see. Over the years, she had grown to hate seeing them in the mirror, but here she was completely exposed.

She would have no secrets from her captors. *None!*

"Imagine my surprise . . ." A man's voice came from the dark. "Such a beautiful woman . . . yet so scarred."

She stopped her struggle and listened, her heart pounding and her chest heaving.

It took her a while to place the accent. Distinctly Russian, once she calmed down enough to reflect on it. She shifted her head right, then left, trying to catch a glimpse of the man. His footsteps echoed in the large room. And she followed the sound with her eyes, her lips trembling.

"You are a woman with secrets, yes?"

Finally, the Russian walked into the light, and she recognized his shoulder length hair. He was one of the men who had abducted her, the one who almost killed her. She swallowed, nearly choking on her next breath.

"Perhaps we share more than you know," he whispered.

He kicked her legs apart and knelt between them. Slowly, he ran his hands up her thighs, not taking his eyes off her. The man looked like a coiled rattler ready to strike, and she couldn't turn away. She tightened her jaw, grappling with fear.

"You wanted to know more about what goes on here. Now you will find out for yourself."

He yanked at her knees and pulled her hips toward him, taking away her leverage to fight back. His body reacted to her nakedness. She felt it. He ran his hands over her breasts and squeezed until she cried out. Now, pinning her to the floor with his weight, he lowered his mouth to her nipple, taking it in his lips. She waited for the pain of his bite, but it never came—*only the degradation.* When he pulled back, he had a sick, twisted smile on his face.

"I get what I want . . . no matter. You tell me what I want to know and you decide. Pain or not?" He rose and leaned on an elbow, glaring at her. "Who is Seth Harper? He is not an easy man to locate, but with or without your help, I will find him."

"Then you don't need my help."

Judging by the look in the Russian's eyes, her feeble defiance struck a nerve. The man took a knife from a sheath on his belt. The blade glinted under the light. He traced the craggy scar along her eyebrow and ran the tip of his blade across her lip, cutting her. She winced.

"A pity that I will not be your first."

She knew exactly what he meant. The man had the mark of a longtime abuser. She watched for the trigger, the instant the Russian would lose control and take what he wanted. She'd seen it before, too many times. The man stared at her now, perhaps reading her mind and torturing her with his restraint.

"You are . . . nothing," he whispered, his face twisted with abuse. She felt his breath on her skin. "This . . . I think you know. I see it in . . . those eyes."

The Russian dragged the blade under her right eye, and she held her breath. He was in complete control and she knew it. He had reminded her how weak she had always been. And no matter who she'd become, she knew a part of her would always be powerless. She had her trigger too, the point where she would give in to whatever happened. The Russian had seen it for himself. He lowered his mouth to her body and she shut her eyes, blocking everything out.

It was happening again and she'd never be free. When his hands groped her body, she fought back tears welling in her eyes. She gritted her teeth and detached herself from what was about to happen.

But a voice bellowed from the dark.

"I've got something you need to see. This won't wait." Another man called out from the back of the room, his voice in panic.

Jess couldn't have been more grateful. Tears drained down her cheeks in relief, but to her shock, the Russian didn't stop. If anything, he grew more determined. She heard the sound of his belt buckle and felt the urgency in his body. She struggled under him, bucking under his weight. She resisted the only way she could.

"Stas, we don't have time for this," the man shouted. She heard his footsteps come closer. "Put her with the others. I need you. Now."

The Russian abruptly stopped—out of breath and seething with anger—the crazed look still in his eyes. In a move she didn't see coming, he slashed across her chest with the knife.

"Aarrgh," she cried, pulling her knees in tight.

The cut wasn't deep, but he had left his mark. Blood seeped from the wound and rolled off her body. Cold chills raced across her skin.

"We are not done. You will see." He rose from the floor and stood over her, pointing his knife. "And next time, you will wish we had finished here."

After the Russian left, two men freed her hands and wrapped a blanket around her shoulders, but not out of compassion. They hauled her down a long dim hallway, past a door that got her attention.

Two uniformed men stood in the doorway, taking orders from the Russian, who glared at her as she passed. Across the room another man was talking on the phone. Although she only got a quick glimpse of him, she recognized his voice. He was the one who stopped the Russian from raping her. She didn't get a good look, but the dimly lit room was filled with computers and high-tech control panels. A silent red flashing alarm spiraled its light through the room. The setup struck her as strange, but she was in too much pain to focus.

Down the hall, her captors tossed her into a dark room. When she fell, she scraped her knees and elbows, her body wracked with pain. Something else had been thrown on top of her, but she hurt too much to check it out. For a moment she lay where she'd fallen, curled into the blanket as best she could. But a sound from across the room forced her to listen.

A whisper. Very faint.

"Are you okay?" The whisper came again, stronger this time.

Jess rolled toward the noise and peered through the murky darkness, her only light coming from under the doorway. In the corner of the room, along the far wall, a shadow moved and then another. Others were with her. She wasn't alone.

"Who are you?" She kept her voice low. "What's happening?"

One of the shadows moved again and crawled toward her. A young girl. When she got closer, the girl spoke quietly.

"These aren't much, but you should put them on. It's cold in here." The girl picked up what the men had tossed onto the floor beside her, nothing more than cotton drawstring pants and a shirt. "There's more of us here, but the others are too scared to say anything."

"How many others are here?" Jess asked as she dressed. Each move made her wince, but the girl helped her put the loose garments on.

"There's only five in this room, including you, but I have no idea if there's more. I haven't been here that long."

"Wait a minute. What's your name?" Jess asked.

"My name's Nikki. Nikki Archer. Who are you?"

Jess wanted to cry, but her tears at having found Archer's niece were tinged with the hopelessness of their situation.

"I'm Jessie Beckett." She stroked the girl's hair with both hands. "Nikki, your uncle came to Chicago looking for you."

"What? Uncle Payton?"

Before she could explain, the girl collapsed into her arms and let go. Without the fear of someone hearing her, she sobbed uncontrollably, her body trembling. Jess knew exactly how she felt. Long ago, she had experienced the overwhelming relief when she knew her physical torment had finally ended.

But unlike what happened with her, no one was here to rescue Nikki—no one that mattered anyway.

CHAPTER 17

Coming over a small rise past a set of railroad tracks, Sam hit the brakes and slowed to a crawl. Seth Harper stood in the middle of the road flagging her down with a flashlight in his hand and looking soaked in the drizzle. Up ahead, lights from a small town shined on the horizon, but she couldn't tell how far it was. She pulled behind Seth's blue van, along the graveled shoulder of the road, and turned to her passengers.

"I need you both to do as I say." She knew Tanu had the discipline of a cop, but Archer was another story. "Do I have your word, Mr. Archer?"

It took him too long to answer.

"Look, I'm not sure what we're going to find, but I can't afford to have you fuck up this search trying to be a cowboy. You could not only jeopardize the rescue of your niece, but other people's lives could be at risk. Now I want your word that you'll do as I say, without question."

"Yeah . . . sorry." He nodded, looking her square in the eye. "You've got my word."

She could see that it took restraint on his part not to say another word; the internal struggle showed on his face. She couldn't imagine his frustration, but maybe tonight, he'd find peace.

To make her vehicle more visible, Sam left her hazard lights blinking for Detective Garza. They cast a yellow light onto scrub brush and mud puddles and gave them limited visibility, without drawing a lot of attention. Sam got out of the car, with Archer and Tanu following her. After quick introductions, Harper filled them in.

"I lost the signal, but I'm pretty sure I saw them turn off here." He pointed across the road to what looked like private property. A recessed gate with an old abandoned guard station. Goodville Textiles. A rusted sign was posted on the fence.

"And see here? With the rain, their tires left fresh tracks." He pulled at her elbow and shined his flashlight to the ground. "We can't be that far behind. We gotta find her before . . ." He didn't finish. He shrugged and turned away.

As a friend, Sam wanted to crash the gate and drive onto the property looking for Jessie. But as a cop, she had to think about the law. She had enough reason to believe Jess was in danger. And even though Harper hadn't actually seen the men drive onto the premises, he'd trailed them to the property and was reasonably certain they were inside, plus the fresh tracks made his statement more credible. She had a witness to give her probable cause to search the premises without a warrant, but had to make sure.

"How certain are you that she's here, Seth?" she prompted, but before he answered, she clarified her point. "For me to have probable cause to search the premises, I need a solid witness, or else I'd have to get a search warrant. And that would take time."

She squeezed his arm and held his gaze until he knew what she was saying.

"Then yeah, she's in there. I saw everything." He nodded. "Definitely."

"Good man." She smiled. "And thanks, Seth."

Her backup, Detective Garza, had her location and was on his way, but she had to make a decision now. She stared through the gate to the deserted textile plant. At a minimum, she needed more intel.

Having made up her mind, Sam pulled Harper aside again.

"Seth, I need you to stay here and flag down Detective Ray Garza. He should be right behind me, but I can't wait for him to get here." She wrote down the detective's cell phone number on a piece of paper. "Here's his cell just in case. When he gets here, let him know I'm on the property, but I won't be alone."

She turned to Joe Tanu and Payton Archer, who stood within earshot.

"Officially, I can't ask you to join me, Joe, but I could use your help." She knew it would be a waste of time to argue with Tanu about coming along, however his sidekick was a civilian. "But Archer stays here."

The retired trooper stared at her, an unreadable expression on his face. She hadn't expected such a calm reaction. When he finally opened his mouth, he had her attention.

"Look, Payton and his sister are like family. If there's a chance Nikki is being held by these people, I'm with you and I'll follow your lead." Tanu looked at Archer. "But Payton won't sit on the sidelines, not with so much at stake. I know him."

When Sam shifted her gaze to Archer, the man shrugged and said, "I never liked sitting on the bench. What can I say?"

Tanu retrieved the Walther PPK/S from his ankle holster and handed it to Archer, who confirmed he had a full magazine and racked the slide checking for brass, safety off.

"If it makes a difference, he's a crack shot," the retired trooper said. "I taught him how to shoot. And I'll take full responsibility. The way I figure it, we could use all the help we can get."

Tanu had a point, but she felt the need to make a point of her own and fixed her eyes on Payton.

"If you make me regret this, Archer, I'll shoot you myself."

The man shot her a sideways glance and shared one of his dimples. "Thanks for the vote of confidence."

"Anytime." Sam peered through the fence across the road and took a deep breath, feeling the rush of adrenaline. "Call me a gear freak, but I've got Kevlar in my trunk. Once we get suited up, we're going in."

"I like a woman with a sense of style." Archer forced a grin, the tension showing through.

"Yeah, you should see my Christmas catalogs."

As soon as they were decked in Kevlar vests and she had her badge visible, Sam breached the fence and crossed the massive parking lot, heading for the old abandoned textile factory with Tanu and Archer. Steady drizzle had drenched her clothes and given her a chill, despite the body armor. And with storm clouds blocking the moonlight, her eyesight gave her fits, making the shadows of the old building seem menacing. She had a flashlight, but didn't want to screw up her night vision or make herself a target. She'd save it for when she actually needed it.

In her head, she said a quick prayer that no one would die, hoping God was listening. In her line of work, she'd begun to think that wasn't always the case.

Hidden security cameras strategically placed on the Goodville Textiles premises had picked up the intruders outside the gate. Another vehicle had joined the blue van, and if cops were involved, Ethan knew more would follow. He'd never pulled the plug on a facility like this before, but now they had little choice.

That's why he'd risked pissing off the Russian, insisting that he forget about the bounty hunter and keep his cock in his pants. Petrovin had the authority and the guts to make the final call. The bastard thrived on power and all that came with it; egotistical bullshit, as far as he was concerned. He knew when he had a losing hand and when to bail, and it had nothing to do with duty.

Ethan also knew there would be fallout over the incident. There always was. But he didn't want to get caught in the middle. There would be no brownie points in knowing when to flush the operation—only repercussions—and he preferred not to be linked to the final decision, no matter how necessary. That's why soldiers like Petrovin made convenient scapegoats, but Ethan was smarter than that.

"We can't risk it, Stas. We have to shut it down . . . now." He urged the Russian to do what must be done. "We can't afford for anyone to find the control room. The rest of the organization would be at stake. Shutting down this facility is bad, but we can still operate elsewhere."

When the Russian didn't respond, he pressed. "It won't take long for them to make it to the building. We gotta go."

Petrovin clenched his jaw, glaring at the security monitors in the control room. The silent red flashing light cast a strange pallor on his face. There were times Ethan was perfectly content to be in ignorant bliss where the Russian was concerned, but not today.

"What are you thinking, Stas?" he asked. "I'm not gonna like this, am I?"

"Make sure they find their way through the garage. Unlock the doors." Petrovin smirked.

"Are you crazy? We can't mess with them now," he urged, pleading his case.

"Don't worry. We will stick to our plan. I am only . . . adapting it."

The control room had been rigged with thermite incendiary devices, primed with other pyrotechnic additives like barium nitrate to enhance their effect and make ignition more reliable. The enhanced thermite had been Petrovin's choice. The chemical mixture burned with an intense white heat, and since it contained its own oxygen supply, it could not be smothered or extinguished by conventional means.

The incendiary devices had been placed strategically through the control room, atop critical equipment to destroy the bank of computers, their hard drives, and any reports left behind. The rest of the makeshift facility didn't matter, but the Russian had C-4 relayed to collapse the dilapidated structure onto anyone who dared to infiltrate the building.

After the thermite detonation was initiated, the rest would be discharged from a safe distance through a series of shaped charges.

A solenoid switch would open the valves of underground propane tanks by relay, releasing heavy propane fumes into the air of the tunnels—the sole purpose for the supply of propane. And after the buildup of gas, a charge near the propane tanks would initiate a white-hot fireball at the core of the building with more C-4 to hit structural supports. The blast would set off a chain reaction through the underground corridors with enough magnitude to drop a structure five times its size.

But that wasn't enough for Petrovin. The Russian wanted to make sure his death trap would take out any cop who crossed his threshold. Someone would pay, and Petrovin would make sure of it.

"Sound the evacuation alarm for the men," he ordered. "The noise will mask the sound of us leaving."

"What about the girls?"

With dead eyes, the Russian smiled and said, "Do not worry about them. I have taken care of everything. I will meet you as agreed."

Giving authority to an egotistical crazy man had its drawbacks.

Ethan had no more time to argue. He hit the evacuation alarm and ran out the door, leaving the Russian behind. When he blew past the room where the girls were held, he tried not to think about them. He'd given up the right to a conscience long ago.

And having a sense of morality was a luxury he couldn't afford.

"What's that sound?" Sam stopped to listen outside a delivery door near the loading bay. "Do you hear that?"

"An alarm," Joe said. "Sounds like it's belowground."

"If we had any doubts about someone being inside, those are all shot to hell. We gotta get in there—now." Payton reached for the door, thinking only of Nikki, but Joe grabbed his arm and stopped him.

"Sam and I will take point. Follow our lead, no question, remember?" Tanu's voice was stern, tempered with the concern of a friend. "If Nikki is here, we'll find her—bring her home."

Home. Payton liked the sound of that word. And the faces of Nikki and Susannah filled his mind, giving him a strange comfort when he needed it. This time when the detective tried the knob, it turned and the door opened. Finding an easy way in had been a stroke of good luck. He followed Joe and the detective into the building, hoping Nikki's ordeal would soon be over.

And as he crossed the threshold with gun in hand, Payton found himself praying, something he hadn't done in a very long time.

CHAPTER 18

"What's that siren?" Jess reached for Nikki and pulled her close. "What's happening?"

"I don't know." The girl gripped her hand. "Jessie, I'm scared."

Beyond the door, an alarm blared through the corridor and a flash of red beat like a pulse under the door, eclipsing the light. Voices were garbled by the sound, and boots scuffed along the cement floor outside their door. Jess didn't mistake it for a good sign. Even if Harper had come through, it didn't leave them in the clear.

"No matter what happens, you stick with me. You understand?" She squeezed the girl's hand. "You and me. We're gonna get through this. I'm getting you out of here, I promise."

The girl burrowed her head into Jess's shoulder and put her arms around her waist.

"I've been so stupid. I can't believe—"

Jess stopped her. "This isn't your fault. These people know how to manipulate and lie. And they prey on kids like you. You did nothing wrong."

Before she had a chance to comfort the girl, a key slid

into the lock and the door swung open. Noise and bright lights flooded the darkness, blinding them. Jess held onto Nikki and cowered in the shadows, but two men carrying weapons swept into the room, yanking the other girls off the floor.

"Get up. Move. Now!" they shouted.

When they came for her and Nikki, she asked the men, "Where are you taking us?"

"Shut up and get moving." One of the cowards grabbed a handful of her hair and pulled, forcing her to stand. Nikki had gotten in line behind the others, but kept turning back, making sure Jess wasn't far behind.

Out the door, they headed right single file. Nikki walked ahead of her, leaving one man on the tail end. Jess had no idea of the layout but caught a glimpse of darker tunnels ahead. All the activity and alarms were behind them. They were heading deeper into a maze, and the air smelled toxic, like gas fumes.

Instinct told her to run. She forced herself to breathe shallow, waiting for her moment. In the confusion and the noise, she and Nikki might break free without being noticed.

When the lead man turned a corner, Jess lost sight of him and the first two girls. Something inside her clicked and she reacted. Biting back pain, she spun and punched the man behind her, catching him off guard. Knocked off balance, he fell against the wall, leaving her to grapple for his gun, but the man held firm.

"You bitch," he grunted.

"Nikki, run! Back the way we came," she panted, struggling for leverage.

The girl moved but didn't take off.

Jess pinned the man's arm against the wall and slugged him in the gut, rapid blows that staggered him. When he bent over, she rammed a knee to his face. In a stupor, the bastard let go of the gun and fell back, his head whacking the cement floor. Even with all the noise, Jess heard the ugly thud. He stayed down for the count. She picked up the gun and caught up with Nikki.

"Come on." She ran back the way they'd come. "How do we get out of here?"

Tears welled in Nikki's eyes. Jess could see that she was losing it, but Nikki pointed straight ahead. "Turn left here . . . I think."

The blaring alarm grated on Jess's frayed nerves, exacerbated by the flashing lights that washed bloodred on the walls. And the gas fumes had become more noticeable, making her nauseous. By the smell, the whole place would soon be a ticking time bomb. Anything could set it off. With a tight grip on the weapon, Jess raced down the passageway as if she knew where to go, clutching the girl's hand. They couldn't afford any mistakes.

And for Nikki's sake, she hoped her luck had changed.

Once inside the loading bay door, Payton followed Joe and the detective into what looked like a small underground parking structure with another secured door to the left. A handful of cars were parked inside. Sam confirmed that the one with the busted-out windows was Jessie's. It proved that something was terribly wrong and her friend was in danger.

They quickly swept the outer chamber and the car interiors, making sure no one waited in the dark to ambush them. Assured that everything was clear, they focused on the only entry left.

Payton took his position on the hinged side of the door. Standing with his back to the wall, he reached over and turned the knob before opening it. It wasn't locked. He shot a concerned look at Joe, who seemed to read his mind. So did Sam. An alarm had blared before they'd opened the outside door. Now a second door was unlocked. Something didn't feel right.

It was too easy.

Joe used the detective's flashlight to check the door for booby traps, then repeated the process with the door ajar. After he gave the all clear sign and Sam had given her thumbs-up Payton swung the door open. Joe and the detective swiftly moved into the room, an efficient team. In a practiced maneuver, they crept through in a bent-legged shuffle, shifting their weapons from corner to corner. Payton followed close behind, taking their lead. But once they got inside, the interior fanned into a maze filled with spiraling red lights, a much bigger underground vault than he had expected.

Before Joe or the detective said it, Payton shook his head in frustration.

"Damn it! Which way do we go?"

Up ahead a door stood wide open. Jessie stopped dead still and pulled Nikki to one side, positioning the girl against the wall behind her. She didn't want any surprises. The men might have evacuated the area, but she couldn't risk getting them caught so close to finding a way out. After sending a silent signal for Nikki to stay put, Jess crept toward the door, gun in hand.

With the alarm sounding, she couldn't hear anything coming from the room. Inching closer, she edged a look across the door frame, peering inside. A sudden motion caused her to flinch. She ducked and pressed her back against the wall. Nikki cowered behind her, wide-eyed and close to panic. After replaying what she'd seen, Jess got the courage to try again. She rushed the doorway with her weapon leveled in a two-fisted grip, shifting the gun hard left, then right. After a better look, she relaxed and stepped farther into the chamber.

It looked like a main control room, the one where she'd seen the Russian and the other man in heated debate, with a bank of computers and monitors along the far wall. She would have kept moving down the corridor, but caught action on the monitors that forced her to stop.

"On my God," she whispered.

Sam had two men with her and all of them were armed. She recognized her friend easily, but the men's faces were not clear. Surveillance cameras had locked onto their movement. And wherever they were, they moved cautiously, expecting trouble.

"Where the hell are you, Sam?"

Nikki came into the room and stood by her side.

"I remember that place," she said. "It's by the loading docks. They brought me through that security door . . . my first day." The girl pointed to the monitor, but her mouth dropped when she recognized a familiar face. Fresh tears slid down her cheeks and her lower lip trembled. "Uncle Payton . . . look, he's here. Oh my God, he's really here."

With Nikki's revelation, a rush of hope flooded through Jess. The girl laughed nervously at the sight of her uncle, unable to contain her emotion—touching humor mixed with tears.

"Do you think you know where they are?" Jess asked.

"Yeah, turn left out the door. Follow the corridor straight, I think."

Not wanting to squelch Nikki's moment of relief, Jess left her in front of the security monitor, watching her uncle. Then she noticed something of interest across the room, tucked near one of the hard drives—a trash can filled with discarded paper. She reached in and pulled out what looked important and official.

"What do we have here?" she whispered. She stuffed what she could into the waistband of her pants under her shirt, and when she looked up, her heart nearly stopped.

Positioned above each computer hard drive was some type of incendiary device, wired to explode. She didn't know much about explosives, except that deactivating one by snipping a wire often set the bomb off. That popped into her mind a moment before she noticed the smell from the rear passageway. Gas fumes. If they were building, a detonation in the control room could trigger a massive blast throughout the whole facility. And where there was one bomb, there might be others.

"Damn it," she muttered under her breath.

They had to get out now! And Sam, Archer, and the other man were in danger too. They didn't have a clue they were walking into a powder keg.

"We gotta find them, Nikki," she said, keeping her voice calm and steady as she stared at the bombs. When the girl didn't respond, she raised her voice to be heard over the blaring alarm, "What do you say, Nikki? Let's go find your—"

Jess stopped dead still. She raised her weapon and swallowed, trying to still her heart. The Russian held Nikki clutched to his chest, a gun to her head. In the murky light, it took her a moment to realize the girl wasn't dead. She was breathing, but unconscious.

Jess clutched her gun tighter, hoping her shakes didn't show. No way she could attempt a head shot, not under these conditions. And the Russian blocked the way out, threatening to kill Nikki. A hellish nightmare, the man wielded his sinister glare like a weapon.

"You leave without saying good-bye, bounty hunter?" He slowly shook his head. "Not on my watch." His voice made her skin crawl.

"You rigged this room to blow," she reasoned. "You really think you have time to mess with me? If this place goes up, you're going with it."

The man had the nerve to laugh. The sound of it echoed in the chamber, making her almost nauseous.

"You're talking to a man with a death wish. Considering

how much you are shaking, I would say life means a great deal more to you, especially the pathetic life of this girl." He sneered. "Put down the gun and kick it over to me."

Sweat trailed down Jess's temple, and the air felt thick and stagnant, making it hard to breathe. She knew she had no choice. She wouldn't force the man's hand with Nikki's life in the balance. Slowly, she lowered her weapon and laid it at her feet, then kicked it to him. The gun skittered across the floor, obliterating any odds in her favor. Her luck had run out, but she hoped Nikki would still have a chance. If the bastard had intended to kill the girl, he wouldn't have knocked her out. He would have taken too much pleasure in slitting her throat and watching her bleed, drowning in her own blood.

The Russian let Nikki slide and drop to the floor before he retrieved Jess's weapon and slipped it into the waistband of his pants. He pointed his gun at her again, a smug expression on his face. Jess took a deep breath and clenched her jaw, waiting for whatever the scumbag would do next.

"You're coming with me."

Wide-eyed, she let her panic show. "What about Nikki? You can't just leave her."

The bastard smiled. "She is expendable. Easy to replace. But you? I have plans."

He'd taken her by surprise. She hadn't expected his reaction. She couldn't leave Nikki behind without a fight. Jess headed for the door, her mind racing with ways to take him out. But he came up behind her and turned the tables again.

A blow to the back of the head staggered her. She dropped to her knees and was shoved to the floor. A warm rush of blood drained down her neck, and the room swirled in a dark haze. She couldn't shake her stupor and lost track of time, her awareness drifting in and out between shades of black. Behind her a shadow moved in the distance, but she couldn't make her body move to see what was going on.

Time stalled and repeated like a skip on a CD, until a

bright heat washed over her face and forced her to open an eye to see what was happening.

On the far wall, the grenades burst and catapulted white-hot sparks high into the air, a blast of hot debris. The computers liquefied under the intense heat, molten metal spewing across the room and setting off a string of smaller fires. She felt the heat around her. And the stench of sulfur hit the air under a cloud of billowing dark smoke. A devastating fireball raged in a chain reaction across the control room, and with it came a blinding fierce heat.

Gotta move. Now!

Pain spiked through her head like a taser bolt, making it hard to see. She tried to crawl, but her body anchored her to the spot she'd fallen. Breathing in smoke and the chemical fumes of the explosion seared heat into her lungs, making her gag.

Without help, she wasn't going to make it. And it was only a matter of time before the rest of the tunnels would explode.

Mercifully, blackness came. For her, the nightmare was over.

CHAPTER 19

Her body moved, a series of sharp tugs. And her head lolled from side to side. Jess sensed the motion and caught only glimpses she couldn't explain. Her legs felt useless, heavy as lead. A relentless blaring sound persisted, surging over and over. She couldn't shut it out. And with the noise came a blinding flash of light. She tried covering her eyes, but her arms wouldn't move.

She strained to see through a dense fog, nothing more than blurred images. But finally her eyes spiraled to a stop and focused, centering on a face. A woman with blond hair. The stranger's lips moved, but the words were garbled and out of sync. She wanted to respond, but couldn't force herself to speak.

Inside, an inexplicable urgency gripped her heart, but her body wouldn't cooperate. She drifted in and out—fighting to stay awake—but had no idea if she was more dead than alive.

Alexa Marlowe had hoped to find the bounty hunter in better shape. When the men attacked Jessica Beckett at the gas station, she only saw the end of the assault. And the woman's associate, Seth Harper, had been hot on her trail and called in the cavalry. She'd seen his distinctive blue van. Planting the GPS tracking device on the bounty hunter's car outside The Cutthroat pool hall had paid off in spades, but her sense of accomplishment quickly faded after seeing Beckett so messed up.

The relentless woman had been a regular pit bull when it came to Lucas Baker. And now she had gotten herself in the middle of Globe Harvest's U.S. domestic operation. She had to give Beckett props for getting the job done. In another life, she would have liked to call the woman a friend, but in her line of work friends were a crutch she couldn't afford.

Having admiration for the woman's guts was one thing, but pulling her to safety had cost her time. Time she didn't have. She'd found an alternative way into the lower levels of the old textile factory but was too late. The evacuation of the abducted kids, the physical abuse of the bounty hunter, and a thermite explosion—it all went down without her weighing in.

But she wasn't one to give up easily. She had that in common with Beckett.

After pulling the bounty hunter into the corridor, Alexa peered back inside what looked like a major control room of the operation. The place was an inferno, belching smoke. White residue covered the walls and desks, and the computers were a total meltdown. Fires with a strange green tinge had sprung up all over. The chemical barium caused the peculiar color, a known component to enhance the effect of thermite. She held her breath and raced through the room looking for anything of value—another lead to follow.

Damn it! Nothing much remained.

In the back of the chamber she found a large fire erupting from trash bins. Covering her face with a hand, she ventured closer, close enough to see that what fueled the fire might be of interest. All around her heat flared. She felt it on her exposed skin. Even her clothes absorbed it and radiated through her body. She gagged from the heavy chemical smell and the smoke, but she had to try.

After several attempts Alexa eventually plucked a stack of badly singed paper from the fire. Blackened scraps with sections of readable print.

"Shit!" She burned her hands and dropped the pages to the floor, stomping out the fire. Afterward, the skin of her fingers throbbed with pain, and goose bumps sent shock waves over her body, but at least she'd retrieved something the bastards working for Globe Harvest had wanted to destroy.

She rolled up the pages and headed for the door, dodging burning rubble and holding her breath against the smoke. Back in the corridor, she debated her next move. The unconscious bounty hunter needed help. She wouldn't survive alone. The bastards who'd beaten her had seen to that. And carrying dead weight would slow her down, maybe get them both killed.

Moving quickly, she stuffed the Globe Harvest papers into the waistband of her pants, then knelt to grab Beckett's arm and raise her off the floor. But before she hoisted the woman over her shoulder, she heard muffled voices in the distance. The cop had brought company.

"Nice," Alexa whispered, lowering the bounty hunter back down. Kneeling by her side, she stroked Beckett's hair. "You've got friends, Jessica. Count your blessings."

With fingers to her lips, Alexa stood and let out a loud shrill whistle that echoed down the corridor. Then she yelled, "Over here. I need help. This place is gonna blow."

She waited to make sure the bounty hunter would get help, then disappeared down the corridor in search of a back way out before anyone saw her. She didn't need the distraction. This was the closest she'd been to finding a division of Globe Harvest.

And she owed Jessica Beckett for that.

With her .45-caliber H&K MK23 in hand, Alexa defied

the dark maze of tunnels and mounting gas fumes to search for the men who had eluded her again. The way she figured it, there was only one way to pay back the bounty hunter. And for once headstrong Jessica might not argue.

"I heard something. A whistle, a woman's voice." Payton gestured for Joe and Sam to follow. "This way."

He raced back to the entrance where they'd come in and turned a corner. One of the corridors was filled with dense black smoke, making it hard to see. Farther down, a fire blazed. And a wall of heat made it hard to breathe.

"There's a fire," he yelled over his shoulder. "And I smell gas."

Sam caught up to him and grimaced. Even stoic Joe couldn't hide his concern.

"Shit! This place could blow," the detective said, covering her mouth with a hand.

"Then we better move." Without hesitation, Payton rushed through the smoke.

He held an arm over his nose, and his eyes watered and stung like hell. The Kevlar he wore made the heat unbearable, but it also protected his skin from scorching. When he got closer to the fire, he spotted someone on the floor. The sight jolted his heart and all he could think about was Nikki. He knelt to get a better look.

The injured woman wasn't Nikki and something inside him broke. He rolled her onto her back and checked her pulse. When Sam got to him, she knelt and smiled.

"It's Jessie. Thank God." But she'd hardly said the words when she looked at Payton with a pained expression. "Sorry. I mean . . . did you find your niece?"

With her question, desperation closed in. "Not yet."

Joe came up, and the two men ran into the burning room, desperately searching for Nikki. They came back nauseous and gagging, covered in soot and barely able to breathe.

When Sam looked up, Payton only shook his head. He

couldn't bring himself to say it. The tunnels were filling with gas, and the fumes made him light-headed and sick. He peered behind him, seeing only billowing clouds of black smoke.

"Maybe she was never here, Payton." Joe reached out with a strong hand and grabbed his arm. "This place is rigged to blow. We can't stay. And Sam's friend needs a doctor."

Payton shut his eyes tight, feeling the sting. A flood of memories washed over him, stemming from the grief of losing his parents. He knew Joe was right. Maybe Nikki had never been here, but it didn't take the pain away. And Jessie Beckett looked in bad shape.

Payton nodded and reached down, pulling her off the floor in one swift move. He carried her like a small child. She was unconscious and pale, her face covered in grime. If he hadn't checked her pulse, he might have thought she was dead.

"Let's go. Now."

As he picked up the pace, a threatening low rumble from the bowel of the tunnels magnified into a massive roar. The whole building shook, and walls tumbled in their path.

They'd waited too long.

"Run!" he cried. "Don't look back. Just go, go, Go!"

Sweat stung his eyes, making them blur. And his lungs were burning. He couldn't get enough air. And sucking in the smoke made his throat burn like acid. He prayed that he'd picked the right way out. The smoke was so dense, he couldn't see fallen debris until he was on top of it. He vaulted over anything in his path. Behind him, he heard Sam and Joe running, trying to keep up.

But another sound overpowered the wailing siren and sent a stab of fear through his chest. A raging fireball ripped through the corridor behind them with roaring force. And like a vacuum, it sucked air in its wake.

Carrying Jessie made his body ache, his muscles burn.

Up ahead a flash of light speared the murky black. A flashlight. He had no idea who carried it and he didn't care.

"Head for that light. Move," he called out to Sam and Joe.

Payton heard voices, and shadows moved through the thick haze. Whoever these people were, they were going the wrong way.

"Get out. Now! This shit hole is coming down!"

He barreled past them, slamming his shoulder against the entrance door, using his body to protect Jessie. As he cleared the door, he heard a loud crash and something snagged his leg. He nearly fell over but managed to keep his balance.

"Joe, Sam, stay with me. We're almost there."

No answer, but with all the noise, his words sounded muffled and distant.

He shoved through the outer door, unable to shake the intense smell of smoke, then sucked the night air into his aching lungs.

A circle of men stood a safe distance from the inferno—cops, firemen, and paramedics. Emergency vehicles had arrived, flashing their lights across a pitch-black sky.

He held Jessie, not wanting to put her down. When he turned, the building had started to implode and fire raged inside, hitting pockets of gas and erupting. In the growing crowd of faces he searched for Joe and Sam. They'd been right behind him.

Payton clung to Jessie, feeling her move in his arms. But when a massive explosion caved the front of the structure into a fiery heap, the only words that came from his mouth sounded like the voice of a stranger.

"Oh, God. Please . . . no."

CHAPTER 20

Running down the dimly lit corridor, Alexa Marlowe heard the explosion deep in the tunnel. The ground shook under her feet and nearly knocked her off balance. She knew in an instant what had happened.

"Damn! Move it, Marlowe."

She secured her H&K in its holster and ran for the underground construction elevator dead ahead—no more than a wire basket with a layer of cement as flooring, hoisted on a motorized steel cable with a hook suspension. If she didn't get ahead of the blast, she'd be cooked where she stood. And if the contraption didn't have power, or juice supplied from a backup generator, none of her effort would matter.

"Come on." She secured the basket door behind her and punched the lift button. "Damn it! Move."

The elevator heaved with an uneasy jolt, and the motor kicked in with a loud whir. It strained and lifted her into a dark shaft, heading to the surface. She couldn't see where she was going, but the elevator was the only escape route possible. Since the corridor below had dead-ended, she had no doubt the men of Globe Harvest had done exactly as she did now.

A loud rumble trailed after her with a huge sucking sound, depleting the air in its wake—a toxic vaporous cloud building momentum in the dark. And a rush of heat swelled around her. Alexa knew she was running ahead of a massive and deadly fireball. The basket swayed under her feet, and between the fumes and the motion, she felt light-headed and nauseous.

She punched the button again and again, unable to stop the compulsion.

"Come on. Almost there."

The darkness of the elevator shaft swallowed her. She couldn't see anything, not even the hand in front of her face. But as an orange molten glow erupted below, she realized that the black void had been a blessing.

"Oh, God."

She looked down long enough to feel the blast on her face. Scorching heat surged up the shaft like a frenzied snake, writhing after her. Waiting for impact, she fought the natural tension in her muscles. When the time came, she wanted to roll with the punch, grappling for safe ground. As she peered through the dark above her, she felt a cool wisp of night air on her cheek and knew her race to beat the fire would be close.

Alexa braced her feet and held on, taking a last gulp of air so her lungs wouldn't cook.

Raging molten flames soon devoured the inky black of the narrow shaft. And for an instant she had enough light to see what lay ahead—shored up stone walls leading to freedom. But when the blast hit, it slammed into her, hard. It catapulted the basket and launched her like a human cannonball, propelling the wire cage with her inside. Her body collided with the metal girding and she narrowly escaped being crushed against the hoisting mechanism. Finally free of the cage, she forced her body to tuck and roll. When she landed, she hit with such force that the impact jarred her knees and back, but she managed to go with the flow and minimize the shock.

Dodging falling debris, Alexa scrambled away as fast as she could and avoided the wire cage that smashed to the dirt near her legs. When the worst was over, she lay on the ground, stunned by what had happened. She rolled to one side, out of breath and completely spent, her body shaking like a junkie in withdrawal. She stared at the blaze that nearly killed her. Like a torch, flames licked the night air, rupturing from the shaft. Yet seeing how close she'd come to becoming a skewered bratwurst brought an unexpected and aching grin to her face.

"Holy crap!" she panted, still shaking off the adrenaline burn. "What a . . . ride!"

At the surface, an old barnlike structure had been built around the elevator shaft to keep out prying eyes. By her estimation, Globe Harvest's evacuation route was a few miles from the abandoned textile factory. Authorities would eventually find it. The old building had started to catch fire, an aftermath of the explosion, the top of the barn blown apart in the blast.

"You bastards had this all under control, one step ahead."

Alexa knew she needed to head for her car before anyone came to investigate the barn fire, but she had quite a hike back, and the way she felt, procrastination had appeal. Sweat covered her body, along with a layer of dirt. And smoke rose off her jeans and shirt. She felt the sting of burns on her fingers and elbows, with hot spots on her legs, but nothing that needed immediate attention. And it took her a moment to feel the rain. It soothed the raging heat of her skin, although her face and body were almost numb. All things considered, she'd been lucky.

But a distant commotion nudged her awareness. Slowly and with great pain, she stood on shaky legs and listened through ringing ears, straining to hear what instinct told her was there. It took time to realize that what she heard was the rotors of helicopters—more than one.

To regain her night vision, Alexa ran into the dark beyond

the barn and away from the fire. She narrowed her eyes and focused on the night sky.

"Shit!" They were running without lights, and she had no idea which way they headed or how many there were. She spun and searched for any signs of movement, but beyond the city lights there was only darkness.

She'd lost them again.

Desperation turned her stomach, and she bent over, exhausted, drained, and still shaking. But when she moved, she felt a crumple of paper at her waist and remembered what she'd found in the control room. She pulled out the documents and examined them in the light from the fire. Nothing but a series of numbers, but she knew where to get help in deciphering the pages.

Suddenly, the hike to where she'd hidden her car didn't seem so daunting—yet one dark thought lingered to taint her small victory.

With luck she might uncover a thread of evidence leading her to another arm of Globe Harvest. The online international organization operated in secrecy and answered to no one, committing heinous atrocities. But tonight any discovery would be too late to help the young girls being flown out of Chicago to parts unknown.

She couldn't handle that harsh reality. Alexa collapsed to the ground and emptied her stomach.

Nikki stared out the window, squeezed next to another frightened girl. The ground fell away from under the helicopter when it lifted, making her queasy. Once they got high enough, she fixed her eyes on the horizon with its glittering patches of city lights in the distance, fighting the throbbing headache instigated when the Russian knocked her unconscious. The textile factory besieged the night with its belching fire, giving the skyline the appearance of sunset, but the sight barely registered.

All she thought about was Uncle Payton. His smiling,

handsome face with that crooked dimpled grin. He came to Chicago to find her, and now . . . he was dead. Her eyes blurred with tears as she choked back her guilt.

All the reasons she'd left home, and her desperate struggle for independence, suddenly felt unimportant and trivial. She'd come half a world away to learn what really mattered, but it was too late to do anything about it. Memories of her mother didn't give her comfort, as they had only hours before. Her mom would be alone to deal with Payton's death and she wasn't strong enough to do that.

Nikki shut her eyes tight, but nothing would hold back the pain . . . or the fear. Now, no one would find her. And she had a feeling with what these men had in store for her, death would be a mercy.

Amidst the moans of the wounded and the commotion of the scene, Payton heard the man say, "Give her high flow oxygen. Fifteen liters per minute for smoke inhalation."

A paramedic gave direction before moving on to the next victim. Each of the injured got a colored triage tag around the neck, indicating the severity of the injury. Jessie had a yellow tag. Payton had no idea what it all meant, but the medics worked with care and efficiency.

"Put her on a heart monitor and start a large bore IV."

Another man in uniform shined a light into Jessie's nose and mouth, assessing the damage.

"Smoke around the nostrils, but rest of upper airway is clear. Voice okay. No need to intubate this one."

She had cuts and bruises on her body, but most critical were the head wound and smoke inhalation. Her head had been bandaged with trauma dressing, and at the hospital she'd need X rays and maybe a CAT scan to determine if she had a skull fracture.

Although Payton had been reluctant to leave her side at the makeshift triage area, he had to look for Joe and Sam, and refused medical treatment for himself until he found them. A barricade had been set up to keep nonessential personnel from getting too close to the fire. Sporadic explosions were still happening deep inside the collapsed structure. When Detective Garza arrived, he helped establish the police barricade, but the fire department was in charge of the scene—a remarkable lesson in controlled chaos.

Payton felt bombarded by the intensity of noise, even with his ears ringing and out of commission. Ambulances came and went, carrying victims. Radios crackled and blared in all directions, filtered through sirens and air horns. Shouts from firefighters and medics could be heard over the racket of generators running lights.

He'd never seen a fire up close. Firemen came in and out of the triage zone needing medical evaluation to keep going. With gear soaked and smoking, each man clamored to get back into the fight. Empty water bottles and discarded dressing wrappers littered the scene, with emergency strobe lights strafing the night sky. And across the asphalt, the fire reflected off the ponds of accumulating water, runoffs and leaks from a series of large and small hoses used by the firefighters. The smell of diesel fuel hung heavy in the air as fire engines operated on high idle, the odor competing with the smoke. Payton doubted he'd ever get the stench of smoke from his nostrils and off his hair and skin.

With all the upheaval, he had a hard time sifting through the crowd, until he found Seth. The kid helped him search the faces of the injured, hoping they'd locate Joe and Sam among them. So far that hadn't happened. And the more time passed, the more Payton lost faith in finding them at all.

Then, silhouetted against the flames, he saw a man and a woman, walking. He couldn't make out their faces but recognized a familiar gait and manner. He squinted into the bright light, narrowing his eyes for a better look at the pair. Slowly, he walked toward the man, not taking his eyes off him. And as he got closer, Payton started to run. By the looks of him, Joe Tanu had been hurt. He leaned on Sam Cooper, grimacing with every careful step.

"Seth!" Payton yelled over his shoulder, slowing down as he got close. "They're alive."

Then he muttered under his breath, "Damn it! They're alive."

Joe was in pain but looked damned glad to be on the right side of the turf. A regular sight for sore stinging eyes. Payton hugged him, fighting the lump in his throat. And as he held Joe, he whispered in his ear, "Good to see you, old man."

"I thought I'd lost you too."

Payton's eyes brimmed with tears as he hugged the man he thought of as his father. When he pulled back, he looked down at Sam and kissed her cheek.

"Thanks . . . for everything."

The detective smiled. "How's Jessie?" she asked.

"She's over here, Sam," Seth cut in, then led them to the tarp where he'd last seen her.

Joe needed help to the triage area, and Payton lent a hand, setting him down on a tarp close to Jessie as Sam knelt and took her friend's hand. Jessie opened her eyes and started to say something, but the words wouldn't come.

"Don't try to speak, Jess. You're going to be okay."

Jess shook her head and tried again, this time reaching for Payton. Her urgency caught him by surprise. He turned from Joe and leaned closer, clasping her trembling hand.

"You don't know me, but my name is Payton. I—"

"I know . . . who you are." She swallowed and pulled down her oxygen mask, wincing at the pain when she lifted her head. "I found . . . Nikki."

At first he thought he hadn't heard right, but his confusion was quickly replaced by urgent concern.

"What? She was in there?" He squeezed her hand when she started to fade. "Did you talk to her? Is that how you knew it was her?"

He had bombarded her with too many questions. And he wasn't sure she heard him until she spoke again.

"I found Nikki. Did I already say that?"

"Yeah, you did," he replied, recognizing her confusion. He'd seen it on the football field, when a guy got his bell rung.

"Here . . . take these." She fumbled for something under her blanket, then retrieved crumpled and bloodied papers, and thrust them at him. "Keep 'em. I'll explain . . . when I can."

Turning her attention to Sam, she insisted, "Don't let anyone take 'em. We need to know . . ." She laid her head back down, unable to finish.

"But they're evidence, Jess," Sam said. "We need to process the paper for fingerprints."

"Then please . . . promise me you'll make a copy . . . for me," Jessie persisted, with a crazed look in her eye.

Sam gave in, reassuring her, "I promise, we'll process the originals, but you'll get a copy. You've got my word, honey."

"What's this?" Payton glanced at the pages in his hands before he handed them over to Sam. "And what does it have to do with Nikki?"

"I found her . . . Nikki." Jessie struggled to tell him more. "The Russian. He left her . . . in the control room." She choked and nearly lost it. A paramedic rushed over to adjust her oxygen mask, but she held him off until she finished. "She was . . . unconscious."

Jessie was practically delirious from head trauma, leaving him to wonder. Had she only imagined seeing Nikki?

"No, that can't be," he insisted, but doubt crept into his mind. "I was there."

Had he checked the control room well enough? Had he somehow missed her? The possibility that he didn't see Nikki through all the smoke made him sick. He stared off toward the burning building and shook his head in disbelief.

"This can't be right . . . we looked." A tear drained down his cheek. He couldn't breathe. "Dear God, she can't still be in there."

In that moment, his world stopped. The noise and the fire, everything faded to a pervasive emptiness—a hollow no one could fill. Sam reached for him, and he became aware of Joe's voice, but nothing sank in.

Had he left Nikki behind?

CHAPTER 21

University of Chicago Hospital

All hospitals smelled the same to Payton—a medicinal tang mixed with odors he didn't want identified. Joe Tanu had been admitted to an area medical center with burns and a broken leg that required surgery. Med staff had him hooked to an IV and a machine for him to administer a dose of morphine at the push of a button. His leg had been propped up and bandaged. Between the flight from Alaska and what happened last night, neither one of them had gotten much sleep over the last two days. It was beginning to show.

As Joe rested in a fitful sleep, Payton kept watch in a chair by his bed, dosing himself with bad coffee laced with liquor from the minibar at his Oak Brook hotel room. He'd cleaned out the stash of tiny bottles and brought a handful with him after making a taxi run to his hotel to clean up and scour the grime off. Even though he'd taken a long shower, he still smelled the smoke from last night. And unfortunately, looking more human, he got attention from hospital staff and others after he returned to the medical complex. Many recognized him from the time he'd played for the Chicago Bears. It surprised him to see how many remembered him in a favorable light, but the critical armchair sports fanatics were more vocal than casual fans.

He had too much on his mind to care one way or the other. He had copies of the pages Jessie Beckett had given him at the textile plant fire, and while Joe was in surgery, Sam made sure he got a set for Jessie. By the look of desperation in her eyes last night, he knew they meant something to her, but he'd gone bleary-eyed trying to decipher their meaning. The puzzle had been a distraction from the futility of his grief for Nikki. But to him, the pages looked cryptic, nothing more than columns of numbers with vague numeric headers.

He wanted to punish the men who had taken and killed Nikki, but making them pay would not bring her back. One thing dominated his mind most of all. He had no idea what to tell Susannah. None of what he'd say would lighten her load. How do you prepare a mother to hear the kind of news he had to deliver? And how would he help his sister let go of her only child?

When he looked up, Joe was awake and had been watching him. Even if he wanted to keep secrets from his friend, the man would see right through him.

"I can smell the alcohol from here." Surprisingly, Joe kept his disappointment in check, but that didn't mean he wasn't feeling it. "And I thought I was the one needing a crutch."

The man never minced words and always knew how to get his point across—his version of a verbal bat upside the head.

"I had to take the edge off. Don't give me a lecture."

"Living is dealing with edges, Payton. And until we know for sure about Nikki, this ain't over." Joe winced with pain. Knowing Tanu, he'd refuse to push his morphine button even if he were gut shot.

First and foremost, Joe had the blood of a cop coursing through his veins. When he talked about "knowing for sure" about Nikki, he meant until recovery crews found and identified her remains. Being a pragmatic man, Joe dealt with the raw truth. It was his nature. Had he been a glass-half-full kind of guy, he might have taken comfort in Joe's words, that there was an outside shot Nikki was still alive. But these days, he didn't feel like a lucky man, and his only fleeting comfort came from single malt scotch and the bottoms of many an empty glass—honesty and truth be damned.

Before he had a chance to respond to Joe, Detective Sam Cooper walked into the hospital room.

"Hey, Joe. How are you feeling?" she asked.

The man shrugged. His eyes had lost their sheen and his dark skin looked pale under the hospital lights. "If it weren't for the pretty nurses, I'd go stir crazy."

"How's Jessie?" Payton asked her.

"She had some pretty deep cuts that needed stitches, but no skull fracture. She got lucky for once, but they're keeping her under observation for the concussion." Sam pointed over her shoulder. "She's on this floor, far corner. I'm sure she'll want to see you, but they've got her on pain meds. She drifts in and out."

With the copied pages for Jess in his hand, Payton got up to leave.

Sam stopped him. "This morning she told me she wasn't thinking clearly last night . . . about turning over the original documents. She figured that if she'd taken something off the premises, it might put me in the middle and compromise my job. Guilt by association, I guess. But Payton, I'm already in the middle. Jess is like family to me."

Sam smiled. "If there's anything I can do to help, you let me know. She's not always the most objective when it comes to dealing with scum like this."

Payton wondered what she meant but didn't want to pry into Jessie's life. He understood the need for privacy. And he certainly appreciated the necessity for leading a solitary life.

"When can I go out there?" he asked. "I gotta know."

The detective didn't have to ask him what he meant. She knew he wouldn't rest until they found Nikki's body. It would be hard on him and Susannah, but they would both need closure.

"Fire crews are still working the scene, making sure it's safe for investigators and searching for—" She stopped herself and shifted her gaze to Joe—a knowing look—cop-to-cop.

"And they'll be searching for bodies," Payton pressed. "That's what you were going to say, right?"

She nodded. "The textile factory is a crime scene. You won't be able to go beyond the barricade, but I'll let you know if . . . you'll be the first to know."

"Thanks, Sam." Before Payton left the room, he looked over his shoulder at Joe. "After I see Jessie, I'm gonna get some coffee. Catch you later."

By the expression on Joe Tanu's face, he had received the message loud and clear. Without saying it, Payton had assured him he would sober up—for now. No guarantees how long his good behavior would last. And if they found Nikki's body, all bets would be off.

When Payton entered Jessie Beckett's hospital room, she had been asleep. He thought about giving her privacy and coming back later, but at some point he lost control of his will to leave. He studied the woman, really seeing her for the first time, minus the desperation and pain of last night. Her pale skin looked flushed, tinged with color that was a perfect contrast to her dark hair. And under the faint scar near her eye, which gave her face character and grit, her lips and the contour of her cheeks gave her a striking vulnerability, a contradiction he hadn't expected.

Her muscular athletic body mirrored the hardness of the scars she bore, yet the soft fleshy curves of a woman's figure were there too. Jessie had the total package, plus an intriguing edge of raw sensuality. Of all people, he had an appreciation for imperfections, both inside and out, and knew there would be more to her story. But for this woman to let him in, it would take patience and time, and he wasn't sure he had either. He felt too messed up to take on a strong woman, and someone like Jessie deserved better. Still, he found himself wondering what it would be like to be with her—to feel capable of returning what she had to give to a man.

When she opened her dark eyes, she gazed at him with all the intimacy of a waking lover. He should have turned away and ignored how she made him feel, but couldn't bring himself to do it.

"Hey," he whispered. Leaning over her bed, he stroked a strand of hair away from her cheek. "Can I . . . get you anything? Water, maybe?"

Payton could tell that it took a moment for Jessie to focus and recognize who he was. He'd taken too much liberty with someone he'd barely met, and he knew it, yet it felt right to be alone with her—a feeling he couldn't explain even to himself.

When she nodded and tried to sit up, he helped adjust her pillow and raise the bed before he fixed her a small cup of shaved ice. Her bedside table had been stocked with the stuff. But when he attempted to feed her a spoonful, she clutched at her hospital gown, reminding him they were nothing more than strangers. And oddly enough, that bothered him.

Damn it, Archer! What the hell were you thinking? He offered her the cup of ice and spoon, for her to take care of her own needs.

"Thanks," she said. "How's your friend?"

Waking up to find Payton Archer so close had unnerved Jess. She took the cup and spoon from his hand, getting a sudden rush when their fingers touched. By refusing his spoon-feeding, she'd wanted to set a clear boundary between them. But she didn't know if the boundary was meant for his benefit or hers.

"Joe had surgery to set pins in his leg," he said. "Guess when he flies home, he'll be setting off security alarms at the airport."

She smiled as she melted ice in her mouth. Payton probably thought she found humor in his remark, but the man had a subtle and undeniable charm. He shared more on Joe's condition, and everytime she caught him staring at her, he turned away and pretended it hadn't happened . . . until the next time. His subtle game came as such a surprise that she had to smile. He had an inherent sensuality that he didn't seem to be aware of, a quality she always found seductive.

"You know," she said, "I remembered you from before . . . when you played for 'da Bears.' "

His sudden change of expression told her she'd said the wrong thing. Idle chitchat was never her gig, especially when she was nervous.

Payton winced and said, "Ancient history. Off the field, I'd sooner forget those years. I wasn't . . ." He thought about what he wanted to say. "I wasn't ready for . . . success like that. My ego was cashing checks my head and heart couldn't handle."

In typical guy fashion, he left most of his meaning between the lines, leaving her to fill in the blanks. When she was younger, she might have been tempted to do that, but these days, she took a man at face value without donning rose-colored glasses. Still, Payton's candor and his willingness to talk about old wounds with a perceptive honesty had hooked her. She definitely wanted to know more about the man—and not just what she remembered from newspaper headlines.

"Sam told me she gave you copies of the pages I got from the control room." When he handed her the document copies, she tried a grin, but failed miserably. Her head ached with a vengeance. "She was right to preserve the evidence and process for prints. I wasn't thinking my best last night. Guess I was pretty out of it."

Payton filled her in on what had happened after the fire. For the time being, he avoided any talk of his niece Nikki, but she knew he would get to it when he was ready. As he talked and paced her hospital room, she listened to what he had to say—to a point.

Jess felt completely vulnerable, confined to a hospital bed wearing nothing but a hospital gown that resembled a hankie with ties. Her battered appearance, both old scars and new, would have made her feel self-conscious around anyone, but being in this small room with Payton Archer compounded her awkwardness. She couldn't remember ever feeling this ridiculous around a man. She found herself counting the steps he took as he paced the floor near her bed and how many times she caught a glimpse of a dimple.

Get over yourself, Jess! He only cares about his niece.

If she thought dismissing him would help her cope, she might have tried faking indifference, but Payton Archer was hard for a woman to ignore. He looked damned fine in those jeans, with his broad shoulders and narrow hips, which only the NFL could produce. He wore his hair long and straight, far too appealing for her taste, the glistening blond streaks giving him the look of a beefy surfer on steroids. And worse, the fierce blue of his eyes against tanned skin had a way of stifling her breath, giving her the heady startling sensation of jumping into the deep end of a pool filled with nothing but ice water. Those eyes could be downright lethal. Yet what surprised her most was the gentleness of his voice when he spoke. It had the drizzle of honey mixed with the gravel of sultry Kentucky bourbon.

Unfortunately for her, he didn't fit the picture of an overindulged self-centered jock, except his breath smelled of alcohol. And at this time of morning, that made him entitled to full membership in the barely functioning walking wounded club. But she knew she wasn't one to judge, being a charter member herself.

No doubt about it, Payton Archer spelled pure trouble. His quiet appeal triggered something she had thought was dead in her. And the fact that he had been in a desperate search for his niece made her want to get to know him all the more. He pushed all her buttons and some she didn't even know she had.

"It took a lot of guts for Nikki to reach out to me, especially when she was so scared," she told him. Despite fighting a burgeoning headache, she set the cup of ice aside and broached the touchy subject of his niece, waiting for him to open up to her.

Sam had told her about Payton's breakdown at the scene after her delirious outburst about Nikki being left in the control room. She had no way of knowing for sure what had happened, and he couldn't have done anything about it in the midst of an explosion, but logical reasoning wouldn't stop the pain of grief. And by the look on his face, he would have a long road toward becoming whole again.

"I don't know what I'm going to tell my sister." He shut his eyes and took a deep breath. "I haven't called her yet, but no sense in putting it off. She has to know. Guess I was hoping this was a nightmare. That I'd wake up and it wouldn't be true. Any of it."

"None of this is your fault . . . or your sister's. These predators know how to manipulate little girls like Nikki. And . . ." She could have gone on but stopped herself, knowing he wasn't ready to hear her tirade or her recollections of the last minutes of Nikki's life. "When you're ready to hear it, I'd like to tell you . . . about Nikki."

He stared at her a long moment, trying to decide what he was prepared to hear. Eventually he nodded and let it go. Jess hated watching him struggle with the unresolved grief, but sooner or later he'd have to come to terms with what had happened to Nikki.

"So how did you find me in the fire?" she asked. "I don't remember much after the Russian slugged me over the head." By his reticent reaction, she wondered if she had pushed too much. But she wanted to open a door for him. "If you don't want to talk about this, that's okay too."

"Actually, I heard your whistle, then you called out . . . asking for help."

"You heard what?" Jess thought long and hard about what he'd said but could only recall vague impressions. "I was really messed up, but I don't remember calling to anyone." She furrowed her brow. "And I definitely can't whistle loud enough to be heard over that damned alarm. That doesn't make sense, but I'm sure you heard what you did or else you never would have found me."

She shuddered at the thought of how close she'd come to dying.

"It was a woman's voice." Payton jammed his hands into the pockets of his jeans. "Do you remember anyone else with you . . . besides Nikki?"

By the expression on his handsome face, the mention of his niece's name took its toll, but when he mentioned a woman's voice, it triggered something.

"You know, I have this memory of . . ." She stalled long enough to pull an image out of the blur of last night. ". . . a blond woman. Her face is stuck in my mind. Last night is still fuzzy, but I think she was there. Sam said I was outside that burning room, but I was in no shape to do that on my own."

Deep in thought, Jess hadn't realized she'd spoken aloud until Payton asked her a question.

"Are you saying there was someone else there? Because I didn't see anyone leave the way we came in."

The urgency in his voice forced her to think harder about what happened, for his sake. Had she imagined the whole thing or was she recalling something from another time long ago? She was treading a dangerous line, threatening to drag him into her delusions if she was wrong.

"I can't be sure, but I think someone pulled me from of the fire," she replied in a voice that lacked resolve. How much could she trust her recollections after what had happened?

When she looked up, Payton had a pained expression on his face.

"What?" she asked. "What are you thinking?"

"If there was a blond woman there, where did she go? I mean, she didn't come through us or we would have seen her. If you're right about this woman, then she got you help . . . and maybe she helped Nikki too. A big place like that? Maybe there were other ways in and out."

Although her memories were muddled, Jess had a vague notion of a back way out. The pieces to the puzzle of last night hadn't clicked into place yet, but Payton was grasping at very thin straws, and she knew it. In her line of work, she'd dealt with the scum of the earth, leaving her more cynical than someone like Payton Archer. The dark thought that percolated in her brain now would not be easy for him to hear, but encouraging him to believe that Nikki might still be alive would only prolong his agony if she was wrong. She considered her words carefully before speaking.

"Listen, Payton." She couldn't look him in the eye. "My memories sometimes get jumbled with a past I'd sooner forget. My childhood . . . I get confused between what actually happened and all the nightmares since . . . I don't want to get your hopes up over something I may have conjured from thin air."

"But—" He stopped short and considered her point. "I can see the pain behind your eyes. Are you okay?"

His astute observation surprised her. Was he talking about her physical pain, or the emotional scars most people chose to ignore? To his credit, Payton didn't ask her any more about her personal recollections. He gave her the privacy she normally craved. And she liked that very much.

"I know Sam has got people digging through that old factory," she said. "We'll know what happened real soon. Maybe by then I'll remember . . . be more sure."

Her words sounded hollow. She wanted to comfort him but had no idea how to do that. She knew how she'd feel if it had been her loved one killed in the blaze. And by the look on Payton's face, nothing would have consoled him either.

But she had to be sure about the troubling thought that plagued her now.

If a mystery woman had helped her from the fire in the control room, that woman may have done the same for Nikki, just as Payton had speculated. But if she was mistaken, and the woman had only been an illusive figment of her chronic bad dreams, she would be leading Payton and his sister down a grim path of false hope. After all they had been through, she didn't want to be the cause of an even greater emotional setback.

Sure it would have been a comfort for Payton to realize he hadn't left his niece behind in the fire, but another scenario remained, with serious implications. Jess shivered at the thought of his niece still in the hands of the Russian. The girl would be no match for the man's cruelty.

She stared down at the pages clutched in her hand, the ones she'd retrieved from the fire. In her mind, Globe Harvest and its obscene network really did exist. And that Russian bastard went to great pains to blow up an abandoned textile plant. The man wanted to bury the proof of his link to the larger organization, but not all of that proof had been burned.

She knew her instincts were dead on. An organization like Globe Harvest operated and thrived on secrecy. Compromising Baker and his laptop connection to the larger system had been the catalyst for what happened last night. And in her hands, she held a copy of the only evidence pulled from the fire. It had to mean something or else those men wouldn't have gone to such great pains to destroy the facility and its control room. With any luck, she'd find a key to open another door into Globe Harvest.

For the sake of Payton and his family—and countless others—she hoped she was right.

Downtown Chicago

After the fire, Alexa had caught a few restless hours of sleep at her downtown hotel room, where she'd nursed her burns and bruises. When she awoke, she'd stretched her sore muscles and took a long hot shower to loosen up. Now, dressed in the white robe of the hotel, sitting at a table eating her room service breakfast, she got a call on her cell phone. Although no number was displayed, she knew instinctively who was on the line.

"Marlowe."

"I hope you're enjoying your time off, Alexa." Over the phone, his low and seductive voice teased her ear as if she lay next to him in the dark. "How is Paris?" he asked.

Alexa contemplated lying to Garrett Wheeler, an associate of a covert organization she knew only as the Sentinels. But chances were that Garrett was only testing whether she'd come close to the truth. She got up to adjust the air-conditioning thermostat, to cut the chill from the room before she went back to her breakfast.

"Paris? I wouldn't know. Why do you take such pleasure in playing these games?"

"For the same reason you feel the need to stall . . . answering a question with a question. You know I don't like it when you keep secrets. What are you doing in Chicago?"

She had taken special precautions to keep her trip a secret from Garrett. But given the man's resources, it was only a matter of time before he would have found her. The Sentinels preferred keeping her on a short leash, according to Garrett, and the alliance had no tolerance for personal agendas—except their own. She had yet to fully understand what mattered most to them—or Garrett. He was as addictive to her as crystal meth to an addict, and she hoped her name might come up on the list of necessities in his life. But she knew he was too secretive to confide such things to her. It wasn't his nature.

"Globe Harvest is here in Chicago," she told him. "I've got a solid lead that I'm—"

"Don't you mean that in the past tense? From what I hear, your lead is nothing but a pile of rubble."

Damn it! Garrett knew more than she had counted on. Alexa tensed her jaw, contemplating her next move.

"I retrieved documents from their control room before the explosion, but I'm sure you know that already or we wouldn't be having this conversation." She sipped her coffee. "I'm confident I'll find another way to track them."

"That is, if a certain bounty hunter doesn't beat you to the punch. Jessica Beckett is an interesting woman, wouldn't you agree?"

A twinge of jealousy jabbed at Alexa, a reaction she hadn't expected. When Garrett found people interesting, it usually meant he'd dug into their background on behalf of the Sentinels, but something in the way he'd said Jessica's name triggered a more personal reaction.

He'd used that same understated word—interesting—to describe her two years ago when he recruited her to be his associate.

"Yes, she is," she said. "I'll be sure to add her to my Christmas card list. What's on your mind?"

"It's come to my attention that she retrieved documents from that fire, and hers are in much better condition than the burned fragments you sent for analysis."

The Sentinels had a web of informants all over the world, but obviously, his list also included someone within the ranks of the local police force, if he knew about evidence the bounty hunter had retrieved.

"So what are you suggesting?"

"The police might've already confiscated her documents as evidence by now, but I hear that the FBI will be involved shortly. Once the feds get their hands on this case, you'll have a much harder time keeping a low profile. You may want to talk to Jessica and pool your resources, whatever they may be."

Garrett still hadn't committed any Sentinels' aid in her pursuit of Globe Harvest. With his access to powerful connections all over the globe, if he chose to help her, she had no doubt Globe Harvest's days would be numbered. And yet he continued to sit on the sidelines, claiming the Sentinels had no interest in intervening. Why?

The most she had been able to ascertain about Garrett Wheeler's secretive alliance and their "agenda" was that he carried out the wishes of an elite group of powerful men from various countries—an alliance of wealthy vigilantes. It appeared that in tough situations, where the court systems of the world would have difficulty rendering justice, the Sentinels intervened to quietly do what had to be done.

For the most part, she agreed in dispensing justice on a grander scale when the case was clearly out of the reach of legal jurisdictions, a common issue in today's international arena. And she relished her role in playing devil's advocate with Garrett and his associates. But there were times when she wondered if these men were treading on a slippery slope. After all, they backed a course of action that came close to crossing a dangerous line between eradicating what they pursued and becoming another facet of it—with the only distinction being their point of view.

For now, the organization still had her allegiance. And from her perspective, the benefits far outweighed the pitfalls. But with her loyalty came a skepticism these men would have to deal with. She wouldn't follow any cause with blinders on. That was one of the reasons she had chosen to pursue Globe Harvest on her own, when Garrett and his backers failed to show interest in her private investigation.

She'd confronted Garrett before when she hadn't comprehended the Sentinels' motives, and she learned that he had boundaries . . . except in the bedroom.

"Why are you telling me about the FBI?" she asked, setting down her coffee cup. "If you wanted to, you could convince your associates to make a difference in bringing down Globe Harvest. I don't understand why—"

"We've gone over this before. These men have their reasons." A phrase she'd heard often from him. "Besides, the world is full of injustice, and they prefer to pick their own battles. However, I will share something troubling I've heard. A Russian by the name of Stanislav Petrovin was in charge of security for the Chicago operation. Stas is a dangerous man with even deadlier connections, Alexa. As we speak, I'm sending you an encrypted file on him."

"You sound like you know Petrovin."

"Just take care of yourself, Alexa." He paused for a moment, then added, "I miss you."

He ended the call without allowing her to respond to his personal message, words that came across her phone as a tender whisper to her ear. Garrett knew how to keep her off balance, but he'd also thrown her a lifeline in pursuing Globe Harvest. Now that he knew about her agenda, could she count on him for more support, or had his gesture been personally motivated? Like all the other mysteries surrounding Garrett Wheeler and his organization, she suspected her questions would go unanswered.

Once she got Petrovin's dossier and quickly familiarized herself with its content, it would be time to call on Jessica Beckett. She headed for her bedroom to get changed. Knowing Garrett's flair for understatement, she would have to work fast if she wanted to orchestrate an encounter with the bounty hunter before the FBI got too involved. But with someone as tenacious as Jessica Beckett, Alexa knew she'd have to be careful, making sure any interaction with the woman would be a one-way street.

She was determined to cut the bounty hunter out of the picture.

CHAPTER 22

Before dawn
The next morning

With the pain meds nearly out of her system, Jess lay flat on her back staring at the ceiling of her dimly lit hospital room, never feeling so useless. Her body ached and her head throbbed, but at least the pain made her feel like she was doing something. She hoped they would release her today, even though her brain felt like mush.

Unable to sleep, she flicked on a small light over her bed and pulled out the pages she'd taken from the textile factory, squinting as the light reflected off the white paper. Whenever she tried to study them, her eyes blurred, which brought on a lingering headache. So while out of commission, she'd made sure that Seth received a copy of the pages. A set was personally delivered to him by Sam. Seth had told her on the phone that at first glance the numeric sequences didn't make sense to him either, but he was willing to look for any obvious patterns in the code. At least she felt that his effort would be something, but it wasn't nearly enough. Not for her.

Yet staring at the ceiling for hours had served one purpose.

The face of the mystery blond woman came into better focus—bits of memory at a time, like kaleidoscope pieces locking into place. And she was able to sift through her recollections and know these images were not from her distant past. They were more current, from the time of the explosion. If the woman walked up to her on the street in broad daylight, she wasn't sure she would recognize her. But with each passing hour, her mind had cleared away the fog, leaving her with one desperate thought.

If the blond woman had indeed helped her, then she might have done the same for Payton's niece. If so, Nikki could still be out there and in the hands of the Russian. The thought made her stomach gnarl into knots. She had to do something, and lying in a hospital bed wouldn't cut it.

When would she tell Payton the truth about what she suspected? And if she did, would he even believe her?

Once again during the night, the helicopters had traveled for hours with only one brief stop to refuel. They landed in a grassy open field where a fuel truck was awaiting their arrival. Every aspect of their departure from Chicago had been planned and coordinated in secrecy. This time, once they touched down, armed men ordered Nikki and the others out of the passenger compartment and into the grass.

When she saw what was happening, panic gripped her chest, making it hard to breathe. Her legs felt weak and unable to move. A man shoved her behind the others. Every girl was forced into the scrub brush at gunpoint. This was it. Nikki believed they'd all be killed—coerced to their knees and shot in the head in mass execution.

"Oh, God . . . please no," she pleaded under her breath.

Terrifying mental pictures flashed across her mind, each worse than the last. But once Nikki saw they were being forced to relieve themselves, she breathed a sigh of relief. Men holding flashlights kept track of the girls as they squatted, giving them no privacy as they watched. What Nikki had imagined had been far worse, so she suffered through the indignity when it came to her turn.

After they got back into the helicopters and took off, Nikki had huddled with the rest and kept an eye out the window to look for city lights or distinguishing landmarks. But it never got light enough for her to see much. She had no doubt their escape had been well planned. They flew by night and through remote areas, making it harder for anyone to track their flight. And with each well-orchestrated move by her captors, she grew more depressed. These men had thought of everything, leaving her without hope of ever being rescued.

At dawn, they landed in another open field, with a shack on the property, a corrugated metal Quonset hut amidst rolling mountains that encircled a clearing. No power lines. No real roads. Only rutted dirt tracks. Nikki didn't recognize any of it. She had no idea if they were even in the United States anymore. And with the noticeable temperature drop, she caught a chill as she followed the others to the only shelter within miles.

"Get them inside," she heard the Russian tell one of the men. "Chain them together, except for the three. I want them on a separate leash."

"We shouldn't stay here long," the second man cautioned, looking over his shoulder and along the horizon.

"Not planning on it, but we may be here for a day or two. I'm waiting for clearance for our next stops," the Russian ordered. "Make sure they . . ."

Nikki didn't hear anything else the Russian said. She got shoved inside with the others, and started to look for the darkest corner she could find. A moldy stench made it nearly impossible to breathe. And their movements echoed in the tin structure as the girls cowered together in smaller packs. Someone struck a match and lit a lamp, casting shadows and the smell of kerosene into the dank space. One man threw dusty, scratchy blankets at them, and some of the girls had begun to cough from the filth floating in the stale air.

But as Nikki found a spot to sit, one of her abductors

grabbed her arm and hauled her to another corner, away from the others. She was handcuffed and chained to two other girls and given half a bottle of water to share. The others across the room got nothing.

She handed the water bottle to the girls chained beside her, allowing them to drink first. When it was Nikki's turn, the youngest kid handed her the water and whispered, a girl by the name of Britney Webber who had a small heart-shaped birthmark on her chin.

"What's happening? Why did they separate us?" Britney's eyes glistened with tears in the dimly lit room.

Nikki shook her head in reply, too scared to speculate. Her lips quivered and the water bottle trembled in her hand as she drank. She'd been culled out with two others for a reason, a purpose she didn't want to think about. She had hoped to get some sleep, but closing her eyes now was out of the question. After her failed attempt to escape with Jessica, she felt certain the Russian's decision to isolate her had more to do with retribution than any treatment for good behavior.

The man had plans for her—something real special. And no amount of speculation would prepare her. No matter what she imagined, the Russian could conjure something much worse.

Nikki fought to keep from heaving the contents of her stomach. She shut her eyes tight and imagined hiding in the darkest corner of her closet back home. As she slowed her breathing, she almost smelled the light fragrance of her favorite perfume, and fought back tears with the memory. And she pretended to listen for the sounds of her mother's footsteps up the stairs. In the not so distant past—a lifetime ago—having her mom outside her closed bedroom door would have angered her. But now she would give anything for such an intrusion. Thinking of her mom brought an undeniable lump to her throat.

And hearing Uncle Payton's soft laughter would have warmed her heart—making her feel safe—until she realized that she'd never hear his voice again. That's when she pictured him dying in the explosion, and the frightening images sent her over the edge. This time she didn't hold back her tears. She couldn't, even if she tried.

"Thanks for everything, Joe. I wish . . ." Payton stood at the doorway to his friend's hospital room, searching for words that wouldn't come. He finally settled on, "Sorry you got hurt."

"Are you kidding me? When I get home, I'm gonna milk this bum leg for all it's worth." Joe grinned between grimaces as a male nurse named Julio slowly helped him into a wheelchair. But his smile quickly faded when he changed the subject. "I know you were out at the site this morning. Anything new?"

"No. Just a whole lot of nothing." Payton shook his head and stared down the hall at nothing in particular, his mind filled with images of the last forty-eight hours.

Hours had blurred into days with nothing accomplished—one big lesson in futility.

Recovery crews had painstakingly sifted through the sparse remnants of the destroyed factory, looking for bodies with cadaver dogs and using other means, without results. He could only watch from a distance behind the police barrier. Sam had warned him that he'd be unable to get closer, but he had to be there when they found Nikki.

It didn't feel right to leave her in the hands of strangers, even well-meaning ones. Payton supposed no news was good news, and a part of him wanted to find hope in that. But being more pragmatic, he had grown to believe no news only delayed the inevitable of knowing what had actually happened to Nikki.

"How's Susannah?" Joe asked as Julio retrieved his overnight bag and packed his personal stuff.

Payton knew that for every hour of not knowing, Susannah

paid an undeniable price. And by the grim look on Joe's face, his friend knew it too.

"Not good." Payton gritted his teeth, fending off the tension headache brewing behind his eyes. "I'm glad you'll be there. She could use a friend."

Susannah's voice had sounded rough on the phone. With every call, Payton had found her more and more on edge as time dragged on without any news. At times, her words slurred and he knew she'd been drinking, but who was he to ask her to quit? She was alone. And with every stone turned aside in that pile of rubble, his sister came closer to confirming her worst fear.

He could only imagine what was happening from a distance. Being unable to console her left him feeling completely useless. Like when they had lost their parents, Susannah balled up in a cocoon of heartache, feeding off whatever was left inside her, giving up. If anyone reached out to help her, he knew she'd probably ignore them. It was her way of handling grief. This time, Payton wasn't sure she could survive the ordeal.

And worrying about his sister had shoved his own feelings deeper.

"She's not the only one who could use a friend." Joe had a way of reading his mind that was downright spooky. "Keep in touch, son. Call me anytime. I mean it."

"I will." He nodded. "Promise."

With Joe in Alaska, Payton knew he'd be losing a lifeline, but it was for the best. When his friend had asked to be sent home, Payton knew Joe had struggled with his decision. He'd explained that he didn't want to be a burden in Chicago, with his bum leg, and taking care of Susannah seemed a worthier endeavor than holding a pity party for one. Payton couldn't help but grin at his justification for leaving the lower forty-eight. Joe feeling sorry for himself was as likely to happen as pro athletes giving up the big bucks and major endorsement deals, to play only for the love of the game.

He stepped back from the door as Julio wheeled Joe into the hallway. "My car's in visitor parking near the patient pickup area," he told the male nurse.

"Not so fast. We've got a stop to make," Joe interrupted. "When does the plane leave?"

"We've got a little over two hours before the charter takes off. Why?"

"Plenty of time." The old man grinned and avoided Payton's eyes. Instead, he stared ahead and directed the nurse with a wave of his hand. "Straight ahead, Julio, my friend."

To Payton, he added, "I promised Jessie that she could see me off and that you'd take her home after. She's being released today."

"Well, isn't that convenient?" Payton narrowed his eyes at his friend.

"Yeah, I thought so."

Jess had signed the last of her hospital release forms and finished packing her overnight bag when a nurse entered the room. Her name tag read LORENA, but she had heard others call her "Smitty." The woman had a voice full of gristle and rolled a wheelchair into the room to haul her to the curb. Unruly short blond hair and sharp eyes tempered with humor gave character to the face of a woman dressed in a crisp white uniform with sensible shoes.

"No thanks. I can walk."

Jess barely looked up, but stopped when she heard, "Sorry, honey. Hospital policy." Lorena smirked, undaunted by Jess's best grimace.

"You don't understand. I've got friends coming to pick me up. I'll be okay." Jess forced a smile. "Save the wheels for someone who really needs 'em."

"Glad to hear you've got friends, honey. We should all be so lucky. But I've never lost this argument and I don't intend to start a losing streak today." The nurse had a glint of amusement in her eyes, clearly enjoying Jess's challenge.

"I wouldn't argue with her, Jessie. Around here, Smitty's got a reputation. They call her Nurse Ratched and she scares the hell out of me."

In the doorway, Payton stood with arms crossed, behind his friend Joe, who sat in a wheelchair and was accompanied by a Hispanic male nurse. If Payton and his friend couldn't buck the system, how did she stand a chance?

At the sound of Payton's voice, the crusty nurse rolled her eyes and fought back a smile.

"Flattery will get you nowhere, young man." She waggled a finger. "If you didn't have such a cute tush, I might take offense and say *póg mo thóin*."

Jess had heard the Gaelic phrase before and knew it meant "Kiss my arse." She shook her head and grinned for real this time.

"Do you mind if I roll her out of here? I swear . . ." Payton made a quick cross over his heart. ". . . she won't budge from the chair until she's free of the building. Deal?"

"Only 'cause it's you, Payton Archer." The nurse heaved a sigh, pretending to be perturbed. "And I'm holding you to your word."

The nurse clutched his hand in both of hers, and in a serious tone added, "We're gonna miss you guys. Have a safe trip back to Alaska, Joe. And Payton? You and your family will be in my prayers."

"Thanks, Smit. That means a lot." He kissed her cheek and the woman blushed, giving Jess a glimpse of the young woman she used to be.

"Now go on. This place is for sick people." The nurse shooed them out.

Complying with Smitty's orders, Payton helped her into the wheelchair and pushed her down the corridor. When they got far enough away, Jess made her move.

"Is she looking?" Gaping over her shoulder, Jess shifted

in her seat, trying to catch a glimpse of her nurse. "I'm blessed with two good legs that work. As soon as I get in the elevator, we're ditching the wheels."

"We're doing no such thing, Ms. Beckett. I made a promise to Smitty, and I'm a man of my word . . . most days." As he pushed her wheelchair, Payton held her down with a strong hand on her shoulder, not letting her up. "Don't make me duct-tape you into this thing."

"When he gets like this, it's best to humor him." Joe winked as he rolled alongside, pushed by his nurse. "Besides, he's wicked with duct tape."

"Who says he needs duct tape for that?" she muttered, and slumped into her seat.

When they got to Payton's SUV rental, Joe had insisted Jess take the front passenger seat since he needed the backseat to put his leg up and stash his crutches. Jess had a sneaking suspicion Joe was playing matchmaker, but she didn't know the man well enough to make that assumption.

At the airport, she got out and stretched her legs, unsure whether she should give Payton some time alone with his friend. But both men made her feel welcome to join them. When it came time for Payton to put Joe on the chartered plane, she was first to say good-bye, making sure Payton had plenty of one-on-one time with his friend. She sat in a chair across the small waiting room of the charter service, gazing out the window and flipping through dated magazines, pretending to ignore the two men within earshot.

"I noticed you left your gun case in the trunk," Payton said to Joe. "I don't think I'll be needing them. Not anymore."

Joe shrugged and fished a key to the case from his pocket. "So return them when you get home. No big deal."

Payton took a deep breath and lowered his head. "Susannah . . . tell her how much I love her. And that I'll call . . ."

The words coming out of his mouth sounded forced, as if he was avoiding a deeper underlying fear, that saying it aloud might make it real.

"I hate leaving you here, especially now," Joe said. "But I'm no good to you like this. And Susannah will probably need someone there when—" He stopped himself.

"When we hear, I may need you to help me make arrangements . . . to bring Nikki home." After a long moment, Payton hugged the man who stood with the help of crutches.

"I love you, old man."

"I love you too, son." Joe closed his eyes.

The two men held each other, sharing what couldn't be captured in words. When Joe pulled from his arms, he wiped a tear from Payton's face, an endearing gesture that seemed natural between them—something a father would do for a son.

Payton walked Joe out to the plane and helped him on board. He came back to the waiting room and stood next to her in silence, watching as the charter pulled away and later took off. For a moment Jess didn't know if he remembered she was there at all. And although she tried not to read too much into the man, it was hard not to respect his open display of emotion for someone he loved like family. That much was very clear. And Payton made no excuses for his sentiment, nor did he make light of it like most men might.

When he was ready, Payton fixed his blue eyes on her and with his deep honeyed voice, smooth as Kentucky Bourbon, he said, "Now why don't you tell me where you live?"

Jess knew she was reading way more than Payton's sad eyes conveyed, but in the instant he focused on her, her world faded to bright white and the sounds of plane engines muffled to nothing. All she heard was the smooth drizzle of his voice. And she felt drawn to the warmth of his body, wanting nothing more than to feel her fingers on his skin and to explore the extent of his tan lines. But reality brought all her enticing images to a grinding halt.

"Yeah . . . right. Home."

Images of the dump she called home flashed in her mind,

especially after Lucas Baker added his decorator touches. If that wasn't enough to deal with, Sam had reminded her that her car had been destroyed in the explosion. Plus, she remembered that the Russian had taken her Colt Python, and thanks to Baker, she didn't even have a backup gun. Since she'd been chasing that not-so-dearly departed bastard and ignoring her pursuit of bounty, she had no cash flow. Marginal though it was, her life had taken a dive into the dumper.

But you ain't the only one who's got it rough, sweetheart, she reminded herself.

None of her troubles measured up to Payton and his sister's. And by the expression on the man's face, he sure looked as if he could use a friend. And maybe a little hope.

"Why don't you let me drive, big guy? We need to talk." Trying not to look too grim, she held out her hand, asking for the keys to the SUV. "But first, I'm hungry and you probably haven't been eating. You trust me?"

He raised an eyebrow but didn't reply. He simply complied by handing over his car keys and following her to the SUV.

Jess had no idea how he would take her suspicions regarding the blond mystery woman and an alternate scenario about the explosion, especially after she'd encouraged Payton to accept that Nikki had been a casualty. She hoped a public restaurant might temper his initial reaction and make him more willing to listen to her reasoning.

But no matter what happened, none of what she had to say would be easy for him to hear—especially if his niece were alive and in the hands of a cruel man. With no leads on how to find Nikki, they'd be as powerless as they were the night of the explosion. The Russian held all the cards, backed by a slick and elusive international organization.

They had nothing.

Innocuous mariachi music wafted from the overhead speakers on the outdoor patio of Jalisco Jim's, a local dive near her neighborhood that had served them a sizzling platter of fajitas to share, along with all the fixings and two mugs of Dos Equis. Under a festive umbrella at a table bordered by a wrought-iron enclosure, she and Payton sat in the far corner of the patio, nearest the back parking lot.

As secluded as the spot was, they were still drawing attention from the other patrons, but she had to get him to consider her scenario of what might have happened the night of the explosion.

"Like you said the other day, if this blond woman got help for me, she would've done the same for Nikki if your niece was in the control room. This mystery woman would've pulled her out too." Jessie narrowed her eyes. "Payton, don't you see? You didn't leave Nikki behind, because she wasn't there by the time you found me. She couldn't have been."

"Then what happened to her?"

As soon as the question was out of his mouth, a look of dread swept over his face. She could have filled in the blanks for him, but she needed Payton to draw his own conclusions.

"Oh, God." He fought to say the words. "Maybe those men didn't leave Nikki behind either."

Jess shivered with his realization. She reached for Payton's hand and held it until he looked at her.

"We're going to find her. I believe Nikki is alive, Payton, and we've got a shot at locating her." She stared into his eyes. "I've seen enough proof that Globe Harvest and its obscene network really exists, and that Russian bastard went to great pains to blow up an abandoned textile plant. He wanted to bury the proof of his link to a larger organization, but not all of that proof got burned. We're gonna find her."

Payton tightened his jaw and pulled his hand away.

"You're mad because I held out on you," she said. "I know how this must sound, but—"

He jumped in, not letting her finish.

"I'm not mad, I just . . . don't know what to think." He shoved back from the table and slouched in his chair, staring at his plate of half-eaten Tex Mex. "If you're right, what the hell am I going to tell Susannah?"

"You see? That's why I didn't say anything before now . . . until I was . . ."

"Sure? Until you were sure? Is that what you were going to say?" He shook his head and didn't wait for her to reply. "Are you still trying to convince yourself . . . or me?"

Now he did sound angry, his tone infused with frustration.

"We've got nothing to go on, Jessie. If she's out there, still alive, how are we going to find her?" He stared off across the patio and muttered under his breath, "How are we going to find Nikki?"

A million-dollar question—a question for which she had no answer. And by the look on his face, Payton knew it too. Her theory on the blond woman was pure speculation. And yet, without any bodies being recovered from the destroyed factory, they had nothing more substantial to cast a doubt on her rationale.

"Sam told me the FBI is looking into the case. They may have jurisdiction. They're analyzing the report I took—"

He interrupted her.

"May have jurisdiction?" He threw up his hands and leaned back in his chair. "While everyone is playing by the rules, in the meantime Nikki's trail is getting colder. And why would the FBI care about one kid . . . a kid who has a history of running away from home?"

Aware he had spoken too loud and had drawn attention, he lowered his voice.

"This isn't right, Jessie."

"For what it's worth, I've got Seth running his own analysis of those pages." When Payton rolled his eyes, she leaned her elbows on the table and continued, "The FBI is not going to share what they find out, unless they have a solid lead. Even if you are family. Hell, they may not even take the case. As far as I'm concerned, nothing much has changed. We're on our own, just like before."

Payton clenched his jaw and stared across the parking lot. She hadn't connected with him.

"Look, you came here looking for Nikki. She could still be in the area. If Sam hasn't found any bodies at the debris, there's a possibility the Russian took her. He must've gotten out like the others. When my head cleared enough, I remembered there was a tunnel out the back. I didn't see where it led, but it was there. Maybe Nikki's trail isn't so cold after all."

Now she had his full attention. He sat up in his chair and propped his elbows on the table, same as her.

"God, you're right," he said. Those gorgeous blue eyes had a spark of fire to them.

"Yeah. Occasionally, it's been known to happen." She nodded. "I've been thinking about this . . . a lot. A couple of days in a hospital bed will do that."

Before she threw out more of her theories, her cell phone rang. She recognized the number.

"I gotta take this. It's Seth." She couldn't help but smile at Payton. Hope had finally settled on his face.

Plus, she'd come to trust her quirky but genius sidekick, Seth Harper. If the kid already had a lead, she could add good timing to his list of excellent qualities.

"Hey, Harper. What's up?"

"Hey, Jess. I just called to tell you the blue monster is yours, at least until you get a new car or settle with your insurance company."

What he said didn't register at first.

"Excuse me?" she questioned, but he didn't stop talking long enough to hear her question.

"I already made arrangements for a loaner—from a friend. So you don't have to worry about me. I parked my van at your apartment, in the visitor's section out front. And

I left a spare key in an envelope, marked with your name. Your apartment manager said she'd see that you got it."

"Gosh, thanks, Seth. You didn't have to do that, but thanks." She smiled at Payton. He looked anxious, waiting to hear what Harper would report. "How's that research coming?"

Silence. Seth didn't answer right away, and when he finally did, he preceded his reply with a heavy sigh. Jess forced a grin for Payton's benefit and waited for the bad news.

"Not very well. I've got nothing. I think there's a pattern that's jumbled on the page, but that only implies an infinite number of possible combos. And I don't have the technology to run all the iterations. I'm not sure where to go from here, but I'm still trying."

"Uh-huh." She nodded, trying to reassure Payton. "Well, stick with it, Seth. I can't think of anyone I'd rather have working on this. I'll call you later."

"Did you hear me? I've got squat. Nada. Zilch." She hung up on Seth as the kid strolled down his mental slang dictionary.

"What did he say?" Payton asked.

She pursed her lips, then replied without thinking, "He's on it. He might have something soon. I'll call you when I hear."

"You better." He reached across the table and gave her hand a squeeze. "What you said is beginning to make sense. I want us to work together to find Nikki. And money is no object. I'll do whatever it takes to find her. Are you okay with taking on a rookie?"

"Yeah, I'm okay with that." She nodded. "I want to help you find Nikki."

As Payton gave her his cell phone number and jotted down his hotel information on a napkin, she pondered what Seth had told her. Payton didn't need another dose of harsh reality. And stretching the truth into the realm of wishful thinking wasn't really a lie, was it? She'd finally gotten him to consider her theory of the mysterious blonde and what it all meant. She couldn't see dashing his hopes now . . . for nothing.

Besides, if she knew Seth—she ignored the fact that she really didn't—the kid would come up with something soon.

He had to.

After 1:00 A.M.

In the wee hours of the morning, Jess awoke in her bed, still wearing her jeans and black T-shirt. Something must have tugged at the periphery of her mind, perhaps a nugget of guilt after her late lunch with Payton. Trying to rebound from a nagging headache, she had taken Advil, hit the sack plenty hard, and hadn't remembered falling asleep, but she supposed she must have. When she opened her eyes, all she saw was a darkened room—an all too familiar one.

Her apartment. Her bed. *Her life.*

Yet she did remember one thing that had lingered. Thoughts of Nikki and Payton had bombarded her, filtering through the violent images of her past to become a jumble of fear and regrets. And a strange haunting melody had played in the background. A song she couldn't quite name. She lay in the dark and listened to a sultry blues song until a peculiar notion bubbled to the surface and struck her with the force of a harsh slap.

If she was awake now—*why did she still hear the music?*

Her eyes grew wide. Holding her breath, Jess lifted her head off the pillow and searched the dark for shadows that moved, listening as the inky black of her apartment closed in on her. She now knew one other thing with certainty.

The haunting music came from her living room. And she wasn't dreaming.

CHAPTER 23

Jess reached toward her nightstand for her gun, but before she slid the drawer open, she remembered that the Russian had taken her Colt Python, the night all hell broke loose. And Baker had stolen her Glock 21, a backup gun she'd kept at home.

Damn it! She peered down the dark hallway, toward her living room. Only a smattering of lights from outside bled through the blinds. Most of her apartment heaved with shadows that played tricks on her eyes.

And the music played. Since Baker had destroyed her stereo, where was the music coming from? Without a gun, it was time for plan B.

She dropped to her knees and fumbled under her bed for the handle of a baseball bat she kept for emergencies. Her fingers groped for the makeshift weapon while she kept her eyes targeted down the hall, searching for any signs of an intruder. After finding the bat, she got to her feet, trying not to make a sound or hit a squeaky floorboard. The music might cover the noise, but no sense in telegraphing her moves.

She clenched the bat and crept down the hall, her eyes alert to any sudden movement. Adrenaline raced through her veins, scurrying a rash of goose bumps across her skin. She tightened her grip, ready to swing at anything that moved.

As she neared the living room, the music grew louder and she finally recognized the source. Flashes of red clued her in and she breathed a sigh of relief.

An old clock radio that had survived Baker's terror was the source. Its red digital numbers were flashing, a throbbing pulse begging for attention. Obviously she hadn't noticed it when she got home. There must have been a power outage while she was away and the clock triggered an old wakeup call.

She took a deep breath to slow her heart, but as she moved to turn off the radio, a voice from across the room stopped her dead.

"I wanted your attention. Thanks for obliging."

Jess had her back to the intruder. She gripped the bat in her hand, unsure what her next move might be, until she heard, "Turn around . . . slowly." She did as she was told.

Her uninvited guest sat in a chair across the room. The woman's blond hair shimmered white in the pale light coming from a nearby window. Most of her body and her face was hidden by murky shadow. Jess had no doubt her intruder orchestrated their encounter, right down to her silhouette.

"I could have shot you," she said, pretending not to be rattled.

"With your baseball bat?"

"I could've had a gun."

"Granted, I took a calculated risk, but you walking out of the bedroom with a bat told me all I needed to know." The blonde moved her head, a subtle shift. "Besides, I searched your apartment while you were in the hospital. I had to be sure you didn't have another gun lying around. A real shame you lost the Colt Python."

She didn't exactly lose the Colt, but the blonde's reminder of the other night triggered a smoldering outrage. She was beginning to think her place had a revolving door on it—first

Baker and now this Paris Hilton knockoff. Having her personal space violated again really pissed her off, but she tried to maintain her composure.

"And if I came out from my bedroom carrying a gun, what would you have done?"

"I'd say . . . it was a good thing neither of us had to find out," the woman said.

Jess lowered her bat but didn't let go. If the woman held a gun on her, the bat would be useless. She took a chance that anyone who would save her life one day wouldn't likely take it the next—at least, not a rational person.

She hoped she'd guessed right.

"If you searched my place beforehand, why didn't you take my bat too?"

"A girl's got to accessorize," the stranger replied. Jess heard the smile in the woman's voice. "Call it my show of good faith."

"I have an urge to thank you for saving my life, but this whole breaking and entering thing makes my memory a little fuzzy. Why are you here?"

"We need to talk. You mind hitting the lights and killing the music? I can only take so much cloak and dagger."

"You're not the only one."

Jess moved toward the nearest light switch and flicked it on. Her eyes adjusted to the light but never strayed from the stranger. Dressed in black, the flaxen blonde was striking. Yet her face had real character—an Uma Thurman type of natural beauty. Her Nordic pale skin and high cheekbones lent elegance to her full lips and an aquiline nose with flared nostrils. Isolated, each feature might not be appealing on its own, but the aggregate was stunning.

The woman's ice blue eyes looked almost gray from a distance—eyes that she imagined could easily switch between good humor and deadly intent. Sprawled in her chair, the blonde appeared tall and athletic, someone who might have played sports at an Ivy League college.

Jess realized that she was nearly the polar opposite. No one would ever describe her as elegant. Yet when confronted by the blonde's intimidating feminine presence, she took pride in the image she'd cultivated over the years—a pit bull on steroids with its hackles up. In her line of work, scrappy with a flair for junkyard mean trumped elegance any day of the week.

"You invade my home and now you want to chat?" Jess grabbed a chair from her kitchen table and straddled it with the seatback flipped. She leaned her elbows on the seatback and continued to play with her bat, an almost threatening gesture if she hadn't added a contradictory smile. "You better talk fast and keep me interested. I get real grumpy when someone interrupts my beauty sleep."

Alexa narrowed her eyes. The bounty hunter scowled from across the room, toying with that worn baseball bat. A nasty scar over Jessica Beckett's eyebrow matched the sinister glare from her dark eyes. Beckett sat on a chair, but clearly looked prepared to fight if she gave her provocation. Seeing the impulsive woman alive and kicking—ready to lay wood upside her head—forced Alexa to back off on her air of superiority. This woman meant business and was dangerous when cornered. If she wanted to gain Beckett's trust, she had to share a little truth.

But how much would she tell her? Too much and the bounty hunter would want in. Too little and the woman would show her the door.

"My name is Alexa Marlowe. I have a similar interest in Globe Harvest. They are an abomination and must be stopped."

The bounty hunter furrowed her brow. "You've got my attention. Go on."

"As you know, I was there at the textile factory. I pulled you out of the control room."

"But you left me. I don't call that very friendly."

"I would've taken you with me, but when I heard your

friends coming, I called out to them. I made sure they found you."

"And if they hadn't come along?"

"Like I said, I would've brought you with me. But in hindsight, that would've been a very big mistake." Before Beckett gave her any lip, she made her point. "If I had done that, we'd both be dead."

When the bounty hunter flinched, Alexa shrugged. "As it was, I barely had enough time to escape through the tunnel. When the explosion ignited the propane fumes, it launched me like a human cannonball." She cocked her head. "All things considered . . . I wouldn't recommend it."

"So you're a Good Samaritan . . . with a penchant for circus tricks. Remind me to send you a Hallmark."

Alexa felt like she was fighting a head wind and not making progress. She had to connect with Jessica . . . now.

"The Russian . . . his name is Stanislav Petrovin. And he flew out of Chicago using helicopters to God knows where. For the sake of the girls he still has, do you think we can dispense with the sarcasm?"

Putting their situation in perspective had done the trick. Beckett's expression melded into one of concern, a far cry from her venomous posturing only seconds before.

"Did Petrovin take the girl who was with me—Nikki Archer?"

The bounty hunter's reaction surprised her. She seemed only concerned for one girl. Finally, the name Archer sunk in.

"I didn't see anyone with you. There was no one else in that control room by the time I got to you." Alexa narrowed her eyes. "So that's why you were with Payton Archer." She hadn't known any of the girls' names before now. "What's the girl's relationship to Archer, besides sharing the same last name?"

"Nikki is his niece. His sister's only child. Payton isn't

exactly brimming over with relations either. She means the world to him."

"And what does she mean to you? I thought you were in this to take down Globe Harvest. Was I wrong?"

Jess pondered the question, struck by the stark revelation about her shift in focus with this case. Her midnight caller had offered her real information about Petrovin and his organization, and her first question had been about Nikki.

What was wrong with her? Had Payton Archer swayed her that much?

"I was concerned about the girl, but Globe Harvest is my main interest." Jess made her face a blank slate. "Why are you telling me all this?"

If the woman was right and Petrovin had flown out of Chicago, why was Alexa here? It made no sense. Jess knew that any resources she had were local and limited, with the emphasis on limited. What did she have that Alexa wanted badly enough to reveal herself?

She didn't have to wait for her answer.

"You have documents taken from the control room. If properly analyzed, they could provide a next step, a way to track Globe Harvest." Alexa leaned forward in her chair. "This organization doesn't usually make that kind of mistake. What you have in your possession could make a big difference in my investigation."

Jess worked hard not to react to Alexa's assertion about the documents. Copies of the pages were tucked in a drawer of her nightstand. She'd tossed them in there when she laid down to rest. How had this woman known about them? Had a cop leaked the information? And if so, whom had they told? Questions flooded her mind, but one loomed ahead of the rest.

"You said you were conducting an investigation. Who do you work for?"

The blonde hesitated an instant before replying, "I'm not

at liberty to say, but I will tell you that the private alliance I work for specializes in tough jurisdictional cases involving criminal activities all over the world. Your work to stop Globe Harvest has given us a priceless opportunity to take them down, a piece at a time. But I'm asking for your cooperation to make that happen."

All she had to do was hand over the pages she'd taken from the control room and her part in this ugly case would be over. But could she trust this woman? Although Sam had the originals, Jess worried that if someone at CPD had tipped Alexa on the documents, those pages might be permanently out of her grasp. After all, evidence could be altered, or disappear and be destroyed for good.

But Seth had copies of the same documents in her possession. Perhaps Alexa didn't know that. Would giving them up be such a big deal?

"Why should I trust you? You broke in here in the middle of the night. You're not exactly my idea of good BFF material." Jess clenched her jaw and glared across the room. "You gotta give me more. Tell me something that might convince me you aren't working for Globe Harvest yourself."

The woman took her time in pondering Jess's request, but eventually complied.

"By the time I got into the control room, most of the documents that remained were nothing but charred remnants. I took what I could and handed them off to be analyzed. I might have been able to retrieve more, but I had to help you."

The woman looked like she had more to say, but Jess had no tolerance for Alexa's not-so-subtle blame game.

"You're blaming me? What happened to all the gratitude for uncovering this priceless opportunity to shut these bastards down?"

"If you hadn't pressed so hard, we could've taken down Petrovin here in Chicago. And we might've rescued Nikki Archer and the others. You ever think of that?"

Alexa's words stung like acid, but the woman showed no mercy. And if what Alexa said was true, she didn't deserve any.

"You're a loose cannon, Jessica. Sometimes that pays off, but it can get you killed, along with anyone innocent caught in your cross fire."

Jess couldn't hide her reaction. She knew all too well that Alexa's accusations had validity. It was one thing to put herself in the line of fire, but quite another to push when someone like Nikki paid the price for her mistakes. She'd spent her life tracking down people like Baker, the Russian, and whoever was behind Globe Harvest—criminals who bartered in human life with entitlement. Being the victim of a similar predator, she had no choice but to expose such men. Reclaiming her life would be an uphill climb. But Alexa's harsh words brought feelings of self-recrimination that were always close at hand, roiling beneath the surface of her thin skin.

Was she capable of being normal? Did she deserve to be happy?

"I shouldn't have said that." Alexa's voice softened. "This job . . . going for the jugular is a tool of the trade. And not one that makes for a stellar human being. I'm sorry."

"But you got your point across. That's all that counts." Jess set the bat down, finding it hard to look the woman in the eye.

"Look," Alexa said, "the partial page I got my hands on . . . the numbers were jumbled to throw us off, but the page I retrieved gave us coordinates where Globe Harvest had a handful of their covert organizations. But since each location is compartmentalized, we would need to hit them all at once to shut them down for good, otherwise they'd fold and disappear, only to regroup in another locale. Petrovin is doing that now, like a damned cockroach scurrying away from the light."

"Nice analogy, but I'd hate to insult the roach population." Jess propped her chin in her hands, prepared to listen.

"Don't you see? With your pages, we'd have a better look at more of their locations across the world. We could hit them at the same time. My organization has the resources to quietly handle it . . . without fanfare."

"Or the pesky intrusion of law enforcement. Right?"

Alexa raised an eyebrow. "Is that a concern for you?"

Jess thought about it. "No, not really."

"Good. I was beginning to think you'd gone bleeding heart liberal on me."

Before Alexa got too comfortable, Jess added, "I want in on this."

The woman shook her head, not giving any thought to her proposition.

"No, the alliance wouldn't allow it." She looked adamant. "As it is, I'm pushing this investigation. Like you, I'm going it alone, but if I can give them Globe Harvest on a platter, I may convince the alliance to give me the resources I'd need. Having you involved would only complicate things."

The woman's expression softened. "I know you have no reason to, but you're gonna have to trust me."

Trust? She wasn't exactly a master of the concept. She didn't always trust herself to do the right thing. How could she place her faith in a ruthless woman like Alexa and her secret alliance? Her organization sounded like no more than a group of international vigilantes. Yet, did she have a choice? If she wanted Nikki to be rescued and play a part in taking down Globe Harvest, she had to trust someone. More lives were at stake. Could she afford to let her ego get in the way if Alexa had a better shot at shutting down Globe Harvest and rescuing Nikki?

Besides, Seth had copies of the pages, she reminded herself again. And Alexa had told her enough about the analysis her alliance had done to locate a few of the Globe Harvest locations. Maybe Seth could benefit by the input if she chose to move forward with her own investigation.

With a show of reluctance, Jess walked into her bedroom

and retrieved the documents from her nightstand drawer. When she returned, Alexa was standing by her front door. But before Jess handed over the pages, she had one more thing to ask.

"If something should come up, how do I get in touch with you?" she asked. When Alexa hesitated, she added, "Come on. Throw me a bone. You said it yourself. I gave you this priceless opportunity. I might have something to contribute after you're gone."

The woman thought about it, and after a moment, pulled a long gold chain over her head. The chain had a gold locket with a beautiful sapphire-cut stone in the center. Jess wasn't much for jewelry, but this piece caught her eye.

"Keep this with you. Press down on the stone only in case of an emergency. And I mean that, Jessica. Only for emergencies," Alexa warned with a stern look. "It'll send out a beacon no matter where you are, and the alliance will contact me. Once I get that call, how can I reach you?"

Jess started to give the number to her cell phone, but stopped when she noticed Alexa wasn't jotting it down.

"Why aren't you writing this down?"

"I don't need to. Tell me once and I'll remember."

Yeah, right. Jess narrowed her eyes, but gave her the number again. After all, she'd already handed over her precious pages. If Alexa wasn't on the level, whether she had her phone number or not wouldn't matter.

"Call me gullible, but I'm gonna ask this anyway. I'd appreciate knowing what happens after your operation goes down. Call it . . . a need for closure. And Payton's niece is still missing. Even if you put a stranglehold on Globe Harvest, that doesn't mean we'll ever find her." The truth of Payton's situation twisted in her gut as she said the words. "Surprise me. Have a heart, will ya? Give me something."

The woman considered her plea and her expression softened. "You've earned that much, Jessica. I'll see what I can do."

When Alexa slipped through her front door, Jess noticed it had begun to rain outside, which contributed to her somber mood. After locking the door behind her late night visitor, she was left with an aching hollowness, a recoil to the nebulous ending of her investigation into Lucas Baker. She had nothing but her hope that Alexa would do as she'd promised. She looked down at the locket in her hand and rubbed her thumb lightly over the gemstone.

"For emergencies only," she whispered.

She replayed the conversation with Alexa Marlowe in her mind and hoped she'd done the right thing. If the woman had told the truth and the Russian had flown out of Chicago, enlisting the aid of Alexa and her mystery alliance might make all the difference in finding Nikki alive. Jess's gut told her it was worth the risk, but she had no idea if Payton would feel the same. Petrovin escaping with Nikki and leaving Chicago would be enough of a blow.

How would she tell Payton? He had to know what had happened. She had no choice but to clue him in that she'd relinquished control to another person—a stranger—who made promises of alliances and resources. Would he be relieved, or would he resent her unilateral decision to leave him out of this very important change in plan?

Jess slipped on the gold necklace and headed for her bedroom to freshen up and change. Payton had given her the number to his cell phone and his room at the Marriott in Oak Brook so she could contact him directly. But what she had to say needed to be done in person.

All she wanted was to give Payton hope. But in her heart she knew it wouldn't be that simple. For her, nothing ever was.

CHAPTER 24

Marriott Hotel
Oak Brook

In damp clothes and hair to match, Jess stood outside Payton's hotel room staring at the peephole of his door as if its glaring eye watched her in return. Once she got out of the rain and hit the air-conditioning inside the hotel, she'd taken on a chill. Her fingers were like ice. At least with her hands stuffed into the pockets of her jeans for warmth, she had two less moving parts to give away her jitters.

Chewing the inside corner of her mouth, she finally mustered the courage to raise a hand and knock, but stopped again to glance at her watch. A little past two in the morning, five minutes after the last time she checked. She wondered why she'd come at this hour. A short time ago, back at her place, driving straight here seemed rational. Now, standing in the quiet hallway, it felt like a colossal bonehead move.

She was about to knock on a man's door in the middle of the night. Even if she had a legitimate reason to speak to him, a part of her felt the awkwardness of her intrusion on a personal level. But if she waited until a decent hour to wake him, he might resent her unilateral decision all the more, as if Nikki didn't rate in importance enough to inconvenience him. Yet rolling him out in the middle of the night had its risks too. She had no idea how he'd take her midnight encounter with Alexa Marlowe.

Jess suspected that no matter what she did, she'd be damned one way or the other, but did she have another reason for being here at this hour?

Her attraction to Payton played more of a role than she wanted to openly admit. If she only had it in mind to talk, she could have phoned from the lobby and given him warning that he had a late night caller. Instead, she'd chosen to stand at his door like a damned schoolgirl, debating what to do next.

And she couldn't deny that she felt completely outclassed by him—a chronic condition on her part, and one of the reasons she'd always made the wrong decisions about men. Venturing a toe into Payton's world implied she felt worthy of the endeavor, and she knew that wasn't so. She'd never tried setting the bar too high; that simply wasn't a consideration. But lowering her expectations hadn't been an answer either. For the first time, a man like Payton had made her feel normal and accepted . . . even attractive. She was wholly unprepared for how he made her feel, and it scared her, yet she couldn't cut and run.

"You're such an idiot, Jess," she muttered, running another hand through her damp hair. Finally, she shrugged. "Oh hell, this is business. This ain't no prom date."

She clenched her jaw and rolled her eyes, raising her hand one more time. Taking a deep breath, she knocked on his door and waited, listening for any sound from inside the room. Other than the faint drone of the ice machine down the hall, she heard nothing out of the ordinary until the slide of a chain and the tumble of a dead bolt told her she didn't have to knock again.

When the door opened, Payton squinted into the bright hallway, dressed only in navy pajama bottoms.

"Hey . . . what's up?" The deep rumble of his voice hit

the pit of her stomach and bolted through her body like a tantalizing spark that she never wanted to end.

"Ah, hi." She grinned and rocked on her heels. "I, uh . . ."

Words failed her as Payton raked fingers through his tousled blond hair, brushing loose strands from sleepy blue eyes. While he was distracted and not fully awake, she took advantage of the moment.

She trailed her eyes down his bare chest and rock-solid abs, not doing a very good job at exercising restraint. She had never seen a man who looked so good in the flesh. His broad muscular chest and arms made her feel petite and feminine, an odd sensation that left her confused about who she was and what she wanted. And the stubble on his chin made him look dangerous and overloaded with testosterone, a serious addiction for her. Everything about this man left her hungry for more.

"I need to . . . talk." She swallowed, wincing after she heard a noticeable gulp deep in her throat. "That is, we need to . . ." Finally she sighed and asked, "Can I come in?"

"Yeah, sure."

Payton stepped aside to let her by, leaving the tantalizing smell of his warm skin in his wake. She walked into the dimly lit room and stared at his rumpled bed, a sight that sent a rush of heat to her face . . . and other parts of her body.

Slowly, she turned toward him as images flashed through her mind of him—of them together—the feel of his hands on her breasts and his warm wet tongue on her skin. She had something important to tell him, but standing here now, all she craved was a simpler life. All she wanted to be was a woman alone with a man, free to do whatever was in her heart.

Gazing at him now, she thought she saw hunger stirring in his blue eyes—or was that merely wishful thinking on her part? She had no idea and didn't care, but she heard the sound of own voice in the back of her mind.

Lord, Jess, what now? What the hell are you gonna do now?

A beautiful woman dropping by his hotel room in the middle of the night sent one clear message to Payton's brain. For him, at this hour, things got real simple. Jessie probably had something important to say.

And generally that involved talking. Talking didn't rate high on his list of favorite things to do with his mouth at this time of night.

And to complicate matters, she looked like she just stepped out of the shower, and smelled of herbal soap and flowers. All he wanted to do was wrap her in his arms and kiss her. She was a strong intelligent woman, but he sensed a part of her was broken inside—a part he wanted to protect. Jessie had an edge of sadness to her, but that wasn't the main thing on his mind right now.

Not now.

Dressed in jeans and a black T-shirt, she hadn't worn anything provocative. But with a woman like Jessie, her sensuality had more to do with her than anything she put on her body. When she walked by him, real slow, her thighs flipped his switch. And with her damp hair and clothes, her nipples had tightened from the AC he had blasting in the room. A major distraction. He wasn't sure he could stay focused. But what always sent him over the edge with Jessie were her lips. He caught himself staring at them all the time, like a starving man eyeballing a thick juicy steak. He had it bad.

And at this hour, with her all to himself in his room, he felt his need for her, exposed and raw. He couldn't hide his feelings, not anymore. Against his better judgment, he took a step toward her and his body reacted. Still, he couldn't bring himself to say a word. Speaking would spoil the moment, sever whatever connection they had between them. He wanted her to make the first move, and searched her eyes for the trigger.

Did she feel the same? Why was she here . . . at this time of night? Payton licked his lips and swallowed, hard. What came next would depend on her.

"I've got something," she began, avoiding his gaze, "that I think you should know."

After a long awkward silence, he finally said, "You came to talk?"

His question stopped her cold. She blinked twice, unable to hide her immediate reaction.

"Well . . . yeah."

By the look on his face, she hadn't misread the situation. It was not her wishful thinking. Payton hadn't expected conversation. It would have been easy for her to make the first move. And only the good Lord knew how much she wanted to do just that. She sensed he would have followed her lead, but she owed him an explanation. If he still felt the same after she told him why she'd come, maybe she'd let sweet nature take its course.

"Damn, it's freezing in here, Alaska boy. You got the AC cranked so you don't thaw?"

"What can I say? I like it cold." He went to the thermostat and turned down the air-conditioning. "I got a jacket you can wear if it'll help."

She might have taken him up on his offer, but by the look on his face, it seemed as if he hoped she wouldn't.

"No, really. I'm good." She rubbed her hands together and began. "Someone came to my apartment a little while ago. That mystery blonde from the explosion wasn't a figment of my imagination after all."

"What happened?" He locked his eyes on her and wouldn't let her go. "What did she want?"

"Besides practicing her breaking and entering skills? She had an interesting way to get my attention." Jess pulled a chair from the desk and sat. When she did, Payton slumped to a corner of his bed. "And she's prone to drama, but basically she told me her name is Alexa Marlowe. She wouldn't tell me much about the organization she works for, except to say it's a private international alliance that specializes in criminal cases with tough jurisdictional boundaries. I figured it for a well-funded vigilante group, but I could be reading into it. I have no idea if she was telling me the truth. At least, not until I can do a little digging."

"What else did she say? Did she tell you anything about Nikki?"

In record time Payton had made the leap she'd expected. If the blonde had been there that night, she could've seen Nikki and helped her out of the inferno. He was shooting for the Cliff Notes version of her story, and she couldn't blame him.

"She told me the name of the Russian, Stanislav Petrovin. And it was like you figured. Alexa pulled me from the fire and had called out to you, so I'd be found. She chased after Petrovin through a tunnel and barely escaped the blast. After she got clear, she heard helicopters, but in the dark she couldn't tell where they went."

Jess got up from the chair and joined Payton on the mattress, touching his arm as she continued.

"Alexa said she didn't see Nikki in the control room. As far as I'm concerned, that means one thing. If Sam doesn't find your niece's body at the bomb site, we've got no choice but to assume she's with the Russian."

It had been days, and they would have no idea where the bastard took her. She didn't say those words aloud, but that thought would hit him soon enough.

"But Jessie, why did she tell you all this? What did she want?"

"She wanted the documents that I saved from the fire."

"What? You gave them to her?" Payton stood and walked to the far side of the room, his back to her, hands on his hips. After a long moment, he asked, "What do you think she's after?"

She got up from the bed and joined him, only getting a glimpse of his profile in the dim room. Partially drawn curtains painted his bare chest with a strip of city lights. And with the rain, the glimmer dappled his skin in rainbow-colored prisms.

She searched for words to comfort him.

"I believe she's after the bastards who took Nikki, Payton. And it sounds like she's got the resources to make good on her promises. But that doesn't mean we sit around and wait. Seth still has copies. I don't think she knew I had another set, and I certainly didn't tell her. She mentioned the pages contained coordinates of some kind. Maybe that tidbit will help Seth make faster progress. Harper's a whiz at this brainiac stuff, I swear. I'll call him first thing, but if Alexa has access to an organization that can track Globe Harvest on a grand scale, I figured we had nothing to lose. I hope you agree."

She watched Payton's jaw tighten, but couldn't read him.

"I just feel so . . . powerless," he said. "If it was a matter of money, I would spend every last dime to get her back, but damn it! We've got nothing, Jessie." He turned and moved toward her, frustration etched across his face. "We've got nothing."

What he said triggered her memory of Alexa. The woman's words surged through her mind. *You're a loose cannon, Jessica . . . it can get you killed, along with anyone innocent caught in your cross fire.* She felt the weight of the chain and sapphire pendant under her shirt, the only lifeline she had to Alexa and her covert alliance. Yet no matter how much it would mean to her to hear that Alexa had stopped Globe Harvest, her part in the victory would feel hollow if they never found Payton's niece. She still felt responsible for the Russian taking Nikki out of Chicago.

"You gotta know . . . I might have made matters worse, Payton. I meddled and put Nikki into a worse situation with Petrovin."

Payton took another step and pulled her into his arms. "No, that's not true, Jessie. You led us to her."

But nothing he said would console her. She fought the tears that stung her eyes. "You may never find her, even if Alexa can rally the cavalry."

And still he held her, despite what she'd told him. She pressed her cheek to his shoulder, unsure she deserved his understanding.

"All I wanted was to give you hope of finding her . . . but I think I've screwed this all up."

He rocked her where she stood, murmuring reassurances in a low voice. His words didn't register at first. Her guilt and pain masked them. But eventually what he said sank in.

"Jessie, you're one of the bravest people I know. You've taken on a battle that's not yours to fight alone. You did the right thing." He raised her chin and brushed back her hair. "You shed light on this organization and now others are involved. People with real clout. The FBI is on the case, plus Alexa's group. As far as I'm concerned, you've gone above and beyond. And I'm grateful. Nikki didn't have much of a chance until you came along."

She couldn't look him in the eye, despite his compassion. Nothing would free her from the blame.

"But Petrovin has taken her to God knows where," she said. "And all we have are the documents I took from the control room. What are the odds that Alexa will find her in the few locations listed on that damned report? My luck is for shit lately."

"I don't know. I'm not much of a gambler, but I'd put my money on you . . . any day."

Stunned, she looked up at him, touched by his faith in her. From almost the first time they'd met, in the chaos after the explosion, she had felt a connection to him. It was as if they'd known each other in another life. He had an ease about him. And yet he was a kindred spirit, wearing his scars on the inside without excuses. This time when she gazed at him, she found more than commiseration in his eyes.

"You were right before." She stared at his lips and felt the warmth of his skin through her damp shirt. "I didn't come here . . . just to talk."

She took the first step and kissed him, taking a chance he'd feel the same. At first the touch of his lips sent a tingle through her body, the subtle thrill of a first-time lover. But after his tenderness swelled to urgent need, she felt an uncontrollable heat raging under her skin.

With every man before, all she wanted was the physical gratification. With lights out, she took what she wanted and never gave anything more. Hot and heavy, quick and done, she knew how to get what she needed. Yet with Payton, she wanted . . . more.

But he stopped and pulled away from her.

"What's the matter?" she asked. A sharp stab of fear seethed through her belly. Maybe he'd changed *his* mind.

"Not like this," he panted. He touched his forehead to hers and stroked her cheek. "I want to remember . . . everything. Take our time."

His expectation sent a rush of dread through her. She was no storybook princess leading a charmed life—far from it. She couldn't understand why he thought she was so special. Panic took hold, and old hang-ups were hard to deny.

"Please . . . can we turn out the lights?" she asked. Nearly forgetting to breathe, she waited for his answer.

"You don't have to hide anything from me, Jessie." He led her to the bed, his hand in hers. But before anything else happened, he turned to ask, "Are you okay with this? I don't want to . . . force you."

"It's not that. I want you, believe me. But every time I get to this point—" She stopped, fighting the lump in her throat, unable to look him in the eye again.

"What?" he asked. "Tell me."

No man had ever wanted to know before, especially at a time like this. With other men, once she gave the green light, talking wasn't necessary. All thrust and afterburners, no subtlety required. If she wondered about Payton being like them, those thoughts melted away like drizzled honey on her tongue, only the sweetness lingered.

"No one's ever asked before," she said. "It's hard to explain."

"Try me. And we're not punching a clock here. Take your time."

She stared at him now, wondering how much to say. Telling him everything meant taking a chance. If she let him into that part of her life, would he only see the damage and run? She took a deep breath and started, unsure where she'd end up.

"I can't control it . . . this fear in the pit of my stomach. It's an impulse that I've learned to live with, but it never really goes away. Right or wrong, it's part of me now." She searched for the words that would make him understand. "Something happened . . . when I was a kid. I know now that it had nothing to do with sex. It was an act of violence, but understanding that doesn't make it any easier. And even though it all happened a long time ago, I guess a piece of the fear stayed behind. It burrowed under my skin, beneath the scars."

She touched the jagged mark that puckered her skin near her eyebrow, an old habit. "Guess you could say X marks the spot."

Over the years, her smart-ass humor had grown into a suit of armor, but tonight it fell flat. Now she only wanted the awkwardness to go away, but she couldn't force a smile. Her old wounds would soon speak for themselves. He'd see her scars . . . or feel them on her skin in the dark. She clenched her jaw, remembering the reactions of other men. Their repulsed flinches, no matter how subtle, had stuck in her mind.

She wasn't sure she could take that from Payton.

Without saying a word, he turned out the lights in the room. When he got near the window, he shoved open the curtains and let the city lights shine through the streaks of rain that bled down the glass. Myriad colors shone into the room, like a kaleidoscope reflecting the shimmer.

"What are you doing?" she asked.

"You wanted the lights out." In the pale glow, his deep voice resonated under her skin like a soothing quiver. "But I've always been a real sucker for rain. And we've got a front row seat."

Payton caressed her face with his hands and kissed the scar on her eyebrow. She closed her eyes, feeling every subtle nuance of his lips on her skin. Her heart pounded heavy in her chest, adding fuel to her growing fire for him.

She expected him to pull the T-shirt over her head and help her undress, but instead Payton surprised her. He held the comforter and invited her to his bed, clothes and all.

"You won't get any pressure from me, Jessie. Nothing has to happen tonight. We're not punching a clock, remember?" And with a smile she always wanted to remember, he added, "We can watch the rain."

If any other man had made this move, she would never have trusted him. But something in Payton's eyes made her feel safe. She slipped off her shoes and cleaned out her pockets, setting her cell phone, ID, and car keys on the hotel dresser. Then she crawled into bed with him and found a spot to rest her head, in the crook of his shoulder. It took a while for her skin and hands to warm up, but as he stroked her hair, she listened to the sound of his heart and counted his breaths.

And together in the dark, they watched the rain paint the canvas of his window.

At first she tried to stifle the onset of tears, a mix of emotion instigated for very different reasons. Eventually she let them flow free, knowing he'd understand and she wouldn't have to explain. She found comfort in their silence . . . and the rain.

Payton's unconditional acceptance of her had opened a floodgate of emotion that she hadn't allowed herself to feel in a very long time. Like an epiphany, she sensed that she hovered over a threshold between her tormented childhood and the woman she always hoped to be. If she wanted to break the negative pattern of relationships in her life, she'd have to open old wounds. So much of who she was had been defined by the violence of her past. She knew how to keep people out of her life, but could she let someone like Payton in without boundaries? Not even her friend Sam had that privilege.

Any time she'd been happy, the feeling didn't last. It was always tainted by the enduring ache that she didn't deserve it. Taking emotion out of the equation, she knew that if she allowed this vile cycle to continue, the bastard who had violated her childhood with his perversions would remain in control. How long would she stand for that?

Whether or not she had a man in her heart wouldn't change things. She had to take back her life and do it for herself. Payton had only instigated the line she now wanted to draw in the sand, but he couldn't be the reason for it.

Eventually her thoughts turned to him as she drifted off to sleep. Payton Archer and his love for rain had found a home in her heart. And strange as it felt, nothing could have been more perfect.

CHAPTER 25

A sustained thunder intensified in her mind until Nikki could no longer keep her eyes shut. She awoke with a start from a fitful sleep and knocked her head against something metal.

"Ow . . . shit."

The jolt nearly stopped her heart, but even after she got oriented to where she was, the shock lingered. The helicopter must have hit rough air, buffeting the fuselage. And with that realization, despair hit her square in the face.

It was still nighttime—nothing had changed—and her nightmare persisted.

She had no idea where she was, and it had been days since her captors let her see daylight. As a consequence, she'd lost track of time. The Russian had kept them on the move, taking her and two other girls deeper into his bent rendition of hell. The fact that he chose to stay with her small group—letting the other hostages go with his men—struck her with an unrelenting fear.

He was with them because of her.

She saw his silhouette in the cockpit of the helicopter. An eerie blue haze outlined his hulking form in profile, making him appear ghostly and more like the monster she pictured when she shut her eyes. To take her mind off him, Nikki peered out a side window, a subtle move so she wouldn't draw attention to herself. She searched for anything that might give a hint where they were. Murky black and obscure shapes drifted underneath for as far as she could see. In the glimmer of moonlight, she thought she saw choppy water below and imagined a vast ocean with no land in sight. She had serious doubts they were still in the United States, and that frightened her too.

Where the hell was he taking them? As bad as it was to be constantly on the move, she dreaded another stop even more. She had a bad feeling the next one might be her last.

Nikki's belly growled and she felt its rumble as they hit another air pocket, a reminder she hadn't eaten in a while. Despite her situation, she'd scarfed down food when they gave it to her, ignoring her stomach nearly retching. She had to keep up her strength. Staying strong might make the difference between living and dying. But she suspected the Russian had kept them dosed with tranquilizers. Nikki fought the drowsiness and tried to stay awake, but knew she'd never win the battle, not if she wanted to eat or drink.

Britney Webber and the other kid were slumped against her now, dead asleep. Their body heat kept the chilly night air at bay but also reminded her she wasn't alone, an unfortunate circumstance for them all. Nikki stared down at the heart-shaped birthmark on Britney's chin, one of the reasons she'd remembered her name. She hadn't bothered to learn the other girl's name and tried not to think about why that was. Normally, the close quarters would have made her self-conscious—yet here nothing was *normal*. Her body smelled, covered in a layer of sweat and grit, but she couldn't do a thing about it. Without access to water, she couldn't clean herself—and she had no privacy.

She felt the aircraft lurch then descend, and the choppy terrain below dissolved into darkness. On the horizon, she saw faint lights, but nothing to indicate a significant town. Fear gripped her more strongly and she felt another wave of nausea.

This is it, she thought. They were going to land again.

When she turned her head, she caught a motion from the cockpit. The Russian had been staring at her in the dark, his face contorted into a sneer. The control panel cast a macabre aura that made him look more sinister, something she didn't think possible.

"Your last stop." He spoke loud enough for her to hear him over the rotor engine. By the way he said it, she knew he was sending her a message, one she didn't want explained.

From below, a sudden show of floodlights signaled the helicopter where to land. Paint on the tarmac marked the spot. In the beams, she caught a glimpse of old chain-link fencing and got the impression of an array of buildings in the distance. A bigger facility, yet it looked deathly still. No other lights. No movement. No visible activity below except for the few men she saw standing near the edge of darkness. They were nothing more than faceless shapes. And the place reminded her of the old factory they had left behind in Chicago, a terrifying image she wanted to forget. A nasty déjà vu gripped her.

"God help me," she whispered, her body trembling.

Once they landed, cold night air swept into a frenzy under the rotor blade of the helicopter as the Russian's men hauled them, handcuffed together, toward an old building. Bound like that, it was hard to walk. Blowing and steady drizzle wet Nikki's face and clothes. With the chill, she knew she'd have a bad case of the shakes to contend with. The rain normally reminded her of home, but now it only made things more miserable and foreboding.

In the dark, and surrounded by more of the Russian's uniformed men, she couldn't get a good look at the grounds, but sensed that the landing site lay in the shadow of a hill, its silhouette framed by the sparing moonlight. And from the light off her captors' flashlights, she caught glimpses of cracked asphalt and chunks of cement underfoot, with broken windows adjacent to rusting metal doors. A musty odor lingered in the air once they got inside the old cinder-block building. But the inside of the dilapidated structure wasn't as run-down as she'd anticipated. A completely different setup, yet similar to Chicago.

The men headed down a corridor that seemed a dead end. By the looks of it, they had made a mistake, but when they didn't appear hesitant, she kept her eyes alert to memorize the way.

Her captors stepped behind a pile of rubble, yanking her and the others with them. They squeezed by fallen cinder-block walls with old rusted rebar jutting from boulders of cement. Once they cleared the obstruction, she saw where they were heading. Farther down there was an elevator door she would have missed in the dark. And when one of the men punched the button, it lit up and the elevator came to life.

Where were they getting their power?

The elevator took them to a subterranean level designated by a series of letters and numbers, none of which made sense to her. When the elevator doors opened again, she didn't see any other kids, as in the last place. The air chilled her skin even more, and a funny odor filled her nostrils, something she couldn't quite identify. The interior of the facility looked more upscale and new. The change surprised her.

Where had they taken her?

She didn't have long to ponder the question. As soon as they got off the elevator, the uniformed men circled her and the other girls. She returned their stares long enough to notice that they weren't paying attention to her. They were waiting for the Russian to give them orders. She held her breath, steeling herself for what would come next. The Russian eyeballed her and the other two girls one by one, as if making up his mind. Finally, his eyes settled on one of them and he spoke with a nudge of his head.

"This one goes first."

He had indicated Britney, and one of his men freed her from the cuffs. It took a while for the girl to realize that it wasn't a good thing. Nikki watched in horror as the drama played out. Britney's eyes grew wide and her face blanched. Her pitiable whimpers gave way to shrieks of panic when one of the men started to yank her by the scruff of her neck toward the set of double doors at the end of the corridor. Beyond that, Nikki had no idea what lay in store for Britney, who managed to dig in her heels and drag her feet, flailing her thin arms.

"No . . . please . . . *stop!*" she screamed, reaching out and grabbing Nikki's arm, forcing another man to pry her fingers free, but not before Britney drew blood.

"Ahh." Nikki pulled her arm away and clutched her scratched skin, not taking her eyes off Britney. "Sorry . . . I can't—"

The girl's body writhed in frenzy, fighting back against the man who held her. Her face had reddened and twisted into a mix of venom and sheer terror when she saw Nikki couldn't help.

Speaking to the Russian, the girl cried, "Why me? Why not one of them?" The kid would do and say anything to save herself, and her fear spread like a contagion.

"What about you?" The Russian grinned at Nikki, then at the other girl. "Would either of you go in her place?"

His offer shocked her. Nikki sucked air into her lungs and held it in, and when she didn't speak up, the man laughed. "I thought so."

The Russian bent down and poked Nikki's chin, a mean jab of his finger.

"You see how it is? Here, there are no friends." He narrowed his eyes. "She would kill you herself if she thought it would do her good." He pointed at Britney. "That one is no saint."

Two men hauled Britney away, kicking and screaming. Her cries echoed down the corridor, magnifying the horror. Seeing it happen had gripped Nikki hard, but knowing she had a chance to step in and didn't do it ripped something from her soul. And she couldn't live with that.

"Take me instead," she blurted, surprising herself. "I'll go in her place."

She said it loud enough for everyone to hear. The words came from her mouth as if someone else had spoken them. Down the hall, the two men holding Britney stopped and turned. And for a brief moment the girl quit crying and looked over her shoulder, tears streaking her face.

Nikki exhaled and waited for the Russian's answer. The man squared his shoulder and raised his chin, looking surprised. Eventually, he glared at her.

"Too late. You had your chance to save her." He jutted his chin to the two men down the hall—the equivalent of an order—and they continued their trek to the double doors with Britney in tow.

"Nooo," the girl hollered. "She said she'd take my place. *stop!*"

"It's not too late," Nikki pleaded. "Please." She made a step toward the Russian, lugging the handcuffed girl with her.

"What are you doing?" the young girl next to her protested. "Are you crazy?"

Two men held Nikki back, as if she posed a threat, but down the hall Britney wailed—a gut-wrenching and pitiable sound. Now Nikki could barely breathe. Her heart hammered inside her chest, an incessant and frantic pulse. Once they dragged Britney beyond the double doors, Nikki only heard her muffled screams until they faded to nothing. Dead silence.

And just like that, she was gone. The finality of it left Nikki drained—and sick. Slowly, she looked up into the malicious eyes of the Russian. She knew he'd been watching her, and as expected, the bastard stared back with smug amusement.

"I said I'd take her place. Why would you offer that if you had no intention of letting it happen?" she asked. "That was beyond cruel."

He let a moment pass before he replied.

"Frankly, I didn't think you'd do it, but I have a whole new appreciation for your stupidity." He stepped closer and whispered, "I have found that people only disappoint. They are not worth a sacrifice of any kind, but how would you know this? You are only a foolish girl."

He stepped back and grimaced, an expression that became a humorless smirk. "Besides, I have plans for you."

With his men still holding her arms, he tapped a finger to the tip of her nose, a humiliating and dismissive gesture. "You will learn a new definition for the word 'cruel.' I will teach you this, yes?"

Bile rose hot in Nikki's belly as she fought for control. She clenched her teeth and blinked back tears, searching her mind for something to express the depth of her outrage, but nothing would come.

"I wouldn't want you to feel left out," the Russian added, measuring his hostile glare equally between the girls. "You will know exactly what happened to that girl." He smirked and with a wink muttered, "I will see to it . . . personally."

Before Nikki could say anything more, she was manhandled down another corridor with the other girl, who looked numb and in shock. Behind another set of double doors, they would wait their turn—to find out what Britney already knew.

Nikki had always heard people say that "not knowing was the worst," but she had a feeling that in this case they'd be wrong.

Downtown Chicago
Early morning

"I don't know where you got these extra pages, but you really scored, girl."

On her cell phone, Alexa recognized the voice of Tanya Spencer, an analyst she'd worked with on other assignments and trusted with her personal investigation of Globe Harvest. She'd met the black woman a handful of times and was always impressed by her intelligence, but her molasses thick southern accent and familiar tone made Tanya feel more like a friend.

"So tell me, what do I win?" Alexa grinned. "A trip to the Bahamas?"

"Damn, I'd like to score me some of that. I could use a little R and R myself." Tanya sighed into the phone. "But you and me have to settle for the big picture, honey. You added fifteen more locales to the grand scheme of things. We had a couple of bogus locations, but the rest look viable. I'd say that was good work."

After she left the bounty hunter's apartment, she'd sent the pages to Tanya in an encrypted file that she launched off her laptop into cyberspace. Wound too tight to catch some z's, she found herself at a twenty-four-hour café drinking way too much coffee and reading an old newspaper. She'd been bored out of her skull until Tanya called with her rushed analysis.

"Bogus locations?" Alexa asked. "How do you know that?"

"My guess is they were input errors," Tanya offered. "When we did further checking to verify the information, a couple of coordinates didn't pan out. One was smack dab in the middle of an ocean, and another one was too remote for the operational needs of our target. We did some homework with satellite surveillance on that one, as I recall. But when we pay a call, you know we like the advantage in our favor. We don't mess with second best. It's not worth the effort or the risk. And you know how partial we are to the word 'discreet.'"

Even though they spoke on a high-tech encrypted phone, Tanya never used names and was always careful not to say anything that would divulge classified information.

"But cheer up," the woman continued. "We've got plenty on our plate. You done good, baby girl."

Added to the few locales she had before, Alexa had now identified a total of eighteen facilities to look at. A major hit list. Coordinating a simultaneous assault on that many locations would constitute a significant operation. She'd have to involve Garrett now, and convince him that her Globe Harvest investigation was worthy of his attention.

The thrill of the hunt always stirred her blood, and with what she'd learned, Alexa could barely contain herself. Her hard work and perseverance was about to pay off, thanks to the help of Jessica Beckett, a local yokel with plenty of grit.

"I'll take it from here. Thanks for—" Before she could finish, Tanya interrupted her.

"The order's been given. I've already provided the coordinates to the man himself. He said to give your work top priority—as if I wouldn't do that anyway. Didn't you know all this? He made it seem like you did."

"Yeah, well . . . we don't always speak the same lingo, you know what I mean?" Alexa hated to look like she was out of the loop on such a big op. Since Tanya always referred to Garrett Wheeler as "the man," it didn't take much to put the pieces of the puzzle together, but was he trying to cut her out of the action? Anger roiled in the pit of her stomach until Tanya defused it.

"He told me to tell you he was coming to pick you up in two hours and that you'd know where to meet him." The woman heaved another sigh. "I sure hope you know what he's talkin' 'bout, 'cause I don't want to get in the middle of this."

Alexa looked at her watch. She had no time to lose. Fumbling in her pocket for money, she paid the bill and gulped down the last of her lukewarm coffee. Two hours would barely be enough time for her to pack, check out of her hotel, and meet Garrett at the private hangar he used at O'Hare. His jet would be arriving soon.

"Don't worry about it. I've got his number."

"Uh-huh . . . I bet you do, honey."

She heard the sarcasm in the woman's tone and had to smile. "Thanks for pushing on this one, T."

Alexa ended the call, flooded by a mix of relief and frustration. Garrett had intervened and taken over. On the one hand, she was happy that he'd finally seen the light on Globe Harvest. Blood had been spilled on this one, and she'd nearly gotten blown into hamburger meat. She knew her investigation had merit. But on the other hand, Garrett always had his own agenda, and she was never quite sure she trusted his motives when it came to the Sentinels.

Before now, he'd all but dismissed her case against Globe Harvest, refusing to utilize the vast resources at his disposal. Yet overnight it had become his top priority. Why?

"What are you up to, Garrett?"

She headed for the café door, making a mental list of what she'd need to bring on this trip. But someone important deserved a bone tossed her way—Jessica's words. Making a heads-up phone call to the bounty hunter felt like the right thing to do. And in Alexa's world, the "right thing" wasn't always clear-cut. Garrett would have no appreciation for her gesture, but she didn't care. Because of Jessica Beckett's help, she'd get a chance at taking down Globe Harvest.

A phone call was the least she could do.

Marriott Hotel
Oak Brook, Chicago
Early morning

Last night, rain on the window might have been magic, but in the light of morning the dresser mirror sure wasn't. The same old face stared back as she sat on the edge of the bed, trying to straighten her disheveled appearance. She had stopped finger-combing her hair when reality bitch-slapped her across the cheek. She'd taken a good long look at her reflection and in the unyielding light of day the magic of last night vanished like a bright gold coin snatched away by a slight-of-hand parlor trick.

"Hey, remember me?" she muttered to herself, but stopped when she glimpsed something else in the mirror—Payton.

Bare chest and wearing his pajama bottoms, he was still asleep in bed, lying flat on his belly with his sun-streaked hair against tanned skin. Wrapped in white hotel bed linens, he looked like a Christmas present, all shiny and new. That thought made her smile until she remembered last night. In Payton's arms, she had nearly forgotten who she really was. For a brief time she had allowed herself to feel . . . normal. But that simply wasn't so, and she had to remember.

The reality of the woman she'd become was plain to see—as immutable as the scars on her face and body. Years ago she had refused to have them removed. Plastic surgery would only improve the outside, denying the person she had to contend with on the inside. She explained it to Sam once, but not many would understand her way of dealing with the past—penance for what she'd done and what had been done to her.

She endured the scars of her past with a fierce determination to protect faceless others from what happened to her. If she'd "fixed" the scars, her outward appearance would have been more tolerable to others, but screw them. If others chose to judge her book by its cover, then so be it. As far as she was concerned, her scars served as fair warning, like the Hazardous to Your Health label on a pack of cigarettes. It hadn't been easy to live this way, but in her mind it had a ring of honesty to it. And she could live with that.

"Good morning. Did you sleep okay?" His gravelly morning voice jostled the insides of her stomach—in a very good way.

She looked at herself in the mirror one last time, forced a smile, then turned around. The pale glow of morning shone through the window, casting a welcoming light on him like a long-awaited invitation.

"Yeah, I did. Thanks." She cleared her throat and avoided his eyes. "Maybe coming here wasn't the best idea I ever had, but it's a new day and we can start over."

"What are you saying?" he asked.

Payton shoved the sheets aside and sat up, staking out his own corner of the mattress. Jess didn't know where she was heading with this, but she felt the need to galvanize her heart before it was too late.

"I mean, Nikki is out there and I think we both have to believe we'll find her . . . so maybe we should focus on that for now."

Payton narrowed his eyes and thought about what she'd said, letting silence build an awkward obstacle between them. Jess watched his reflection in the mirror, her way of distancing herself. Nibbling the inside corner of her lip, she had no idea what he was about to say, and waiting for him to do it was making her miserable with regret . . . and expectation.

"Jessie, I thought we—" He stopped and fixed his eyes on her through the mirror. "I agree Nikki should be the focus, but searching for her is not the only thing between us."

"I'm just saying we have a clear priority here, that's all." She wanted to distract him from the personal connection they had made last night. In the long run, it would be best for him. "For you and your sister, it's important to keep hope alive and give it all your energy."

She coaxed another smile and went on.

"Until you know for sure, you should hold onto the hope that you'll find Nikki alive, Payton. Hope can get you through some pretty tough times." She reached for his hand and clutched it. "Believe me . . . I know."

With her touch, he looked into her eyes and listened. Jess searched her heart for what to say next, but what she found completely overwhelmed her.

"The thing is, Nikki made a mistake. She trusted the wrong person and believed what they told her. But a kid's mistake isn't supposed to be a death sentence, damn it. This wasn't her fault. And when we find her, she's gonna need a lot of help to recover, Payton. She's gonna have an uphill battle each day. It angers me when I—"

She stopped herself, stifling the rage. Nikki's plight had hit far too close to home. And the urge to tell Payton what had happened to her felt like floodgates opening, the force of water not to be denied.

"When I was a kid, I was taken from my mother. I was too young to remember all the details of that day, but I do recall images, you know?" She swallowed and edged closer to him on the bed, shoulder-to-shoulder. His warmth gave her the courage she needed to continue.

"A bright sunny day. Fall colors. And a woman's smiling face, playing with me at a park. She must have been my mother. They were the last happy images I remember, and I'm not entirely sure if they were . . . real. I just know that they've stayed with me even after all that happened. I guess they were real." She nodded. "Truth is, I need to believe they were."

Jess always pictured vague fragments of a woman's face and wondered who had meant so much to her that she recalled her face even now. Over the years, she had clung to the belief that the woman had been her mother, but the truth was that she really didn't know.

"Wait a minute. You mean you never got to see your mother again?"

"No." Jess shook her head. "The police never found her. I became a ward of the state."

With all the effort the police had put into finding her family, it was surprising that no one ever claimed her. That weighed heavy on her mind over the years—and still did, if she were being honest.

"I'm so sorry, Jessie." He squeezed her hand.

She fixed her eyes on Payton, surprising herself with how easy it had been to open up to him. "But the man who took me left me with plenty to remember him by, as if I would ever forget what he did to me . . . and the others."

"There were others?"

His question reminded her that the truth about her life was ugly—gnarled and twisted like a destructive and malignant tumor leaching life from the living. No one wanted or needed to hear about it. And the last thing she wanted to do was rob Payton and his sister of hope. Hope made for a terrible first casualty, and she had no intention of adding to their misery.

"I shouldn't be telling you this. Not now. I only brought it up to say that I made it through and Nikki can too." She tried to pull away, but he stopped her.

"I don't know who did this to you, but I hate the sorry bastard. I'd sure as hell like to beat the crap out of him."

Men always thought they could fix things with their fists, but underneath his anger, she knew Payton only wished he could have protected her from a lifetime of pain.

"You'd be too late. Cops shot him the day he got caught. He's dead, but picturing you beating the crap out of him still works for me. Thanks."

She wielded her sarcasm like a shield, unable to bring herself to tell him more. She had blocked much of her degradation from her mind, mercifully banished into the oblivion of time and distance. And there were things in her memory that no one would ever know. Things she hadn't even told Sam. But as she saw it, nothing would be gained if she continued.

"If I tell you much more of what happened to me, it won't be any comfort to you. And that's not my intention. I just wanted you to know that it's not in my nature to give up, and I get the feeling you're the same. We can't give up on Nikki." She let go of his hand and pulled away. "I'm sorry. I thought I could talk about what happened to me, maybe give you a pep talk, but . . . I can't."

"That's okay." He leaned toward her, closing the gap she'd made. "We haven't known each other very long, but time doesn't always play a part in how close you can feel to another human being. In hard times, you get to know who your friends are. What I'm trying to say is, if you ever want to talk . . . I'd listen."

"Thanks, Payton." She smiled and clasped his hand again. "I appreciate that."

Something in her gut told her that placing trust in Payton would not be a mistake. And he'd been right about knowing who your friends were during hard times. Her friendship with Sam had endured over the years. But why had she opened up to him? Perhaps, in her heart, she knew it was time for the healing to start. If she would ever wrestle her life back, it had to begin with a first step. And Payton might be hers.

He was a good listener, and she had a feeling she might eventually get an opportunity to test those listening skills. If she was right about Nikki—that the girl was still alive and in the hands of the Russian—she might need to confide how she'd found the will to endure her own ordeal. And she prayed Nikki could dig deep and do whatever it took to survive.

Now, after what she'd said to Payton about Nikki, she realized there had been a change in her way of thinking.

She'd allowed Alexa to take over, which made sense. Alexa seemed to have the resources to handle the international magnitude of Globe Harvest and not be hampered by the rules of fair play. Her trust in Alexa had surprised her, but her unflinching need to find Nikki—one girl—had taken on an equally surprising urgency.

But when she thought about it, it made sense. Kids make mistakes, but an error in judgment should not be a life's sentence. Nikki was an innocent kid who had come into the crosshairs of ruthless and cruel men. If Nikki wasn't to blame, then was *her* story so different? If Nikki could be forgiven, she had to admit that she could too.

For the first time, the weight she'd been carrying on her shoulders all these years started to budge. And it felt . . . good. Damned good.

"I could sure use some coffee." She crooked her lip into a smile. "Maybe something quick to eat. I've got to call Seth to tell him about Alexa." Jess rose off the bed, but stopped short when she heard her cell phone ring. Reaching for it on the dresser, she said, "That's probably him now. The boy has a way of reading my mind."

She answered the call, "Beckett here."

"Just wanted you to know that your contribution netted us fifteen more hot spots." The woman didn't identify herself, but she recognized Alexa's voice. "Can't tell you when this is going down, but I wanted you to know. Thanks to you, we've improved our chances at shutting down this target for good."

"I didn't really expect you to call, but . . . thanks for the bone." Before she'd finished, the call went dead.

Alexa had spoken her mind. No frills. No ticker tape parade. She had to satisfy herself with the subtext of the cryptic message.

"Was that Seth?" Payton asked when she shut down her phone.

"No. Alexa," she replied with a grimace. "She's a woman of few words, but I think she may have given us just enough information for Seth to work his magic."

The woman had identified fifteen locations from the pages she'd given her. Now she'd have something more for Seth to work on. And that was all the ticker tape parade she'd need. Just because Alexa had what she wanted, that didn't mean Nikki would be found. Payton's niece was a needle in the proverbial haystack. And any attempt she and Payton made to find her would be at even worse odds. Still, she had to try. Rolling over and giving up wasn't an option.

"Come on, Payton. We may not have the resources behind us like Alexa, but I've got a feeling we're back in the hunt for Nikki. And Seth is gonna show us the way."

For his sake, she sounded more confident than she felt. Seth would be a long shot, at best. And she had no idea how to find Nikki, but doing anything was better than sitting around waiting for a call from Alexa that might never come.

The odds were definitely stacked against them, but she knew what it felt like to be an underdog. The way she figured it, a woman with nothing to lose should never be counted out.

CHAPTER 26

Peninsula Hotel
Downtown Chicago
Morning

"So tell me . . ." Payton said as he watched her punch the elevator button heading for Seth Harper's suite. "What do you pay this summer intern of yours? If he can afford this place, you gotta pay pretty good. Where do I apply?"

"Sorry, the last time I put money on a quarterback, I got burned on the bet. You cost me money, as I recall." She crossed her arms and narrowed her eyes at him as the elevator moved. "Believe it or not, this girl's got standards."

"Well, sorry I didn't come through for you. If I had known you back then and knew you had money on me, I might've tried harder to win." He grinned, looking like his old cocky self, back in the day.

"Oh, you won, Archer." She raised an eyebrow. "I was betting against you at the time."

The elevator doors opened and mercifully saved her from an explanation, but the grimace on Payton's face had been priceless.

Down the hall, Seth Harper's suite door had a DO NOT DISTURB sign on the knob. After she knocked, her well-worn employee and friend greeted her.

The tall and lanky kid looked like he'd been up half the night and just crawled out of bed. His large dark eyes had shadows, the inherent sadness in them intensified from his lack of sleep. Gone were his upscale "hotel" clothes, replaced by his usual *Jerry Springer* tee and worn jeans. Room service dishes made it apparent he hadn't left his room in a while. And once again, Harper looked as if he was living temporary, only taking up a small portion of the suite with his meager belongings.

The kid was a real puzzle. One day she'd wrestle him in her grip and work him like a Rubik's cube to figure out his story, but not today.

She pulled Seth aside, out of earshot, while Payton stepped into the main living room. "You look like a DUI booking photo. Are you okay?"

"Yeah, I'm . . . okay. I know you may find this hard to believe, but not everything is rosy in Harperworld twenty-four/seven. Lately I'm not exactly riding the rails of the happy train, but I'll figure it out . . . soon. No worries."

She didn't buy his answer. But before she could quiz him further, he changed the subject and headed for the living room, raising his voice loud enough for Payton to hear.

"I've been trying to decipher the random numbers on this report of yours, but I've got nothing so far. When you called this morning, you mentioned you had a visitor last night. Catch me up, okay?"

The living room had maps strewn over the sofas and chairs, turning a part of the space into a jumbled mess. And in the study, with his laptop cranked up and room service dishes set aside, the desktop looked cluttered too. No wonder Harper didn't want maid service.

She gave him the short version of her story, unsure what he would need to know for his analysis of the document, versus what he'd want to know as a player.

"Okay, so tell me exactly what Alexa said about these numbers again," Seth pressed.

"She said that some numbers were jumbled up on purpose, to throw us off. She implied that if anyone unauthorized got their hands on the documents—like us—they'd need a decoder ring to make sense of it. Apparently she had her super powers in high gear, because she figured it out. Or maybe she just knows more about these jerks than we do. But she told me that the numbers were coordinates to where Globe Harvest had some of their operations. Something like that."

Jess chewed the inside of her lip as she replayed Alexa's words in her head, then added more.

"She said that each location was compartmentalized and that it was important to hit them all at once in order to shut them down permanently, otherwise they'd spread the word, evacuate, then crop up somewhere else. That's why I thought she should get copies to our pages. If she's got the resources to do this, it's our best chance at shutting these bastards down. We could never pull off something on this scale."

"But she called them coordinates. I mean, she used that word, right?" Seth persisted.

"Yeah, she did. I'm sure of it." She nodded. "And she said that on the pages she got from me, there were fifteen locations. I figured that if we back into that number, we might figure out the arrangement and decode the hodgepodge."

"Yeah, I think I know where you're heading with that. But if she used the word 'coordinates,' we might have a better shot at cracking this report format. Give me a minute."

Clearly, Seth had other things on his mind. He looked frazzled, like he had one foot in the room with them and the other in some alternative universe where only genius types had membership cards. He disappeared into the study but emerged again, pointing a finger at her.

"Oh, and if you're hungry, order room service. We might be here awhile." He turned to head back the way he'd come, but changed his mind. "And order plenty of coffee. I think we're gonna need it."

"The guy needs food and caffeine to think." She shrugged. "Who am I to argue?"

After room service arrived, she and Payton ate while Seth worked in the study. Harper had embraced his alone time and refused to stop, but he did take the food and drink she offered. That left her and Payton killing time in the other room while Seth worked.

She used the time by contacting Sam to do a background check on the mysterious Alexa Marlowe, but wasn't surprised when her friend came up empty. Chasing someone like Alexa would be like trying to grab smoke. Sam did pass along to Payton the information that they hadn't found a body at the destroyed factory yet. For him, her update was a mix of good and bad news. Good that Nikki wasn't a confirmed casualty, but bad that his niece was still in the far-reaching tentacles of Globe Harvest.

After Sam's update, Jess's mood grew more somber. She and Payton speculated on their next moves in the search for Nikki, but mostly they split their attention between the discussion at hand and the guy in the next room, slaving over his high-tech laptop.

"I've been thinking about this," Payton muttered under his breath to her. "We don't have much. If what Alexa said was right, Nikki was transported out of Chicago and we've got no place to look. Even if we hit all these locations at once, like she said, that still doesn't mean we'll find her, does it?"

Payton had indeed been thinking. And he'd come up with the same conclusions she had.

"But I'm not willing to throw in the towel, Payton. Are you?" When he didn't reply and only stared at her, she continued, "You see, this is what I was saying about hope." She leaned closer and grabbed his hand as they sat on the sofa. "Now, Sam said they hadn't found a body in the rubble, right? So far, that supports what Alexa said about your niece being shipped out. If she's still alive, then we've got a chance at finding her. That's all I care about. And if that kid in there"—she pointed toward the other room—"can find one shred of a direction, I'm willing to take that next step. What about you?"

"Yeah, I'm with you . . . coach." He crooked his lips into a half smile. "Thanks for the pep talk. I needed that."

Jess watched Seth from the living room and caught glimpses of his face in the blue haze of his computer monitor. And she heard the sounds of his quick fingers on the keyboard. The kid was completely engrossed in what he was doing. He had gulped down the java and devoured his scrambled eggs and toast as if he hadn't tasted them at all. She could have served *Fear Factor* food—worms al dente, beef brains sashimi, or mystery contents from the dreaded Blender of Fear—and he might not have noticed.

In a short amount of time, Harper had endeared himself to her and become a part of her inner circle. And without flinching, she believed in his ability to pull a rabbit out of his bag of tricks. Strange as he was, he'd become a friend. She only wished she knew more about him.

Finally, after nearly two hours, the kid yelled, "I think I've got it. The pattern."

She heard the smile in Harper's voice, and his excitement was contagious. Payton followed her into the study.

"Here—look at this." He pointed to a column of numbers on his monitor. "Like Alexa said, they jumbled the format, but once you told me she used the word 'coordinates' to describe the locations, it got me thinking. Longitude and latitude."

He grinned up at her until he realized she needed more to catch the wave of his enthusiasm.

"Once I figured out the pattern of how to arrange the variables, I started pulling numbers off the list and compiling them into viable longitudes and latitudes. It wasn't hard from there."

"If you say so." She grimaced and shrugged to Payton, who looked just as lost. "Geography was never my thing. If I had to sum up my questions, I'd say, what the hell are you talking about?"

Seth grinned and took a breath, searching for a way to explain what he'd found.

"Any location on Earth is described by two numbers—its longitude and its latitude. If a pilot or a ship's captain want to specify a position on a map, they would use these numbers as *coordinates*." He stopped and corrected his explanation. "Actually, it's more accurate to say there are two angles, measured in degrees, 'minutes of arc' and 'seconds of arc.'"

"That's not what I meant, genius boy," she said. "Let's try a less accurate way to describe it. Can you dumb it down a hair? What's the bottom line?"

"If the world were a transparent globe, the lines of constant longitude, or *meridians*, would extend from the North Pole to the South Pole like segments of a peeled orange. And latitude is the radius of this transparent globe at its center, broken down by its northern and southern halves in degrees from the equator. Bottom line is that every location on the planet can be in the crosshairs of longitude and latitude to give a coordinate for a specific location."

"So by finding these coordinates, Alexa thinks she has an idea of where Globe Harvest has some of their operations?" she asked.

Seth nodded. "Yep, but here's the strange thing. Alexa told you that she'd located fifteen Globe Harvest operations. On our report, I found seventeen coordinates."

"Do you think she missed some?" Payton asked.

Jess was very much aware of Payton looking over her shoulder. Her skin tingled with the heat of his intimacy. And the smell of his skin was intoxicating. She swallowed and took a deep breath, feeling her cheeks flush with warmth when memories of last night filled her mind.

"No, I don't." Seth's reply reluctantly pulled her back into the present. "Someone with the resources to figure out this report didn't just miss a couple. I think she ruled some out, but for what reason, I don't know. To figure that one out, we're gonna have to locate each of these places on a map and see if something hits us."

"What, like a two by four?" When both men stared at her, she shrugged. "Sorry. Sarcasm is one of my skill sets. So what now . . . we're gonna stick pins in a map and count to seventeen?"

"You've got it," Harper said.

He reached into his desk and pulled out a plastic box of multicolored pushpins, not exactly standard issue with every hotel room. Seth hadn't been caught flatfooted by this latest news of coordinates; the maps strewn in the living room should have been her first clue.

"You look like you were expecting this, Harper . . . unless pushpins are part of the deluxe package here at the Peninsula. 'Cause I'm telling ya, you can't get nifty office supplies at just any old five-star hotel. You gotta have real clout to score pins of this quality."

"Can't a guy conjure a little magic without you spoiling all the fun with how it's done?" Harper sat back in his desk chair and swiveled, looking up at her with a big sheepish grin on his face. "You think those pushpins are hot, you should check out my stapler collection."

"You need some fresh air, Harper. Being cooped up in this hotel room has seriously warped your perspective on reality." She shook her head. "Let's get to work."

It didn't go unnoticed that Seth had never answered her about the pins. He joked it off as usual. Normally she would have pursued him with questions until she got a reasonable explanation on why Harper was Harper, but she'd grown to accept a certain element of mystery surrounding the kid. For now, she'd accept his idiosyncrasies and be grateful for his help.

Seth coached them through another explanation of how

longitude and latitude worked, then pinned his largest world map to a wall in the study, and they stuck pushpins into the coordinates he gave them. By the time they were done, they stood back and looked at their creation, having no greater insight.

"Okay, so we have colored pins on a map. I'm not seeing much that stands out except that one up there." She pointed to a blue pin in the middle of the Bering Sea. "You think Globe Harvest went on a three-hour tour with Gilligan and went down with the boat?"

Seth narrowed his eyes. "I can see why Alexa might dismiss *that* coordinate. Obviously someone made a mistake when they entered the code. It could happen. So that leaves us with one more to figure out. What about these others . . . you see any that stand out?"

Payton walked closer to the map, focusing at first on the blue pin in the Bering Sea. He then shifted his attention to the other locales.

"Well, if I was looking downfield for somewhere to unload the football, I'd be looking for an open man . . . someone isolated," he began, almost muttering to himself. "But I've got a feeling that wouldn't be the case here."

With a furrowed brow, Harper gave her a quick look, but kept his mouth shut. Genius boy clearly didn't speak jock.

"Go on, Payton," she said. "What are you thinking?"

"Globe Harvest hides in plain sight. Maybe they think they're too smart to get caught. I mean, they did that here in Chicago, operating right under the nose of the cops. These guys are savvy and they know how to fold up shop. But a location too remote might draw unwanted attention if it doesn't have good cover for their comings and goings. Being isolated might work against them. Does that make sense?"

"Yeah, it does." Seth looked at the map over Payton's shoulder. "So maybe this location in South America would fall under that category. I don't see a city of any size nearby, plus it's all by itself in the middle of nowhere." Harper pointed to a red pin.

"So maybe the Bering Sea and the Amazon jungle might be the two locations Alexa discounted, thinking they might be some kind of error." Jess chimed in. "Not a bad theory, Payton. It definitely makes sense."

"But should we assume that?" Payton questioned.

"What're you saying?" she asked.

"If Alexa has fifteen locations covered, then that leaves us with two. Now I'm not proposing we hire a guide into the Amazon jungle, but what if this location on the Bering Sea was just a little off?" He pointed to a spot on the map, a place near Russia.

"The closest landmass to that coordinate is St. Lawrence Island, Alaska. And look how close St. Lawrence is to Russia. No more than forty or fifty miles, tops," he said, his enthusiasm mounting. "And don't you think it's too much coincidence that the son of a bitch we're chasing is Russian?"

"He's got a point, Jessie. A damned good one," Seth agreed. "I mean, what have we got to lose?"

For a moment, Payton stopped and stared at Seth, then quickly shifted his gaze to the map on the wall. She was sure Harper's question was the reason. In fact Payton had a lot to lose. If his energies were focused on some wild goose chase, his niece's trail would grow ice cold and they might never find her.

Was pursuing his theory worth the risk of losing Nikki for good?

"Well, I've never been good at sitting on the sidelines," Payton muttered under his breath, as if he were alone and trying to convince himself. "I've gotta be doing something or I'll go crazy."

Silence filled the room. Seth avoided her eyes, but she could tell he felt the awkwardness.

"Well, I'm sure you're not suggesting we row a boat to the middle of the Bering Sea and have a look around," she said, picking up the slack in the conversation, "but I bet your friend Joe Tanu can help, him being a retired Alaskan state trooper and all. We could check out the island real quick."

"We?" Payton questioned, looking over his shoulder at her. "Oh, no. This could be a rough trip, with no frills. I was planning on leaving right away, be there by nightfall, island time. Hell, Jess, there's not much to St. Lawrence except for the small Native villages of Gambell and Savoonga. A sparse population. Once I hit the island, I'd be roughing it and camping out, keeping a low profile until I rule out the location. But if I get a hit, those Globe Harvest bastards won't get another chance to vacate like they did here. Even if Nikki isn't on the island, I'm gonna see to it that someone from Globe Harvest pays for what happened to her."

Thinking about what he said, she swallowed hard.

"I hear ya." She raised her chin in challenge and crossed her arms. "But are you saying you don't think I can rough it, Archer?"

"Oh, hell, Jessie . . ." Payton cocked his head in exasperation. "Please don't make me answer that."

He looked to Harper for support, but found none.

"Don't look at me. I'm out of this." Seth held up his hands and ditched male bonding in favor of more coffee.

For nearly an hour Jess gave it her best shot, trying to convince Payton to bring her along on his trip into the wilds of Alaska. She presented her case in a clear and logical manner, while he countered with his version of reality—male rationale run amok. Eventually the gloves were off and cool heads warped into mouths on autopilot.

"Look, more than likely St. Lawrence Island will be nothing more than a Hail Mary pass in the final seconds of the game," he said as he stuffed his hands into his pockets, leaning against a door frame in the study.

"Why do men always resort to sports analogies?" When she caught his glare, she said, "Did I say that aloud?"

"Jessie, come on. The world is a big place—"

"Wait, let me write that down," she interrupted.

"—and Nikki could be anywhere," he continued. "This is gonna be a long shot. We've got less than nothing to go on."

"Then why are you shutting me out? Hell I'm good at . . . nothing," she countered. "You said it yourself—it's unlikely Globe Harvest would pick such an isolated place. If you think this is gonna be a walk in the damned park, you should have no objections to me coming along. I can handle myself."

Payton dropped his head and took a deep breath. She had him on the ropes.

"You know if we don't go together, I'll just find a way to follow you there. And that's not an idle threat," she said. "I doubt the state of Alaska would be ready for Jess Beckett gone wild."

"I'm not either." Payton rolled his eyes and shook his head. "I'm just . . . worried for you, Jessie." He'd softened his voice, and another wave of memories from last night took hold of her heart. "You've been through so much already. You almost died in that explosion. I'd never forgive myself if . . ."

In a nearby chair, Harper had found a ringside seat to their verbal skirmish. All he needed was a bucket of popcorn. Jess caught Seth's eye and nudged her head, asking him for privacy. If Harper hadn't gotten the message before, when the arguing had started, she wanted it spelled out now. She needed alone time with Payton. The kid took her hint and left without a word, ousted from his own study.

Jess walked up to Payton and placed a hand on his chest.

"And how do you think I'd feel if you went alone and something happened? I'd want to be there to watch your back and I'd trust you to do the same for me," she said. When he wouldn't look her in the eye, she stroked his cheek with a finger until he did. "You and me, we aren't sidelines people, Payton. We get into the game one way or another.

It's part of who we are. Now, I made a promise to Nikki, to get her out of this, and I'd like to keep it."

She rose on tiptoes and kissed his cheek, loving the way her lips felt on his warm cheek. The arousing smell of his skin left her feeling light-headed. All she wanted was to hold him—to feel her arms around him. But before that could happen, she needed him to concede her point.

And she'd saved her best argument for last.

"Besides, I know what Petrovin looks like. If it comes to it, I'll be able to spot him from a distance. His ugly mug is hard to forget." She tightened her jaw, with memories of the Russian careening through her head.

When Payton gazed down at her this time, she knew by the look in his eye that their bickering was over. She had pleaded her case and won, if the word "win" described it. Urban girl Jess Beckett was heading for the Alaskan wilderness—remote and sparse, where grizzly bears and alpha males roamed free. Once her feet hit the tundra, she'd be nothing more than part of the food chain.

St. Lawrence Island was dead ahead. And she'd be in the thick of it before nightfall.

CHAPTER 27

Chicago O'Hare
Private hangar

Overcast skies from the early morning had burned off, leaving the promise of a beautiful day. Rays of sunlight breached the clouds and speared light through billows of white. And rain had settled into puddles on the side of the road, sparkling like gems under shimmering light, a vestige of last night's storm.

In theory, the change in weather should have lightened her mood, but her more philosophical nature made that impossible. She liked to think that a renewing rain could cleanse the world, but even in her imaginings, mankind would find a way to screw up the idyllic notion. As long as humanity preyed on itself, the world would only reflect the worst of mankind's cruel intentions. And Alexa felt helpless to alter the breadth of society's sins . . . except one covert operation at a time.

Doing something about Globe Harvest felt right, even if she'd be taking the law into her own hands. She knew what lay ahead. An operation of this magnitude always put her on edge. She liked to think of it as mental preparation, but in all likelihood her restlessness had been forged by the reality that this day could be her last.

She drove up to the nondescript metal and glass structure, the one without a name and only the designation 4569 on its front door. She knew from experience the number was a blind that led nowhere. Garrett Wheeler and his people knew how to be discreet. On the tarmac to the side of the building was the man's private jet, glistening in the sun. And despite her wish to take her encounter with him in stride, she couldn't help but notice her heart beating faster as her eyes searched for him.

"Whose bright idea was it to get personal?" she muttered under her breath, gripping the steering wheel tighter than usual. "Oh, yeah. Me. I was the genius."

Once that ship had sailed, she figured shutting down the damned harbor made no sense, but she wasn't sure which was worse—the first time or every time since. She'd never been a woman to curb her appetites, and neither was Garrett. That made for a dangerous combination.

She parked the car in a spot near the front door marked for visitors. When she stepped out of the vehicle, the sound of planes taking off from O'Hare filled the air and mixed with the hum of traffic coming off the interstates. As if on cue, a man emerged from the building and approached her. Alexa recognized his face and knew the drill. She handed over her car keys and rental agreement, knowing he'd return the vehicle to the rental agency for her.

"I'll take care of everything. Have a safe trip." The man acted as if she were going on vacation.

"Let's hope," she replied.

Although she tried to be subtle about it, Alexa watched for Garrett as she readied for her eminent departure. She got help with her baggage from a crewman in uniform who loaded her bags onto the jet. But when she was done, still no Garrett. By the time she looked at her watch a second time, she heard a lusty male voice behind her.

"Glad you got my message and could join me."

She turned to see Garrett coming out of the building with

his usual swagger and a coffee cup in hand. Dressed in a sharp navy suit, crisp white shirt, and a bloodred tie, he looked like he'd stepped off a magazine cover with his swarthy good looks, resembling a highly successful financier. No one would guess the man had powerful yet deadly connections all over the globe. He dressed in sharp contrast to her more casual attire of jeans and a brown leather jacket.

"And may I ask what changed your mind?" she asked. "I thought I'd still have to convince you of the merits of this case. Imagine my surprise when I find you'd set the wheels in motion for this trip before I barely had my morning coffee. Fortunately for you, I like surprises, especially when I get my way."

Set against tanned skin and dark hair, his steel gray eyes took her in without restraint as he slowly sipped coffee. He gazed at her from top to bottom, as if he was starving and she was a leg of lamb. He didn't miss a curve, and looked at some parts twice. But when he finally grinned, his slick smile disarmed her, as it always did.

"I aim to please." He winked, and moved toward his jet. "I brought more appropriate clothing for you. Everything's on board. We can both change en route."

He dangled a well-played carrot before her, not saying where they were headed. The man loved his games.

"At the risk of overindulging you," he added, "I'll give you first picks of your accessories."

Alexa knew he meant she'd get first crack at the weapons locker he carried with him on assignment. The man really knew how to treat a woman.

"We've got plenty of locations to choose, all coordinates needing immediate attention," she pointed out as she climbed into the jet. "Tight timing, but I'm sure you've got a logistics plan."

Once they were inside and had their privacy, the ground crew secured the outer door and Garrett replied, "Yes, I have. You'll be in charge of the primary entry team. I've got the snipers and Stanton has support and perimeter. I'll go over the details for the other locations to get your input once we're airborne. We'll launch our assault soon after we land. Does that work for you?"

She smiled and buckled into her seat as the jet began to move. "Yeah, that works."

Knowing Garrett, he'd picked a top-notch team to accompany him into the field. The man had a taste for the best, and no one was more thorough when it came to planning an operation.

"And we may have a line on Petrovin, although there's been no confirmation as yet." His face suddenly became more solemn. "I thought you'd want to know."

Garrett had tossed out that little morsel as if it meant nothing, but she could tell that wasn't the case. She suddenly understood why he'd gotten involved in her personal investigation. What moved the man to act sometimes baffled her, but his motives usually warranted closer examination.

"My, you have been busy. Impressive. By the way, where are we heading?"

Although he hadn't committed to a specific location in his briefing with her, she had a strong suspicion that if Garrett had a lead on Petrovin, that's where he'd want to be. Alexa had to admit. She wanted another crack at the Russian too.

"By your own admission, you're a woman of mystery who likes surprises," he said, arousing her interest when his lethal smile returned. "I wouldn't want to spoil it for you."

Two hours later

In the dim light of the security control room, Stas Petrovin had read the encrypted message downloaded from the local server and crumbled the paper in his hand. He glared at one of his men, staring straight through him, then shifted his attention to the bank of security monitors linked to state-of-the-art digital cameras positioned at all points of the compound.

Had he made a mistake in coming here?

"Issue a facility alert to all the men. Be on the lookout for any suspicious activity. No one comes or goes without me knowing about it." Slowly, he shifted his gaze again, looking the man directly in the eye. "And I want a systemwide alert. We're shutting down this location temporarily. The shipment we just sent out will be our final one until I make the call otherwise."

"Yes, sir. I'm on it." The uniformed man left the control room, leaving Stas alone with his thoughts and the handful of guards manning the security station. The room had grown nearly silent, the tension mounting. In the murky light, he felt the men's eyes on him as he contemplated his next move.

After days of planning and the constant maneuvering to make sure he hadn't been followed from Chicago, he had been ready to land and get his life back, carrying on where he'd left off. But now all that looked up in the air.

The online alert had been precautionary. His superior was a careful man, to be sure. And for the most part, he appreciated Anton Bukolov's conservative nature. Globe Harvest had survived and thrived because of his wariness and shrewd manner.

No, he would not question what had transpired to make Bukolov anxious. Nor would he second-guess him. Who could blame the old man? He had anticipated fallout after the explosion of the Chicago facility, but this alert had come on the heels of a few tiring days with him on the run. He only wanted things to get back to normal, whatever that meant.

Somewhere within the organization, pressure had been applied, and like a lizard with its tail caught, sometimes it was better to sever an appendage to save the whole. Perhaps that was what Bukolov had intended, and he would give the old man the respect he deserved.

Petrovin got on the phone and called an extension in

logistics. When the call was answered, he recognized the voice of the man on the line.

"A mere precaution, but make sure my helicopter is fueled and hidden away from the compound. You know the location. Do it now, Mitchell." Without waiting for the man's reply, he ended the call, accustomed to giving orders.

Similar to what had happened in Chicago, he would ensure he had a way out and be prepared for any eventuality, a prudent move on his part. But the success of his mission would be paramount. He would protect Bukolov and the organization at all cost. If he had to evacuate *this* time, he'd be traveling light.

No hostages. And no witnesses.

The face of the blond girl wavered in his mind. Although she showed backbone and had stood out from the rest, she would be a casualty, pure and simple. One way or another, he'd be dealing with her. After a quick look at his watch, he knew the girl's time was nearly upon him and he must prepare her soon. Dismissing her from his mind, Petrovin headed for the door with one thought lingering.

All men stared death in the face. Ironically, it was a part of life. And when his time came, he didn't want to die a feeble old man. No, that would be unacceptable. He wanted his passing to be memorable, perhaps in the line of duty. Being second in command and strangely indifferent to his own mortality, he had chosen to live his life on a razor's edge and hoped he'd have similar control in the manner of his death. At least, he hoped it would be so.

Rank had its privileges . . . and its cost. And he embraced both.

During the flight, Alexa had changed into a battle dress uniform in camo and set aside other gear and the weapons she would bring. She sat across from Garrett, who was reading the *Wall Street Journal* as if he were on a business trip, dressed in full tactical uniform. She marveled at how the man looked as good in his BDUs as in his pricy suits, but that might only be her taste. She loved complicated men.

Alexa shook her head and fought a smile, then glanced out the window.

By checking the position of the sun, she figured they were heading west, but that was all she had. Soon he'd brief her about where they were going; until then Garrett Wheeler would revel in his surprise, as he always did.

But she was no stranger to the concept of keeping secrets herself. She had Tanya Spencer working something personal for her, so when her cell phone vibrated, she suspected the call might be from her. On her cell phone display there was a disturbing text message from Tanya.

Target left Chi via air, west. More to follow.

The night she met the bounty hunter face-to-face at her apartment, she'd been given a way to contact the woman if something came up. Having Jessica Beckett's cell phone number had its advantages, her GPS location being one of them. That night, she'd had a hunch that having a means to track the bounty hunter might eventually pay off. And apparently her ability to read Jessica had been dead on. According to Tanya, Beckett had left Chicago and was heading west via airplane.

Alexa found it ironic that in a world filled with technology, she relied most on her instincts for human nature as the best tool in her arsenal of tricks. And something in her gut had told her that Jessica wouldn't stay put in Chicago, waiting for a status call. But being right wasn't much consolation. Where in the hell was the woman going?

She'd never seen anyone more stubborn—except when she looked in the mirror.

Damn it, Jessica. What are you up to now?

She deleted the text message and stowed her cell phone, making sure Garrett hadn't noticed. Being on her own mission left her no time to fret over Beckett, but she couldn't help the fretting part. She respected the bounty hunter's abilities, even though her methods were often questionable. But somewhere along the way, she found herself liking the woman—completely unacceptable.

If Jessica Beckett got killed because she was in over her head, Alexa didn't want to feel responsible. But she knew it was already too late for that.

Savoonga, Alaska
St. Lawrence Island
Dusk AKDT

Payton had helped her pack for the trip, making sure she brought the bare essentials and enough layers of clothing to keep her warm. Their trip from Chicago to Alaska would gain them three hours, giving Payton enough time to arrange for a private charter, make a few other logistical calls, and get them to the island before nightfall. She understood his sense of urgency, even in the face of a staggering wall of unknowns.

Since the village of Savoonga was centrally located on the island of St. Lawrence, he had elected to fly there. It had been a long flight, but she hadn't slept much on the small plane, only fitful dozes. She had too much on her mind and her past bubbled to the surface again, threatening a repeat of her recurring childhood nightmare. But she'd refused to succumb.

Now their plane was preparing to land and made a pass over a sparse airstrip near Kookoolik Cape on the Bering Sea, the island's northern coastline. The sky was overcast and metal gray, giving the land a drab and listless feel. Barren tundra with small ponds and marshy areas dotted the landscape below. And from what she could see, dwellings were built for function rather than aesthetics, and butted up against one another in clusters between worn dirt trails. The word "bleak" came to mind.

When Jess gazed down at the tight grouping of houses and buildings that represented the whole of the community, the plane lurched when it hit an air pocket. Her stomach leapt too, but not only because of turbulence. She'd never seen a community like this, so foreign to what she knew. Payton wasn't kidding about roughing it. At that moment she felt she had no business being here, though she wasn't about to admit it to him.

"Did you know that from the western tip of the island you can actually *see* tomorrow?"

She spoke loud enough to be heard over the engine and forced a smile. She explained to Payton that the International Date Line crossed between the western tip of the island and the Siberian coastline, allowing a person to actually *see* tomorrow.

"And the island is only thirty-eight miles from Siberia."

She was full of useless information about St. Lawrence, things Seth had shared with her off the Internet before she'd left Chicago. Harper had compiled a file of tidbits that she'd read on the plane as a distraction when she couldn't sleep. And she'd picked out a couple of choice ones to bestow upon her travel companion, but Payton only smiled politely, looking preoccupied and tired.

During the flight, he'd taken a drink, but she noticed he stopped at one, something she imagined didn't happen often. She suspected he walked a tightrope with his sobriety, and most days it probably didn't take much to topple him. But the situation with his niece had tested him. All things considered, she thought he'd shown remarkable restraint, but Payton had a problem he had yet to deal with. And she knew what "coping in denial" was all about.

Nikki weighed heavy on his mind, and it showed. He'd spent time on the phone with his friend, Joe Tanu, arranging for someone to meet their plane when it landed. And Joe had updated him on his sister's condition. Waiting for word on Nikki had spiraled Susannah headlong into a nightmare that only another parent could fully appreciate—or an uncle who loved his niece like a daughter. For his own reasons, he hadn't told Susannah about his rush trip to St. Lawrence Island. He probably figured another dead end would be too much for her.

Payton had to feel powerless to help his sister. And Jess had been connected to his family's plight long enough to feel his pain.

"How's your—"

Jess stopped talking when the aircraft made its final turn, and looked out the window to watch the landing, a glutton for punishment. The plane swung in almost sideways when a strong gust of wind buffeted the fuselage. She gripped her armrest and refrained from comment until the charter landed with a series of bumps that jarred her teeth.

"Smooth." She let go of the armrests. "Real smooth."

"The landing's over and no longer a problem." He cocked his head. "And complaining isn't allowed."

"Who's complaining? My compliments to the pilot, for cryin' out loud." She furrowed her brow. "He didn't kill us. I'd call that a good flight."

The airport terminal was nothing more than a metal Quonset hut that she would have mistaken for a warehouse if not for the wind sock on a flag pole, thrashing in the gusts. A smattering of small planes were tied down outside, with wooden blocks at their wheels, and signs were posted for Frontier Flying Service and a couple of other carriers.

While Payton took care of offloading the plane and their belongings, she contended with the steady wind and gazed over the horizon, assessing her surroundings. The terrain was mostly flat and boggy, not much more than a wind-battered finger of land surrounded by a turbulent sea.

And as far as her eye could see, the beachfront was made up of peculiar gravel, stones that looked like large marbles under her boots. She was thankful Payton had insisted she wear sturdy hiking boots, but this type of turf would be difficult to walk for any distance. Her feet sank into the stones and shifted under her weight, making each step a little unstable.

"Good call on the footwear, Archer," she muttered, zipping up her jacket against the wind that caused her eyes to water. "So this is the last frontier."

Natives of the island had come to check out the newcomers, mostly curious dark-haired children with dimpled round faces and narrow squinting eyes. They had on bright print clothes and colorful smocks under their jackets, and some wore rubber boots to walk the shoreline. The seasoned faces of older Native men and women stared blankly from a distance, their eyes hard to read.

She felt out of her element as she took a quick look around. No big city noise. No traffic. Nothing familiar. And an odd stillness closed in on her, prickling her skin with a chill—aided by the realization that she'd entered a world so radically different from any she had experienced.

Even the air had its uniqueness. It carried a salty mist that covered her skin with grit, but the seabirds thrived in it. They shrieked and drifted overhead, suspended in place by the stiff breeze, scavenging the beach and a nearby dump.

But on the wind, the normal odor from the ocean carried another smell. She tried to identify the stench, focusing on the refuse dump that was filled with an assortment of debris from rusted metal barrels to what looked like massive and decaying driftwood blanching to a dull gray in the sun. In the dying hours of the day, a swell of seabirds hovered over the discarded heap and dive-bombed the rubble, foraging for food in near frenzy.

What was the attraction?

"That smell. Is it coming from the dump over there?" she asked Payton when he got within earshot. He shifted his gaze to where she pointed.

"That's not your standard dump, exactly," he said. "Most of that is whale carcasses."

"Well, that's something you don't see every day on Michigan Avenue."

"And the smell is rotting blubber left on the bones," he added. When she winced, he said, "Don't worry. The wind will shift and make the odor more tolerable. After a while you won't even notice it."

She stared at the garbage heap again, trying to picture Moby Dick, but gave up. "I'll never eat sushi again. I swear to God."

"Well, you gotta remember these people subsistence hunt off the sea like their ancestors have done for two thousand years. They probably have access to a small grocery, but most of their meat comes without plastic wrap." He brushed back a strand of her hair that had blown across her cheek. "Since they don't get much sunlight in the winter, they cache or stockpile their food during the summer, when they have longer hours to hunt and no ice to contend with."

"What do they eat—exactly?" she asked. He'd piqued her interest.

"Berries, roots, and greens from the land, but mostly they fish and hunt for walrus, seal, whale . . . maybe the occasional reindeer or game bird."

A couple of Native kids zipped by them riding an all-terrain vehicle. The ATV was throttled on high and the wheels kicked up a rooster's tail of gravel as they barreled down a worn path.

"That looks like fun." She grinned and watched them drive away.

"ATVs in summer, snowmobiles in winter. And yeah, they're fun, but around here they're a necessity."

"Do you know the population of the island?"

"Not exactly, but I would guess around fifteen hundred people. Mostly Yup'ik, from what I understand." He took her hand and led her toward the makeshift airplane terminal. "Come on. We've got a guy to meet in the office here. Joe set it up."

Following him, Jess realized she'd asked her questions for a reason.

The more she understood about the people who inhabited St. Lawrence, and as she got a better look at the island, the more she wondered if they'd made the right choice to come here. If Globe Harvest steered clear of isolation to better cover their tracks and mask their operational needs, St. Lawrence Island would be the last place on earth they'd want to be.

She wondered if Payton would eventually come to the same conclusion. And she knew if he did, it would break his heart.

Although she steeled herself for what might happen, she was suddenly glad to be with him . . . as his friend. If the search for Nikki ended here, they might never pick up another trail to follow. Even if Alexa suddenly sprouted a heart and called with good news that Globe Harvest had been shut down in some areas of the world, that didn't mean those bastards would be out of commission for good—or that Nikki's whereabouts could be traced at all.

Conceivably, they might never find her—or her body.

And that would mean no closure for Payton and his sister. They'd be devastated. Before this moment, she hadn't realized what the trip to St. Lawrence Island meant to him. But now, she had no doubt in her heart that he did.

Payton knew exactly what this trip meant—and what was at stake for Nikki.

CHAPTER 28

"Are you Frank?"

Payton didn't wait for an answer. Jess watched him offer his hand to a man in the airstrip office.

"My name's Payton Archer."

A man wearing an Alaska State Trooper uniform was filling a coffee mug and making himself at home. With her body clock turned upside down by the time change, the coffee smelled good.

"Yeah, that'd be me." The man grinned and shook Payton's hand. "Frank Toyukak out of Nome. Your friend Tanu and me, we go way back. I'll be happy to help any way I can."

Trooper Frank had a distinctive oval face with high cheekbones. His dark skin was weathered by age and marked by laugh lines. His black hair and spindly moustache were peppered with gray, and his eyebrows had a pronounced arch. They made him look as if he had a constant surprised expression on his face. The man had a quiet voice and reserved manner that Jess liked immediately. He looked like a straight shooter.

Payton introduced her. "This is Jessica Beckett, out of Chicago."

"Hey, Frank."

"You're a long way from home," the man remarked, and shook her hand. "Good to meet you both. You care for coffee? It ain't Starbucks, but it's plenty hot."

The trooper poured coffee into ceramic mugs, but let them add any cream or sugar. While he played host, he said, "Sorry to hear about your niece. I read the missing person report after Joe called. And he filled me in on this Globe Harvest organization you're chasing. Do you really think they're operating here on the island?"

"We have reason to believe it's possible, but I admit it's a long shot." Payton took a gulp of coffee and glanced her way, a worried look on his face. "We want to pursue any lead we've got. That's why we're here. And Joe said you might help."

"I'll do what I can, but it's a little late in the day to do much now." The trooper set down his coffee and stepped over to a desk to spread out a topographic map of the island. "Speaking of that, Joe said you might be camping overnight and may not have time to pack. I brought a duffel bag of personal gear and a cache of food and water for a few days if you need it."

"Days?" Jess tried to keep the question out of her voice but failed.

"Ah . . . thanks, Frank." Payton shot her a sideways glance. "That'll help. *We* appreciate it." The fact that he'd emphasized the word "we" had not escaped her notice.

"But if someone is abducting young girls and using St. Lawrence as a base of operation," the trooper continued, "they'd stand out for sure. Let me give you a map tour of the island. It might speed things up since we'll lose the light soon. Or maybe you'd prefer I find you a place for the night and we start fresh in the morning. Your call."

"No, I'd rather do what we can now," Payton said, directing his attention to the map.

"Joe told me you'd say that, so here's what I know."

According to Frank, the island was sparsely populated and mostly inhabited by Natives. The man gave them a rundown using the detailed map. At first Jess suspected there wouldn't be many places for Globe Harvest to hide their operation, but the trooper shared his thoughts on other activity on the island. If Globe Harvest was there, they could cover up their actions a number of different ways.

"Two Alaska Native Corporations own St. Lawrence Island and manage the resources. The Natives who live here are considered indigenous shareholders and are allowed to excavate sites for old bones, artifacts, and walrus ivory to barter or sell. We get traffic through here from that too."

"I hate to ask this, but isn't that looting?" Payton asked, raking a hand through his hair. She could tell he expected to get more direction from the trooper, a place to start their search, but the man only gave them more to consider. The island seemed like a haystack with Nikki being a needle.

"Here they call it subsistence digging for old stuff." The trooper shrugged. "We also get oil and gas companies sending reps to scout out offshore locations for exploration. What I'm trying to say is, things happen on the island from time to time, but generally I know about it."

He gave a broader overview of the terrain and offered his Robinson R-44 Clipper II helicopter for them to see the island firsthand when the time came. After he was done, Payton looked more dejected, but he pressed the trooper for more.

"No, this can't be it. There's gotta be something . . ." He leaned over the desk, staring at the map in frustration. "In Chicago they'd taken over an old textile factory. The place looked deserted from the outside. Do you have anything like that here?"

Payton was grasping at straws now. And by the look on his face, he knew it too. From what she had seen, St. Lawrence Island had little that could be construed as a substantial commercial property, but when Frank didn't answer Payton right away, it gave Jess hope that she was wrong.

"Well, there is the old Air Force station at Northeast Cape, but it was shut down in the seventies." The trooper pointed to a section on the map. "As far as I know, no one goes there except . . ."

"Except who?" Payton sounded hopeful.

"More like . . . except for what," the Native man corrected. "That facility was mainly a radar site, an Air Force listening post back in the early fifties, but later they abandoned it." His face grew more somber. "Many of the local Natives used to camp and hunt in that area until they started to get sick. Real sick."

"Sick?" she asked. "From what?"

"Cancer mostly," the trooper replied. "But other diseases too. Some say from PCB exposure."

"That's awful." She couldn't imagine such a thing, getting struck down by disease that might have been brought by outsiders. Life on the island looked hard enough without the added complication.

"Yeah, many died before they finally figured it out, but it was too little, too late." Toyukak shrugged. "No one goes there anymore. They know to stay away. The government conducted a clean up program in 2003. They say it's clear, but we get the occasional air traffic for inspections, soil testing, or remediation efforts. If that land is supposed to be okay, then why do we still have government types flying through? I doubt we'll see an end to it anytime soon."

"Take us there," Payton insisted, unable to hide his enthusiasm.

"I told you, it may not be safe. And if this organization is doing anything illegal here on the island, I'd hear about it."

Jess knew he wasn't trying to be difficult. More than

likely, Frank was concerned for their safety. Imagining an organization like Globe Harvest operating here was hard to believe, even for her.

"Would you hear about it? Or would residents mistake any activity for just another government inspection or test and dismiss it?"

Payton let his question sink in, allowing the trooper to come up with his own conclusions. After a quick minute, the man did.

"Come on. This may be a wild goose chase, but it's worth a look. We can be there before the sun goes down, and my helicopter is fueled and ready." Before the man left the office, he turned to Payton. "Joe said you'd be carrying. Are both of you armed?"

Payton told him about the weapons Joe had loaned them. Jess missed her Colt Python, but there had been no time to replace the weapons she'd lost to Baker and the Russian. She had Joe's .45-caliber Glock 21 and wore it under her jacket in a holster. And Payton had his .380 Walther PPK/S. Frank might have understood the need to carry weapons as a precaution, or perhaps Joe had vouched for them. Either way, the trooper didn't ask for permits or question them further. But he did insist on taking charge.

"We're only checking the old radar station for recent activity," the trooper clarified. "If I see anything suspicious, I'll call for backup and we'll wait until help arrives. Are we clear?"

"Yeah, crystal." Payton forced a smile, but she couldn't read his face.

On the surface, he looked reasonable and in control, but she knew better. If Globe Harvest occupied the radar site and evidence supported that theory, she had no doubt that when it came to saving his niece, Payton Archer would be a hard man to stop.

She had bet against him once—something she wouldn't do again.

An hour later

In a ravine hidden in a stand of evergreen trees, Alexa looked through binoculars at the quiet setting below her position. Her team of five men was within eyesight and awaiting her order to proceed. She felt their presence more than saw them.

The sun would be down soon and she'd have the cover of darkness to make her move. Night vision gear and the element of surprise would give her team an advantage. She looked at her watch again. In less than fifteen minutes their sweeping raid would be under way. And once Garrett gave the signal, nothing would stop it.

An advance team had done an initial assessment of this site and communicated their findings via the device she wore in her ear. Thermal imagers indicated warm bodies were inside. For an abandoned enterprise, the presence of people on the property gave her a warm and fuzzy feeling that their assumptions about Globe Harvest having a location here had merit. Working with trusted locals, the advance team had also acquired a blueprint of the facility, giving them entrances and exits that would be invaluable when the time came.

Alexa was prepared to proceed when Garrett's voice came over her earpiece.

"Inbound aircraft, stand down until further orders. Anybody have a visual on the passengers, call it in."

Like a racehorse champing at the bit, Alexa's adrenaline kicked into high gear. She hated being forced to stand down now, so close to the launch of the assault, but she understood the need for taking precautions. And an inbound craft could change things significantly.

"Acknowledged," she replied.

She heard the sound of a helicopter but couldn't see the aircraft through the trees. Nearly ten minutes later, with the sun slipping below the horizon, no one made contact with intel on the new players to the party. If they moved forward with the plan, it would be Garrett's call.

"We've got nothing on the inbound."

She heard disappointment in Garrett's voice, but she had a job to do.

"Does that change things?" she asked.

To keep chatter to a minimum, she didn't say anything more. Garrett knew her well enough to read between the lines. They had too much riding on this operation, here and at other locations, and he knew it. Timing would be critical. In less than five minutes the maneuver was set to go. Only Garrett could pull the plug on the whole thing, but she hoped he wouldn't.

"No. We proceed on schedule . . . on my order," he replied.

All hell was about to break loose, and Alexa hoped no one had to die—except for any Globe Harvest bastard who fought back. She gripped her weapon and gave a hand signal to her men, preparing them to move on her mark. When Garrett gave the order, she wanted to make a good first impression on Globe Harvest.

Despite her posturing with Garrett—that taking down the organization behind the abductions was vital—she knew what mattered most in an operation like this. She risked her life on the front lines to rescue hostages, a countermeasure that tipped the scales against the necessity of killing. The hostages ranked above everything. Seeing the relief on their faces when they knew their ordeal was over, especially after they'd given up hope, had kept her in the game and able to sleep at night.

In the end, it was enough for her.

Nikki remembered how, back in Chicago, she was thrown into a dark room with other girls. She'd been confused and nearly paralyzed with panic, but when she sought comfort and answers from the others, they rejected her. They cowered in the shadows, too afraid to move or speak. Eventually, their silence wore her down. And their fear leached under her skin, infecting her too.

But here, she was locked in a cell, completely alone. And she didn't know which was worse.

The small cell had one recessed bulb in the ceiling, and it cast a pale light. She had a narrow bunk, a nasty sink, and a stainless steel toilet that had seen better days. Reluctantly, she chose to sit on the bare mattress. And as minutes turned to hours of silence, her mind wandered.

She even watched a roach scurry across her cell, and hadn't been repulsed by the clack of its small legs on the concrete floor. In a strange way, she felt comforted by its presence until it finally slipped under the door and was gone. At that moment she wished she could trade places with it. Even a roach had more freedom.

You're losing it, Nik.

Before her abduction, she thought she understood who she was. But sitting alone in this place, waiting for what would happen next, she realized she'd been wrong. And images of home and the way things had been drifted cruelly through her mind, more of a torment than a consolation. She would have given anything to feel her mother's arms around her, even though being home again wouldn't be the same without Uncle Payton. His death would always be a reminder of her blinding and selfish stupidity.

Grief and regret swelled through her belly, making her nauseous until a steady thrum resounded down the hall. It took a while for her to recognize the sound of footsteps. The noise brought back horrid memories from Chicago. She knew what it felt like to pray that the footsteps down the hall weren't coming for her, even if it meant someone else would be targeted.

But today, when a key slid into her lock, she knew they'd come for her. The Russian was first to enter her cell. His depraved eyes slowly traveled down her body. Two men came with him, standing in his shadow. What had they come for?

Oh my God! This was it.

Her heart thrashed in her chest and she choked on her next breath, shoving her back into a corner behind her bed. She had no place to go. Her eyes grew wide and filled with tears, and she couldn't make her body move, not even to defend herself. The rush of fear had paralyzed her into someone she didn't know.

She was convinced they intended to rape her—all three men—when the Russian leaned against a wall, amused and entertained by her panic.

"I have come to reunite you with your friend. That is all. Come. She is waiting for you." He grinned, then waved a hand. He'd taken the normal bite from his voice. "It is not far."

As she walked down the dark passageway behind the Russian, manhandled by the two guards at her side, she caught movement behind sealed doors. A small finger at one portal, an eye looking through glass from another. She had no idea how many were being held here against their will, but the sight sickened her.

The Russian turned a corner, and at the end of the corridor, another light filtered into the murky hallway. It shone through a small window on a door. Instinctively she knew he'd be taking her there, but a peculiar odor distracted her. She remembered the smell from the other night when they first arrived, the odor she couldn't quite place.

When the Russian opened the door to let her inside, she had to cover her eyes from the intense brightness. It blinded her, and she raised a hand to shield her eyes. When her vision cleared enough to look around, she was surprised by what she saw.

A surgical room, pristine in white and stainless steel. Large overhead lights hung over an operating table, the main focus of the large room. An observation window was positioned above, but that room was empty. And a man dressed in pale blue hospital scrubs and a white lab coat stood across from her, looking like a doctor. His eyes were on her, but his expression was unreadable.

Now the smell made sense. It was the medicinal odor of iodine and something else more pungent—coppery and sweet.

When she turned to ask the Russian why he'd brought her here, she discovered the answer on her own. A body on a gurney, not much more than a bloody heap, had been shoved to a corner of the room.

"Oh God," she gasped, stumbling back with a hand over her mouth.

No one had bothered to cover the remains. The sight horrified her, but it wasn't until she saw the small heart-shaped birthmark that she finally understood what the Russian had said in her cell.

I have come to reunite you with your friend.

The bloody heap on the gurney was Britney Webber.

"*Nooo!*" Nikki screamed. Her voice echoed in the chamber. "But why? Oh my God, what did you do?"

In shock, she asked questions aloud while her mind grappled with unfathomable answers, trying to understand what had happened. It didn't take long for her to piece the truth together. The girl's eyes had been hollowed out, leaving darkened pits. Her chest and abdomen were splayed open like some science experiment gone terribly wrong. And the coppery sweet tang of fresh blood hung in the air, a morbid reminder.

The Russian had killed Britney for her body parts.

"Here at this facility, we harvest and sell to the highest bidder, quite a profitable enterprise. Capitalism at its finest," the Russian said. The humor in his voice and the smirk on his face made a mockery of Britney's murder and forced a simmering rage to grip her.

The contemptible man stepped toward her and stood close enough for her to smell alcohol on his breath.

"You see? I have found a way for us to leave this place . . . together." He mocked her too now, his voice barely a whisper for her ears alone. He stroked her cheek with a vile finger and she felt his hot breath on her face. Choking back a sob, she pulled her chin away, finding it hard to take her eyes off the corpse on the gurney.

But her revulsion toward the Russian didn't shut the man up.

"Once again, you will be with me, just not in a manner you'd prefer." The arrogant man barely stifled a laugh.

"You're wrong, you sorry son of a bitch. Being dead is the only way I'd ever be with scum like you." She didn't know where she'd gotten the courage to say it, but it felt good. And bonus points, it made the Russian mad.

"Prepare her!" he demanded. "This one I will witness personally." He thrust a hand at the doctor, punctuating his order with a warning. "I have business to attend to, but don't start until I return. Call me when you are ready to proceed."

The egotistical man left the room without a glimmer of remorse or even a glance over his shoulder.

Stunned, with tears blurring her vision, Nikki couldn't take her eyes off the grotesque and misshapen hull of Britney's body, pitted with the bloodied hollows left by the surgeon who'd taken her life. A heart-shaped birthmark on a pallid chin was all that remained to identify her.

In her head, Nikki raged against the injustice, and she felt as if she'd aged a thousand years. But she couldn't force her mouth to speak or convince her legs to move. She imagined the terror of her own scream and what it might feel like to run until she dropped, but that wouldn't be possible. A guard grabbed her arm and shoved her toward the doctor.

On the order of the smug Russian—who had hijacked her life and now wanted to snuff it out entirely—she'd suffer Britney's fate and be powerless to stop it.

CHAPTER 29

Northeast Cape
St. Lawrence Island

On Frank's order, an Alaska State Trooper chopper pilot, Gary Coburn, flew over the site of the deserted Air Force radar station to get a bird's-eye view before they landed. Jess craned her neck, helping Payton look for any activity, but she saw none from the air.

She knew not to expect much from a facility that had been abandoned over fifty years ago, but this place was in worse shape than the textile factory in the boonies of Chicago. Seeing it brought a backwash of doubts that weighed heavy on her heart. She saw the same misgivings on Payton's face when he avoided looking in her eyes.

In the dying hours of the day, the facility looked like an old ghost town, gutted for anything of value and left for the wind and other elements to wear it down. Shattered windows, toppled walls, and rooftops that had caved in were all that remained. A small mountain range stood on one side of the old military grounds that had been carved out of a cluster of evergreen trees.

"We won't fly too low." Trooper Frank's voice came over her headset. Noise in the cockpit made it nearly impossible to hear conversation without headgear. "The rotor blade could wipe out evidence of activity. The wind is bad enough out here, but no sense being foolish." Frank pointed in the distance. "We'll land beyond the trees and trek back."

They nodded, and the pilot swung hard right and prepared to land. The maneuver left her feeling like she'd left her stomach at the top of a roller coaster. Once they landed, the foothills at the back of the radar station eclipsed the sun. Although the sunset shed a faint reddish glow onto the scene, visibility wasn't good at ground level. Soon they'd have to resort to flashlights, and she was thankful the troopers had brought extra gear.

Trooper Gary took point, and Frank walked in silence with them, his complete focus on the path they took toward the old base. At times the trooper stooped down to get a closer look at the ground, but he never said much. The beam from their flashlights drew bugs from the gloom like a magnet, making her wish that she'd applied a liberal dose of repellent. She tried to ignore the insects, but the little buggers made her feel itchy.

Despite being plagued by flying vermin, Jess felt the adrenaline rush of the hunt, though the odds weren't with them that the trip to the island would pan out. But when they got near the collapsed gate of the old facility, things changed.

"Hey, Frank, check this out," Trooper Gary called over his shoulder. When they caught up, he shined his light onto the ground. "See these long scrapes on this flat boulder? These marks are new. And along here, something heavy landed in this spot. You can tell by the way the soil and rocks have been disturbed . . . pressed down."

"What does that mean?" Payton moved his light around the perimeter of where they stood. Shadows ebbed and flowed with the motion, creating an eerie tableau.

"Another helicopter maybe?" Frank asked, directing his question to the other trooper.

"I'd say more than one, considering how these markings

overlap," Coburn replied. "But what if this is only a government inspection trip? How are we gonna tell the difference?"

She hadn't thought of that, but it was a damned good question. She despised rain on her parade.

"Actually, you bring up a valid point," Frank said, "but before I flew to the island, I had an opportunity to contact the officials responsible for the inspection activity here. I found out they haven't been here in the last three months and hadn't planned another trip until early next year."

Frank had withheld information. He'd savored a nice tidbit, waiting to spring it at just the right time.

"You were holding out on us. Why didn't you say anything about this before now?" Payton pressed.

"I didn't want to expose any of us to harm. And I didn't think we'd find anything out here, but this . . ." He heaved a sigh and shook his head, staring at the markings on the ground. "This is different."

On the surface, the trooper took the discovery in stride, but Jess could tell he was shaken by it. When he had time to consider his next step, he spoke again.

"Look, Trooper Coburn and I are going through the gate, looking for footprints or some other proof of recent activity. You folks stay here. If we find something more, I'll call for backup and we'll wait like we agreed. Is that understood?"

"Yeah, sure. We'll wait right here." Payton nodded and grabbed her hand. The sudden gesture surprised her but she went along and smiled at the troopers.

After they took off in the dark, Jess followed their progress by their light beams. When they were far enough away, she whispered to Payton as he let go of her hand.

"I didn't like the way he said 'if we find something.' Frank needs a lesson in the powers of positive thinking. You think they'll find anything?"

In a bold move, he grabbed her flashlight, but kept his eyes on the other men.

"I'm not waiting to find out." He doused both their lights, leaving them standing in the dark. "We've come too far to give this a casual once-over. I'm going in."

"Oh no." She shook her head, still speaking in a hushed voice. "You're not leaving me out here to be the girl. I'm with you, big guy."

"Look, it won't be easy breaking and entering into this dump in the dark."

"Now you're talkin' my language, Archer. Nothing like a little B and E to get the heart pumpin'."

"It'll be risky. We can't use our flashlights until we get past the troopers. Hell, we could get whacked by friendly fire if Frank mistakes us for armed trespassers." He kept his voice low. "Frank's gonna be pissed."

"You said the words 'we' and 'us,' Archer. I heard them distinctly." She grinned. "Even your subconscious knows you're not leavin' me behind. Embrace the concept."

She heard his sigh and saw his shoulders slump, a tantalizing silhouette she'd come to recognize.

"No matter what happens, we're stickin' together," he said.

"I wouldn't have it any other way, Archer. In fact, I like the sound of that."

She followed Payton through the opening in the gate, careful where she stepped so she wouldn't fall in the dark and break her neck. She felt the weight of the pendant Alexa had given her, hanging around her neck, and recalled her words.

Press down on the stone only in case of an emergency. It'll send out a beacon . . . and the alliance will contact me.

Jess realized how futile her backup plan had become in this remote place, but decided to err on the side of caution for once in her life. She reached under her shirt, pulled out the necklace, and pushed down on the gem. The stone clicked and held in place. If the bling alert worked, Alexa's alliance would put out the word on her emergency, and eventually she'd get a call from the woman herself, if her social calendar had an opening.

Of course, if she and Payton ran into Globe Harvest here on St. Lawrence Island, it would be too late, but there was always a bright side. At least Alexa would know where to find their bodies.

As Payton had warned, none of this was going to be easy, but they'd come too far to give up now. She wanted this as much for herself as she did for Nikki. Never giving up on this case had fueled an inner strength, and she felt empowered by the newfound sense of control.

They'd make one last push to find Nikki, and Jess prayed it would be enough.

In night vision gear, Alexa moved with her primary entry team down a short slope, holding her H&K MP5/10 submachine gun fitted with a suppressor. She kept her eyes alert for any suspicious activity as she shuffled in bent knee stance with weapon raised, making her way toward the breach point.

In her bag of tricks, she carried flash-bangs, stingers, and tear gas grenades to create a diversion as her team launched their initial assault. Others would follow behind her men, a planned attack. The perimeter had already been contained, and Garrett had responsibility for the sniper unit. She trusted these men to cover her backside.

Without being detected, she and her men converged at the entry point. As expected, the place was in shambles and looked deserted. Hard to imagine Globe Harvest operated in this dump, but thermal imagers confirmed the presence of warm bodies, and they had picked the optimal entry point to maintain the element of surprise. Shock and awe was the name of the game, their objective to overwhelm the hostage takers inside with their firepower and quick assault, giving them no time to react.

Her team waited for her order. She took a deep breath, but

nothing would stop the sensation she had come to accept. She felt the rush of adrenaline assault the inside of her ears, and her heart pounded into her throat, part of the deadly game. If all went well, their siege would be over in a matter of minutes, hopefully without loss of life.

At least, she prayed that would be the case. Rock steady on the outside, she gave the hand signal, and all hell cut loose in her world.

"Sir, we have a breach."

Petrovin heard the man's voice from across the security control room. He shut his eyes and clenched his jaw until he could continue.

"That helicopter from earlier, is it them?" he asked.

Just before he'd taken the girl to the operating room, he'd gotten word that an aircraft was circling the perimeter of the compound. This happened from time to time, mostly government types collecting soil samples. With the notoriety of the radar station and the PCB contamination, it had been a perfect deterrent for curious eyes. He had hoped that the intruders would have moved on by now. But apparently they had stopped for a closer inspection.

"Yes, sir, I think so," the man replied. Stas shook his head, amazed at the man's ineptitude, but his man redeemed himself when he clarified, "With our surveillance, I spotted two Alaska troopers, but there's a man and a woman who've gotten inside the outer compound. There could be others, but we've got to counter, sir. What are your orders?"

Stas imagined firing a submachine gun into the fools who dared to mess with him. In his head, yet not entirely absent of personal experience, he heard the meaty thud of the bullets and imagined bloody carnage at his feet. But he knew what Anton Bukolov would want, and he'd reluctantly comply.

In a line, Alexa's team moved through shadowy corridors in a stack formation, using her free hand on the shoulder of the man in front as a guide. Her other hand gripped her weapon, always prepared to use it. Her team cleared one room at a time, prepared to deal with resistance as they went.

"Go, go, go."

One of her men blasted down another closed door with a battering ram. Night vision gear painted the interior in eerie shades of green as she tossed in a flash-bang, then diverted her eyes so the blast wouldn't blind her.

BOOM!

She knew from experience that a blinding white light would sear the dark. And a glowing ball of fire would radiate like a shock wave in all directions, followed by a billowing stench. Even now, the blast resonated into the corridor where she stood ready to move in.

The fierce image would leave its imprint on the eyes of anyone inside the room. The white light would hang suspended in darkness then splinter into spangles, blurring the vision of anyone looking directly at it. In a daze, those affected would have minimal hearing, registering only muffled sounds.

Her team had only seconds to gain advantage.

She had entered the room in a rush through the smoke, leaving tail-end Charlie to provide cover outside the door. As soon as her team broke through the threshold of the door, they split apart to avoid becoming easy targets. Each carved out their piece of the pie—their responsibility—breaking down the room into sectors, with trust in the team a necessity of the job.

She heard screams of men through the haze and caught movement in the far corner of the room, a ghostly image in night vision green. But she had her assignment.

"Clear right!" she yelled. Her section of the room was clear of targets, but she moved to her next position, tightening the circle.

Other members of her team weren't so lucky. A short spurt of bullets erupted, and even through her com set she heard the muffled yet chilling sound of bullets pounding flesh. A body dropped to the floor and the shrill scream of a girl reminded her why they'd come. The hostage shrank into the corner, too afraid to move.

"Clear left," her man called out instinctively, following protocol.

Their circle tightened toward the center of the room, her team carving a wedge between the freed hostages and their captors. Fast and brutal, they neutralized the room with deadly intent. More gunfire. More men died. Hostages scrambled to get away. Her team sorted through the chaos and took control. In minutes it would be over.

She heard a man pleading for his life in Russian. For a second she hoped it was Petrovin, but she knew better. Stanislav Petrovin would not go down easy. And the man would never beg for his life.

"Clear center." The last all clear sign came.

It was over.

They'd taken care of the last room, the stronghold where these men had made their final stand with the hostages. The smell of blood played second fiddle to another stench. A man had cleared his bowels as he died. She recognized the odor.

Even through the ringing in her ears, she heard the low moans of the wounded and dying. Walking through the smoke and carnage, her team flexicuffed everyone in the room, even the hostages, the wounded, and the dead got their hands tied until things were sorted out and everyone was questioned.

By the time Garrett found her, she saw the relief in his eyes that she'd made it through the operation. He rushed to her, careful not to reveal too much to his men. But the look in his eyes said it all.

"Are you okay?" he asked.

God, she loved the sound of his voice.

"Yeah. Did we lose anyone?" She ventured a touch of his sleeve.

"No, thank God. A couple of injuries, but they'll live. It was a good op, Alexa."

She fought a smile, unsure what part God would have chosen to play, but she gave Garrett the benefit of the doubt that he had a direct line to a higher power. When he looked beyond her, searching through the murky haze of the room, Garrett smiled uncharacteristically, a strange sight in a room colored by bloodshed.

"Well, I'll be damned," he said.

"What?" She turned and shifted her gaze to where he looked. "What's so funny?"

"I had intel of Petrovin being here, but that's Anton Bukolov himself. The guy behind Globe Harvest."

Garrett pointed to the old Russian who had pleaded for his life. When she'd seen the old man on his knees, she wondered if he was a victim. Now her sympathies for the old guy drifted away with the smoke. Bukolov would pay for what he'd done to all the innocent lives they'd never know about.

"Before you leave, thanks for sticking with this," Garrett told her." We never could have pulled this off without you. The Sentinels are pleased."

She didn't exactly count it as a blessing to be on the radar of the Sentinels—a far-reaching global organization that had confederates in every country, allowing Garrett's alliance to operate in secrecy—but something he'd said stuck in her mind.

"What were you talking about . . . I'm leaving for somewhere?"

"Your bounty hunter is about to put her foot in it. She sent up a flare. Tanya tracked her to St. Lawrence Island. When she couldn't get ahold of you, she made sure I got the message. If you hurry, you can keep her breathing for another day."

Jessica knew not to contact her unless it was an emergency. And knowing the bounty hunter, she'd be in the thick of a firefight before she'd admit she needed help. After all, she had first met Jessica in the midst of a thermite explosion.

What are you up to now, Beckett?

Once she heard about St. Lawrence Island, it only took a moment for her to connect the dots to the coordinate they'd dismissed in the Bering Sea. Somehow Jessica must have figured out the erroneous location was a hair off. *Damn it!* The island could have been part of their assault plan had they thought more out of the box and not played it safe.

With her current location outside Providenija, Russia, Alexa did a quick calculation in her head on how long it would take to fly to St. Lawrence Island, but Garrett interrupted her.

"Take your team and the AW139. I customized it so it's got speed and enhanced range, a bird tailored for our kind of ops. Tanya will feed you the exact coordinates when you get airborne. I'll clean up here, but stay in touch. If you need backup, call me."

Garrett didn't look surprised by Tanya's message to her, or surprised that she'd been tracking Beckett. As she rushed from the room, grabbing her team and making quick arrangements for the next order of business, she yelled back to him.

"You knew, didn't you?" She narrowed her eyes. "You could have picked any of the coordinates to assign me, but you picked here. You knew I was tracking Jessica. With us being so close to St. Lawrence, we might have a chance to help her."

"If you persist in believing I'm all powerful and have a magic crystal ball, then go ahead." He shrugged.

"I don't know anything about your crystal ball, but if I had to guess, I'd say you had a pair . . . of brass ones."

Despite the grim setting, some of the men chuckled. But

Garrett only shook his head and said, "Your bounty hunter—she's an interesting woman."

Alexa raised an eyebrow and said, "Yes, she is."

Jealousy was an ugly affliction. Even now she'd been struck by it when Garrett gave his personal insight on Beckett. But as she raced for the helicopter, with her team following, she prayed she'd be in time to help the headstrong bounty hunter.

Jealousy be damned.

Northeast Cape
St. Lawrence Island

His men awaited his order. Petrovin shifted his gaze from face to face, thinking over his position on the breach in his security perimeter. Although he didn't know the extent of the problem and would have handled the situation differently, he knew what Bukolov would want.

And Stas didn't want a repeat of Chicago. He'd blown apart the evidence, but not before a handful of cops turned into a multitude that he'd narrowly escaped. And similar to that situation, there might only be a few intruders outside now, but more might come. No, he wouldn't toy with them today.

He simply wasn't in the mood.

"Immediate evacuation. And this time, no hostages," he told his man. "I will handle the detonation myself. We leave in twenty minutes and I wait for no one."

Every man in the control room stared at him.

"You know what to do," he prompted. "Make sure they are all locked in their cells, except for the girl in the operating room. She will get my personal attention."

He was done talking. For the sake of drama, he hit the silent alarm, a button on the console in front of him. Immediately, beacons of red rotated through the room and his men rushed to their duties, an all too familiar sight for him these days. Before he left the security room, he would set up for the detonation of the facility, an act he would control.

But first he placed a call to the operating room. One matter remained unsettled.

"We have no time for precision, Doctor," he said. "Harvest what you can from the girl now, and leave the rest. I will be there shortly."

Calmly, he walked out of the security station toward the operating room. In controlled chaos, his men scrambled down the halls, securing prisoners and making their way to freedom—an escape tunnel where the helicopters would be fueled and ready.

He would soon join them for their final farewell of this hellhole, but not before he had the girl's heart and other sundry parts in a box. This would be one delivery he'd make personally.

CHAPTER 30

Northeast Cape
St. Lawrence Island

Tanya Spencer had provided Alexa the coordinates where she believed Jessica Beckett had last signaled. The woman hadn't tracked her cell phone this time, but used the beacon signal off the necklace Alexa had given her for emergency use only. A more reliable means.

While they were en route, Tanya had also given Alexa a quick yet thorough summary of what to expect once she got to the island. But once she arrived, Alexa had a hard time believing her eyes. What would Jessica be doing on this remote island? And why would the bounty hunter send up a high-tech distress signal here?

Searchlights from the helicopter strafed the ground around the old Air Force radar site, giving her perspective on the scene. Bright white swept the ground and the rubble below, washing everything out. The place was a pit, looking more like a war-torn village. From what she could tell, this part of the island didn't have much of a population. Yet according to Tanya, this was the place.

Eventually, Alexa saw something to clue her in that she'd arrived at the correct coordinates. Several red flares burned on the ground near a collapsed cyclone fence. And a man in a trooper uniform came out of a dilapidated building and was waving his arms to flag them down.

Speaking into her headset, she gave an order to her pilot, "Set down near that gate." And to the man next to her, she said, "We're going in to lend assistance to the local law and get a quick assessment of the situation, but once we hit the ground, I want you to head out again and do a perimeter search."

"Anything in particular you're looking for, Marlowe?"

"Yeah, a stash of helicopters on the ground or a locale to hide them." She briefly explained what had happened in Chicago and how the Russian got away. "I want a tracking device on any aircraft you find. I don't want any of these bastards getting away from me a second time."

"You got it."

Before they landed and talked to the trooper, she made another judgment call. She wasn't in the mood for flack.

"Now that we're back in the good old USA, break out your FBI credentials. And I'll do all the talking. I'm not in the mood for a delay from the locals."

Alexa switched colors with the ease of a chameleon, and without flinching, so did her men.

As he walked down the corridor, Petrovin steeled himself for what he would see when he entered the operating room. Although organ harvesting was a means to an end for his superior Bukolov, he himself did not care for the whole distasteful mess. And despite the fact that he resented the privileged life of this blond American girl—his own life had not been so agreeable—she still stood out in his mind as someone with backbone. And he had to admit to having an inkling of respect for her.

But duty meant everything to him. Without it, he had nothing.

When he shoved open the operating room door, he looked for the carcass of the girl and expected to be repulsed by it.

He hoped that seeing her dead might end the peculiar admiration he had for her. The defiant girl would fade from his recollections, replaced by images of the dead one. And corpses had always been easily dismissed from his mind, more a matter of convenience.

But instead of seeing the girl, he found the room in complete disarray and one of his men unconscious on the floor with blood pooling near his head. The girl was nowhere to be found. When he looked up, the doctor rushed to him, his face red with agitation.

"When the alarms went off, one of your guards left to save his own skin. And this one allowed the girl to get away." The doctor pointed to the guard on the floor and went on, "She punched him in the gut with her elbow, and when he bent over, she shoved him into the wall. I think he may be dead."

The man was speaking faster now, out of breath. Spittal came from his mouth.

"She looked like she'd taken martial arts. I couldn't do a thing against her. Where do you think she learned that?"

"Focus, Doctor. Where did she go?"

The man pointed to his right. "She took off toward the elevator. She's got the guard's gun, and I think she took his keys too."

Stas clenched his jaw, working hard to contain his anger. He had to think clearly. But no matter how hard he planned for every contingency, whenever he involved others to carry out his orders, things got fucked up. And today had been no different. In the end there was only one person he could trust. And he had to remember that.

"Why bother with her?" the doctor said, trying to downplay the incident and justify his own cowardice. "We should be going. Besides, she'll die in the explosion anyway."

"You make a good point, Doctor. Very sound reasoning from an educated man, such as yourself." He waggled a finger at him. "The men are waiting at the helicopters. Perhaps you should go. I will follow shortly. Since I'm a man of duty, it falls to me."

He turned to go, but stopped short at the door.

"You know, Doctor. In many ways, we are men cut from the same cloth." He could tell the good doctor believed he'd been insulted, but the medical man forced a grin. When he did, Petrovin added, "That's how I know."

"Know what?"

"That you have no heart." He smiled and ventured a laugh until the man relaxed. "Because if you did, I would cut it from your chest and take it with me."

The doctor looked up, but before his eyes registered full recognition, Petrovin raised his weapon and pumped a round into the man's heart and throat. He caught him just right, freezing the moment when the man's expression switched from pompous to startled. Stas didn't wait for the body to fall.

He turned and walked away, muttering, "A bullet is a sure cure for stupidity."

He left the operating room, but once he got to the corridor, considered his options. He stood outside the room, awash in the red lights of the alarm system, and gazed down the hallway where the doctor told him the blond girl had run. Down the other way, his men waited at the helicopters. It didn't take long for him to make up his mind.

Above all else, he trusted his instincts and made his choice accordingly. A man of duty always weighed the consequences.

"What was that? Did you hear that? Sounded like gunfire." Gun in hand, Payton ran into the dark with his flashlight sweeping through the dusty haze. The crunch of dirt under his boots echoed down the gutted corridor. The air felt thick and muggy, making it hard for Jess to breathe.

"I think it came from over here," he cried out to her, not caring who else overheard.

She raced after him, gripping her weapon and casting her flashlight in front of them both. She heard the shot and knew exactly what it was. But as she looked ahead, the corridor came to an abrupt end. Stone and rubble blocked the way. It didn't look like there was a way around it. And her heart sank.

She could have sworn the sound came from this direction. Hell, it wasn't like they had a minivan full of options.

But as she slowed, Payton picked up his pace, maybe seeing something she hadn't. When he got to the end of the corridor, he reached to the floor and grabbed a handful of dirt. He tossed the dirt into the air, letting his flashlight pick up the particles as they drifted. To her surprise, the finer particles of dust drifted forward and got sucked through a section of the collapsed wall. Payton had found an opening large enough for them to squeeze through.

As sure as she was that the gunshot came from behind the rubble, she was game to try whatever he came up with—his Hail Mary pass at fourth and long.

"How did you see that? I would have missed it. Damn, you're good." She grinned.

"I used to watch *MacGyver* reruns in the off season."

Before she could reply, Payton grabbed her hand and tried to rush her through the small opening, but she stopped him.

"We better mark this spot for anyone to follow."

"The troopers?" he said. "Good idea."

"Yeah, right—Frank and Gary." She would take any help she could get, but she was hoping Alexa might still find them.

Payton fumbled through his pockets, fishing out fifty-dollar bills and a clean white handkerchief. The hankie caught her eye and she considered using it, but she had something more noticeable in mind.

"At the risk of sounding prudish, turn your back." When he did, she fished her arms under her shirt and pulled a Houdini. "Okay, we can use this."

With only a smile, she held up her lucky red bra and raised an eyebrow. This time she hoped for a different kind of good fortune.

"That would get *my* attention." He winked.

Jess wedged the lacy garment into the debris near the opening and followed Payton through the wreckage. When they got to the other side, it didn't take long to find an elevator. Locating a working elevator in this dump had seemed like winning the lotto until they got inside and looked at the button panel. Now they had way too many options to choose and no time to do it.

Before Payton started to do the "man thing," and hit all the buttons in a typical testosterone-driven shotgun approach, she reached out her arm and stopped him.

"Don't touch it. Hold on." She bent over and flashed her light onto the elevator panel. When she found what she was looking for, she smiled and said, "You may have *MacGyver,* but I've got my rebellious youth in the foster care system and my felonious friends to fall back on. Check this out. Only one button has layers of fingerprint smudges. I'm thinkin' that's the place to be."

"And I'm with you. Punch it." He nodded.

When she hit the button and the elevator started its descent to God knew where, Jess reminded herself that what had drawn them here was the sound of a gunshot. She clutched her Glock and took a deep breath, nudging Payton to do the same. When the elevator door opened, no telling who would be on the other side.

Nikki heard the gunshot but didn't stop. She knew instinctively to run faster. She had no idea where she was going, relying only on her sense of direction and what she had memorized of the layout. For the first time since her abduction, she was alone. She had to take advantage of it.

The rotating beams of red—even though they flashed without sirens—made her anxious, but at least they enabled her to see in the darkened corridors. She'd taken the guard's keys and had his gun but had no idea how to use it. If it took more than pulling the trigger, she'd be toast.

As she ran, her lungs burned, making it hard to swallow. Her throat was parched. And whenever she heard footsteps running toward her, she ducked around a corner or squeezed behind fallen debris. But she knew her luck wouldn't hold.

Gripping the keys in her hand, she realized why she'd taken them. She might not have known the other girls' names, but she wouldn't leave them behind—not if she had a chance to make a difference. She wasn't able to help Britney, but for the sake of the others, she had to try.

This has got to be it. She finally found the hall she'd walked down only a short time ago, where she saw the other girls locked in their cells. She rushed to the first door and slipped a key into the lock, but it didn't budge. Her fingers trembled and she kept looking over her shoulder. Her eyes played tricks on her. Shadows moved and undulated in the red flashing light.

"Please . . . get me out." A small voice came from the other side of the door. Nikki felt tears welling in her eyes—tears of frustration and fear.

"Shhh. I'm trying," she whispered back, shoving another key into the lock.

This time the key worked. When she opened the door, a little girl reached for her, clutching her in an embrace, her body shaking. She couldn't have been more than eleven years old, a scrawny little thing with blond hair, big brown eyes, and freckles across the bridge of her nose. All Nikki wanted to do was hold her. She needed someone to do that for her too, but neither of them had time.

"We've gotta go—get the others." Before she left the room, she had to ask. "What's your name?"

"Shelby."

"I'm getting you out of here, Shelby. No matter what happens, you stick with me." She took the girl's hand and squeezed it. Her fingers felt so small and fragile.

Nikki had used the words that Jessica Beckett had said to her, a memory from a lifetime ago in Chicago. And Jessica had also taught her a move or two that had helped her take out the guard in the operating room. She wasn't sure she'd ever see the woman again, but remembering her now had given her strength.

The key to Shelby's lock worked on the other cell doors. She found six girls in all. And now she had to find a way out, back to the elevator, but had no idea where to turn. She huddled the girls together and squatted near the floor around a corner. They stared at her, waiting for words of wisdom she didn't think she had. Hell, she was just a kid herself. But for their sakes, she had to be more.

"It's important we stay quiet," she whispered. "No matter what you see or hear, no one cries or makes a sound." Forcing a smile, she reached out and stroked the cheek of Shelby, the youngest, until the girl grinned back. "We stick together, no matter what. And hold each other's hands. Does anyone remember where the elevator is?"

"I think it's down this way." An older girl, named Bethany, pointed down the hall behind them. "At the end of that hall, we make a right . . . I think."

Nikki didn't like that Bethany wasn't sure, but some of the others nodded. Once they had a plan, they had to move. She felt the weight of the gun in her hand but hoped she wouldn't have to use it.

"Okay, that's it, then. When I say so, we'll move out. And stay behind me." She forced another smile, then crept to the corner and looked both ways. "Let's go."

The alarm was still flashing, but she hadn't heard footsteps in a while. She prayed the men had gone, but didn't feel luck was on her side. Holding onto Shelby's hand, she crept down the hallway, her gaze shifting in front and behind them as they walked single file. But when she got to the end of the corridor, nearly to the corner where they needed to turn, she heard a noise that echoed off the walls. With the sound repeating, she had no idea how many were coming.

"Oh my God. Not now."

She considered making a run for the corner, but the footsteps were coming in their direction, closing the gap between them. She'd never make it with six girls. She let go of Shelby's hand, shoved the gun into the waistband of her pants and reached for the keys she'd taken off the guard as she raced to the nearest cell. They'd hide until they could move again.

Nikki fumbled the keys in her hands, but remembered the door was already open. The lock could only be secured from the hallway. Once they got inside, the door would be open to whoever walked in. But she didn't have time to think about that, not with the footsteps getting louder. She rushed the girls inside, keeping them as quiet as possible. At the last instant, she did remember to flip the light switch on the outside wall of the cell. When the room went black, the girls gasped. She didn't blame them for being afraid. Hell, she was too.

"Get to this wall and press against it," she whispered.

She picked the best spot in the room for the girls to hide. She didn't want a guard to look in the portal and see them. If someone hit the light switch, she wanted them to see only an empty room.

"Remember, not a sound," she whispered.

She waited until they were all behind her, hugging the wall, before she gripped her weapon and pointed it at the door. In her mind, she pictured herself pulling the trigger like in the movies. Because if someone walked through that door, that's what she'd have to do—without hesitation.

She wracked her brain trying to recall what little she knew about guns. If the weapon she held in her hand had a safety lock, she'd have no way of knowing what it would look like or how it worked. That scared her bad enough, but what if she fired and missed and the guard fired back? She grimaced with the thought and pushed it out of her head, except to make up her mind that when the time came, she'd step into the center of the room, away from the girls. She didn't want them caught in her cross fire.

In the dark, Nikki felt Shelby reaching for her. The girl's touch reminded her why she had taken a stand. Yet as much as the gesture meant to her, she had to stay focused. It took both hands for her to hold the weapon as badly as she was shaking. For the sake of Shelby and the others, she prayed for the strength to pull the trigger, a strange prayer. She felt the weight of the gun and the sweat on her palms. And her eyes blurred with stinging tears. That's when she saw it.

At the base of the door she caught movement, a subtle brush of a shadow backlit by the faint pulse of the red flashing alarm. The shadow of a man stretched farther into the room, like unwanted fingers. Someone stood outside. She held her breath and aimed the weapon higher.

The next person through that door—she would shoot to kill.

CHAPTER 31

Outside the perimeter of the compound, some two kilometers from the old radar site, the men waited for Petrovin to show up in the two choppers that would take them to safety and a new location. Both pilots had started their aircraft, but in the one nearest the escape tunnel, tension had grown to a fevered pitch.

"Where is he?" one man asked. His eyes darted to the other faces in the dark.

Another man looked at his watch.

"Twenty minutes is long gone." A security guard clenched his jaw and heaved a sigh in frustration. "He would leave any of us. He said so himself."

As soon as the man said it, the others stared at him. They'd been thinking the same thing, but it was as if Petrovin himself would overhear and heads would soon roll.

"What?" The man shrugged. "We have no idea what is going on in there. And he is the only one who controls the detonation. All I'm saying is that it's risky for us to sit here, not knowing, that's all."

"If we take off and he's left behind, he would find each of

us. You know how he is." The co-pilot turned his head and spoke loud enough for them to hear, punctuating his commentary with curses under his breath.

A few minutes went by, without a sound coming from anyone, but the tension could be cut with a knife. From time to time the men gaped over their shoulders and stared at the tunnel in hopes Petrovin would emerge and the waiting and uncertainty would be over. If he did show, they could forget what had been said and keep each other's secrets. But the Russian never came.

Without a word, the pilot took matters into his own hands and gave the thumbs-up to his counterpart across the makeshift tarmac. As the man made final preparations to leave, not another word was said. The helicopter lifted off the ground, hovered for an instant as the pilot gave the tunnel one last look, then flew into the night sky.

Petrovin would be on his own.

"May God have mercy on us all," the pilot muttered under his breath.

For anyone who heard him, they might have thought he had included Petrovin in his prayer, but that hadn't been the case. A man like Petrovin had no use for God. And if the Russian made it out alive, every man here would require divine intervention to stay one step ahead of the man's inevitable retribution.

Swallowing her next breath, Nikki aimed the weapon toward the closed door, preparing to shoot whoever opened it. She felt the weight of the handgun shaking in her hands. How hard would she have to pull the trigger? Could the gun go off accidentally?

But more important, could she kill?

All these thoughts raced through her mind, clouding her judgment as the shadow under the door moved in the red pulsing light. Down the corridor, she heard doors slamming.

The guards were looking for them. She pictured the Russian's face, and heard his voice as if he stood next to her in the dark. Fresh tears rolled down her cheeks.

Damn it! How had all this happened?

The culmination of her terror came down to this moment. When she put a face to whoever was outside the cell, only one pair of eyes came to mind, and she nearly threw up thinking about it. Could she do it? Did she have what it took to kill him? If the Russian walked through that door, she wasn't sure she could pull the trigger. That was the kind of control he had over her.

But whether she was ready or not, she'd run out of time. The knob turned and the door creaked open.

Oh my God, please no! Inside her head, she screamed. Her heart thrashed in her chest and pounded the inside of her ears. She gripped the weapon and stepped away from the wall. As Nikki moved to the center of the room, she felt Shelby's small fingers fall away. She had never felt so alone.

Now, the dark silhouette of a large man stood in the open doorway. Her eyes blurred with tears, but she couldn't stop crying. She started to pull the trigger. And she would have done it, except movement behind the man distracted her. A face she recognized. In the red glow, she saw Jessica Beckett, the woman she never thought she'd see again.

Nikki's sobs came in a torrent. She lowered the gun, her muscles too drained to keep the weapon hoisted. She wanted to say something, yet the words wouldn't come. She was happy to see Jessica, but when the woman flipped the lights on, Nikki couldn't believe her eyes. The man from the shadows who'd stood in the doorway was Uncle Payton.

And she'd almost killed him . . . again.

Before she could say anything, he swept her off the floor and clutched her to his chest, cradling the back of her head with a hand. In his arms, she felt safe. In his arms, she never felt so loved. And in his arms, she wasn't alone anymore.

"I thought you were dead," she whispered into his ear

and burrowed her face into his neck. "And I almost . . . pulled the trigger. I could've—"

"Shhhhh. I've got you now, baby. You're safe, Nikki," Payton's low voice reassured her. "Oh my God, I love you so much. I thought we'd lost you for sure." Eventually, he lowered her to the floor and pulled back. "Let me see you. Are you okay?"

When he had assured himself she was all right physically, he grinned that same crooked smile she'd grown to love. She could see he'd been crying, and it broke her heart to imagine how close she'd come to losing him a second time.

"How's Mama? I can't believe I did this to her . . . and to you." She pictured her mother's face, and a devastating wave of regret hit her hard.

With a gun in her hand, Jessica kept watch at the closed door, searching out the glass portal, then shifted her gaze back to them, listening.

"You didn't do anything wrong, honey . . ." Payton kissed her cheek and pulled her to him again. ". . . except maybe trusted the wrong folks. But they're the ones who're to blame here, not you."

"That Russian man killed Britney. He took her heart and her eyes . . . they had an operating room." Nikki knew she wasn't making sense, but the words kept coming and she couldn't stop holding her uncle. "He was harvesting body parts, selling them to the highest bidder . . . and he killed her. He almost did that to me, but I got away. That's how I stole this gun."

She handed the weapon over to Payton, glad to be rid of it.

"The Russian? The same one from Chicago?" Jess stepped closer and stroked Nikki's hair. When the girl nodded, she said, "We saw the operating room, honey. These men will pay for what they've done."

Before she and Payton found the row of holding cells and

began their search of each one, they had located the operating room. An unconscious man lay on the floor, and another one dressed like a doctor had been shot to death; the gunfire they'd heard earlier. They'd also seen a crematorium where bodies had been destroyed in an industrial-size furnace, remains reduced to dust and bone fragments. Emissions from the crematorium probably got chalked up to the contamination in the area, perhaps sustaining the belief this part of the island was still at risk.

She and Payton had discovered Globe Harvest's setup while looking for Nikki, but Jess had no intention of telling the girl what they'd found. It would be hard enough for the kid to recover from her ordeal without adding to her night terrors.

To distract Nikki, Jess turned to face the others.

"We're getting you girls out of here—now." She held out her hand to the smallest girl, a blond kid with freckles who was crying. "It's okay, honey. We're gonna take you home."

Many of the girls had ventured timid smiles, hesitant to move until Jess said the word "home." Then one by one they rushed to her. And when she felt the press of their warm bodies, Jess was overwhelmed with a flood of emotion, one that had been building in her for a very long time.

The sensation propelled her back to the day when *she* was rescued. She'd been a severely abused child who only existed in the moment, without a future or a past—and she had no one to call family. She thought she'd forgotten what it felt like, but in a rush everything came back.

"I hate to break up the party, but we're not out of this yet," Payton said. "We've got to get these girls out of here, Jessie."

She looked up at him and nodded.

"Yeah, he's right, girls. We gotta go." Jess wiped her face and retrieved her Glock from the waistband of her pants. She headed for the door and did a quick look through the glass, then fixed her eyes on Payton.

"I'll take point. We'll keep the girls between us." And to the kids, she said, "Everyone keep real quiet, okay? *Shhhh.*"

Jess opened the door, trying to minimize the creak, and crept into the hallway. With one hand, she clutched the little blond girl's fingers, and she gripped her gun in the other. And when she got to the end of the corridor, ready to turn for the elevator, she stopped short—not believing her eyes.

Standing between her and the elevator was Alexa Marlowe and an entourage of men dressed in black and sporting FBI gear. Alaska State Troopers Frank and Gary were with them. Every last one aimed a weapon at her. If she had more of an inferiority complex, she might have taken offense. But as it stood, she never felt safer in her life.

"Damn, am I glad to see you." Jess grinned. "Whoever said there was safety in numbers really knew what they were talking about."

Once Alexa relaxed and lowered her weapon, she pulled something out from her BDU pocket, an item Jess knew well. Shaking her head, the woman twirled her red lacy bra in one hand and raised an eyebrow.

"You really know how to send up a red flare, bounty hunter. Thanks, you saved us time." As Alexa approached, she got a good look at the girls behind Jess and added, "Well, I'll be damned. Good work, Jessie. But if it's all the same to you, I'd rather not end up a slab of bacon. I'm partial to my ass the way it is. I'm sure Globe Harvest has this place rigged to blow."

"It's worse. Nikki told us Petrovin is here," Jess said. "If he's in charge, we gotta get out of here fast."

Alexa clenched her jaw in anger. "Let's roll—*NOW!*"

Without hesitating, she and Payton grabbed Nikki and the smallest girl, and Alexa's men reached for the other kids. The Alaska State Troopers took point with weapons drawn, and Alexa followed close behind, armed and dressed to kill. They all ran for the elevator.

Mercifully, Jess didn't remember much about the explosion in Chicago, but this place felt different. There were no propane fumes and no shrill alarm to grate on her nerves. Still, she knew Alexa was right. If the Russian had been here, he'd have the place wired to blow. She only hoped they'd have time to get ahead of the blast.

And she prayed Nikki's good luck had rubbed off on them.

Out of the shadows, Stas Petrovin emerged from the escape tunnel in time to see his men fly away in both helicopters, leaving him alone to face the enemy . . . and his fate. He glanced at his watch. They had waited nearly forty minutes, well beyond the time he had warned that he would have left them.

What more could he have asked of them? *What more indeed.*

He shut his eyes and took a deep breath of the cool night air and looked up into the heavens. This place reminded him of Siberia, and he had mixed emotions about that. Casting a bluish haze over the foothills, a full moon shone above him. The sight of it should have made him feel small and insignificant, but nothing could be further from the truth.

He felt powerful and in absolute control.

In his hand, he had the means to bring down the underground facility and implode it under the feet of his enemy, perhaps taking the lives of many with the blast. If he did his duty, Bukolov would be protected once more. Yet for the first time, he sensed he had a choice.

Perhaps that was why he felt in control. He stood on a precipice of change and he knew it.

He contemplated his actions, then made his decision, reveling in the fact that the call was his alone to make. Without further thought, he initiated the detonation, knowing he had a time delay for his escape. But instead of thinking of his own safety, he pushed the envelope and chose to stay, standing in the glow of the moon. After all, it was a night for indulgence, and he had the heart of a poet beating in his chest.

Of this, he was certain.

After leaving the elevator, they barely had enough time to clear the collapsed wall when Alexa felt a familiar rumble under her feet. Self-preservation sent a second surge of adrenaline through her brain.

"Oh shit, not again."

They raced for the way out, but with the first impact, the ground swelled under her, then dropped out. The quake nearly knocked her down as she ran. She saw one of the troopers hit the dirt, but the man scrambled to his feet, hardly missing a step. And, good man, he never dropped his weapon. The older girls ran one step ahead, their age giving them an advantage. And her men kept the kids out of harm's way like a team of bodyguards or a strong defensive line in the NFL.

"Pedal to the metal, people. This place is gonna blow," she yelled, keeping her legs pumping. Her lungs heaved and her thighs were on fire from exertion.

Dust and debris fell from over their heads as they ran. The whole mountain could come down on their ears any minute. She took a quick glance back and saw that Jessica hadn't let go of Nikki's hand and Payton had the other. In his left arm the quarterback carried a little blond girl who had his neck in a fierce grip. He didn't look like he minded the extra burden. She couldn't blame Jess and Payton for not wanting to let go of Nikki and the smallest girl. The four weren't making the best progress as they ran, but some things were worth the risk.

A hot vaporous cloud of gases and dirt swept by them as they finally made it outside. Alexa remembered how it felt to barely escape the carnage in Chicago.

"Keep moving. Don't stop." And under her breath, more

to herself, she added, "And whatever you do, don't look back."

A wall of fire belched from what remained of the cinder-block structure they had used to enter the old radar station. She felt the heat crawl up her back as if she'd caught fire. Eventually, cool night air touched the inflamed skin of her face, and she knew she'd beaten the blast once again. When she got free, she did a quick head count and was relieved everyone had made it through, until she saw Jessica ranting up ahead.

Alexa's hearing had been hampered by the siege at Providenija, where they'd captured Anton Bukolov earlier, the aging captain at the helm of Globe Harvest. But as she neared the bounty hunter, she heard what the woman was complaining about. In the distance, the sound of helicopters brought back a feeling of déjà vu.

Only this time Alexa knew things would be different.

"That bastard got away again. Damn it!" Jessica cursed, and flung her arms out in sheer rage, stomping her foot. "We were so close."

Although the bounty hunter's words sounded muffled, she heard enough to approach the woman with details she'd been waiting to share. She raised her voice, unsure how loud she sounded, and told Jessica the good news.

"I learned my lesson in Chicago. When we first touched down here, I had one of my men search the perimeter, knowing how the Russian and Globe Harvest liked a back-door escape plan." She forced a smile, though she ached all over.

"And?" By the smirk on the bounty hunter's face, she knew what was coming.

"We've got tracking beacons on those birds. He and his men won't get far this time."

With that news, Jessica grinned and turned to listen as the helicopters flew south. Once again Alexa saw Petrovin and his men were airborne without lights, but even in the distance the rotor noise was unmistakable. They were making their escape, only now she couldn't help but match Jessica's grin.

Until the night sky lit up like the Fourth of July.

"What the hell?" They both cried out in unison.

Two huge explosions erupted in the distance like a supernova up close. Alexa could have sworn she felt the force of the blast from where she stood. Out of reflex, Jessica grabbed her arm, but kept her eyes fixed to the sky. Her mouth gaped open until she finally spoke.

"Oh . . . my . . . God," she muttered under her breath. "Did you have anything to do with that?"

"You may not believe me, but no, I didn't." Alexa hated thinking about what had happened to the men onboard. No one deserved to die like that . . . except for Petrovin.

Jessica never took her eyes off the fireballs that pierced the night. The unexpected explosions shredded both fuselages. The airborne wreckage fell to the earth like heavy globs of molten steel, and where each piece landed, the ground caught fire. The inferno would rage for a while, but Alexa thanked the heavens that this part of the island had few inhabitants. As it was, the residents here would not soon forget the Globe Harvest facility explosion and the helicopters that had been blown out of the night sky . . . and neither would she.

Alexa stood alongside the bounty hunter, staring into the bright light on the horizon. Eventually, she felt the presence of the others, her team, the troopers, the girls, and Payton Archer, but none of them said a word. After a long moment, Alexa wasn't sure what to say to Jessica, except that the woman had been through hell and needed to hear something good.

"It's over, Jessie. This time . . . it's over."

The bounty hunter looked at her for a brief moment with tears welling in her eyes, only nodding in agreement before she turned away.

But even as Alexa had said those words, she wasn't sure

she believed them. Helicopters don't just fall from the sky without help. And it might take weeks to uncover what happened, too late to do anything about it. Any trail would be ice cold.

Once the shock and the numbing realization that they'd almost died had worn off, each of them would grasp that they had no idea if anyone was left behind. Nikki had done her best to save the girls she had found, but were there others?

Only time would tell . . . *and an army of cadaver dogs.*

But she knew that wasn't what Jessica needed to hear. The bad news would follow soon enough. No, the woman needed to feel her ordeal was over. They all did.

Away from the compound, and in the quiet of a darkened clearing of evergreens, a lone figure crept toward an Alaskan State Trooper helicopter, taking great pains not to be seen. In the confusion of the massive explosion and the aftermath of the sabotaged choppers, it would not be difficult to steal the aircraft from under the nose of the American law enforcement officers.

The man had not anticipated such a random convenience, but he was not above taking advantage of low hanging fruit. In no time he had hot-wired the aircraft to start, a skill acquired from a misspent youth. Once the helicopter lifted into the air, he felt freer than he'd ever been. Years had gone by since his military training, but flying an aircraft such as this was like riding a bicycle, as the Americans said—a proficiency for which he would forever be grateful. Now he'd let the stars and his instincts guide him wherever he wanted to go.

Like a phoenix rising from the ashes, he felt the significance of his newfound opportunity to reinvent himself. He knew how to disappear. And by doing so, he would eliminate the need for looking over his shoulder if the great Anton Bukolov got the urge to look for him.

For all anyone would know, Stanislav Petrovin had died on St. Lawrence Island, Alaska.

And by the time the Americans had concluded their investigation of the explosion and the helicopter crash—and sifted through the remains of those who had died—the actual truth might still not be discovered for some time . . . if ever. Who could say? The name Petrovin might even become legend. He liked the sound of that.

But he knew that the euphoria of his escape would not last long. Eventually, what had happened in Chicago and on St. Lawrence Island would eat at him—personally—until he could no longer bear to remain dead.

Perhaps if revenge was a dish best served cold, Stas Petrovin could learn to be a patient man—and bide his time.

CHAPTER 32

Talkeetna, Alaska
Three days later

Susannah had gotten up early that morning to make blueberry pancakes from scratch, Nikki's first choice for breakfast. The house smelled of coffee, fresh squeezed orange juice, honey-smoked bacon, and a buttery maple syrup courtesy of the Roadhouse Inn in Talkeetna. After getting Payton's call that he was bringing Nikki home, Susannah had rushed to clean the house and fill her refrigerator with all her daughter's favorite foods, then anxiously waited to see her sweet face.

The longest wait of her life.

She knew it would be an uphill battle for Nikki to reclaim her life. The same could be said for her too, but the little girl who had run away from home was not the same young woman Payton brought back. She saw it in her daughter's eyes. An underlying sadness remained and might never go away, but Nikki also had a newfound strength that Susannah hoped would stay. And like a good batch of pancakes, she felt like they were starting over . . . from scratch.

"Nikki, breakfast is almost ready," she yelled loud enough for her daughter to hear upstairs. Calling the girl's name, even doing the simplest daily chores for her, had become a blessing she never wanted to take for granted.

But she also knew they'd have their bad days too.

Every night since she'd come home, her daughter had horrible nightmares. But when she woke up crying, she had been there to hold her. Nikki had taken to sleeping in her bed, an arrangement a mother could get used to. She'd become addicted to the natural smell of her daughter's skin and the sweet scent of her hair after a shower. And another memory lingered in her mind as she set the table.

On that first night after Nikki was home, Payton stayed over. He was too big for all three of them to fit in one bed, so they slept on the floor in the living room. Her brother never asked to sleep over. It was something they all wanted, and it just happened. She hated the reason that they needed the comfort that night, but she would always treasure the memory when they'd been reunited as a family.

So far, Nikki hadn't wanted to talk to her friends or see anyone else since coming home, but maybe later that day it would change. After her painstaking cruise through a living hell, life had certainly gotten simpler, and Susannah didn't mind that at all.

"Nikki? I'm makin' pancakes. Your favorite." She listened for the sound of her daughter's footsteps upstairs, but hadn't heard movement in a while.

She set the pancakes to warm in the oven and went searching for Nikki. She looked in her bedroom, the one they'd been sharing, but her daughter wasn't there, and the upstairs bathroom was empty. She tried Nikki's bedroom and didn't see her there either. For a moment she felt a rush of panic, a mother's reaction she found hard to contain.

"Nikki?" Her voice cracked and she slumped on her daughter's bed, listening to the quiet of the house. That's when she heard it. She walked to the girl's closet and found her kneeling on the carpet, crying.

"Oh, honey." Susannah dropped to her knees and held Nikki close. "I'm here. You're okay."

"One thing I remembered was the smell of my closet." She sobbed, her voice sounding fragile and small. "And I remembered the sound of your footsteps outside my door. It's good to be home, Mama . . . with you."

Susannah held her daughter tight, kneeling on the floor of Nikki's closet. Payton had come through on his promise that she'd get her second chance. Now it was her turn to make good. And from here forward—for Nikki's sake—she'd take it one day at a time.

Jess lay in Payton's bed, listening to the soothing sound of his breathing as he slept. She kept her eyes closed, content to let the morning's peace wash over her. With the quiet patter of rain on the rooftop of his cabin, nothing could have been more perfect. She smiled and nuzzled against his chest, feeling the warmth of his bare skin next to hers.

For the first time in years she'd slept through the night. And considering what they'd just been through, that was a major miracle.

But when her mind and body clock wouldn't let her rest anymore, she got up, wrapped a blanket around her naked body, and shuffled off to his bathroom to take care of business, bleary-eyed. The cabin was still dark, with only slivers of light coming through the windows. She could have gone back to bed, but changed her mind and walked outside in all her glory. In another life she would have dressed in the dark and slipped out of his life, but not today. Today, she had to drink in the seclusion of Payton's wooded acreage.

And being alone to do it seemed important.

She stepped onto his front porch, with the blanket around her, to watch the rain drip off his roof and turn the dense treeline and shrubs into a deep slick green. In the distance she heard the steady rush of a river on the crisp morning air, a gentle hush she could get accustomed to. And the smell of the damp earth nourished her soul. Alaska was the best-kept secret on the planet.

Yet despite the mood-altering scenery, she had other things on her mind. Staying with Payton for a few days had been chicken soup for her heart, but at some point she knew she'd have to face reality. Not everything had turned out well.

The Alaska State Trooper chopper had gone missing. Jess tried hard not to let her imagination run wild, but she wondered if the Russian had somehow survived. Anyone from Globe Harvest could have taken the helicopter to escape the island, but her fatalistic nature was hard to deny.

And the Russian was impossible to forget.

The other day, Alexa had called to say that the report her alliance used to derive the coordinates looked like a black-market summary of "transactions," bartering in human life on all levels. When they compared notes, and Jess told her what Seth had uncovered on the Globe Harvest Web site and the secret entry code to access it, Alexa said she'd take the information and put it to good use. Because the online system was set up across international jurisdictions, it would be difficult for traditional law enforcement to catch them. Although Alexa's organization was anything but traditional, Jess wasn't sure she felt comfortable with powerful vigilantes operating on an international level with no one to answer to—judge, jury, and executioner all wrapped in one covert well-funded alliance.

Except for the heartache of leaving Payton behind in Alaska—his family would need him now more than ever—Jess couldn't wait to get back to her life in Chicago.

After the ordeal on St. Lawrence Island, she'd called Sam just to hear her childhood friend's voice. She downplayed the incident on the island so the woman wouldn't worry, saving the details for when they would talk face-to-face, but Sam had good news of her own to share. She told Jess that no bodies were found in the rubble of the textile factory outside

Chicago. No one had died there; that wouldn't be the case on the island.

But when Sam launched into her second tidbit of good tidings, she asked Jess to contact Detective Ray Garza when she got back to town. And that smacked of trouble.

Before her friend explained, Jess groused, "What the hell kind of good news is that? The man wants to book me a one-way stay at the gray bar hotel, doing life with no chance of parole."

She heard the smile in Sam's voice when she replied, "He only wants to wrap up your part in his investigation into the death of Lucas Baker. The good news is that you're no longer a suspect."

"Generous of him. Did Seth come through on my alibi? How hard did you have to sweet-talk Garza before he gave in?" Before Sam answered her questions, Jess teased, "As I recall, Detective Ray was more than a little easy on the eyes, girlfriend. You should get you some of that."

"Ray? What are you talking about? You're crazy. I work with the man, for cryin' out loud."

Sam had leapt to her protest far too fast. Jess knew she had hit the bull's-eye on the attraction her friend had for the ruthless detective with the sexy eyes.

"Speaking of Seth," Sam changed the subject deftly, "I went to check on him, like you asked."

Harper hadn't answered his cell phone for the last several days. At first Jess took it in stride. She'd gotten used to the guy's mysterious ways. But finally his disappearing act got to her. She asked Sam to check on him at the Peninsula Hotel.

"Did he freak when a cop showed up at his hotel door?" She joked, but her heart wasn't in it. Jess wanted to hear Harper's voice. But most of all, she wanted to thank him for his part in bringing Nikki home. None of this would have happened without him. *None of it.*

Sad-eyed Seth Harper had been the *real* hero.

"He wasn't at the hotel, Jess. And get this—no one there had ever heard of him. And when I described him and told them which suite he'd been staying, they said that room hadn't been booked in the last two weeks. What do you make of that?" Sam asked.

Jess felt a sudden disconnect from Seth, as if meeting him had only been a strange dream, like none of it had been real. She flashed on the last time she'd seen him. The tall lanky kid didn't look as if he'd slept in a while. And she recalled how he'd dismissed her concern by saying, "Not everything is rosy in Harperworld twenty-four/seven . . . but I'll figure it out soon. No worries."

Well, now she *was* worried. Why hadn't she pressed him more . . . to find out what was going on with *him*? She vowed, when she got back to town, to look for him in earnest. After all, she still had the blue monster, his butt ugly van. When she found Seth, she'd uncover the truth even if it had to be at gunpoint. She hoped the kid would contact her, as he'd done before, but she wouldn't wait for that.

Maybe *he* would need saving. And she wanted to be there, holding his lifeline.

With bittersweet memories of Harper on her mind, and a swell of darker recollections scratching beneath the surface of her skin, Jess discovered that she'd wandered into the rain. And oddly enough, she didn't mind it. She had learned to appreciate the healing properties infused into each precious drop. Payton Archer had taught her that.

As if on cue, the man himself joined her, naked and under wraps the same as she was. Without hesitation, he joined her in the rain as if he did it every morning.

"Hey lady, this town might be small, but we do have a dress code."

"Then it's a good thing you live in the boonies, Archer, where people can run butt naked if they want." She threw open her blanket and flashed him, long enough for him to pull her into his embrace, skin-to-skin.

After all they had been through together, she still didn't know much about him—except for what really mattered in a man's character. She hoped she'd have time to "discover" him, but out of the blue she asked Payton a strange question she'd been wondering about since meeting him. And being naked with him—standing outdoors in the rain—seemed the perfect time and place to chat.

"You ever wish you had your glory days back, Payton? I mean your time in the NFL? If you could do it all over, what would you change?"

"Looking back only stalls out your life. Living in the past is not really living at all," he said, nuzzling her in a monster hug. "I know that now, more than ever. And I don't wish for my time back with the pros, not half as much as I wish my parents' plane hadn't crashed. Or that this vile thing had never happened to Nikki. Football and all the money in the world doesn't even take a close second to family . . . and the people we love. That's what matters most to me, Jess."

She pulled him closer and pressed a cheek to his bare chest. She liked a man who had his priorities straight. Two nights ago they had made love for the first time in his cabin in front of a cozy fire. In the light, her scars were clearly visible, but nothing felt more natural than making unabashed sweet love to Payton Archer.

That first night in his hotel room, she realized that her nervousness hadn't been about sex or breaking in a first-time lover. It had been about letting him under her skin, letting him get to know her, scars and all. But Payton had burrowed into her heart when he gave her a front row seat to watch the rain. So when it came time for the physical part of their relationship—well, that came easy, so to speak.

"Joe Tanu has invited us over for breakfast. He just called." Payton's low voice rumbled through his chest and into her ear, sounding muffled and sweet. "You feel like going? If you don't, I'm sure he'll understand. Joe is a very patient man."

"Patience runs in your family. I can see that." She grinned and rubbed her hands along his muscled back. "Sure, I'd love to eat Joe's cooking."

"Yeah, the man owes me a couple of eggs anyway. I've cut him enough slack."

When she looked up at him, she could tell there was a story behind Joe and those eggs. And from the quirky expression on Payton's handsome face, Jess firmly believed *everyone* should have an egg story buried in the closet, suitable for sharing . . . between good friends.

With his arm around her, Jess walked back toward the warmth of his cabin, never feeling so alive. She might have resembled a drowned rodent at the moment, but later on maybe her changed luck would kick in and she'd have a good hair day. A girl could only hope.

"I promised to troll the main street of this little burg later today with Nikki," she said. "She and Susannah are taking me shopping, apparently. For what, I don't know. I'm not much of a girly girl, but I'd do just about anything with your niece. And I'm looking forward to getting to know Susannah."

"Nikki hasn't wanted out of the house since we've brought her home. I'm glad she and Susannah are taking that first step . . . with you."

"Yeah, me too."

Until now, Jess didn't know much about first steps. But with Payton Archer, she'd be willing to learn.

And now a special early look at

Jordan Dane's

THE WRONG SIDE OF DEAD

The next in the Sweet Justice series

Dirty Monty's Lounge
South Side of Chicago
9:20 P.M.
Late Summer

At the end of the bar, Seth Harper slouched, nursing his lukewarm beer and keeping his dark eyes on the door. Waiting. Not even a good beer buzz made him forget why he'd come—or why he still sat alone.

Given the grand scheme of the universe, he distracted himself by contemplating the big picture. Dirty Monty's and places like it existed for a reason. And several libations had given him the clarity of mind to reflect on it. Sleazy dumps gave the socially unacceptable a place to hang out, even on a Thursday night. And if these folks packed a thirst, Monty's served the cheap stuff and charged enough to trick its marginal clientele into believing it was worth it. When alcohol was involved, things *always* got real simple. And he appreciated the irony of his half-tanked epiphany, especially since he'd be counted among the socially unacceptable here tonight.

Yet he was a few beers shy of being easily duped by any redeeming nature of the shoddy bar. The pungent odor of cigarette smoke, liquor, and cheap perfume had marked him. And the carpet smelled of mold, a borderline improvement over the collective tang of the bar patrons. His dark tousled hair, well-worn jeans, and favorite black *Jerry Springer* tee already reeked of the bar's seedier elements. And well into the night, he'd be hearing a steady thrum of bass in his ears, courtesy of the nonstop jukebox music—a mix of country, classic heavy metal, and top forty pop. He sighed and stared into his beer mug, bracing himself to accept what had happened and hail a cab home.

What the hell are you doing? The question had stuck in his head, reminding him that he'd been played for a sucker. She wasn't coming *this* time.

And insult to injury, the piss factor had kicked in again. Every time the bartender shot tonic into a glass or hit the spigot for a draught beer, his bladder reacted. He made a quick trip to drain the vein and slumped back on his stool. But after another fifteen minutes of nursing his beer and a fragile spirit—shifting his gaze between the front door and his watch—Seth decided to call it a night. He downed the rest of his drink and fumbled in his pocket for a tip.

As he stood, he caught sight of a blond woman near the door.

It *had* to be her, but from where he stood, her face had morphed into an unrecognizable blur. He narrowed his eyes and struggled for a better image, but nothing more would come. When he moved toward her, he staggered against the edge of the bar, feeling suddenly light-headed. The sensation took him by surprise. He hadn't drunk *that* much.

"What . . . the hell?" he slurred under his breath.

When the room undulated in shadows, he knew something was terribly wrong. He felt sluggish and weak. Out of sync voices and warped music amplified into an irritating blare. He looked around, but everything was the same. Faces of strangers and the distant memory of a blond woman jutted in and out of the dark, distorted and overlapping in a jumbled mess. Blinking hard, he couldn't change what he saw. Colors bled from the ceiling and walls, creating a macabre and shifting canvass.

Fear took a firmer grip.

"Help . . . m-me."

He imagined calling out, but wasn't sure the words were his. Could *anyone* hear him? His arms went slack. And when standing became a chore, he collapsed. Before he hit the floor, strong hands grabbed him. He turned to look for a face, but the room spiraled out of control. His world switched off.

And he was powerless to stop it.

Hours later

Seth stared into blackness, his thoughts the consistency of primordial ooze. Although his brain sent a questionable message to the rest of his body that he could move, he chose not to try. His senses were gathering intel and he was content to let the process happen at its own pace.

He blinked his eyes—slow and easy—the only motion he could muster.

It took time for him to recognize that something else moved in the dark. A faint edge of red stabbed through the shadows, a light blinking at a steady and insistent rhythm. He had no idea where it came from and didn't care. The left cheek on his face hurt, and his head throbbed at the same measured beat as the light, inflicting a growing ache from behind his eyes and through the base of his skull. And with it, a chill sent a rush of pinpricks over his skin that cut deeper, especially with his back pressed against something cold and hard.

In front of him, images gradually took shape and emerged from the dark, pieces of a puzzle for his consideration. And like an artery, the red light pulsed, repeatedly teasing him with a glimpse and swiping it away. Crimson lunged across a blanched palette like a strobe effect, capturing a wild array of blotches that marred the surface. At first the scene over his head looked like a harmless rendition of an artist gone berserk, until a metallic sweet odor triggered something else.

Now a strong feeling of dread spoiled his creeping drift through oblivion. Muddled thoughts mercifully tempered the sensation, but he felt it all the same.

Do something!

Urging his body to move, he lifted an arm and dropped a hand to his belly, a sluggish awkward struggle. His fingers felt dampness on his clothes. And a second bout with the cold swept over him, causing his teeth to chatter. He fumbled a hand to his cheek. It felt warm to the touch and throbbed a little, but he had no idea why. To get his blood moving, he rolled to his side and shoved an elbow under him, the cold tile pressed hard against his joint. When he lifted his head, dizziness instigated a surge of nausea. He nearly gagged, but managed to control it.

What had happened? He pried through his memory, recalling nothing of how he ended up here. And where *was* here? He peered through the shadows of what looked like a cramped bathroom, and beyond where he was, the remnants of a cheap motel room. But none of it looked familiar.

Through it all, the flashing light persisted. Its grim red doused everything. He looked across two small beds and saw the light came from a window with thin drapes partially drawn. Outside, a neon vacancy sign flared its message, but he couldn't see all of it. And after only a quick glimpse, the light sent shards of pain through his eye sockets and challenged his night vision. To recover, he shifted his gaze to the dark corners of the bathroom again, looking for anything that would trigger a memory.

Instead, he came face-to-face with a nightmare he would never forget. Dead eyes stared back at him from the edge of a tub, opened wide and accusing. A slack head tilted at an odd and unnatural slant. A woman. Her mouth gagged with a soiled towel. Dark hair matted to her head, a bloodied mess.

"Holy shit!"

He gasped and shoved his back to the far wall, scrambling for a place to hide. But he couldn't shift his gaze from the white filmy eyes and gagged mouth. A face frozen in terror and awash in flashing crimson that stippled eerie shadows over the corpse.

"No . . . no. What . . . ?" His mind couldn't grasp what he saw.

The body smelled of violent death, the metallic sweet odor tinged with something more than he wanted to imagine. And the artist's blotches he had seen when he first opened his eyes had morphed into the reality of blood splatter. He clutched at his damp shirt and pulled away his hand to see it colored by a dark substance. He knew in an instant that it was blood.

"Oh, God."

This time Seth couldn't hold back. He emptied his stomach, even knowing dead eyes stared down at him as he retched.

Sick and confused, he got to his feet and backed out of the bathroom. When the eyes of the body followed him, he turned away from the gruesome scene, staggering off balance. To catch himself, he leaned a shoulder into the doorjamb and gripped it with a hand. His legs barely supported him. And even in a stupor, he realized his brain was fried. Trusting his senses and his perceptions would be out of the question.

When he stumbled into the next room, he caught the motion of a shadow outside the window. He only had time to blink but it was too late. A loud crack and the door burst open. He lurched backward, his spine jammed against a wall, the only thing that kept him from falling.

"Move . . . *move!*" Everything happened too fast.

Lights flooded the room. Beams spiraled through the dark, zeroing in on him. He raised an arm to shield his eyes.

Angry voices filled his head. Words whipped by him and through him. Only a few stuck long enough to register a meaning.

"On your knees . . . *now!*"

Seth tried to react but panic gripped him, making him sick again. He froze where he stood. His whole body shook. And he knew he had only heard a fraction of what these men had been yelling. Everything surged off balance—too fast for him to keep up.

What the hell was happening? Who were these men?

"Hands behind your head . . . Do it!" One man's voice pummeled his ear, louder than the rest.

A bright glare blinded him. His eyes watered. He squinted between his fingers, filtering what little he saw through his muddled brain. It was all so surreal, like a bad movie, not happening to him. But when the silhouette of a man eclipsed the window, more shadows blocked the red blinking light. Now he felt the men close tighter around him. And in the flashes of light, he realized they had guns.

"Don't shoot . . . *please* don't shoot me," he begged, raising his hands.

This was real. It *was* happening. And when the yelling intensified, he shut down, too numb and afraid to reason it out. All he wanted to do was collapse and throw up again.

"Oh, God, I'm . . . gonna be sick," he mumbled, unsure they'd heard what he said.

When he bent over to empty his stomach, they rushed him. Strong hands grappled him to the floor. A knee dug into his back.

"*Arrghh.* Please," he pleaded. His face was pressed hard to the carpet, muffling his voice.

"Relax . . . *relax,*" a man shouted. The way he delivered his message would do little to calm anyone. "Don't fight," he added, yanking his arm back.

"He's down. We got him."

Seth felt the harsh slap of metal on his wrists, and for the first time realized these men might be police. He forced his body to give up the fight, but that didn't translate to those who hauled his ass off the floor and frisked him. They manhandled him, but he knew the drill.

He'd grown up knowing way too much about how cops operated.

"Let's get light in here," one man said.

An overhead light came on, blinding him again. When he recovered, he watched two uniformed cops holster their weapons and sweep by him to look in the other room. They stopped before they crossed the threshold into the bathroom.

"Damn." One cop cursed under his breath and turned an angry glare on him. "You're some kind of freak, boy."

Another cop stepped closer and stared at his face, saying, "Yeah, and I suppose you got those scratches on your cheek from shaving." The cop shook his head in disgust.

Scratches? With eyes wide, he sucked a rush of air into his lungs, unable to let it go. And when all eyes turned on him, he avoided their stares, probably looking guilty as hell.

"I know you're not gonna believe me, but I didn't do this." He swallowed. His throat was parched. "I don't know how I got here. And I don't know that woman."

"Well, you're right about one thing, kid," one of them said. "I ain't gonna believe ya."

A cop behind him chuckled, but the ones closest to the bathroom weren't laughing.

While the cops worked at containing the scene and starting their investigation, Seth tried hard to think, connecting the dots through his doped-up brain. No doubt he'd been drugged, but he couldn't remember how or when it had happened. His memory had been wiped clean. And by the looks on these men's faces, another cold fact was undeniable.

In the next room, the brutally slain body of a woman lay sprawled in the tub. The shocking image was forged into his brain when he caught a better glimpse of the dark-haired woman steeped in gore, courtesy of the harsh light overhead. He looked away, but that only made things worse when he noticed his clothes covered in blood. Too much blood to be considered an accidental brush with the body. And the cuts on his cheek ached, another not so subtle reminder of how crazed he looked to the cops.

By the deranged splatter on the bathroom walls, he knew only a certifiable maniac with anger issues would have done such a thing. And Seth figured every cop in the room was convinced *he* was that maniac.

For them, the truth was as plain as the scratches on his face.